The
Save Your Planet
Show

JOHN KLAWITTER

The Save Your Planet Show

ISBN: 978-1-938674-05-01
Printed in the United States of America
Published 16 November 2013

Double Spin Publishing
A Division of Dancing Bear Ent., LLC

TO LYNNIE

Always.

ACKNOWLEDGMENTS

I owe a great deal to a wildly eclectic assortment of scientific and cosmic thinkers, creative artists, magical musicians, positive tinseltown players and never-say-die pitchmen, hard running scribblers and makers of vids, films and webmashes I have had the good fortune to study and read and occasionally meet and work with. Some few of the many who deserve mention: Richard Feynman, Michio Kaku, Bob Dylan, Waylon Jennings, Percy Rodrigez, Ray Bradbury, Danny Dark, Steve Zuckerman, Dick Francis, Elmore Leonard, Peter Turchi, Sid Field, Desmond Loden, Thomas Perry, Robert B. Parker, Flannery O'Connor, Lajos Egri, Marvin Harris, Walker Percy, J.Richard Jacobs, Rod Serling, Iwao Takamoto, Mark Henderson, George Petlowany, David Viscott, Larry Elder, Nelson B. Winkless, Jr., Bill Hanna, Joe Barbera, Phil Mendez, Wally Burr, Danny Ellithorpe, Arthur Pierson, Natalie Wood, Ali McGraw, Genevieve Bojold, Leslie Nielson, Nikita Knatz, Jacqueline Bisset, Jacquie Rogers, Ann Charles, Leo Burnett, Dick Marx, John David Moore, Richard Harris, Carl Hixon, Charles & Ray Eames, the Disney pirate-gang of writers, artists and storytellers, the Warner Bros Animation Loons, the free-lancing dreamers, the dancers, the singers and the musicians.

Thank you, one and all. I have tried to take your lessons to heart, some few experiences published in Tinsel Wilderness, where I thank some few of the great and even famous creative people were kind enough to boot me along my own way. Particular thanks with regard to The Save Your Planet Show to story teller guru Robert McKee for his advice, "Every scene must move the story forward."

The Save Your Planet Show
Title Song: Interplanetary Game Show opening :60-90
Bright, whimsical music with a Milky Way Galaxy flavor
Lyrics by John Klawitter, ASCAP

Ha Ha Ha and Ho Ho Ho/ It's the Save Your Planet Show!

Sacred nuts & clever nerds/ Heads of state & mortal foes
Yeah Yeah Yeah and Yo Yo Yo/ It's the Save your Planet Show!

CHORUS:
Mergatroids, asteroids, insured by Lloyds
Collapsing sun, muon gun, death by fun

Got a planet made of granite?/ A lava top about to blow?
Have an earth that's doomed from birth/To go in a sunny glow?
Yes Yes Yes and No – Oh No!/ It's the Save Your Planet Show!

CHORUS:
Viper voids, Sigmund Freuds, Planetoids
World colliders, Doom abiders, Deep Space Spiders

Are you the creatures smooth and rare/ Ready to accept our dare?
Are you so smart, good at debating? Winning scores galactic rating!

CHORUS:
Don't say die, do not ask why, or tell a lie
(unless you have to)

So
Click Click Click and Go Go Go/ For cosmic fun we're number one!
It's the Save Your Planet
Save Your Planet
Save Your Planet Shoooooooowwwwwww!!!!!

One

I was born in 1938. I used to be an ordinary old person, but I'm not any more. Not old. And certainly not ordinary.

My name is Lucy Weiler and I have abilities that, just looking at me, might surprise you. I can communicate with a creature half way across the galaxy, and I saved the earth from fiery self-destruction…well, that last one, I had a little help from my friends.

It was ten years ago, early in 2013 and there was a bad storm brewing on the horizon. Something cruel and evil was moving in on all of us, and we were like butterflies dancing in the sunlight. I am not referring to the unfair crippling of old age that at the time I saw all around me, and felt in my own bones. It was something worse, something unimaginably violent…and terminal.

Put yourself in my sensible walking shoes and try to imagine it was you living back there almost a decade ago. Try to get some idea of the way it was for me: imagine back then, and it is the year 2013. *Welcome to Chermundo Villas, where the living is stylish and easy.* That is what the brochure says. At this time, I lease at the Chermundo, and so I can tell you firsthand that this is a place where old people come to spend their last days, and hopefully keep their wits and then die as gracefully as possible before they run out of money. So far, I am one of the lucky ones. I have a few friends, a comfortable suite of rooms and finances that, with luck, should see me through to the end. Hey, it is okay; I like to think I am a tough old broad. Like the song says, *Do not cry for me Argentina.*

My name is Lucy Weiler. My story – our story – this story I am about to tell you – I guess the best way is to start right in, and let us see where the bits fall or however Writer's Digest teaches their rapt students to scribble it down in those writing courses I never took.

Pay attention now, because I am about to tell you something a little confusing that you may immediately jump to the conclusion must be impossible. Or you will decide I am nuts. But come on, give an old lady a break, lend me a bit of your time and I promise I'll tell you a few things that you could find worthwhile and even helpful in your own life.

I'm sure you have heard about young minds trapped in old bodies. There are a thousand cruel jokes about old people who forget all the mileage they have on their beat up frames and go ripping about acting like young fools. Well, I am the opposite of that; I am an old person presently living quietly and happily in a young person's body. My story could be a page ripped out of *Ripley's Believe It Or Not:* I was born on April 17, 1938. It is now April 21, 2023. I currently live in rural Washington state in apple country, and my driver's license says I am 28 and when I look in the mirror I think I can pass for a hot, young soccer mom. I know I can, actually. But I could not pass for that at the time my story begins back in 2013. That was ten years ago, back when I was in my seventies at the retirement home. Back then, if I had looked at these words I am writing, I do not know what I would have made of any of this. About my driver's license, of course it is not accurate, and in the strictest sense, it is illegal. I had to bend a few minds to make that happen. These days, I can do things like that. Gently bend peoples' thoughts to avoid the trouble of being discovered. I have to practice that paranormal art, if I am to have any sort of a *normal* life at all.

I am not bragging and certainly not complaining, I am just telling you how it was and is with me. How does an ordinary old lady discover the fountain of youth? Well, in a way, it found me. And no part of what I went through was easy. So I believe I earned my second spin at the game of life.

You do not have to believe any of this unless you have a mind to, but for me…well, the part of my life that started about a decade ago was interesting and different, and it changed everything, and so it is natural for me to feel moved to write about it. What happened was deadly dangerous and nearly wiped us out, although, when all of us were in the most trouble, we did not know – or maybe simply were unable to admit – how bad it was.

Although there is reason to believe it began much earlier on, I like to think the story starts the day that my friends Wheelchair Jack and Delrina, the rowdy, curly red haired flapper, Showboat George and Millie, the pudgy farm girl and groupie grown old before her time, and I catch the Chermundo van ride over to Albertsons to pick up some things they do not regularly stock up on in the Villas pantry.

At this time we call ourselves the Old Bunch. We all live as guests at the Chermundo Villas retirement home in Encino, and while the staff takes fairly decent care of us in exchange for the outrageous monthly sums of money we fork over, it is a joy to take a little frolic off the grounds for personal provisions – you know, the special stuff, like fresh oatmeal cookies, dark chocolate M&M's and Honeycrisp apples that make living at an advanced age almost worthwhile.

Our bunch is six in number, although Herbert – known to us The Old Viking, or simply Herbie – did not make that particular trip with us. He was going to tag along, but at the last minute he got a fax from overseas, and then he said there was something important that needed attending with one of his largely non-existent business clients and so we should go on without him.

If you know anything at all about old people and retirement homes maybe you are thinking the makeup of our group is a bit against the odds, three guys and three gals in a little clique of our own, if only because women live longer than men and it should be two or three women to every man. You would be right about that, but our gang of six came about mostly because we are settled in our ways and feel comfortable around each other.

Just why did the Old Bunch come together in the first place? I have asked myself that question without coming up with a real answer, though I do have my suspicions. We are all financially okay, but in some other ways we have lost at the game of life. None of us have any close family, not even Wheelchair Jack with his not-really-his-own daughter. Of course, Jack loves her and his granddaughter as well, but I get the feeling loving him back is a duty, at least the way the daughter sees it.

One way to think about how we live is that retirement homes are a little like boarding school, with the wishers and the doers, the predators and the teasers, the vain and the timid.

Remember back in high school, you had the extremes of adolescence? Then you got promoted (shoved along) to middle age where everybody concentrates on sex, making babies and making money. Then, just about when you think you are tottering into some quiet refuge of old age where things are calm and balanced, by some unlucky trickery, you slip back into the same extremes that plagued you as a teenager. Maybe not everybody, but lots of oldsters are like that. This makes finding people you can get along with more important than you might imagine.

Anyway, on the day my story starts, the van leaves us off at Albertsons where Jack latches on to a big bottle of Mondavi Cabernet Sauvignon, *the red swill of forgetfulness* he calls it, although I believe it does not work for him. It certainly does not for me. And he buys a small flask of cheap brandy for his pal Herbert. *On consignment,* he says, which means *Herbie damn well better pay him back.*

Delrina scoops up her special Luna energy bars with the white chocolate and macadamia nuts, a bottle of Golden Blush Scarlet hair color and that wrinkle removing cream that, judging by the limited results I am fairly sure is not worth the money.

I select a dozen apples, four tangy Honeycrisps, four even more lip-puckering green Granny Smiths and four tart little crab apples and when we get back on the bus we each have a bag or two of goodies that we have convinced ourselves we need, but really are just an excuse to get out of the Villas for a little while.

Paradise can be boring too, or so I have been told.

"What are those dinky, puny little things?" George asks, pointing at my bag of crab apples.

"Old fashioned farm apples," I tell him. "We had them on our farm when I was a little girl."

"Where was that – Dwarf Land?"

"No, Chatsworth, Mister Show Biz."

We girls go out of our way to show George that maybe he used to be Mister Wonderful at the studios but around us he is just Georgie-Porgie pudding pie.

"Crabby apples," Millie grins mischievously. "Like you, George."

George gives us a fake frown. "Herbie's grouchier than me."

That is true enough, and Millie broadens her smile, "I'll tell him you said that."

However, on our return to the Villas, old Herbert is nowhere to be found. This is odd, because he should be there, religiously banging away at answering his emails in the Villas computer and games corner. That area is recessed at one end of the lounge, and we have to walk right past it. We would have seen him right away, but he is not there.

Two

Jack and I give each other a questioning look. This could be trouble; Herbie is always in the lounge when we return, hoping to scrounge a free cookie or a handful of caramel popcorn.

I am ready to shrug it off and get on with my day, but Jack has other ideas.

"Let's check it out, Lucy," he says.

I hand him my apples and he sets them on his lap with his big bottle of red swill. We head for Herb's place, Jack rolling along in his wheelchair and me scurrying to keep up from behind. Did I mention Jack's legs are hopelessly paralyzed? The story is, he had a terrible accident at his wife's funeral and has not been the same since.

I like Jack Hamlin, and I do not like very many people. It is not that we have a relationship like Millie and George. Not at all anything of that extent, but, well, a girl has to have a few select friends or go stark raving mad in this crazy world. Since my own personal disaster with a member of the opposite sex, I am not likely to try anything closer than friendship again in this life, and Jack knows it. Everybody knows it. We have our share of hungry black widow gals and black widower males here at the Chermundo, and I have found it pays to be clear and even forceful in declaring my limits and boundaries and to say exactly what I do not want from those rusty iron pumper males who go around flexing their muscles and showing off what they have to offer gals like poor lonely old me. I have not actually had to fist or knee anybody, but I have come close.

Jack lives in the rooms adjoining Herb's. We arrive at the living room Jack shares with the Old Viking. Herbert is not to be seen, and he is also missing from his private rooms.

But somebody else is there, Big Bert with a few of his *hombreros*, Mexican day laborers he pays next to nothing because they are illegals and live their lives too scared to say anything and he has told them he will report them and have their butts kicked back to Tijuana. This is no secret. Bert tells everybody. He is proud of it. I think he is one of several Villas employees that we see too much of. He is in charge of cleaning out rooms after a guest passes to the great beyond or when one is moved to the Z ward.

Bert is an ill-formed fellow with a surly disposition. His nickname is Big Bert because he has narrow shoulders that slump over a thin chest that in turn slumps over a gigantic stomach that sags in front of him like a spider's abdomen. He is a bully, and my heart skips a beat when I see him. He treats us guests like he is just too busy with important work and we had better stay out of his way. Jack says it is because Bert is afraid of us, but I do not think so. He is a naturally mean individual; maybe he came out of the womb that way, or maybe it was something he picked up along the way. I want to scamper back to my own room, but Jack, who usually is the drift-along dreamy sort, picks this time to take a stand against the forces of evil.

He starts slow, but I know Jack. The enemy has been engaged.

"How come the fuss?" he asks, looking around the living room. In spite of his problems, Jack is anything but stupid or slow; he already knows the answer.

I shake my head no, trying to warn Jack we will do better to get out of here, but he raises his voice as he repeats his question, "Hey, Bert-boy – I'm talking to you. Where's Herbert?"

Bert's sneer shows he would rather talk to a Howdy Doody puppet. He is an important person, in charge of moving Chermundo guests around. He does not take questions from guests. He tries to puff his narrow chest as he stands in the middle of the living room, clipboard in hand. Most of the help is not like that, but there are a few you have to watch out for.

"What are you, the press or something?" Big Burt snarls at us, and then turns his attention back to his clipboard as if by miracle or magic that simple gesture will erase us from his presence.

"Somebody made this mess," Jack persists.

"Oh, now you're the man from CSI? Sorry, I can't answer your questions, detective."

Jack takes his voice up another notch. Our quiet Wheelchair Jack is actually moving out of serenity into the milder fringes of aggression, "What happened here, Bert?" For a few seconds, Bert looks like he is tempted to take hold of Jack's wheelchair and shove him out of the room or off a cliff somewhere, but he sees me standing there, arms folded, and I manage a frown so he cannot tell how frightened I am. Bert decides answering Jack's question will be the lesser pain in his life. But he is as unpleasant as he can possibly be about it.

"The problem with dementia is you never know you got it." He smirks as he says it.

That might be funny coming out of some guttersnipe nighttime TV comic's mouth, but Jack and I are old people, and we do not find it amusing. We think Bert is the embodiment of stupid as he smiles at his clipboard.

"But me and a few of the other-side nurses helped the old gas bag see the light," Bert gloats, full of himself.

Jack and I are certain Herbert would not go anywhere he did not want to without a fight, and we see a mess of entry books, shipping invoices and fax papers scattered on the floor.

"How many goons did it take?" Jack asks.

"Just two orderlies and a nurse – once they got the needle in." Bert gives us a quick, knowing look, a glimmer of triumph in his eye.

10

"And you," Jack says. "You were there, too. Helping out."

"Yeah, and me," Bert agrees.

"Whatever is becoming of this place?" I shake my head in disgust.

Bert's grin turns cruel, "Nothing you or the gimp can do about it."

But Jack is already out of the room and wheeling his way down the hall.

Three

I rush after my friend. "Jack! Wait up! Where are you going?"

"Doctor Daniel," he grunts.

The Office of the Geriatric Doctor is closed, and no light is on behind the locked door. Jack spins his wheelchair back and forth in an impatient little arc.

"Damn it, damn it, damn it…"

"The Old Viking will be alright," I say. I am not feeling okay about what has happened to Herbert, but the rational side of me is thinking it may be time for all of us to face the facts; he does display early signs of Alzheimer's disease.

Jack does not agree with me. "Director's office," he says, and heads off down the hall, back the way we came.

This is a new experience for me; I am usually the one shaking Jack up, trying to get him to show a little interest in the world. Okay, sometimes I can get him to peep out of his shell, but this time he is already up and running full speed. I think some things are better left alone. But Jack is on his horse, galloping full tilt, his lance aimed at a windmill that I am sure he must see more clearly than I do. I have to admit it; maybe Jack is right on this one.

He does not knock or announce himself; instead, he rolls past Janie, Goozeman's secretary, and barges in through the director's open door with me panting close behind him. Did I mention I have diabetes? It's hard for an old girl like me to keep up with an angry man on wheels.

"What's up with Herbert?" Jack asks. The way he spits out the words, it is a challenge.

Goozeman looks up at us, his face registering his startled surprise, but when he sees who it is, he recovers enough to try his hard ball attitude. I do not think he has ever seen Jack upset about anything, and, come to think of it, neither have I. The director lurches to his feet and looks around as if he wants to call an orderly or two and solve the problem with a little stuff-and-shove, but with me standing there, he is not going to get away with that kind of rough stuff. Believe me, this is not my moment of heroism. I have not suddenly grown big brass balls. I am actually quaking in my boots and I do not want to be there; but I keep telling myself the *Goozer* does not know that. Nobody knows what a pantywaist wuss I am inside. With my sullen stare and thin features, some of the guests have taken to calling me witch with a capital B. They do that behind my back, of course. The look serves me now; I put on my best glare and it has to count for something because our director takes a step back. He seems to shrivel a bit. And then he huffs and sits back down.

"I can't talk right now, Hamlin. Not with you either, sorry, Lucy," the director talks fast, like he is a recorded voice, some sort of a Dictaphone playback. "If you have anything of relevance to discuss with me, make an appointment."

A sallow young man with an unhappy look on his face is sitting in a chair on the other side of Goozeman's big wooden desk. The pinch-faced geek wears a snappy beige silk shirt with big maroon magnolias printed all over it. Jack and I recognize Herbert's nephew, the one who wormed his way into an auditing overlook position on the Old Viking's finances until he proved untrustworthy and Herbert put the kibosh on the deal. The little rodent pulls off his wrap-around Oakley sunglasses and his eyes flicker a quick, uneasy look from us to Goozeman and back again.

"I'll handle this," our pompous director assures him.

"Mister Hamlin to you," Jack says. And this is Ms. Weiler. You work for us."

"I know who you are, Jack." There is an ugly tone in Goozeman's voice. "And I certainly don't work for you."

"Where's the Old Viking?"

The director bites his lip as he realizes he will not be able to shoo Jack off like a pesky fly. "You see, folks, there was a situation…" Goozeman says this like a politician, but his delivery is in that whiny nasal voice of his. He has not said anything specific, and yet he lets his voice trail off as if he has made the definitive clarifying statement, end of topic. He extends both hands wide, palms down, and makes a patting motion. "But we took care of it."

"The Old Viking launches no more ships," Herbert's nephew says. But, in spite of his cocky expression, the nephew is not all that sure of himself. He brushes muffin crumbs off the front of his shirt and wraps both hands around his Starbucks grande latte as if there might be a nice prize inside that paper cup.

Jack is showing a new dimension I find attractive. He takes in the scene and the look on his face hardens. "Sidney Orton Miller," he says in a voice that is like a low growl. "Herbert's younger brother Alfred's son. Herbert's nephew Sidney. That covers it all, doesn't it?"

Jack must have some kind of magic because the younger man gets to his feet, clutching a thick wad of papers to his chest. His Starbucks latte tips over on Goozeman's desk. Luckily, the cup appears almost empty, but a spatter of foam appears, and a light brown puddle runs down the side of the director's desk and widens on the floor.

"You can't just invite yourself to a private meeting in my office!" Goozeman's whine is working its way up into the high octave where mosquito wings hum and catbirds chirp. He furiously gestures in the direction of the door, "We're busy, Mister Hamlin. Come back later, if you must!"

Jack spots one of the big green Z ward ring binders open on the director's desk. I can see this new, unexpectedly animated Jack Hamlin is not going anywhere until he wants to.

"Herbert doesn't have Alzheimer's," Jack says. He points to the binder to show he knows what is going on.

Goozeman slaps the flat of one hand on his desk. "Now the patients are diagnosing!" He rolls his eyes to the ceiling as if seeking special guidance from Jesus and his band of merry saints. But the Goozer's only response from the Almighty comes as Sidney's cup rolls off the desk and hits the floor with a hollow little thunk. There must have been more coffee left than I realized; the plastic top flies off and the pool of creamy brown liquid on the floor quickly becomes impressive.

"Guests," Jack corrects him. "We're not your patients; we're paying guests of Chermundo Villas."

Bluish neon glare from the ceiling lights reflects off Goozeman's rimless glasses. "I said, get out of here Mister Hamlin – I'm in a meeting!"

But Jack still is not finished. He recognizes the thick wad of legal papers that Herbert's nephew is clutching to his chest with both hands.

"So Sidney, I see you've got a copy of The Old Viking's will there. I bet it's not the most recent one. You know – the one where you get nothing!"

Sidney darts a quick look at Goozeman. That is enough for Jack and me to guess the rest, and suddenly the ropes of worry and fear are loosening around my chest.

"You're in tro-uble," I chant like a teasing schoolgirl. "You're both in tro-uble!"

You see, it is a slam-dunk triple play. Herbert's lawyer, Tom Fennerman, is Jack's lawyer, and my lawyer, to boot. In practically less time than it takes to tell, Jack rolls out of the director's office and down the hall and we are in Jack's room on a conference call to Fennerman.

Long story short, before five o'clock that very afternoon, some people in suits show up in the Goozer's office. Voices are raised, and before sunup the next morning, feisty Herbert is back in his old room, maybe still a little woozy from the drugs, but already yelling to anyone who will listen that he is going to sue Sidney, his rat of a punk nephew, and Doctor Humphrey Goozeman, and anybody else within a hundred yards for anything he can think of. Lucky for Goozeman, Herbie's brain actually has gone somewhat in the direction of Swiss cheese, and while The Old Viking is long on vengeance, he is somewhat short of memory. A worrisome week or two passes and no legal papers show up, and our ambitious and conniving director starts to breathe a little easier, and pretty soon he is back to his rotten old self.

Four

Let me tell you what you already suspect about Jack: He is smart and loyal and good to be around, and he has some unexpected steel in him that nobody realized before that incident with The Old Viking. And he knows how to get things done. The other, not-so-together side of Jack…well, my take is that he has about 90% given up on his own life. He can be drifty-minded, like he is in some other world. I believe people tend to underestimate a person like that, and I do not mean just younger folks. I have to confess, though I was there and I saw how he snapped out of his dreamland to do what he did for Herbert. I myself have been worried about Jack for quite a while. One moment he is right there with The Old Bunch, a part of whatever we have going and the next he is staring off into space. And worse, I do believe that lately he has been having conversations with invisible people.

A retirement home like this one, what everybody used to call an old folks home, is the first place where people who do not understand us might think we are all about ghosts and spooks and messages from the other side. Some of those false assumptions come about because our hearing gets fuzzy and tinny and our vision blurs and we see spots and dots and halos around lights. There is an entire bag of tricks that old age plays on us. But while you may hear a lot of talk, a retirement community it is the very last place to expect anything like a real actual ghost or witch or alien from another planet to actually show up. Say you were looking for hot sex with a human, or good rich blood to suck, or slaves to take back to their home planet. Why would you bother with us?

And another thing: I do not believe apparitions have the patience to mess with people who are too worried about something else – the approach of their own personal end-of-days, that moment when each of us crosses over to nothing or to whatever else is out there.

Be that as it may, should Villas elders like we were back then ever begin to experience even the slightest out-of-the-ordinary things, we certainly would do our best to keep such odd events to ourselves. Nobody around Chermundo wants to end up in the Z ward.

Beyond questioning my sanity, you may now wonder how I can be any judge of paranormal happenings. Admittedly, my days up until the times when these things started to manifest themselves were not much to write about. Well, I did marry the wrong man and that just about ended my life, but enough women have done that so you would not classify my personal misstep as anything extraordinary. That story of mine was sad and maybe even tragic, but it was nothing out of this world.

I am going to tell this as if it is happening right now, and maybe it is, somewhere, in another part of the world or in a parallel universe or another part of the galaxy. From here on, my story is something that you may read about in Stephen King novels or see on an old episode of Star Trek. You may not be willing to stretch your believing that far, but you have to admit, we do live in uncertain times. Actually I think all times are uncertain. That is because time for us in our limited dimensionality only moves in one direction, and it does not give a lot of clues about what lies around the next bend, much less the one after that.

I know this is not the way professional authors write, the common procedure being to put it down past tense, as if it happened last week or a million years ago. But here we have my story, and it is my very first and maybe my only one, so I do not have anything to lose. And when I run into trouble along the way, I will find a way to fudge it through, or, failing that, will add the pages up, hit the delete button and wander off to fry up some bacon and eggs and see if my son and daughter have finished their homework or are trying to levitate the tractor again. In which case, you will never read this and so it absolutely does not matter, does it?

At the time my story begins, back in 2012, I am nearing seventy years of age (well, over, actually, but give a girl a break, why don't you?), and I am five foot seven inches tall and weigh just over one hundred and twenty pounds. (Well, okay, one hundred and thirty) I show up for the yoga classes they offer at the Chermundo a few times a week and I walk alone or with Delrina a mile or two most mornings before the sun comes up, and so I am in relatively good shape in spite of the diabetes, though I seem to have lost a bit of the oomph and stamina I had even ten years ago. I have short-cut dark grey hair with a few last streaks of black, and fair skin freckled with unpleasant age spots. My face is of the lean sort with a nose and high cheekbones that used to be considered by some who comment on such things to be Roman and aristocratic, and by others, in combination with my dark stare, discomfiting.

Weiler is not the name I was born with, but I do not see how that matters much in the grand scheme of things. After all, it was not my husband's real name, either. I never did figure him out entirely, though I got most of it, and suppose I could have crossed that particular finish line if I had set my mind to it.

Five

The second movement in my wonderful, horrible and terrifying adventure begins – at least for me – early one afternoon in the lounge and game area on the guest side of Chermundo. This happens in early March and the staff has already strung up green and gold bunting and pinned cutout shamrocks and grinning cardboard leprechauns, the tricky little rascals hugging their shining pots of gold. They stuck these merry little imps all over the corkboards even though St. Patrick's Day was over a week away. Back East, the groundhogs have decided there will be more winter, but here in Southern California the spring songbirds are in full chirp and the white false pear tree blossoms are out, though the realists among us know the rain and cold can return at any moment. I am certainly not complaining. Lucky to be alive, call it overtime or extra innings, Shut up and make the best of what life gives you, I say.

The Villas lounge is the hub of our social life, a big community area next to the dining room and kitchen, and today it is alive with the usual chatter and activity. There is a peppy game going on, something designed to keep our ageing minds from drying up like old prunes. Melody, one of our young candy-striper volunteers, is squinting at questions she reads from a prompting page set out on a little stand on the table in front of her, and a cluster of a half dozen or so oldsters are competing to guess the answers. I guess you can say I am part of the group, though I am sitting a little apart from the semi-circle of participants, folded in my favorite deep maroon leather La-Z-Boy chair with the leg section up.

Remember, I told you that at that time I was old. I had Type 2 diabetes back then, and my legs cramped up quite often, particularly after a good walk in the morning. The things they do not tell you about growing old! I've got Doctor Daniel advising that my thighs and calves might ache less if I back off on chocolate. See what I mean about a lot of bad choices and very few good ones? If I will only use a little willpower, I might have fewer leg and back aches but no See's California Dark Chocolate Brittle. What kind of choice is that?

Anyway, there is a bit of irony in my getting on with my story at this moment in time because I have my laptop on my lap and am trying for the ten millionth time to begin writing the romance novel of my dreams. But for the life of me I cannot even get past the title. I have tried Clarissa's Golden Promise and Clarissa's Life Story and The Dreams of Clarissa, and nothing seems to work. I give a frustrated sigh and close the lid.

Jack Hamlin is there, resting in his wheelchair at the far end of the semi-circle from me. He is smiling that serene little smile of his that makes everybody wonder which side of Chermundo he belongs on. He nods his approval as he observes the game. Apparently it is enough for him just to be there.

That is the thing about Jack; when he switches off on the world, if you did not know him well, you might think he is an idiot child grown old. I know a bit more about him than most, because we both have Tom Fennerman as our lawyer, and because Jack is a part of our inner circle, The Old Bunch. Without taking a closer look, anybody can see he is the quiet one with nothing of interest in any direction out of the ordinary. Lord of mercy was I wrong about that one!

The word game is in full play. Candy-striper Melody, who is nearsighted and trying too hard for a husband and so kept at a distance by the handful of eligible male staff members, narrows her gaze and squints at the page in front of her. "Okay, what is the fastest animal on earth?"

"A cheeter!" Show Biz George yells with his customary annoying enthusiasm. George is a bit of a shouter due to the multiple failings of his drawer full of cheap hearing aids. He is wearing his crown of grey hair in the Ben Franklin look and he owns a closet full of designer suits and lounge lizard outfits by a North Hollywood clothier named Sy Devore. Everybody in the movies or television knows Sy Devore is the place where *Hollywood Players* used to go for that *totally today* look. The manly silver screen look is of the highest quality and built to last forever, but George was in his glory in the 1970's and his outfits went out of style when Dean Martin, Frank Sinatra and the rest of that rat bunch were doing movies. Today our Pal Georgie is sporting a red silk shirt and a heavy gold chain that resembles castoff jewelry from that big black guy on The A Team. I am just grateful George's pal Millie has talked him out of wearing his pukka beads.

"That's 'cheetah', George," she shouts in his ear.

Millie is the merriest member of our over-the-hill mob, not looking for a permanent official arrangement but clearly enjoying George's steady male companionship, which she handles in her own endearing, if bossy, way. With her strong features and blond hair with shocks of grey strands, Millie is looking like somebody's Norwegian grandmother out of a YA book about growing up in dairy country with goats and pigs. Her story is that she actually did live on a farm in the Central Valley. It was a hard and somewhat isolated life and her mother died young. After that, Millie ran away from the barnyard chores and became a Kingston Trio groupie and had too much LSD and two coat hanger abortions, all of which slaked her fire for rock and roll. And after *that*, she felt she had no choices left other than to come home and take care of her bossy old dad until it was too late for her to get married. Lucky for her there was oil on the back thousand acres.

She knows crafts and has lots of rural bits of information, like which weeds the California Indians used to make tea for headaches or to power up your spirits and what Mic Jagger liked for breakfast. Maybe she takes her own medicines because she is energetic and spunky enough for two or three of me.

"That's what I said, Millie!" George grumps.

"Yes, Georgy-Porgy," she says, just to get the last word in. George and Millie really are like an old married couple, only they do not know it. When they are around each other they mostly act like spring chickens, sometimes they get so goofy you would think they are fluttery in love. But in the next moment they will be going at each other like a pair of cranky old muskrats.

I sing "Georgy-Porgy pudding pie…"

Except for Herbert, we were all in a cappella singers or glee club at one time or another in high school or college and so, hardly missing a beat, The Old Bunch picks up on it, "Kissed the girls and made them cry/ When the boys came out to play/ he kissed them too, it's all okay!"

Jack is solid in the middle with his steady baritone.

Even The Old Viking manages to get in on the last phrase "…it's all okay!" with that quavering old falsetto of his.

Our spoofy ballad is impromptu and a little raggedy around the edges, but we are all laughing and the quality of our singing does not concern us. We are the Old Bunch, and we know we are good.

"Hey!" George voices a mild complaint, but he does not mean it. I heard his bass in there too, and the quick-brewing spat with his Millie is behind us.

Now let me warn you, here is where my story starts to get the first faint touch of weird to it. This is the moment, one afternoon a week or so before St. Patrick's Day, when a man who does not belong anywhere on the planet walks into the lounge area and sits next to Jack on a sofa to one side of his wheelchair. Jack said he had met him before, and there were times the Stranger had tried to talk to him, but what the fellow said had never made any sense to Jack so he has been doing his best to ignore him. Anyway, this is the first time the odd fellow has showed up when Jack is not alone. Still, it does not make any sense to Jack one way or the other at the time, because in the crowded lounge area, Jack is the only person who can see him.

And me. I do not know why, but I swear to you on a stack of bibles, I can see him, too!

Six

Something happens to my eyesight. This Stranger absolutely is not there, and then there is a moment when everything is brightly swirling patterns like I am falling into a carnival mascara color wheel and I think I am going to faint, but when I shake my head things seem to clear, and I see that we humans on the planet earth are not alone.

No. I am not describing it exactly, and this is important if you are ever going to believe me, so let me take another shot at it.

One moment there I am, looking across the lounge in Jack's general direction. He is just sitting there by himself. And then there is a sort-of disturbance next to him, something in the air space, an unusual something on the very edge of what ordinary people ever get to see with their own eyesight.

The thing-whatever has a shape about the size of a person, but while distinct, it is not solid. It is not an outline, either, and it is not wobbling or wiggling or waffling. What can I say about it that makes any sense? It is…well, sort of dull reddish at first. Then it somehow modulates itself from transparent to translucent red, and then solid red. And then it quickly shifts itself through the light spectrum like it is looking for a color on which to settle – red, orange, yellow, green, blue, purple and into violet. When it reaches violet it reverses itself from solid through translucent to transparent. And then it briefly winks out, leaving me blinking and thinking my old eyesight is playing tricks on me.

But that only lasts a second, and then this happening shifts itself back through to solid, assumes somewhat accurate coloration and finally settles a look that is on the dull side of a rather common everyday reality.

What I have witnessed apparently materializing out of nothing is an ordinary looking man with grayish skin and slicked back hair. He looks like he could be one of Dr. Spock's Vulcan cousins from Star Trek, except that he is not wearing a future suit or anything. He is wearing a severe black jacket. And he has on a pair of cotton khaki cargo pants, and sandals from ancient Rome or the Banana Republic, I cannot decide which. He has the cocky attitude of a television game show host, and I find myself thinking Jack Nicholson could play him, a cross between Jack's role as the devil in Witches of Eastwick and the loveable if mentally off-center author in As Good As It Gets.

At first, my mind cannot accept what is happening. I am thinking I fuzzed out for a moment in a swoon or near-faint, and when I am alright again, there he is. I try to hang on to my wits, saying to myself, Do not go whacko-bird here, Lucy, or they will haul you off to the other side. Still, irrational thoughts flash through my mind. The guy owns a cloak of invisibility or whatever it is. On the other hand, except for his novel way of entering a room, he does not seem that much out of the ordinary. I tell myself maybe I am imagining things. Maybe he is a schoolteacher pal of Jack's, or one of those fellows from JPL Jack met when he worked with them on his Mars Rover ideas. Or maybe he just wants to sell Jack an annuity or a condo in Baja. That must be it; he must be some slick sales guy and that seems right because my first impression is that I do not trust him as far as I can spit, which was not very far at all -- even when I was a kid and used to practice with the farm kids in the back of the schoolyard at Chatsworth High. But now this strange newcomer is talking.

"Hi, Jackie-boy," he says. "I'm back again and I've got big news!"

Jack's frown deepens and he looks away, pretending to ignore the Stranger, but this does not deter the odd newcomer's enthusiasm in the slightest.

"Jack, you get to partner up with me on the 998th Cross-Galactic Save Your Planet Show!"

Jack still does not see him, or if he does, he chooses to ignore him.

The Stranger waves his arms wide and twirls them in a grand and somewhat goofy gesture, "It's us, Jackie-boy! Ta Daa! Ta-Daa! Ta Daa!"

On the one hand, that was almighty perceptive of me to pin this guy as a sleazy game show host; on the other, it merely serves to alert you to what deep manure I have stepped into. There is no "Save Your Planet Show." Bright smiling fellows do not materialize and offer prizes to the residents of retirement homes. And yet, here this strange newcomer is, still fine tuning his color a bit, now concentrating on the shades of grey in his skin tones.

I find myself thinking, Beige pallet, you moron! That was just automatic on my part. Call it instinct or early training. I was not trying to be mean; putting on makeup is something women learn when they are little girls.

It was just a thought that popped into my head, and yet the Stranger was instantly rattled, as if he could hear what I was thinking. Some talk show host, letting a casual aside from an old lady from Chatsworth throw him off his game!

Regardless of who he is or what he thinks he is doing, the next moment he puts on his game show face and does a little humming "Save the Planet" tune as if singing to himself or a camera hidden somewhere, and he pats his hair, looking around the room, his quick eyes darting here and there as if he is trying to spot something or somebody. I pretend to be interested in my laptop, but in truth I am stunned by the magical appearance of this odd bird, a wannabe wild and crazy guy who claims to be running his own whacko-bird Save the Planet show. What will he come up with next – enlisting us all to collect our ice cubes from the refrigerator and ship them to the Arctic circle to cure global warming?

I am Lucy Weiler, grade school teacher retired, and this sort of thing does not happen in my real world. After all, I have lived a normal, sane life and I do know what can and what cannot be so.

I take a calm breath and cast a furtive glance in his direction. This oddly animated, almost human looking stranger looks to me to be an old guy, somewhere in his mid-70s, maybe ten years older than Jack. It does not matter that he is neither on staff or a guest here, or that he should not be here, because nobody notices him enough to say anything one way or the other. And, you know, on an ordinary level, the guy does almost fit in. He sits there on a chair next to Jack, full of excitement with his news as he nervously munches on a peanut butter sandwich. He is certainly the right age and dressed well enough to actually be living as a guest at the Chermundo Villas, though that Nehru jacket of his went out a long time ago. But I get it right away that the fellow not only is not a guest, he may actually be invisible to everybody but Jack and me – because when Jack's pal Herbert comes over to ask him to spell something or other, the newcomer has to stand up quickly and scoot out of the way and then The Old Viking sits right on the spot where he had been sitting. I find myself thinking this must be reassuring to Jack, maybe, in an odd way, that he is seeing a real invisible person, if you catch my meaning. But then I guess, if Jack really is thinking that way, this realization only serves to reinforce his notion that he is making it all up in his mind. Jack has to be thinking there is not and never will be an invisible stranger. Life goes on, dull and monotone, at the Chermundo, without such happenings.

And I am right in there with Jack, thinking maybe I also am taking a trip in the Crazy Car. Maybe there is no invisible newcomer. You see, Herbie does not think much about other people's feelings, and he would be the one to ignore anybody and push them aside, particularly when he has business on his mind. Still, I am getting shivery tingles, what my students a decade or two ago used to call bad vibes.

This new guy certainly blew in like a paranormal perception, and he absolutely is unusual looking, something not quite right about him. Maybe it is his jet black hair, all slicked back and shiny, and maybe there is something reptilian in his features, like he is trying to be ordinary but cannot quite get it right, and maybe it is even the grey-blue pallor of his skin, which seems to be off-color and smooth as if it does not have any pores, like he is wearing a light application of makeup, a thing that one or two of the old men still on the prowl at the Villas have taken up, particularly to hide the dark bags under their eyes. Come on, Lucy, maybe he is just a sales guy, I keep trying to reassure myself; maybe that is it.

The Stranger leans closer to Jack and speaks to him. "Stop ignoring me, Jack. You're on Celestial Celebrity Apprentice and it's not good for the cameras!"

And I can understand what he is saying! I am certainly out of range of a low whisper, and it is a few sentences before I am aware of something stunningly impossible – I am not hearing sounds, I can hear this fellow's thoughts in my head! What an incredible moment this is for me! Me, Lucy Weiler, the most common person on the block, reading minds! But even as this realization boots me in the head, I do not really believe it. It is just too out of the ordinary for me to accept and I go looking for other explanations. You know how some rooms seem to magnify the sounds depending where you are? That is what I am thinking. I am in a little sound-cove or something like that, and so I can hear their conversation.

"Hello, Jack," he says. "We're live here, beaming across the galaxy, and you've got to give me something, I'm dying here."

Jack continues to ignore him, which on the one hand is not at all out of the ordinary. As a general rule Jack pretty much ignores everybody and everything except his roommate, Herbert and sometimes me. Living in his own world, is how Dr. Daniel describes the way he is.

But the strange fellow persists. "Jack, Jack, Jack. Earth to Jack." He snickers to himself, as if he has said

29

something funny. "Hello, Jack. Come on, Jack, I know you can hear me."

Stop pestering him! I think without any premeditation, the thought just blurts out of my brain. The Stranger blinks. He looks around in surprise, and catches that I am looking at him. Our eyes lock, and in that moment I am dizzy with what I can only describe as a download of information. "Not one human in a million! Stroke of pure luck! I am trying to help! Twenty Two contestants!" All this, and a flurry of images hit my consciousness, weird looking octopus creatures and green monkey boys and feathered jackals waving goodbye, visuals of a long voyage streaking across what must be billions of stars, maybe the Milky Way. Loneliness. Empty space. And finally, an arrival.

Amazing! Jack may not get it, but ten seconds and I am already a true believer! We are at the Chermundo Villas in a room full of guests and there absolutely is a creature from somewhere in deep outer space who says he wants to help us, and Jack and I are the only two who can sense this creature is here. But who is he? What does he want? He says he is trying to help us, but help us to do what?

But the Stranger does not answer my concerns or continue looking at me. Then I realize he is talking in another direction, "Through an amazing bit of research and wizardry," he announces to a camera lens that I cannot see, "I have just made contact with Lucy Weiler, one of prime team leader Jack Hamlin's close allies!"

Jack looks straight ahead, his eyes on the word game and with just the gentle smile on his lips maybe stiffening a little. His gaze flicks to me and then settles on Herbert Miller. The Old Viking is half-sitting, half crouching nearby, furiously keying a computer, one of four in a row with big print screens designed for the percentage of guests who cannot afford their own machines or have not bothered to update their eyeglass prescriptions.

Seven

I came here looking for a quiet refuge from ordinary life, not weird alien strangers. I had enough of strange surprises, of rotten husbands, of secrets and hidden lives. I was an only child and, thanks to my lying, cheating Ted, when I entered Chermundo Villa had no children of my own.

I would say most of us are relatively happy and carefree, at least we pretty much are that way until Doctor Humphrey starts his propaganda campaign about the benefits of incorporating the Villas with some big combine of old people's homes. A few days after the kidnapping of the Old Viking incident, the chubby little man in his well-worn, shiny suit slithers up to me in the lounge. I am alone, of course, in my favorite chair, trying again to begin my romantic fantasy story about Clarissa and her love life. This is the way our director operates; he tries to cut his prey from the herd, to get them alone so he can work his evil magic.

"My dear Lucy," he begins.

"I am not *your dear anything*, Mister Goozeman."

"*Doctor* Goozeman."

"You see I am busy, Goozeman. Please take your business somewhere else."

"It is not strictly my business, Ms. Weiler. It is our business, and it is a matter vital to your staying on here at Chermundo Villas. You have not returned the new agreement we mailed to all the guests."

"Do not worry yourself about it. It looked like you were trying to *replace* our old agreement, so I sent it to my lawyer."

His face flushes red and his cheeks puff out, "There was no need for that. It is just a simple addendum to the normal leasing contract."

"We think there was sufficient reason."

"We?" He clenches his fists and throws his chest out like an aggressive little schoolyard bully.

"Yes. We." I know he is an insecure little worm and I am not about to illuminate him whether we means two or twenty guests. Let him worry about contracts, lawyers and lawsuits. I give him a cold glance of dismissal, "Now get away from me. I'll be in touch if I have a complaint you need to hear about. Or my lawyer will."

He struggles in a vain attempt to mask his anger and then he storms out of the lounge. What does Goozeman want? The contract he has asked us to sign is a long mess of legal gobblygook, so I can only guess. We guests at the Chermundo technically lease space here; I say technically, because if you have ever been an oldster or been involved in signing up an older person in your own family for retired living, you know you need a lawyer like our Tom Fennerman to make sure things are set out straight.

You would think everything would be cut-and-dried, but it is something like a time share lease promoted by slicksters; once you have committed to the deal, they have you in their clutches for the length of the lease. And, if you are unhappy and alone, then what are you going to do, pay big money to go somewhere else that is probably just about the same?

The Villas has the architectural air of a sprawling Spanish hacienda; the ambiance speaks to the unknowing observer of pleasant informality and few restrictions. I think that is actually a carefully thought out design for success in the old folks housing business. At our place, there are two connected buildings; each is a distinct section, with the more exclusive, hidden and expensive one offering complete and guarded hospice care. There is a big garden courtyard in the center of the complex between the two sections, with chairs and tables for outdoor moments and wide, curving sidewalks for the semi-serious walkers who do not wish to brave the urban streets of Encino, and behind that, the mandatory community swimming pool with its heated spa.

Our pal Herbert the Old Viking is a good example of how not to sign on for an old folk's home. The situation for such unfortunate oldsters comes up suddenly and is pretty much unexpected. Their reaction is I don't want to live with that bunch of old people – that's not for ME!? That is clearly how Herbie feels, and quite a few others I see around me at the Chermundo.

When my time came, I was the other way around. I did not want a replacement husband or a special best friend or a brand new significant other, but I also did not want to be alone, and so I researched and tried to get into the best place I could. I wanted a private life, and yet felt the need for the touch and crush of ordinary people around me, and medical help if I would need it. After Ted departed, our neighborhood had endured a rash of home robberies. That ugly business encouraged me to put my old Victorian farmhouse up for sale. So I made my choices and I live here in my own small suite. I lease a small living room, tiny kitchenette, bath and bedroom. I have a big Victorian sofa, some few pieces of antique china and silverware, a narrow, high-topped Elizabethan writing desk, and a single bed with one of those adjustable motors to ease the back and leg pain. Everything just-right-sized as the bears in Goldilocks might say and absolutely no room for a new fellow who would like nothing better than to sign his name where Gregory Otis Mittelbaum's had been on my checking account.

As for the smaller section of the Villas that I mentioned earlier, that is called The Z section, The Z ward, or simply The Z. That is where the Alzheimer's patients are penned in, though talking about it like that seems a little cruel; maybe I should have said cared for, after all, there is no guarantee I will not end up there myself. The tone Z-side is, the brochures comfort us, as similar to the warm Chermundo Villas family atmosphere as possible. We may be old, but we are not idiots; we can see there are locks on the doors, and Z section guests may show up for holiday celebration luncheons, but they are always escorted to and from their rooms, and they cannot leave the Z whenever they want. If you are not of a certain age, maybe you will not understand when I say there are some benefits to an early death.

Eight

But let us return now to the first time I meet the Stranger. He appears somewhat marvelously out of nowhere. He plagues Jack about participation in some weird galactic game show. Jack ignores him. He tries to cling to his sanity by focusing on the real world madness and delusions of his pal, Herbert Miller, otherwise known as the Old Viking.

Herbert has a dark complexion, a pencil moustache, and jet black hair. His is the flashy smile of an old used car salesman, a confident smirk that shows his perfect set of stark white implants. He is certifiably nuts, what I will have to describe as a furtive oddball; by that I mean he is the perfect cliché of a conspiratorial old guy who is so obvious that he draws attention to the variety of silly things he is trying to hide from everybody – from the doctors, the staff, the regular guests and even us, his own gang of six. These socially awkward little mannerisms of his range from snitching handfuls of sugar packets from the self-serve line in the restaurant section of our dining room to snatching his mail and faxes from the startled hands of the junior orderly entrusted with the unfortunate task of delivering them.

To me, Herb's impatience, his casual rudeness and sudden flashes of anger are signs that his brain is melting faster than a lemon flavor snow cone at Sunset Beach in the summertime, but I am no expert and Herbert does not really bother me; live and let live, you know. And he is interesting, what the heck, I have been thinking for some time that maybe I can use him as a colorful, unstable and erratic character in my romance novel, a bit of comic relief between all the lustful looks and heavy panting. You know the formula for writing pulp romance, guy meets girl, guy gets girl, guy loses girl, and guy gets girl again for a happy ending. Shakespeare had his Falstaff and maybe my muse has granted me Herbert the Old Viking.

At this moment, when Jack tries to avoid his invisible visitor by looking over to see what is up, Herbert is growling to himself, "Ring-rang, ding-dang, bing-bang, lousy no good rotten English language, nothing spells like it sounds…fricking, fracking—Jack…hey, Jack!"

And Jack, even though he is looking right at his pal Herbert, is having thoughts that are a thousand miles away. Now that I realize Jack has a visitor from an extremely long distance, I find it impossible to blame him.

Wheelchair Jack comes back to ordinary, everyday reality with a start, "Yes, what, Herbert?"

"Jack, good buddy-friend-pal. How do you spell 'senile'?"

"S-E-N-I-L-E.

Herb still thinks of himself as un-retired, and his business schemes are much bandied about by the scoffers and the wise crackers here. He is the subject matter for lots of bad jokes and general laughing matter among us guests, sometimes me included, if truth be told. If he is not dickering to buy a time share in Katmandu, the Old Viking is shouting on the phone to negotiate transfers of funds from a surprise inheritance in some far-off place like Cairo or Belgrade, found money from a distant relative he has never even heard of who died in a tragic accident and left him everything.

Jack gives Herbert a bit more of his attention. "Herb, don't let the orderlies or the nurses catch you talking to your damn Nigerian friends."

"Friends?! Them bastards owe me thirty-five million five hundred thousand dollars! That's three five comma five zero zero comma zero zero zero dollars and no cents, Jack, in case you can't count no more."

Jack shrugs and looks around the room. His gaze returns to the Stranger, and he notices I am watching him, and that is when Jack starts thinking seriously that something out of the ordinary really might be happening, that is, something outside his own imagination. The odd fellow smiles back at him and shrugs, as if he is agreeing, Yes, Lucy is looking this way, and she sees me, too. Come on, Jack, we've got trillions of couch poopers across the galaxy hanging on your every word – only you're not saying anything!

Jack shakes his head and looks away, in the direction of the computer nook. He knows the Z ward beckons, and he is not going to play the fool for an imaginary apparition of his own making.

"Herbert, you're an idiot," he says. "The Nigerians don't owe you anything. It's a scam to make you think there's an accounting error."

The Old Viking slams both hands down on the keyboard and glares at his best buddy, "Don't tell me stuff, Jack! I once shipped big ticket items all over the world, my dubious friend! Fire trucks and ambulances and telephone poles to Dubai!"

This is what I mean; one moment Herbert is fairly reasonable, and the next he is a raging ranter.

"Telephone poles?" Jack asks.

Herbert nods emphatically. He is back to Mister Totally Sane again. He stabs in the general direction of his roommate with a crooked forefinger, "Shows what little you know, Jack! Pine trees don't grow on the desert; the A-rabs gotta get them from North Carolina. Jack-buddy, I done it all: steam engines to Jordan, containers of Pentax cameras shipped in right here from Kyoto, pen-lights and car key lights from—"

"Right. Okay, Herbie. I know you were a big success; but you only had six people working for you, not 600. You didn't do multi-million dollar deals and you never shipped anything to or from Nigeria.

But Herbert is back on full vent, "No stupid Chermundo dicto-crats is going to stop me, Jack! I'm a person! I got my rights, you know!"

Jack forgets about his invisible visitor, at least for the moment. He looks around to see if any staff members are in the room. If Herbert gets caught emailing scam artists, the Villas personnel will take away his internet password and he will become insufferable. Chermundo does not want to be liable, even though The Old Viking has his own laptop back in his room that they cannot legally do a thing about. But at least when he loses everything he owns, disappointed relatives will be less able to turn vindictive and trace it back to a Chermundo machine.

Herbert goes back to his keyboard and, at least for the moment, everything seems okay. Nearby, the Sharpen-Your-Brain Game continues.

Melody squints at her cue page. She leans forward and pulls the clear plastic stand within range of her myopic vision, "The capital of Rhode Island?"

There is a pause. I can see nobody knows. George finally guesses, "Quebec?"

Millie gleefully jumps on his answer, "George, you don't just say the first thing that comes to your head!"

"You know what Marilyn Monroe said about Canada?

"No, George, what?"

"She said she thought it was up in the mountains somewhere."

Jack is trying to be patient. He is reluctant to continue his going-nowhere argument with Herbert, but now he is worried not only about seeing an invisible visitor, but about the Old Viking getting in trouble. Everybody knows Herbert is a silly and hopeless over-the-hiller-bird, but still, the wily old geek is Jack's friend, one of his few friends. "Yes, Herb, you have rights. Everybody has the right to be made a fool. But that's not the point. The policy here at Chermundo-"

"I know they got a ding-dang policy, Jack! Stop riding my ass about it!"

"Herbert. Last time, they took away your internet for a month. You get scalped by African crooks and they will not want a law suit from your nephew.

"What does that bling-blang little rat turd Sidney have to do with it?"

"That's not the point, Herbie. The point is Chermundo doesn't want to be held liable."

I am watching Jack and Herbert from my spot at the corner of the semi-circle around Melody. I am more interested in the Stranger and in hearing what is going on between him and Jack than the capital of Rhode Island."

"Providence," I say, just to keep the game going.

And, would you believe it, my pal, that henna-headed she-devil trickster Delrina complains about this, just like she always does. "It's not fair," she says. "Lucy was a schoolteacher. She knows everything about everything. I say she ought to sit out every second question."

"Now who is the sore loser?" George pipes up.

I can see Herbert bending over to Jack, speaking conspiratorially, but, deaf like he is, anybody half-listening like I am can easily make out what he is saying.

"I got my own internet in my very own room," Herbert growls angrily. "This big screen's too public anyway. Every-stinking-body is able to poke in my privates."

This, in turn, upsets Jack. "Herbie, you asked me!"

Actually, I am pleased to see a little fire in Jack. He has shown himself to be a friendly force and so I am worried about him. I like to see his attention is still at least a little bit in the real world. As I may have mentioned, the people on this side of the Villas have to band together to keep each other out of the Z zone. But clearly this is going to get a touch more complicated for both of us now that we are having parallel delusions about visitors from outer space. The nuts should stay together in the same bowl, because there is security in numbers.

"Yeah," Herbert is saying, "but just to spell a word. I didn't ask for no fricking, fracking international economic advisor to show up."

But there is little enough reason to be worried about Jack actually losing his temper. In the next minute he is off in another world, looking at nothing and talking to his invisible visitor. Even if you are not as old as Jack and me, try to grasp the dilemma:

Jack does not know for sure that I can see the Stranger and actually communicate with him. How can he convince himself that he is really not a crazy person seeing crazy things nobody in their right mind ever could explain? You or I certainly would not want to try to explain them. That is why people with real jobs in the real world refuse to put their hands up when the Las Vegas or Laughlin lounge entertainer looks out at his audience and asks, *Anybody ever see a flying saucer?* All this, and the newcomer is not going to let up on Jack.

"Hello, Jack," the Stranger says. "Welcome from the CBC."

"Canadian Broadcast Company?" Jack gives him a derisive look.

"Cosmic," the Stranger corrects him. "Broadcasting across the sentient...err, from a long way away..."

Jack sighs and tries to hide his response. "Shhh. Go away."

That is when Herbert angrily slams his hand on the computer monitor. It has gone blank screen on him, and apparently for no reason, though with Herb's shaky hands, you never know. "God damn it! Bumped off again! Talk about scams, this service is criminal, that's what!"

Herbert grabs his papers and the notes he has scribbled on any paper he could find, and scrunches himself away from the computers. He is bent over like an old crab as he angrily makes his way out of the room.

In the background, George exclaims, "A-ber-ham Lincoln!"

And Delrina pats her reddish-black curls and jokes, "You would know, George! You were alive back then!" She's talking to George, but her dark eyes follow Herbert as he scoots out of the room, and for maybe the tenth time I wonder if she is a little sweet on the old coot.

But Jack, well, about then our friend Jack is getting a little wild-eyed.

"He dropped a paper," the Stranger persists.

Jack's worried glance darts around the room. He catches my eye again, shakes his head and looks away. He speaks quietly through gritted teeth, "Lucy, would you do me a favor and pick up that paper Herbie dropped?"

I retrieve it and hand it to Jack, but not before I see the fancy letterhead. "Bank of Nigeria," I say. "Impressive."

"Thanks," Jack says, but he is shaking his head. "Just another scam."

"Poor Herbie," I say.

"What's it say?" the Stranger asks.

Jack and I look at each other. Jack shrugs and gives me a look, welcoming me to his weird world of the unusual and the unknown. "It says the Bank of Nigeria will release funds in excess of thirty five million dollars U.S. transferred directly into his account when Herbert Miller pays the transfer, holding and administrative fees of twenty four thousand dollars U.S."

"So it begins," the Stranger says. He is not looking at us. He is talking into a camera that we cannot see. He continues, "An accomplished crook in a place half way around on the other side of this planet starts out to swindle a small packet of gain from an elderly businessman and inadvertently sets in motion a complicated string of events that will end in the destruction of the sentient life on this solar system."

Candy-striper Melody says, "Planet closest to the sun."

"Mercury," the Stranger says. He smiles patiently as Jack and I stare at each other.

"*Merc*-ury!" George shouts.

Melody launches a new question and Millie answers "Roosevelt."

"Teddy or FDR?"

Jack throws up his hands. "Lucy, what is going on?"

"Intergalactic Entertainment has spent a lot of resources to get here," the Stranger tells him. "I convinced them to shoot the whole wad, grease the entire pig, and blow the bundle. Now I need you to convince me it was worth it."

"And how do I do that?" Jack sounds bewildered.

"Just give me a couple of one-liners here, pal. This place is a jewel. Blue skies. Waving fields of grain. Anything."

Jack is dumbstruck, no help at all and the Stranger looks frustrated and more than a little angry, so I figure What the heck, give it a shot, and I sing, "Oh beautiful for spacious skies/ for amber waves of grain…"

Without missing a beat, The Old Bunch picks up on it, "For purple mountain majesties/ Above the fruited plain! America! America! / God shed his grace on thee / And crown thy good with brotherhood / From sea to shining sea!"

"Now that was more like it!" The Stranger shouts his approval, apparently to the entire sentient galaxy, "It's me, good old DS, yes, the spin-spinner himself, coming your way from Contestant Planet Number 20, a beautiful blue sky place with amber and fruited grains, worthy of your most excellent consideration!"

It feels nice that our singing is appreciated, except nobody in the lounge except Jack and me hears him.

The perk-your-brain game continues. Melody asks, "The biggest planet?"

"Nerphonius P-3," the Stranger says. "At least in this slice of the galactic pizza." Jack and I shrug at each other.

"JU-pit-er!" George yells.

"The biggest ego," Millie wise-cracks, "That would be George!"

Their laughter is interrupted by Mason. Mason is a young black guy, our daytime orderly here at Chermundo. He is a big man, but even tempered, and he is one of the good staffers, a person we feel we can trust. "Movie time!" he announces. "It's 'Shane,' starring Alan Ladd!"

Jack looks at the Stranger, "The shrimp who won the west."

"Don't change the subject, Jack."

Jack frowns and turns his head away from his invisible companion, still about as certain as I am that we are both crazy and the odd, nearly-human looking fellow is just another abominable sign of advancing old age. The brain game breaks up and the players rise and begin to move slowly from the room.

Nine

I am caught on the horns of a galloping dilemma. Naturally, I want to stay in the room and, after everybody goes, rush up to Jack and the Stranger and make some sense out of what is happening. Come on, if you were living in my beat up old gym shoes, you would too. But Mason wants to know if I am coming along to see the movie. I delay by waving him and Melody on. I make a fuss about getting out of the chair by myself for the exercise.

As the Old Bunch starts to make their exit, George is blathering knowledgeably about the filming of 'Shane,' "Short little Alan Ladd couldn't have been more than five seven. He did his scenes by walking on apple boxes so he looked tall as the other cowboys."

"Oh, George," Millie says, "Everybody who lives here in Southern California knows that."

I reluctantly begin to fold my tent, figuring I have no choice but to tag along. It takes me a moment to close down my laptop, and my latest failed attempt at novel writing is now completely vanished from my mind. I have written nothing, not even decided on a title. I use the lounge chair's auto-lifter to give me the usual slow grind of a boost to my feet. By this time, most of the guests who want to see the movie have already left for our small auditorium.

Mason grins, happy because he assumes I am joining in. He pauses in the doorway, "You coming, Jack?"

I slow down even more, wondering if Jack will come, and if he does, will the strange visitor come along, too? I cannot seem to settle my thoughts. I do not know what to do.

But Jack is again talking to the Stranger. This is not good, because Mason is standing not two dozen feet away, and he cannot see the visitor or he would have mentioned something. The worst thing is, Mason will now think he is seeing proof that Jack talks to thin air.

When Jack finally turns to the orderly, he shakes his head. "No, thank you, Mason," he says politely. "Shane rides away into the sunset at the end, or is that giving too much away?"

Jack returns to his other conversation, "Why are you bothering me with this crap?" he asks.

I am half-way across the room before the Stranger answers. "Because everybody is ahead of us and we're such a pig head and we're almost out of time," he says. He looks apologetically in the direction of his invisible camera, "That is what is called tough love here on this lovely blue planet earth set on the far away rim of our mother galaxy."

Now I know you will probably think I am just as crazy as Jack, but I heard all of it, including that last sharp warning, "we're almost out of time." And my head is full of questions; who is almost out of time? Late for the movie? Something else? Was Jack now taking both sides of the conversation, turning his monologue into a dialogue? And then I realize it was the pure thought again, a mental illumination, an energy-thought in my own brain, straight from the strange being to me, "we're almost out of time!"

Melody the candy-striper has lingered to straighten up the chairs. She puts a hand on Mason's arm, and they exchange a moment of mutual understanding. I can see the two of them have not heard any strange voices or seen any odd strangers.

However, they both have seen Jack, clear as day, talking to empty air. Mason and Melody are looking disappointed. Everybody likes Jack, and they see the dark shadow of the Z ward moving ever closer, getting ready to pounce on him. Mason shakes his head and they leave, heading for the movie. I go in the other direction, toward the kitchen serving line which is now empty while waiting for a flock of aluminum trays for the evening meal. From the open alcove, I can watch Jack and the Stranger.

Jack is raising his voice in a rare display of anger. "Great! They overhear me talking to an empty chair! You can't do this! You have to leave me alone!

"As if you have a lot of visitors."

"You're not a visitor; you're a – a figment!" Jack grips the wheel rails of his wheelchair and rolls himself out of the room. The Stranger remains seated, watching him leave. A moment before, the odd fellow was wearing a confident show biz look along with an almost smug air of superiority, but now he looks vulnerable and uncertain. He sees me watching him and gives me a sad expression. *You humans are hopeless. And I thought I had a shot at the big time.*

It does not seem right to say nothing, so I blurt out the first thing that comes to mind, *So you are only thinking of yourself! You do not care one way or the other if Jack ends up in the Z ward.*

Z ward? Of course I care. That's not the game we are playing here. We're not playing a game. He pauses, evaluating what he has just said. *Well, maybe we are, but it is bigger than you think. Everything is at stake for you. Everything!* He looks vulnerable and I think maybe I have been too hard on him.

Do not give up on yourself, I tell him. *Or on us puny earthlings. Maybe it will work out alright.*

He gazes at his half-finished peanut butter sandwich, takes another bite, and then sets it on a nearby end table. The sandwich remains, but the image of the Stranger slowly does a rippling fade to invisibility.

I hope you are right. The stranger's thoughts drift into my head. *From your mouth to God's ear.*

Okay, so now I may be hearing voices out of nowhere, but I recognize the blessing. *So you're Jewish then?*

No. Inner Plaiedian, actually. He is almost gone before he fades back into view and I can see him studying me. *You are an extremely intelligent being.*

Not really. I automatically dismiss his comment, thinking he must be buttering me up for some reason.

You figured out Ted Weiler, didn't you?

I am too stunned to think clearly. This odd apparition knows about the tragedy of my life! "S-some of it," My voice stutters my startled response out loud; I blurt out the first thing that comes to mind. I really must be cracking up.

There are incidents and accidents, he says, *but true coincidence is universally non-existent.*

Before I can shape even the first of the hundred questions that burble up in my mind, his image does a fast left-to-right zip to nothing, and he is gone.

Ten

Back in the day, that is, when I had just turned thirty, the man I married had told me his name was Ted Weiler. 'Ted' turned out to be a keeper of many secrets, not all of them pleasant, and looking back, I can see that when I met him I was little more than a naïve and trusting San Fernando Valley farm girl who had gone away to Pomona College, which was itself at that time little more than a respectable and ambitious backwash educational institute of higher learning. I lived my early adult years thinking the world was a wholesome place full of decent people trying their best to live their lives in a responsible way and do good things for one another. I tell myself I still travel that yellow brick road, but my bottom line is that deep down I no longer believe "gooderism" to be a universal definition of the human condition.

As a child, I was raised at the far northwest end of the San Fernando Valley, north of Chatsworth in the shadow of the Vasquez rocks. Those were the days, the late 1940s and early 50s when it was still mostly corn, horses and giant strawberries.

When I was in my gawky teens, my mom and dad took the grapevine, that winding two lane blacktop over the mountains to the Central Valley. The goal of their trip was to pick up a load of hay bales for our few dozen cows and horses but, while heading north and negotiating the sharp downhill curves on the steep and winding northern side, the brakes on their old Ford pickup gave out and the truck accelerated until it was going so fast it went flying off the road. In those days, similar accidents happened with such frequency the state highway repairmen eventually installed gravel traps. That downhill run is so dangerous that those traps are still in service even though today the grapevine is a major freeway. But that was too late to save my parents.

I had been packing my books and clothes for my second year at Pomona College at the time. I may have been naïve and awkward, but I was of age and a responsible sort. I missed the first semester, but was determined to get my education. With the help of my father's lawyer, I sold the land and kept the farmhouse and a few acres, and hitched a ninety-mile ride with two other students east to Pomona in a faded green DeSoto, making it in time for the start of the second semester.

After college, I had my busy life as a third grade schoolteacher. I met Ted at a high school reunion in Chatsworth. I did not remember him from school, and neither did anybody else, and I guess that should have been a warning, but I was head over heels in the usual way and blissfully unaware of the things that might happen. In the everyday experiences of my life up until that time, fakes, liars, thieves and murderers did not pop up pretending to be ordinary people. And Ted was very good at deception, so good, in fact, that I was only able to find and fit together some of his missing parts after he died.

"You don't want to know about it, kiddo," he told me. "I work for the U.S. of America government, for a quiet little company that sub-contracts from the FBI."

"Oh," I said. I had not really asked, and continued to fold the dried laundry from a basket I had brought in from the clothes lines strung in the back yard.

"My work," he continued without prompting, "my job is very hush-hush, and really too boring to even get into."

"Okay," I said.

"I spend most of my time tracing crooked money that is being slipped back into the economy as legal profits."

"Uh-huh," I said. I did not know what to say. It was like playing a bit part in a gangster movie, the faithful wife of one of the G-men who had no idea what her husband did.

49

"The international bad rascals doing this – you would know their names, sweet-cheeks, if I should have the bad judgment to say them out loud and jeopardize your well-being – these bad guys are very good at what they do and you must never know about them or your life will be in danger."

"Okay," I said. "Can you take the laundry basket out to the back porch for me?" He agreed to do that and we never said another word about it.

The hardest parts for me were the times when Ted was called away for weeks. There would be no way to get in contact with him, but, as he explained over and over again, that was for my own good.

It was only after his terminal accident that I found out Ted Weiler was not his real name, and he himself was one of the bad rascals, probably one of the worst individuals I would ever personally meet. And, looking back, even though we were legally married at that time with golden wedding rings and all, I was in fact little more than what an unkind observer might call his West Coast lay.

After I said yes to the man, we were married in a small white Lutheran church and he moved in with me in my old family farm house. He converted the deserted farm workers quarters into a two car garage and an office at one end where he did his secret job. I was never allowed in there. Papa had grown some eucalyptus trees to rim the half dozen acres that remained of my property and there was enough land for two horses and a little strawberry patch that still grew giant succulent strawberries in the shadows of a rectangular patch of sweet corn. Over the years that followed, Chatsworth became more and more of an outlying suburb of Los Angeles, but as our house was tucked back against the sandstone outcropping of the Rocks, the urbanization mostly took place out and away from us.

Looking back, most of my life with Ted was not bad at all. We settled down and had our years together. We went on trips around Arizona and New Mexico in the summer months when my school kids were out on vacation. Those were the best times for me.

One April we had the AAA Indian Country road map out on the dining room table. We were going over plans to explore some two lane blacktops in Northern New Mexico.

"Look, look, look, honey-pie!" Ted said. His stubby forefinger pointed out a road running south out of Albuquerque. "Turquoise Trail! Parallels the road to Silver City!"

Ted knew I loved turquoise probably more than diamonds, which was good for him because he had never given me a sparkler. Still, as I studied the map, the roads seemed to go from black lines to black dashes and then to beige dots, and some of them dead ended in what looked like nowhere.

"Isn't that kind of a desert area, Teddy-Bear?"

"Lu, Lu, Lu – Look! Turquoise Trail! They show seven or eight mines all within fifty miles! We could get some big chunks of the blue stuff, right from the source!"

I was not totally convinced, but he was very excited about it, and with my husband along what could go wrong? We were looking at the book that listed motels along the way when the phone rang. Ted rushed to pick it up as he always did, and, sure enough, it was for him. No big surprise, nobody ever called me except to renew my subscription to Writer's Digest or to inform me little Billy had the flu and would not be in class for a few days.

Ted's call was important. One of his front burner projects had gone hot, as he used to say. "Change of plans," he told me, and he did look a little flustered and even annoyed.

He packed in an hour, gave me a peck on the cheek, and headed for the door. He had already called a taxi. The cabbie drove him to the Burbank airport and the man named Ted took off out of my life forever.

I was to make the motel arrangements while he was gone. Los Angeles to Flagstaff to Gallup to Santa Fe, and then wandering back roads on down the Turquoise Trail to the Silver City-Deming area. He said he would be back in three weeks, plenty of time to pack our bags and shoot off motoring east across the Mojave. But after one month went by I had to cancel the Best Western reservations, and after a second month, I panicked and had a locksmith out to make a set of keys for his office, hoping I might find some clue as to his whereabouts. It was three keys, actually, a regular lock and two deadbolts. Once I had the keys, I was able to open the door into my Teddy-Bear's other life. I did not see all that much, but it was enough to cure me of my lingering naïveté on life, love and the pursuit of personal happiness.

Ted Weiler had another family! He had another wife and grown children, a boy and a girl, that, from the photograph on his desk, looked to be in their early teens. In the later years of our being together, he had worked from a laptop, and he had taken that with him. I searched every inch of his office, but there was nothing as to how to contact his family or his business or even anybody who might know him. There was, however, an old metal roller skate carrying case from the 1950s. When I saw it, I remembered it as my case. The skates were mine from when I was a teenager, one of the last Christmas gifts I had received from my parents. Ted must have gotten it from the crawl space under the house and decided to take it over for his own. The white leather skate shoes were dry and cracked and one of the shoe strings was missing. They were gathering dust in a neglected corner of the room, and I wondered what they were doing there. I found the answer when I opened the cheap metal carrying case itself. There was no room for the skates. That case was full of wads and packs of twenty and fifty dollar bills. The money was folded and flattened in a haphazard fashion, like an afterthought; cookie jar money set aside for a rainy day or a fast escape.

After that, the bad news kept hitting me in shock waves. Get this – I am in my sixties at this time and I find out that Ted may have wanted me, but, in spite of all the sweet and endearing things he had said over the decades we were married, he had not wanted children. In the bottom drawer of his desk I found a big stack of his yearly calendars. Decades of calendars from hardware stores and realtors and even one or two sexy numbers from a barber shop in Chatsworth where Ted was a regular customer. I studied the odd pattern of days marked in red, until I solved the puzzle – that lying bastard had plotted me out, calculating the rhythm of my life cycle! He had calculated exactly when it was safe to enjoy the pleasures of my bed without fear of any encumbering consequences, if you get my drift. No babies for you, Lu!

And one other thing, in the bottom of that same drawer I found a checking account in my name with over a hundred and fifty thousand dollars in it! It was not reassuring to see my forged signature on an account I had not opened and did not know anything about. Nor was the fact that the other name on the bank papers, in case of my untimely death, was that of a man I had never heard of.

I googled the name Greg Mittelbaum and found a single hit, an obituary for Gregory Otis Mittelbaum, his wife Alice, and children Grace Anne and Benjamin, died instantly on impact when a light plane piloted by Greg lost its way in a fog and crashed into a mountain in a remote wooded area of Maine up near the Canadian border. The article said the loving husband and father had been an insurance adjuster whose job frequently took him all over the country. Was that true or was that another cover story? I would never know. I did figure out there was no real chance Greg Mittlebaum or Ted Weiler would ever be coming back.

The life I thought I had built with my husband caved in around me. I tried to keep what I could of my balance. I had the rest of my life to live. At that time I had a few years yet before I could walk away from my school teaching chores at the full retirement. But everything I believed in had been taken from me, and for the first time in my life I felt truly alone. I fought depression and notions of suicide as hard as I could. I was not going to allow this bitter, frustrating experience to crush me. Worse things, I told myself, had happened to plenty other women. And, after a lot of storming about and yelling at empty rooms, I did find some comfort in meditation…and in my own version of the Lord's Prayer, which I still recite to myself:

Our Big Everything whose exact Name we do not know
Who art in some other place or plane or elevation we can only imagine
Hallowed be thy Name, whatever it is.
Give us today whatever we need that is good for us
And forgive us our weaknesses, chief of which is stupidity
As we forgive the stupid, cruel and evil things others do to us.
Lead us not into further stupidity
And deliver us from bad fates and painful endings
(As you have already once done for me)
Amen.

I think I mourned my own loss of innocence as much as the loss of the man I never really knew. It was some months before the realization dawned on me that, had Ted not crashed into a mountain, I myself was set up to disappear in some unexpected but totally plausible way that he could well make appear like an accident. I could almost see the newspaper obituary, "Lucy Weiler, wife of grieving husband Ted, wandered away and lost while on the Turquoise Trail in the dry desert badlands south of Albuquerque."

So, in spite of everything, in at least that one small way, Lucky me! Thinking on what might have happened, my spirit began to mend and after some time I did start to get my life back in some sort of order.

It was a year after Ted went missing that I went to see the lawyer who had handled details of the sale of our farmlands after my parents were killed. Bob Fennerman had gone on to his maker, but his son Tom was running the business. It was an interesting roll of the dice that on the day I went in to see my old lawyer's son I met Jack Hamlin.

But lately I have been having disturbing thoughts in another direction…did not the Stranger tell me there were no coincidences?

Eleven

Jack tells me he has had enough weird visitations from his outer space figment for the immediate future. He does not look back to see if anything else is going on in the lounge. He rolls his way down the wide corridor, headed for his room. Once there, he has to wheel through the living room he shares with Herbert to get to the somewhat smaller room that serves as his study, kitchenette and bedroom. Both Herbert and Jack's bedrooms and bathrooms have their separate entrances off the shared living space. Their private rooms are tight and cozy, like most of our accommodations at the Villas.

Their shared living room is large enough, but Herbert has set up this community space as if it is his office, and decorated it as much as possible to look like The Old Viking Shipping Company did back when it was in its prime.

I have seen that place in a complete upheaval when the gang came to collect Jack for one of our weekly food runs in the van, and, of course, when Jack and I went looking for Herbie the time Goozeman and his underlings tried to put him away.

The room is cluttered with junk mail, a fax machine, a printer, a letter postage machine, a hole-puncher and clutters of period piece office brick-a-brack, much of it so out-of-date it looks like it belongs in a "Back To The Future" movie. Technically, Jack has the right to half of this common space, but the Chermundo administration lets Herbert get away with his obvious delusion, reliving his glory days as a big time importer-exporter, because, well, Jack does not stick up for his rights and they both pay their bills – and, until Jack complains or the Old Viking gets in financial trouble with the many people trying to scam him, Chermundo will not have much say in the matter.

One look around and you can see Herbert goes the extra mile and then some to keep the legend of his glory days alive. There is a big green sputtering neon sign on the wall, "Old Viking Shipping," and a cork bulletin board with memos, shipping line schedules and grocery store coupons push-pinned in a haphazard pattern. His desk has an oversized bronze painted plaster bust of a mustachioed guy wearing a helmet with horns on it, and there is a thick metal nameplate, "Herbert Miller, President & Owner," with the holes where it had once been screwed to a door.

As Jack rolls by in his wheelchair, Herbie is hovering over his massive old desktop computer, busily pounding out a letter on a worn keyboard. A fat file rests next to him on his desk. The folder cover has "Official File - Nigerian Contracts" handwritten with a thick black marker. Jack drops the letter I retrieved for him back in the lounge on top of the file.

Herbert grunts, happy to see him, "Jack-boy! I thought you would be doing the movie."

"Seen it a hundred times." Jack starts to wheel past Herbert, heading for his own room, but Herbert reaches out and grabs one arm of his wheelchair, stopping his progress.

"Jack, Jack—wait! Take a look at this. You think it's strong enough?" He pushes a printed copy of the email he has been working on in Jack's direction. Jack sighs and takes a look. It has dozens of spelling and typing errors. In fact, counting the ones where he has accidentally activated the caps lock, almost every keystroke is an error.

Jack reads it out loud, "MY DEAR PRINCE KUAZI yOU MUST THINK WE ARE A FUNKY CHICKEN. wE HAVE bEEN in BUSINESS OVER 50 YEARS WITH NEVER ADVANCING MONEY! nO PAYMENT tO yOU UNTIL MY $35 MILLION and 500 THOUSAND DOLLARS IS IN THE BANK hERE iN tHE uNITED

sTATES! sTOP BEING A GREEDY BUZARD! yOURS
tRULY, Herbert mILLER, pRESIDENT, oLD vIKING
sHIPPING

Jack grins, amused in spite of his dark mood. "Huh.
Buzzards and chickens! That's nice use of bird analogy,
Herb." He hands the paper back and wheels on to his own
room.

Herbert's voice follows him from the outer area,
"Yeah, but is it strong enough?"

Jack's smile broadens; he is sure his friend cannot see
the expression on his face. "There's two 'z's' in buzzard,"
he says.

"Thanks," Herbert's voice floats in from the other
room. There is a click-click-clack as he corrects the error.

Twelve

Jack's rooms are Spartan by comparison to Herbert's. As he wheels himself in, the strange friend that apparently only Jack and I can see is already there, sitting in a far corner of the room on the floor beside Jack's bed. He has a plate piled high with Ritz Crackers loaded with peanut butter. "Hey, Spin-Spin Fans, catch this," he says to his invisible camera. He takes three of the loaded crackers and begins juggling them. This is impossible, as the sticky combos should fall apart or stick to his fingers, but Jack is growing accustomed to physical impossibilities on the part of his unusual and unwelcome guest.

Jack sighs, "Stop that. And you just were eating. Inventory is going to start noticing all the missing crackers. We're not supposed to feed our guests."

"Note the honesty in our team leader! Honesty, a virtue prized throughout the galactic pancake!"

"I said 'Put them down!'"

The Stranger sighs and the objects circle down and return to their plate as if by magic. But in the next second a grin lights up his face as he thinks of something else. He shows off one of the crackers in the direction of his hidden camera, "Peanut butter! Best thing on this extraordinary planet! Nothing grav's a body up quite the same as peanut butter!"

Jack shakes his head. "Not all the people who live here like peanut butter." He is puzzled and annoyed at the same time. "Grav-ing up sounds like something one of my students might invent when they forgot their homework."

The walls of Jack's room are decorated with a few reminders of his glory days as the top math and science teacher in his school district. There is a Kern County Teacher of the Year plaque, a JPL commendation for a suggestion he sent in for some modifications to make some device on the Mars Rover more functional, and several small, framed letters from former students, these leaning against the wall to the back of the tiny writing surface on his battered old desk, the one piece of furniture he brought from home when he gave up on his past life and moved to the retirement home. A framed photograph of his daughter Emily and granddaughter Amanda is in a prime position on his small desk.

"Grav-ing up is a real thing, Jack…well, in another language, but still real."

"My guess is that, assuming the logic of my delusion is correct, you come from a planet much larger than this one."

"Why?" the Stranger says, showing a sudden interest.

"Because you need energy to keep from exploding, otherwise you'd puff out like a rockfish pulled up from 100 meters on the ocean floor."

Instead of directly agreeing with Jack, the Stranger turns to his camera, "And there you have it! First rate deductive logic! You don't find that on any of the other 21 doomed planets!" He pauses and cups one hand to an ear. "Ah, that's other 19…yes, right." The Stranger's voice turns private and nasty as he talks to someone half a galaxy away, "Blew themselves up, did they? What about the other one? Wow, some accident! Keep me briefed, idiots; I looked like a fool on that one!"

The Stranger turns his attention back to Jack. He waves one long fingered hand at the plaques on the wall, "You won all these, didn't you, Jack Hamlin?"

Jack looks bothered and pained. His years as a schoolteacher are not of much interest to him. "I should win something. I was a high school teacher my whole life. That's at least worth a bronze medal for patience."

The Stranger points out one award, "And a prize winning science essay!" The Stranger has somehow conjured up a miniature solar system. "Catch this!" he says to his invisible camera. He plucks some of the planets out of their orbits and begins juggling them.

"Would you stop doing that?" Jack raises his voice, "And remove that solar system – get it out of here! I have no room for orbiting masses." Jack shakes his head as if to clear the sight from his mind.

"Tell me about your award-winning essay," the Stranger says.

"Honorable mention. Not a big deal. It was my take on The Theory of Everything. I might have done better, but they said it was a cross between speculative science and religion."

"Religion as speculative science," the Stranger nods knowingly to his hidden camera.

Jack watches the planets go round and round. Those still in orbit are intersecting at right angles with the ones being juggled. "Would you please stop doing that?"

"Why?"

"It's annoying, that's why."

"It's easy. Here, you try." He hands Mars, Venus and Uranus to Jack.

Jack sets the balls down on his lap. "No."

"Why not?"

"I can't do this. I'm the klutz of the century. And they're not real, anyway."

"Just try."

Jack picks them up and does an awkward attempt. He drops Mars, tries again, drops all three, tries again and finds himself awkwardly keeping the balls in the air. In spite of himself, he is interested. His pace picks up. It is impossible, but he is juggling, something he has never even attempted before.

The Stranger adds Jupiter with a warning, "Watch out, this one is a bit heavier."

Jack's brow furrows as he concentrates on the balls. "I can't really be doing this. I am really off the deep end.

Here I think something and it's real. That's called loony-
tunes to infinity squared."

"It's just an unconscious thing. You do it by not
thinking about it. Humans can do more than they know,
Jack." The strange man snatches the balls from Jack and
gives his galactic audience a serious look, "Lots more."

Jack looks at the planets, now all back in their orbits,
but he is still thinking about what he did with his life,
"Back forty years ago there wasn't much call for cosmic
physics," he says. "I liked math, I was good at it, I had to
do something to earn a living, and I became a teacher."

"Always room for another Einstein or Feynman."

"Right. But I went to State College, not Harvard."

The Stranger eyes the planets, back in orbit. He
conjures up a smaller one and gets it rotating on the outer
fringes of his little solar system.

"What's that?" Jack asks, pointing to the tiny little
whitish grey ball rotating out beyond the known planets.

"Inarapi. One of those frozen mudballs out past Pluto.
Your astronomernauts haven't discovered it yet."

"Astronauts," Jack corrects him. "Or astronomers. I
suppose some guy named Inarapi discovers it?"

"No, you just did. But he gets the credit." The
Stranger does a knowing take for his invisible camera.
Then he causes all the planets to wink out, one by one, with
grand gestures like Mickey in the "Sorcerer's Apprentice."
He leaves the sun for last, and confidently flicks it out with
the long forefinger on his left hand, "If you don't believe I
exist, Jackie-boy, why do you talk to me?"

"Can't think of even one good reason." Jack shakes
his head and reaches for a bottle of pills. He shakes two
out in his hand.

"What are those for?" the Stranger asks.

Jack looks at the pills in his hand. "Anti-illusion
meds," he replies. "They make all known varieties of
figments go away."

"Do they work?"

Jack eyes him, "We'll see."

"No, wait – not when we're on the air!"

Thirteen

Bella is the nicer of the two full time nurses on our 'guest' side of the Villas. Do not get me wrong, they are both okay, but Bella has been my favorite since I saw her in a flat-out sprint to get Doctor Daniel when one of our old codgers fell over at dinner and started spitting up blood. She did a pretty good hundred-yard dash for a gal who is at least sixty pounds overweight, and they did save the poor fellow's life.

This afternoon, Bella seems to be wasting time around the lounge, taking some swipes at the furniture and chairs with a Swiffer duster. Since the Goozer has taken over, the on-duty nurses are expected to straighten chairs and do light housework in addition to making certain we get our meds, do our exercises and are eating properly.

I am sitting in my favorite chair, and I notice she has had her hair straightened and is bleached platinum blond.

"Nice hair," I say, looking up from my laptop as she whisks a nearby lampshade. Her new look is nice in a startling sort of way, the light color contrasting against her dark chocolate skin.

She gives me a conspiratorial grin. It's a wig," she confesses. "Me and Jane is going for the Doris Day appearance. At least I am. Jane thinks she looks more like Twiggy, you know that British twat you see on the shopping channels?"

Jane is nearly dark skinned as Bella, and nearly skinny as Twiggy.

"It is a good look," I tell Bella.

"Oh yeah, we make a statement on Saturday nights."

"Dancing?"

"Oh, yeah. Gots to get away from this place. No offense; it's not present company."

"None taken. We all try to get away when we can."

She puts on a serious look. "Lucy. You like that Jack-boy, right?"

"He is a friend, yes."

"You tell him I overheard the Goozer saying he going to get Jack something bad."

I shake my head and frown. "This place has not been the same since they hired Goozeman."

"Jane, she from New Orleans, she know some French. Jane say Chermundo supposed to mean *sweet place.* But we see what is happening; we think maybe they lost their way."

"I have to admit, it does feel different with Goozer as the director. Harvey Goozeman struts around like some little Hitler, but the guests here all have legal leases. I do not know how much trouble he can cause Jack. Or anybody, for that matter."

"Oh, he is slimy, that one. Everybody knows about how he tried to kidnap the Old Viking off to the Z ward. And that isn't the first time! And I tell you something else – the staff know he ain't no real doctor at all!"

Our director is so disliked that I am wondering how much of this is truth and how much rumor. "He has a diploma on his wall. Jack and I saw it."

"You should look real close sometime, Lucy. A doctor degree from some university in Northern Italy nobody ever heard of. Supposed to be on some island – Elba, that be it – off the Italian coast." The nurse's voice drops to a conspiratorial whisper, "But you know that Jane is a smart one. She called people who live on that island and they don't got no NIU university on Elba. Lucy! There's such thing as Northern Italy University! Hell, from what Jane says, they barely got a high school!"

"How did they ever hire somebody like him?"

"He's a bottom-line money guy. People who own this place, they appreciate a skill like that."

"Did you tell Doctor Daniel?"

"Well sure, but what is Daniel going to do about something like this? He works for the Goozer." She gave a quick look around and moved on to dust something else. That little frightened gesture of hers was to the heart of what was making me more and more uneasy about my stay at Chermundo Villas. Everything seems proper and friendly on the surface, and the place certainly maintains the air of a prosperous upper class retirement home. But underneath prim and proper something feels almighty wrong. I resolve I am not going to let the Goozer matter slip my mind. But for the moment, I have other pressing matters to attend to. After all, unless I am being scammed by my own delusions, there is a world to save.

Fourteen

Meanwhile, half way around the world from Southern
California, in the steamy African coastal city of Lagos,
Nigeria, the phones are ringing off the hook in a crowded
room they call The Bloody Boiler Room, at least they
would be, if the phones there had hooks, which indeed,
some few of the older ones still do. The action is taking
place in a battered corporate board room that is located in
offices on the tenth floor of a shabby high-rise building
once owned by a British company and now taken over by a
scam operation. Looking out the window, the view is of a
broad, flat and muddy sweep of a wide river that can be
seen making its sluggish way south to the Atlantic. To a
person unacquainted with the geography of the area, this
idea that the river runs in a southerly direction might seem
wrong, until one realizes Lagos is located on the bottom of
the western bulge of Africa. From the coastal city of Lagos
the jungle lands spread to the north as well as to the east,
and the ocean is directly to the south. So, in this area
where the river reaches the sea, urbanized coastal
swampland stretches away in both eastern and western
directions into the smog-hazed horizon, while to the north
the glazed air, shrouded with the smoke of tens of
thousands of charcoal cooking fires, makes indeterminate
where exactly the coastal swamplands begin to blend into
the interior of West Africa. This is the month of March,
and the rainy season has begun, but this year it has started
in a spotty way with plenty of humidity punctuated by
intermittent heavy squalls of warm rain, and so the

atmosphere is burdened with an overbearing sensation of mugginess.

But none of this stops the primary Nigerian industry, the business of exporting oil, or the second largest, the swarm of ingenious scams that have extracted large sums from the bank accounts of greedy, unsuspecting and naive individuals from more prosperous economies all around the world.

Can you imagine what it is to work in such a place? The crowded ex-corporate conference room on the second highest floor of the Reign Victoria Building bustles with enterprise. The phones ring and bleep and blat, the incoming emails bling cheerful alerts and there is a babble of different languages, similar only in their messages, which are dedicated to the emotional cajoling, whining, pleading and demanding of money.

The Nigerian known as Big Mo, or simply Mo, leans against one wall, picking the remains of the fried chicken sandwich he had for lunch from the sensitive area of his big golden front tooth with a blue plastic cocktail olive spear as he watches his team perform. His eyes flick from person to person around the room, trying to be aware of everything, to miss no important detail. He is a tall man, somewhat overweight as he moves into middle age, and a striking rugged masculine type, strong featured rather than handsome. When he was hardly more than a baby, his mother had migrated from the interior Igbo tribal region to the heavily populated lowlands of Lagos. She had her hard times, but Mo learned the ways of the city life enough to survive, and finally, to prosper.

A common 18th-century sea chantey of the slave trade went, "Beware and take care of the Bight of Benin, where few come out though many go in." Today, thanks to the marvels of modern communication and the internet, Mo and others who ply his trade have given fresh meaning to the old warning. The modern chant might well be "No money comes out, though much goes in."

Mo looks on with bemused interest as, from their station in one corner of the room, BuBa and his wife BeBe open envelopes, scan the contents, scoop out the cash and checks, and then address larger size envelopes, stuff in white "prayer shawls" and toss the envelopes in the outgoing mail bin. They have three cardboard boxes always in plain sight in front of them, one for stacks of checks, a second for money from Europe, and a larger one for piles of U.S. dollars of all denominations. The happy thought flickers in the back of Mo's awareness, "Let us hear a cheer for the rich and greedy Americans—how we love our plump American fools!"

In another corner of the large room, a handful of operators punch up or dial outgoing calls. The moment they get a hit, they swiftly connect to the talent, a group of a dozen people sitting around a conference table relaxing while they wait for their next act to begin.

Mo is an enlightened and results-oriented captain of industry. He does not care where his help comes from or what they look like in person. His band of troopers and specialists is of every ethnic shade from darkest, deepest blue-black Afro to rich brown mixes of Caucasians, Arabic, Middle Eastern and Asians.

Rene and Maba, two of the ladies sitting in the talent pool, have their blouses unbuttoned, revealing their bare, rounded breasts.

Rene coos, "Me, me, me, me!" as she presents herself to a sweet faced little black baby that is poised to crawl back and forth on the table between them.

Maba shows a robust alternative, "No, child, you no go over there! I got the good stuff over here, right here now, baby child!"

The baby is not unhappy, but it is doing its best to puzzle through the moment, trying to make up its mind what to do with this wealth of feeding opportunities. The little creature, still too young to stand, is believed to be a child of the Yoruba tribe, but nobody is really sure, the mother having been brutally carved to pieces and her remains cursed forever with the common voodoo rituals, the fatal result of a forbidden love that was discovered by those to whom it deeply offended. The murdered mother had been a chit runner and a favorite of Mo's, and his team is adopting the baby as a group project.

Both of the women presenting their breasts to the infant are barely out of their teens, and both are beautiful. Rene has ebony black skin, while Maba is brown like cherry wood. It is a good-natured contest, and yet with a serious note because personal money of all types and denominations is hitting the table.

Star-Power Charles is enjoying the show. He is a splendid spectacle in his colorful designer workout threads. He wears a newly acquired lounge lizard outfit that a New York pimp might strut about in, something like a tiger's coat if tigers had chartreuse fur with grey streaks. He watches the Best Mamma contest with the usual avid male interest, grateful for the break in his otherwise boring day. Charles is Mo's up-and-coming star actor because he has the right combination of talents, including a nimble mind to go along with his quick fluency in English, French and Spanish, as well as a variety of accents. He is quickly able to snap into the persona of a British-born businessman or a down-on-his-luck general or a politician ousted from power that just happens to have millions in the Bank of Nigeria that he is desperate to get out of the country. But Mo worries that Charles is young and his success has come perhaps too quickly; the young buck loses interest easily. For the moment he is resting easily between calls.

"I'll lay a fiver on Rene. Five Nigerian," Charles says.

Charles' assistant Albert, clean shaven and fresh looking in his shiny new silk suit and a tie the sales girl assured him was a Yale prep design, looks up from his often interrupted attempts to read a battered Book of Mormon, and shakes his head, turning down the bet. Still, he cannot resist commenting, "If you're so sure, do five U.S." Albert thinks about it for a moment, "Of course, she'll go for her mother."

Charles grins, "It's an orphan, stupid. And stop reading that evil book. Allah will strike you dead."

"Allah loves all religions. And black is beautiful. Baby-baby go for the dark skin. Dark be delicious."

To a raucous round of hoots and jeers, the baby crawls to Maba, the lighter-skinned woman. Maba gathers her in and prepares to nurse her. Money passes hands around the room.

"You lose, man! Give me that fiver!" Charles grins delightedly.

Albert waves him off, "I never bet you no fiver!"

"Lucky thing, too!"

Maba cuddles the baby to her left nipple and it sucks contentedly. "Baby like milk chocolate!" she croons.

"Hey, hey, hey!" One of the phone dialers goes on alert. "Hot one here—Maba!"

Maba tosses the baby girl across the table to Rene who neatly catches the infant and begins nursing.

"Dark chocolate de best, anyhow!" Rene chortles.

The baby doesn't seem to mind the difference, and starts right in where she left off.

Mo warns them from his position against the wall, "Quiet, people! On speaker!"

The room goes silent. Over a loud speaker system scratchy with static, a querulous old man's voice is heard. The people in the room grin at each other as they listen to Old Leonard, just another confused and angry sucker from that wonderland of America, as he pours his rage out on the telephone. "Damnation! Don't you people ever get it? Just plain rude! You got no respect at all for a man's private life! Why, it's middle of the night here!! I told you never call me at this hour!"

Mo has been waiting for the proper moment. Now, like a movie director, he signals Maba, who looks up from her notes and cuts in on the old man's rant. "Leonard, baby! It's me, Maria!

Old Leonard grumbles, "I don't know no Maria."

Maba continues in a smooth tone, spreading oil on troubled waters, "Oh, Leonard, Honey, it's me, Maria...Maria Achabara, the poor widow of our dear president, now cruelly murdered and gone these six month and more. Leonard, how could you forget to me? You say you would help me move my $12 million dollar to your bank in America. You promised it to me!" She hesitates, referring to her notes, "You going to forget a poor old comradely Catholic woman in her time of distress?"

Leonard's voice comes over the intercom, now sounding weak and confused, "I—I well—right, Maria, then."

Maba soothes him, "Sure, Leonard, sure…of course, yes, you remember Maria."

Leonard is still not mollified, "B-but I went to Hopkins International like we agreed…you were not on that plane like you said you'd be!"

Mo makes a churning motion with one hand; directing his actress to pick up the pace a bit. She nods with a grin, "Leonard that is exactly what I must tell you about! I buy my ticket and I pack to come, but they stop me at the airport! Right here in Lagos! Men with guns force me off the plane! Leonard, you must help me or I am a lost ruin!"

"What? Who did that to you?"

"Bad men with guns! They were very cruel to me, Leonard!" She grins at the others around the table as she flings up one hand and dramatically weeps into the phone, "Cruel and mean—they did things to me, Leonard!"

"Well, they are-are-are…scum suckers!" There is a pause while the old man tries to catch up with the new events as Maba has presented them. "But I can't do anything about that, can I Maria? Not really, no…I'm here in Cleveland and I'm frustrated, too…." His voice trails off, and for a moment Mo is afraid they have lost the connection. He looks to the operator, who reassures him the American fish is still on the line.

Maba slides into the active side of her pitch, "They accuse me of stealing, Leonard! They will throw me in jail! They want money, Leonard! But my money is tied up by the bank! It is just a small amount what they demand, when you think of the millions I am going to share with you when I come to America…but I do not have it here and now."

"Well, gol-dang it, how much we talking about here?"

Mo nods and signals the dialer to dial down Old Leonard. As his voice fades, Leonard is heard complaining, "But I already sent you five thousand dollars the last time!"

The general hubbub in the room resumes. Rene, nursing the baby, cheerfully accepts a handful of paper money for winning Best Mamma. "No child can resist me," she says.

Charles frowns, "Well, technically he went to Maba first."

Rene grins as she snatches the money, "Technically, your ass, Super Charley-boy. Maba never even got started. It was 'who gonna nurse the baby.'"

Charles shakes his head. His ready grin fades as he reads an email from the monitor screen in front of him. Mo is alerted by the expression on his young star talent's face. He leaves his position by the wall and moves to stand behind Charles and read over his shoulder.

Charles vents his outrage in an English accent, "The bloody sod calls me a buzzard! A buzzard and a chicken!"

"Who?" Mo asks.

"Crabby old Herbert, the president of…" Charles scans the email to refresh his memory, "…Old Viking Shipping."

Mo shakes his head, "Look at the way he types. And the rotten old fart has the nerve to call you senile! You be wasting your time, Charlie-boy, and you know time is buckos to us."

Mo goes back to his regular post, leaning against the wall, but Charles does not agree. He sees himself as the young stud star, vital to the operation, and he oozes confidence.

"Since when we stop taking money from old people?"

Mo doesn't respond right away. He considers himself a tolerant man. He thinks back, remembering he was young once, as well. He smiles patiently and decides to take a moment to explain, "Old, yes, Super-Charles. But a guy like that, his family controls his finances."

Charles is unable to let go his end of the disagreement, "We do not know this for certain, Mo – I myself am making the calculation this old crapper may be loaded for the bear. He is just a little light on the brain power. AND...I do have his bank account number, AND his social security number AND his home address!"

Mo's expression warms into a cautious half-smile as he considers the possibilities that kind of financial information makes possible. He decides on a last parting warning, just to make sure everybody knows he is still the boss. "Well, that's something, Super-Charles...but don't spend too much time on it.

Charles grins and salutes him. "I'm motivated here, *mon Capitan.* This bloody ass calls me a chicken-funker, he deserves to have his big Viking dick nailed right properly to the wall."

Mo laughs and waves the subject off; Star-Power Charles can go ahead and handle it, Mo is the boss and he has much bigger fish to fry.

Fifteen

I have just enjoyed a hot shower and have sleepily wandered into my living room while scrubbing at my bristly, still-damp iron grey hair with a bath towel. I am wearing my purple robe with the embroidered violets on the collar and my favorite pink fuzzy slippers, and thinking to heat up some water for tea. And there he is, the Stranger from deep outer space or wherever, sitting on my Great Aunt Clara's Victorian high-back stuffed sofa, reading my copy of "The Golden Treasury of Myths and Legends," which he has obviously taken from my crowded bookshelves. I find his unexpected presence annoying. Sure, he is a wonderful alien or whatever, but how would you like a game show host popping into your life whenever he wants. Thank God, at least he did not show up in the shower.

I put on the water for you, he lofts at me in mental-speak. *Vanilla Ginger Green Chai for the mornings, right?*

He does not wait for an answer, instead indicating the page he has opened in my mythology book, *Why do you think this writer tells us Prometheus has stolen fire from the heavens?*

Because that is the way the story goes, I reply in my newly acquired talent. *And put that back where it belongs when you are finished.*

I'm already finished, he says, and as his thought is completed the book flies back on the shelf next to Joseph Campbell. *I was just using it as a visual device.*

To introduce what subject? I snap at him. I am not in the mood for games, particularly not from visionary creatures with questionable motives.

Oof—you're quick! He says. *Well, we'll get right to it. There's lots of ground to cover.*

How much ground? I raise one skeptical eyebrow.

Maybe just the high points since Gilgamesh.

In that case maybe I better have a sip of tea first, just to jar my old brain cells.

Oh, oh. He says.

Oh, oh—what? I was annoyed by his unannounced arrival and I am tired of his skating around from subject to subject as if I am a child or some animal of lesser intelligence.

Oh, oh, station break, he says, sounding flustered and a touch out of control. He may have a galactic show, but he certainly acts like he is in vaudeville, or maybe Loony Tunes. In the next second he goes all wavy and dissolves into my tea cup. I give it a distasteful look and carry it over to the sink in my small kitchenette and am about to pour it out. Now I am going to have to put the water back on and brew a new pot for myself.

But then, for no particular reason I stick my finger into the water and it is like walking through a doorway in Alice's Wonderland. I am in some other place, a weird and futuristic recording bay with cameras and wall banks of monitors and the oddest assortment of creatures from green crab-like things to cyclopean monsters with big red hands with thick fingers.

"Oh, oh," one of the crabs says, and I blat him with the first of my big lies, *It's okay; our game show host knows.*

He turns his big fish eyes away from me without a second glance and goes back to squeezing tools with his claw-hands that make some camera shots appear on the big screen and others disappear. There is a commercial for a cream to go on the skin of an unbelievably ugly parrot-faced squid. I spot my strange alien acquaintance on one of the smaller monitors. He is talking to a stern group of elders clad in grey robes. They look like his people. With their grey frowns and grey faces, it looks like he is having a tough time.

Sure. Pleadian Royalty, my crab buddy blats at me, *Why are you giving him such a hard time?* I use that odd word 'blat' because his particular method of mind-communication has a remote and guttural effect, like talking to somebody through an empty cardboard wrapping paper roll.

I decide to give him attitude. *Hey, who asked you, crustacean-boy?* George is always talking about who does what on the set, so I think I know something about this. *You want me to file a grievance with your union?*

Nooooo," he blats with a cowed expression on his face.

I cannot explain where all my new-found courage is coming from. Maybe I am just so tired of being used and dumped on by my ex-husband that it does not matter to me what some odd creature from some unknown faraway place thinks of me.

Okay, but you owe me.

Owe you what? He gives off a bleeping moan.

Never mind. Just remember when I call on you.

I think to pull my finger out of the cup, and I am just in time as the strange alien materializes like a little cyclone out of the tea.

You expect me to drink that after you've been taking a bath in it? I ask him.

He gives me a guilty look that makes me think I hit the nail on the head on that one.

Where have you been? I ask.

Why...I...station break, I told you. He flummoxes it; I do not know for sure what he is up to, but I am sure he is lying.

That is just so much crap. Look, sit down.

Interesting; I tell him to do something and he does it. I start to put on water for another cup of tea.

Here, let me do that. He holds his hand over it for ten seconds and it is boiling hot. *Microwave,* he says with a pleasant smile.

I liked it better when I thought it was magic. I put a new teabag in the liquid and stir it around with one of the silver spoons I inherited from Aunt Clara.

What is Niagara Falls? He asks. He has read the imprint on my old spoon, a popular collector's item over a hundred years ago. I am sure one or two of his cameras are lit up on me right now and in a room somewhere both close and far away crustacean boy is happily focusing on our conversation.

It is a huge waterfall in the Eastern United States. It is thunderous and beautiful. Newlyweds used to go there on their honeymoons. I can imagine that my crab buddy in the control room is scrambling on Wikipedia to find some photographs. *But do not get me off track – I have been meaning to talk to you about something.*

That perks the Stranger up right away and he gives me a big beamer of a smile. I find myself wishing he could get his makeup right; his sharp white teeth against that gray skin make me uneasy.

Oh, joyful wonder across the cosmos! He burbles happily, *Okay, lucky Lucy-lu, how can I help?*

As if I was not in a rotten mood before, I hate the way this slickster calls me Lucy-lu as if we are pals or kissing cousins or something. But I let that one slide on by. I do not want to be distracted from my real gripe. I take a deep breath and start right in on him, *Well, I told Jack about how when I first met you, it felt like you were spot-lighting around, going through a color chart to somehow assist my limited, second-class eyesight to see your magnificence.*

He seems uneasy, and the smile wilts a little. I think maybe it is the dripping satire in my voice. *Err, yes? You have a question about that?*

Oh, I have a million questions, but none that I think you are ready to answer. Now, here is my concern, I described my impressions to Jack and he said the oddest thing. Jack told me that shifty color business was because you had to fish around to find the right wave length. Jack said that on our world our eyes see the spectrum of light our sun gives off. But where you are from, you might have a different sort of sun. In fact they have different suns in lots of solar systems, suns that give off different radiations.

Well? He looks amused but puzzled. I am thinking this slickster is not all that smart, and I am reminded of that old lawyer's cliché: never encourage a question of a witness if you do not know where it will lead you.

Jack says that you might have X-ray vision, or see using ultraviolet light.

And so? You probably know the game rules won't allow –

I am not asking you for anything. I just want you to know I quit.

That stuns him. *Quit?! No! You can't! Why?*

I realize I am going to have to spell it out for him. *If you can see on other wavelengths that means you can see right through our clothing!*

Well, sure. Of course we can. That's it?

That's quite enough for me!

Lucy-lu, don't be a silly mud-baller!

You are not endearing me or helping your cause in any way by calling me an earth-slug.

But Lu, he protests. *Clothing is nothing! From edge to edge of the platter, every sentient creature knows that. In the greater universe, clothing certainly does not make the man. Or woman, for that matter.*

Stranger, I do not have to recognize that anything you tell me is fair or even accurate. I am sorry, my odd alien acquaintance, but I do not agree with your advanced ways. I will not parade myself like a naked baboon or a happy little fruit fly in front of your trillion kabillion viewers! I am out of this game of yours! And I think I can convince Jack, as well. We quit, Mister Save-Your-Planet Game Host!

This possibility clearly has not occurred to him. He gives me an open-mouthed stare. *You would endanger the very existence of your planet for petty vanity?*

I like to think of it as pride. You go talk to your – your cosmic executive producers and your big-time game show director and you tell them we wear dignified clothing on all wavelengths or we quit.

My strange companion begins to wobble to invisibility, but I point to the teacup, *Be my guest.*

Are you sure?

Yes, but be careful. You're jumping into an irreplaceable antique Dalton china cup.

He does his little cyclone maneuver into the tea and I take hold of the spoon. I do not know exactly what the science is, but I am thinking that silver is a good electrical conductor and -- wonder of wonders! -- my peculiar notion proves right, because I am sucked along on his slipstream not only to the studio but along with him through some complicated transporter. Then I am locked with both hands clinging to some long, shiny thread that follows behind him as he races away from our solar system on an incredible flight that is as stunning as it is swift. In less time than it takes to tell it, some semblance of us has flown past blackness and energy flares and magnetic sucking things and stars beyond calculation, only to end up entering the same dull grey room he visited before with the same grim, grey ancients staring at us. Well, rather, they are staring at the Stranger. I think I am invisible, and I am sure the Stranger has no idea I am there. But then one of the ancients winks at me and gives me a quiet nod to indicate I am not to say anything. Incredible as it seems, I, Lucy Weiler, presently living a quiet life at Chermundo Villas, am daring an out-of-this-world adventure, and so far at least I am getting away with it!

I watch quietly as the Stranger presents my gripe to his committee of grey-faced bosses, and I have to admit, he is a good pitchman. He argues that we must have our distinctive precious and valuable clothing because it is our identity, and if we cannot maintain our sense of pride we will walk off the set, as he puts it.

The angry firestorm of disapproval is nearly universal with this bunch of grey individuals, but the fellow who winked at me raises his own idea, *I think these lower-life sentients-of-earth show uncommon realization of their own worth, and our viewers like that sort of thing. Good for the ratings, you know.*

Foolish pride! Someone else grumps. *Lunatic egos! Idiots!*

No. No mass-package mulling! Think for yourselves for a change! These earthlings rely almost entirely on primitive vocal communication. They have only evolved into the basic beginnings of mental-speak, but it proves what they may be capable of. The poor creatures cannot consume energy directly. Try to live in their simple pods; just imagine if you had to survive by eating your fellows!

A wave of disgust sweeps around the room.

Someone shouts, *I say blast them now! Good riddance, filthy beasts!*

But the lone being that is defending us puts up his hand for attention. *Do not our own legends say that is how we ourselves began?*

That silences this crowd of colorless vultures. Our benefactor gives me the slightest motion of his head, and I realize it is time for me to leave. I do not know exactly if he helped boot me on my way, or if I started on my own back across the galaxy, but I experience the same rocket-like flight across the unknown cosmos. I reach and zip in and through the alien recording room before my crabby pal can blat even a single syllable, and in the next moment after that I find myself back in my kitchenette, stirring my cup of tea, and this not seconds before the Stranger himself pops back out of my teacup.

Greek gowns! He exclaims with a triumphant flourish, some sort of courtly bow accompanied by a grand gesture with both arms. *The women get Greek gowns and the men will be presented as in Roman togas!*

Quirky, but acceptable, I say and I hold my hand out for a shake. *All right then, let us get on with it.*

Sixteen

Sunday brunch time at the Chermundo finds many of the guests and their invited family members celebrating St. Paddy's day in the dining area with a special Irish heritage menu and a giant rectangular slab cake with green shamrocks on top of a thick layer of white vanilla frosting.

I go through the serving line for a plate of scrambled eggs (dyed light green) and ham, and I claim an empty place at a table already occupied by George, Millie and Delrina. I see Jack has company. He waves to me from a nearby table where he is sitting with his daughter Emily, and Fargo, his son-in-law. They have shown up for the Cheerful Chermundo Brunch that today features the just-like-home-cooked menu of regular staples with a celebratory twist – roasted chicken with wine sauce and a parsley sprig, pork chops over basmati rice baked with a Blarney Stone kiss and meatloaf a la Villas Dublin, and that Irish holiday special, corned beef and potatoes. The kitchen is also offering side orders of cabbage or parsnips, but those items smell too strong, like the cooks left them on the boil too long. A quick look around the room assures me nobody is brave enough to try those particular bits of ethnic nostalgia.

George is telling a story about Saint Brennan, an Irish saint less well celebrated than Saint Patrick.

"Brennan is on his way to discovering Greenland. But half way there he is already out of food and water. He is delirious when he thinks he spots a knight on a horse."

"Georgie, he's in the middle of the sea!" Millie scoffs.

"I know, Mills. But there he is, this knight in shining armor, galloping over the waves. Brennan is astonished, of course, and so he stands in his little sailboat and yells, 'Halloo, there…what are you doing riding across the ocean on a horse?' And from a long distance away he hears a voice call back, 'Halloo, there…and what are you doing rowing across the desert in a boat?'"

"Where did you hear that story?" I ask, realizing it was in that same book of mine that the Stranger borrowed from my bookshelf.

"Must have read it somewhere," George shrugged. "It came to me in a dream last night, so I looked it up. It's an old legend, that's for sure."

George goes on an unrelated tangent and starts talking about a new television series, something about a romance soap writer getting involved with a lady cop, and I should be interested, but my mind starts to wander. I try to pick up on Robert McKee's book "STORY," which Jack has loaned to me, while at the next table over Jack's daughter and son-in-law quietly pick at their food.

Jack knows I want to be a novelist, which is why I had trouble trying to understand why he would give me a book on writing screenplays. But Jack is a teacher at heart and he knows a lot, too. He reads just about everything he can get his hands on. He got "STORY" from George, who was throwing out all his books in an impulsive gesture to clean up his life. Jack says that in the old days when George actually had a life, he worked at places like Warner Brothers, Paramount and Universal Studios. You would never know it today, to hear old Georgie-Porgie enthusiastically bat his words around like he does not have a brain in his head. But now his story about Saint Brennan has me thinking about what is real and what is not. What caused him to dream up that particular story, anyway? I find myself remembering the Stranger's comment that there are no coincidences, which feels more and more like a warning, a serious wake up call for me, or maybe for all of us.

Jack took some time to pass on to me how George explained to him that storytelling is storytelling is storytelling, and the rest is just the details, what the professionals who do it for real call format.

Thinking about the happy wreck that George is today, I have to stop and remind myself here is a guy who wrote a dozen Movies of the Week that ran on network television back in the day. I admit there was a time when I underestimated all of drifty-minded Jack and his loud and loony bunch of pals. Sure, Herbert was – and still is – a hair-trigger emotional explosive device, and George had so much bluster you can be sure his brain is light as taffy and airy as a balloon and Millie is an imitation of some backwash girl from "Little House on the Prairie" who ruined herself along the way, and Jack himself is seeing things—but again, who am I to talk? Every now and then if I concentrate hard enough, I think I can catch a glimpse of the real people The Old Bunch used to be. Come to think of it, there is old Delrina, who probably still has more under those tight henna curls than one would think, you know, plenty of active grey matter behind the reddish fluff and frolic. It is easy to underestimate old folks when you see us in our present diminished state, the screwed up and—face it— deteriorated way we are now.

Most of us have a daily fight just to get past the aching bones and the meds that make us loopy, dull and dizzy, just to clear our minds and sort out a decent thought or two. At least give me this; I know what I am. I am old, and these are the hills I myself climb every day just to get out of bed and rub the numbness out of my fingers and toes and bring the feeling back to my wrists and the backs of my legs. Old Age Mountain gets steeper as you climb it. Realizing that, I have to remind myself to give a little more slack to my pals around me; they probably see me in the same light – or worse!

Anyway, I have been grinding away at McKee for weeks and I am about half way through "STORY," but how can I stay interested now that the shenanigans of weird outer space aliens are taking over all my attention?

Seventeen

I set aside my speculations about how or why George was blessed with his Saint Brennan dream at this particular place and time, and pretend I am reading a paragraph or two of "STORY" in between nibbling at my ham and eggs, and nobody at my table bothers me, they go on talking about the topic of the day, which has drifted from saints in rowboats to scrapbooking, or "scrapping" as Millie calls it, because they can see I am not good right now at conversation. That leaves me free to not only mull McKee's pronouncement that every scene must move the story forward, but also to look around at everybody else in the room, you know, looking for color and motivation for the characters in my novel…if and when I ever get the courage and the know-how to write it. And, as Jack's table is within my hearing range, I catch an earful.

"You're not seriously advising me to become a taxi driver," Jack's son-in-law Fargo is protesting. His face is a study in mild social outrage, his cheeks an unhealthy reddish blush that I doubt comes from skin rash.

I can see Jack is just passing time, but his son-in-law is not that sharp today. Jack shrugs, "Well, you're out of work, right? Los Angeles always needs taxi drivers; never around when you need one. You do still have your driver's license, don't you?"

Fargo gives every indication that he is not going to become a cabby. He shoots Jack a sullen stare and waves the suggestion off with an impatient gesture. Unfortunately, the hand is holding a fork with a gravy-moist piece of Irish Legend chicken on it, and the goopy morsel goes flying in a little arc that settles with a plop on the white gym shoe of a passing busboy. I doubt whether McKee would have let one of his screenplay students write that into a scene – too improbable, and yet, so perfect! The busboy does not even notice and continues on past, but Emily's face says she is mortified.

"Dad," she says with a heavy inflection, "Fargo is a marketing sales executive."

"He's an unemployed bum, is what he is. Last time I looked, you were the breadwinner, Em."

The flush on Fargo's face deepens and a vein stands out on his neck, but he does not say anything. I am guessing he is afraid of Jack and that is why, in situations like this, he lets his wife do the heavy lifting for him.

"Fargo is not going to drive a taxi," she says. "Let's talk about something else."

Emily is a good sort, but probably a little too much in the direction of her mother. I did not know Jack's wife, but in a place like this I have heard the rumors, particularly from George, who says Jack's missus always did the proper social things, that is, until she unexpectedly fell over stone dead of a stroke. Everybody always points out the dangers of the wild rocker lifestyle, but, while you may not have noticed, prim and proper can kill you, too.

Just how do I know this personal stuff about Jack's life? Well, George's kids used to go to school with Jack's daughter, and they actually had Jack one year as their trigonometry teacher. George tells Herbert and Delrina everything, and they tell everybody else. Now, aren't you sorry you asked?

"This is very tasty," Emily says. "I like the salmon; done just right, still flaky. It's my favorite. Dad, do you like your meat loaf?"

"Where's my granddaughter?" Jack asks. He gives his daughter an unhappy look.

Her reply has a bad pause in it at just the wrong spot. "Amanda...has a sleep-over with friends."

Emily is a terrible liar, and that could not be more obvious. Fargo cuts in to try and save her, "Little kids shouldn't be subjected to grown-up things." I can see how that comment only makes matters worse, but it is evident he does not care about Jack's feelings.

"That's just more blather from you, Fargo," Jack says. "I like to see her." Jack is not half the dull blade people might think, and his eyes narrow slightly. "What grown-up things would you like to talk about?"

Emily frowns, "I know you were expecting to see her, Dad...but..." There is an awkward silence, and, as Jack's attention seems to have drifted, Emily retreats to her chatter about the lunch, "Oh, dear...well, the food should be good, with the top cook they have here. The Villas newsletter said he was a chef at a big Four Star restaurant downtown near the sports arena." She looks around, taking note of the items from the menu that people are eating at nearby tables. "Yum, it all looks very good."

Our glances cross and she sees I am watching her. She frowns and shakes her head to dismiss the unpleasant notion that her little group might be displaying an overage of public transparency, and again she finds saving grace in the food situation, "Fargo, you haven't touched your chicken at all; not one bite."

Fargo gives her a startled look, wondering what he missed. He was gazing out the window.

It is not that I am super smart or a mind reader—that comes later—but anybody can see Fargo is bored out of his gourd; he cannot wait to leave. He confirms this with a casual comment about professional basketball, "Lakers are playing the Knicks this afternoon. Game starts in a half-hour."

"Wouldn't want to miss that," Jack grins at him. He knows how to push his son-in-law's buttons. "Basketball is a sissy game. You should get busy and get me a couple more grandchildren."

Fargo's lip curls. A curt shake of his head says it all, but he adds, "You only had the one."

"Keeping score, eh?" Jack says. "Really, it's not like round ball."

Fargo frowns. He cannot think of a snappy reply. His eyes fall to the small imitation cut glass vase in the center of the table holding up a green carnation and a sprig of white baby's breath. He eyes Jack's plate, "You going to eat the rest of that meatloaf?"

Jack has barely touched his food. His gaze wanders around the room, as if he is looking for someone, or maybe watching out for something that might be about to happen.

"No, you can have it, Fargo." Before anyone can think to stop him, Jack hands his plate across the table and reaches over to snatch Fargo's.

"Oh, no!" Emily's mouth opens and her gaze darts around; she is embarrassed, afraid everybody in the room is watching and afraid of what they must think of her family sharing meals as if they could not afford their own! In the hurried transfer, the plates land with two loud thumps and some of the gravy from Jack's meatloaf slops on the white tablecloth.

I catch Emily's eye again, trying to be a little sympathetic, but she frowns as if daring me to say anything.

"Dad, wait!" she says, but it is too late, and her exclamation only brings more unwanted attention to their table. She snatches up a napkin and angrily mops at the small gravy spot on the tablecloth. This serves to make it a much bigger brownish mess.

No matter what his daughter says Jack is no longer paying any attention to her. But he does look annoyed, or at least preoccupied. It seems there is plenty reason for his distraction, as his new acquaintance, the strange invisible man with the sickly pallor to his skin is sitting down in the empty chair at their table, joining them to make it a foursome. There he is with his game show grin, and his pallid grey complexion and slicked back hair. This unusual apparition or accident of nature or whatever you want to call it has a paper plate with a peanut butter sandwich. He eyes it fondly and takes a bite.

"Peanut butter!" he says. "Food for the gods! Err, demigods," he adds, with a flicker of a glance in my direction.

Jack gives the Stranger a curt nod and mutters in a low voice with his hand over his mouth, "My daughter, Emily. My son-in-law, Fargo."

The Stranger looks them both over and then gives Jack a look of mild interest, "As in Fargo, North Dakota?"

Jack nods grimly, "The very same."

"What are you saying, Dad?"

The damage has been done. Fargo gives Emily an I-told-you-so look. There is iron in his voice as he asks his father-in-law, "Yes, Jack, what are you saying to the invisible being in that empty chair right next to you?"

The remark hits its target; Jack knows Fargo would like nothing better than to have him tied up in a straightjacket and dragged by his feet over to the Z ward. "I...I was just muttering to myself."

"You said my name."

Nobody can ever accuse Jack of being a slow thinker. Remote, yes, but not slow. He replies, "Yes, if you must know, Fargo. I remarked that you are named after a town. That seems a little unusual."

Emily sighs and jumps on her father's remark, hoping to fend off yet another argument before it starts, "You've known Fargo for over ten years, Dad."

Unfortunately, she is too late and the runaway train is now off the tracks or thundering down the rails or however that expression goes when real writers like Hemingway or Danielle Steele use it.

"How quickly time passes." Jack shakes his head. He seems half-in and half-out of their conversation. "Ten years...that long," he says to the apparently empty space where the Stranger is sitting. "It seems like a lot longer."

"Time is relative," the Stranger says. "Or, so I've heard."

He takes a bite from his sandwich and shoots Jack with a finger as he gets up to leave the table.

"My name is DoubleSpin," he says.

"What?" Jack is surprised.

"DoubleSpin," the strange man repeats. "You didn't introduce me to your family. It would have been a good bit for the show. My name is DoubleSpin."

"That's a funny name," Jack says.

Emily's face reddens, "Come on, Dad, it's Fargo's real name and the given name of my husband is really not a subject of humor."

"I agree," Jack says to Emily. "There is nothing funny about Fargo."

This further upsets his daughter, "Of course you agree. You agree, you apologize, but you don't mean it and you just go out and do it again!"

Jack looks around, knowing he is going to have to deal with her anger and there is no easy way out of the situation. But the Stranger is gone.

"DoubleSpin," Jack says, puzzling over the oddness of what has happened. He stares at me, but I have to shrug; I do not have any answer for this one.

Fargo looks from Emily to Jack and then decides to throw a little fuel on the fire. Maybe Jack can push his buttons, but he certainly knows how to push hers.

"Now Em, it's just your father. You know how he gets."

Emily explodes, throwing down her napkin and standing. "Dad, why do we always, always, always end up arguing about everything?"

Jack gazes around the room, still looking for the odd intruder that he alone can see. But Jack realizes DoubleSpin is not going to help; the odd fellow gives him a little finger roll goodbye as he slips out of the wide dining room entryway. And, I swear, he waves at me too, just before he winks out of sight.

Jack looks at the table, at the place where his unwanted guest was sitting. DoubleSpin has left the plate with half his peanut butter sandwich. Jack idly picks it up and chews it.

Fargo gives him a puzzled look, and I realize he cannot see the sandwich. I think that was when I had to admit something beyond a simple delusion shared by two people was going on. One half of a simple peanut butter on white bread sandwich, and there I am, just as loopy as my pal Jack. He takes a bite from it, and the bite disappears into his mouth. He can see it and probably taste it, and I can see it, but nobody else in the room has the slightest idea. And then Jack is looking at me.

"Peanut butter," he says, silently mouthing the words to me.

"I know," I nod.

Did I imagine it? At the moment I was not sure, but that little scene was enough to make me wonder for the first time since I was a little girl what things are real and what only exists in my imagination. I know what everybody says about writers. I had wanted to be a writer as badly as I had ever wanted anything, and people like me supposedly make things up in our heads…but why couldn't I have conjured up a fairy prince or a pot of gold? Some rotten fictionista I turn out to be! I cannot even materialize a ham-on-rye from Jerry's Famous Deli!

Looking back over the years, realizing there are no coincidences, I can see now how the story of Saint Brennan influenced my thinking that day. How many ways are there to interpret the same reality? Well, at least two, and probably more. But why was any of this important? Suppose one night you had a brilliant and yet confusing message from some unknown creature from another solar system halfway across the galaxy? Amazing, yes, but let us not get lost in the wonder and the magic – would not the responsibility still be on you to figure it out?

There is little more to tell about that meeting in the dining room at the Chermundo. Not much happens after that. The threesome at Jack's table finish their brunch in stony silence, and the combatants separate and return to their neutral corners, which means Jack goes to his room and Fargo and Emily leave for home. I turn my attention back to Robert McKee's "STORY," but I can no longer concentrate on the print, which seems to keep slipping off the page. Or maybe I fall to a bit of dozing, you know, we older folks do that from time to time.

Eighteen

So I wake up and look around and I know I am in a dream because I am wearing a white linen gown, and I am myself but it is me the way I looked in my twenties: long, jet black hair and one of my boobs is showing only it is upright and pert and full the way they used to be. I am walking along with DoubleSpin in broad daylight. I gasp and try to tuck my boob in but this causes a look or two from passersby.

"Isn't the temple beautiful in the early morning hours?" he says. For some reason, he decides we are to use verbal communication.

"I said dignified clothing," I grumble.

"Don't quibble. I assure you, your garments are 100% correct for the time. That was our deal. And I'll let you keep your necklace." The fact that it is made of crude heavy golden links calms me down. I guess I am easy, after all. Any old alien can ply me with jewelry and I am putty in his hands.

"W-what are we doing here?" I manage to gasp.

"Time is a river. We just went back up-stream a bit."

"W-why?"

"Analogy. These people believe they have fire for their cooking and incense offerings and such because Prometheus stole it from Zeus. And stop fiddling with your breast. It is unbecoming."

"B-but – am I on camera?"

"Of course…about thirty trillion sentient couch potatoes are gaping at you. But most of them have no idea what a breast is for. And I already told you, it is technically accurate in every respect. I am living up to my part of the deal. Now, back to the point; how did earth people actually come to use fire in the first place."

I find that by fidgeting with my hair I can cover most of my naked breast at least part of the time. "I do not know. How did they?"

"I don't know either. Probably lightning hit a dead tree and they figured it out. But you see when you live in a society, you need rules, and guilt is a very helpful commodity – am I going too fast for you?"

"No. You do not seem to be going anywhere at all."

"Your early cave people didn't know what fire was, so they explained it by magic. Here we are in ancient Greece and the magic has been crystallized into a myth. Prometheus stole it, so it assumed a rightful importance. It could do things; warm them throughout the night, provide light in the dark, cook meat – but it was also dangerous. But the important point I am trying to make is that there actually were – actually are – demigods."

I turned and gazed at him in quiet astonishment, "And you are one of them."

"Well…yes. The problem your latest pack of religious imagineers gave themselves when they created their God was that they cast out the demigods. That was wrong. They shouldn't have done that."

"And that made you angry?"

"Of course not. It made us less effective. We had to find new ways to help you."

"Like coincidence…" I can feel a slow, irrational fury building in me. I stamp my foot like a child, "So we have no will?! You shape everything we do? I do not want to play this game!"

"Calm yourself, Lucy – you'll make a scene."

"I do not care if 40 trillion – "

"Thirty some odd trillion," he corrects me. "But not them – *them*." He points in the direction of the Greek passersby and indeed, several of the citizens of ancient Athens have stopped and are watching us. "Quickly; we don't have all that much time," DoubleSpin says, "The demigods did not give you fire. You discovered that on your own."

"But…" There are a thousand questions whirling around in my head, but what he is saying is so important to me that I cannot think which one should come first.

"Over the years since, we may have kept you from burning your house down a time or two, but we don't casually interfere. There are rules against it."

"You are like…guardian angels?"

"No, that's somebody else. The GAs are very empathetic, but they don't deal in long term sentiency growth. We used to be more like instructors, but once sentiency spread everywhere that was impossible."

"So what do you do?"

"We help out as best we can?

"You interfered in my life," I whisper.

"You fell for the man who called himself Ted. We had nothing to do with that."

"You killed him and his wife and family!"

"No, we did not! That would be horrible – and illegal! We suggested a few paths of action to him, and of those available, he chose a flying frolic to the mountains. As you say it in The Lord's Prayer of the Christian religion that you yourself chant from time to time, 'Lead us not into temptation but deliver us from evil.'"

"But you killed his wife and family."

"No, he lost his way in a fog. The projections were he planned to kill them anyway. Poison. Wild mushrooms gathered on a hike. Nearly one hundred percent certainty. He was cashing out his chips, making ready for a new life in Rio."

"But you knew he would be flying into that fog."

"I'm afraid we did. And, as he was not the praying kind, there was no GA to deliver him from evil."

"But his children…" My voice was now a faint whisper.

"He was raising them in cruel ways. There was a very high probability they would have ended up like him…or worse, even. Your world already has too many of that kind."

"But you are not sure of that."

"I accept your reasoning. That one is on my head."

He gives me a sad look that feels genuine to me. Maybe he can be accused of running a shallow and uncaring galactic game show, but I feel at least some of the weight of what it is to be DoubleSpin.

As I look on ancient Greece, everything seems to fade except the pained expression in his steady gaze, and I wake to find myself alone in gathering darkness. I am lying on my favorite lounge chair in the deserted Chermundo community lounge. Somebody, probably Mason, has thought to throw a fuzzy comforter over me. I let the chair raise me and then I slowly come to a teetering standing position on my numb feet and stretch my aching limbs, and in so doing I am struck with the unfairness of being a young mind in an old body.

Nineteen

Late that same evening, as Fargo and Emily prepare for bed, Fargo is still nattering at his wife about her father. Even before the St. Patrick's Day brunch, it was Fargo who wanted to escalate the hostilities. At least, that is what Jack tells me he was able to piece together from the events that take place in the weeks that follow. Maybe some might think the way events are turning out is coincidental. Certainly, stranger things have happened. By now maybe you are listing my story as the fictional last ticks and tocks of a worn out old brain. I will say one thing – the hard knocks of personal experience lead one to find less and less serendipity in the world. Maybe I have come to think this way because I am a veteran at the game of living. Or maybe I am just whacko-bird, one of the favorite expressions of us oldsters. We will be talking about some shifty liberal politician who wants gas at twenty bucks a gallon, or loony greenie who wants to cure global warming like it is an infectious disease, and we will put the whacko-bird tag on him…still, if anybody had seen Fargo talking to Emily about Jack, I know who you would say was the angry bird-brain.

"He's got money we don't know about," Fargo spits out angrily. "He's hiding it from us!"

"Why do you think that?" Emily frowns, not knowing what to believe or why it should even matter. She has been trying to keep the peace, but since Fargo lost the latest in his string of jobs she finds him more and more argumentative and difficult to be around. Lately, he seems to be running hot, a line of sweat on his forehead when there is no reason for it. Yet, when he lets her take his hand it is cold and clammy. She hopes he is not going to have a stroke, fall over and die like her mother. Maybe he has already had a stroke, or a small series of strokes. She has heard all about this from one of those quickie television network news medical reports, there are secret strokes that can happen and the person who gets clobbered does not even know it, and that can change the victim's personality and nobody is the wiser for it.

"I can see it in his face!" Fargo snaps. "Your father is a natural-born liar." Fargo takes off his shirt and throws it toward the clothes hamper. He misses, but he does not bother to walk the few steps to pick it up and put it in the hamper. He stopped doing that a long time ago.

This little gesture frustrates Emily. It is just one small thing, but she is going to have to do it herself, and he does a hundred small, thoughtless things like that every day. "Fargo, we don't really need to do anything about this. We have enough money."

"You can never have enough money, Emily."

They do not say any more. She storms off to the bathroom and he climbs into bed. A bit later, Fargo feels he might like to hug and smooch a little and who knows where that might lead? He throws an arm over her bare shoulder. Again, his hand is moist and unnaturally cold on her back. Emily moves away from him. She is quiet, staring wide-eyed at the wall with a worried frown on her face. She stays still in that position long after she knows he is asleep.

Twenty

"Move over, Joe," The Old Viking says as he pulls a chair up to the table already occupied by other members of the Old Bunch.

Delrina grins at him, "What you call me, gringo?"

"Ohh…" Herbert looks confused for a moment. "Sorry, Del. I was remembering my dream from last night."

"Hoo, boy! I was in your dream? How did I get so lucky?"

Herb's face flushes beet red, "Well…yes, you were. Well, not really you. Somebody who looked like you, but named Joe. And we had one of those beds with drapes over it."

"Sangre de Christi! Amigo! We were sleeping together?!" She sounds amused and mildly outraged, but I can see her face has a little color, too, and she cannot help but be pleased, even if it is only her old fart pal Herbert.

"No, no, no! Nothing like that!" Herbie's stammering protest is like that of an embarrassed schoolboy. "This woman named Joe. She looked a little – a lot like you."

I find this interesting. I time travel to ancient Greece and at the same time The Old Viking dreams he has a smoking hot, bodice ripping scene with our pal Delrina in a four poster bed. I look over to DoubleSpin, who is quietly eating his regular Peter Pan Peanut Butter sandwich. He shrugs and looks away, guilty as sin. He sends me a thought, *With Herbert it was only a dream. Real time travel is expensive. It would blow our budget to warp both you and Herbert on the same night. They would fire my butt at light speed. By the way, your necklace is in the bottom drawer of your dresser.*

"Women are never named Joe," I tell Herbert. "Maybe you mean Josephine."

"That's it!" Herbert's face brightens at the thought. "She was telling me not to go out tonight."

"That's Portia," George says. "You got your Shakespeare all mixed up."

"I tell you it was Josephine!"

I think the conversation has become complicated, so I interrupt before The Old Viking becomes too upset. "Zip it for just a minute, Georgie-Porgie. Go on, Herbert, tell your story. What then?"

His face clouds, "Well, you know how dreams is. One moment I'm going to bed with…" his eyes stray to Delrina for a moment, "with Joe, and the next I'm on some battlefield and somebody who looks a lot like my fat little rat nephew Sidney, only he's wearing red coattails, if you could believe it, and he's done some kind of trick on me with cannons and I'm going to lose everything."

"And then what?"

"And then nothing. I wake up feeling chilly as an iceberg and thinking maybe Jack here put the thermostat down again."

"Did not," Jack grunts from his wheelchair. "You dreamed you were Napoleon, which makes a lot of sense, because in real life you are actually a crazed and doomed hero of commerce."

"Jack, if them cannons was brass metal they have to be worth a million bucks!"

"Napoleon lost everything at Waterloo," I tell him.

George breaks out into his version of an old rock and roll song, "Josephine, why can't you be true?"

And the rest of us around the table join in, "Josephine, why can't you be true? Why can't you start doing the things/ like you used to do?!"

99

I am thinking that rock and roll has to be good from end to end of the galaxy, and from the grin on DoubleSpin's face, I have to be right about that one.

"Joke's on you, smart-asses," the Old Viking says with a derisive snort. "I am rootin' tootin' certain for sure that was 'Maybelline!'" And with that, he gets up and heads for the computer nook to blast away at his Nigerian friends.

Twenty one

Emily brakes to a stop at the curb in front of Amanda's school. Amanda has been sitting in back. She gathers her knapsack, gets out of their small crossover wagon and comes to the open window on the driver's side. She kisses her mom.

"How was grandpa?" she asks.

"Oh, he was alright, honey." Emily's tone is such that her daughter knows she does not want to say anything more than that about the St. Patrick's Day lunch with grandpa.

"I missed seeing him."

"We had to talk about grown-up things," Fargo tells her from his seat on the passenger side.

"Oh, so it was your idea that I shouldn't go," Amanda says.

Fargo frowns, "Why do you say that, little brat child of mine?"

"I heard you yelling at Mommy." Amanda gives her mom a hug. "I love you, Mommy."

She hikes her heavy knapsack over her shoulder and turns away.

"No kiss for Daddy?" Fargo asks.

Amanda walks away without looking back.

Once they pull away from the school and are on their way again, Fargo instructs Emily to drive them right past her high-rise building to Tom Fennerman's law offices, located a few blocks down on Figueroa Street. Emily argues that she will be late, but Fargo insists.

"They won't mind if you're a little late, Em. What we have to do now is much more important for our future. For Amanda's future. For the future of our family."

Emily relents, telling herself she has to go along to make sure he does not make an even bigger mess of things than he already has.

The couple sits in Fennerman's waiting room for over twenty minutes. Emily is nervous; she thumbs through a Vogue and a GQ and then throws the slick magazines back on a pile. She didn't expect to have to wait like this and now she will be late for work.

"Fargo, this isn't a good idea."

"We have a right to know," Fargo insists, his lower lip jutting out like it probably did when he was a pampered little boy.

"I don't like having a meeting behind Daddy's back. It's not the way we do things in our family."

"Things are different now," Fargo says.

"Tom is Daddy's lawyer, too. He won't be able to tell you anything more than what you already know."

"Tell us, Emily. Us."

Emily shakes her head. She is about to inform him it is all his own stupid idea and she wants no part of it. She grabs her purse and gets to her feet, ready to storm out and leave him to his own devices. But before she can go, Tom Fennerman enters the lobby. He picks up his messages from the receptionist and recognizes Emily. He is surprised to see them.

"Emily! And, err…Fargo. What can I do for you? Did you have an appointment?"

Emily looks at Fargo. It is his idea, and he is going to have to carry the ball on this one.

Twenty two

I have been living out my days at the lovely
Chermundo Villas ever since my dear Ted, or whatever his
name was, slapped himself into some foggy mountainside.
I can tell you, unlike many of the guests, I came here and I
stay here of my own free will…or, more to the point, as my
new alien acquaintance might say, I believe I tucked my
life in here because of my own fears. I put on as crusty a
front as possible, but, truth be told, I am generally afraid of
everything.

When I lived alone at home, I had started to be
unsteady on my feet, and I even fell a time or two. Once I
blacked out in the bathroom, and when I came around to a
dizzy awareness I was sitting on the floor next to the sink.
I had a big purple bruise on my forehead and a headache
the size of Alaska. The docs tell me it is my weak heart.
Nothing traumatic, just getting old, you see.

Now do not misunderstand me. I am not looking for
pity; I am simply telling you how things are with me. I
already explained about the diabetes, and now this heart
thing. You can take it as a warning, if you are of a mind to.
You will get here, too, you know, unless you intend on
dying young, which I do not recommend, either.

My point is, having been at Chermundo Villas for this
amount of years, when you are a guest here, the days and
weeks and months drift on by with an effortless flow that
makes you unaware that time is actually passing. The
rhythm of the seasons, call it the pattern of the holidays, it
all dances on by like jolly paper Santas and Easter Bunnies

hopping across a cork board. The very order of these
things makes for a mindless and even numbing sense of
repetition – as if any more obfuscation was in order! The
ones of us who notice the days flowing by comment on this
occasionally like passing ship wrecks joking in the night, or
however that saying goes…we make light of it, but there is
nothing anyone can do about the passing of time.

"How do you do, and how do you do, and how do you
do again?" as the old Mother Goose rhyme asks. You do
not know it? "One misty, moist-y morning, when cloudy
was the weather, I chanced to meet an old man, clothed all
in leather."

But my own mind drifts…Nothing anybody can do, is
there, about the relentless march of their days? If you find
a solution, let me know. Hey, come to think of it, I found
one…but here is the irony: it is not for the faint of heart.

Regardless, the days pile up and there are no more
revelations by the strange fellow who calls himself
DoubleSpin. Without saying a word to each other, Jack
and I have formed a secret pact that we are not going to talk
about it.

Then late one day a few months later, evening falls on
Herbert and Jack's suite and Jack gets to know something
more about the purpose of DoubleSpin's visit. I think it
was June because by then the days were longer and the
nights shorter. Late June, for sure, because I remember
there was talk of a fireworks display in the park for
Independence Day, and they had tacked up a sign up sheet,
maybe we would get enough signatures to fill a van with
the still not totally brain-dead and chug on over there to see
it.

Herbert's room is dark. He is still at dinner. But there
is light and the noise of conversation from Jack's room.
The Stranger is sitting sideways, stuck to Jack's wall, about
three feet above his desktop. I know this is impossible, but
there you have it, just as Jack told me once our truce of
silence got itself broken, so you can take it or leave it.
Jack's weird visitor has a plate of gravity-defying peanut

butter-and-Ritz crackers, but he is only nibbling at them. Jack is lying on his bed, staring up at the ceiling.

"Why do you always argue about everything with Emily?" the sideways Stranger asks.

"I was a teacher," Jack says.

"I know. Big time math wizard."

"Nothing like that. High school. I taught at a very small, private, expensive high school. I taught math, trig… some physics."

DoubleSpin nods to the plaques on the wall, "But you did alright."

"Yeah, I guess. But you asked the question, and the answer is simply that I probably didn't pay enough attention to my kid. Doreen handled all that, you know, and now she's gone. As for the rest, it was 'Earth to Dad, Earth to Dad – anybody home?' most of the time and let's face it, nobody was."

"I like that analogy, Jack. But why was nobody home?"

"It takes special talent to be a good dad. I don't think I had the aptitude for it."

"You seem to care."

Next door, Herbert has quietly come into his room. He is about to turn on his light, but he overhears Jack talking and thinks Jack is talking to him. He goes to Jack's door and is ready to say something, but he holds back, which is a very rare thing for The Old Viking. He stands there, watching Jack talk at thin air.

"You know the knock on us math guys – all brainy abstraction and no real emotion." Jack thinks for a moment and eyes the Stranger, "You know what they say about all reality being experience-based?"

"Well – yes...but I'm not allowed to affirm or deny."

"I just wondered if you had any idea where science fiction comes from."

"Jack, not one in a billion sentient creatures has any idea what you are talking about."

"Do you?"

"Not really. I know how crystals grow and what a photon is."

"That's something. What are you doing here, anyway?

"Right now? Refueling."

"On what?"

"Gravity.'"

Jack screws up his face. "That makes no sense at all."

"Just because you don't know a thing doesn't mean it isn't true."

"Well spoken. How's that gravity thing working out for you?

"About half full."

"Yes, you are," Jack grins. "But I meant are you absorbing it?"

"Well, yes, you could say that…" The Stranger smiles at him in a patronizing way, like a man petting a dog.

"Nice story," Jack says. He gazes at DoubleSpin, thinking about the oddness of their conversation, "You're not going to tell me, are you?"

"Can't," the Stranger agrees. "Against the rules."

"I could write your story. We could win a prize in Scientific American. 'The Man Who Ate Gravity,' or maybe 'Mass Equals Crunchy Peanut Butter Squared.'"

"Plus these cheesy crackers," the Stranger says. But then something occurs to him. "Then you do believe I exist…at least a little bit."

"Of course. I also believe in Mickey Mouse, Tweety Bird and the Tooth Fairy."

"You've got to believe in me, Jack. I'm here to help you, but I can't if you don't let me."

"Help me do exactly what?"

"I can't say right now. Just keep your eyes open and you'll see." DoubleSpin looks toward the doorway.

Jack follows his gaze and sees Herbert.

"Hi-ho, Old Viking."

"Hi Jack," Herbert answers. He shakes his head and retreats to his own room without saying anything more.

Twenty three

The meeting with Tom Fennerman shows no results at all that are to Fargo's satisfaction, but Jack's son-in-law is not about to give up. He has convinced himself he is on the trail of vast riches – or at least that he has found a way to shake loose some cash from Jack, and maybe in that way solve his desperate need for bridge financing to carry him along for a while until he can straighten out his life, and nothing is going to stand in his way. If only he had control of the family cash flow instead of his hopeless, financially retarded wife! Sounds crazy, I know, but dope head thinking can be more whacko-bird than even what goes on in the dizzy brains of ancient hobby horses like Jack and me.

The week after the 4th of July fireworks displays, Fargo acts against all common sense and sets up an appointment at the Chermundo with Doctor Daniel. The administration offices are on the street side of the Villas, so Fargo is pretty sure his father-in-law will not get wind of it. Emily again tags along, but by now she is thoroughly steamed. She does not really want to be there, but she has found some pills Fargo has been taking without her knowing about it, strong stuff prescribed by a doctor she has never heard of. Oxy pain meds for back pain that she is fairly certain he does not have. Not a good sign. What with his lying and irrational behavior, she is beginning to fear for her own safety, and for that of her daughter. But Fargo no longer seems to care about her feelings. When she brings up the medication, he goes on the attack, tells her she is an emotional mess and a butt-in-ski, and you know that round did not end peacefully. Truth is both of them are beginning to look shabby around the edges.

Jack has not spoken with Emily about this – he is convinced she would never talk to him about her personal life with Fargo – but the Jackster is smart in more ways than math. He tells me he thinks Fargo is taking meds, hopefully not crack. Jack knows the physical signs, and more than a little bit about the mean addict world through his teaching days, but he is unable to bring up the subject to Emily – he knows it would make her go nuclear.

Emily feels she has no choice other than to tag along with Fargo to this meeting at the Chermundo. She is going to do her best to keep matters from getting further out of control. Maybe it is a good thing she is there, the way Fargo paces around the good doc's office, all impatient and angry over supposed slights and insults he believes his father-in-law has inflicted on him. Dr. Daniel, whose specialty is geriatric medicine, is thinking that if he was a psychiatrist he could make a big pile of money right here, because this pair has a ton of problems that could use fixing. However, they are not the subject of the meeting.

Fargo's voice rises, "Hey, Doc – I was right there; I saw it!" Fargo is sporting the three days without a shave look made popular by beer commercials and pop rock stars, but his clothes are sloppy and mismatched, and on him the style seems more befitting an out-of-work street bum, which, behind the façade, is pretty much what he actually is. He glares at his wife as if she might contradict anything and everything that comes out of his mouth. "You saw it too, Em. Don't say you didn't! Your dad was talking to someone who wasn't there!"

Emily's lips are pressed in a thin line and she does not say a word.

"You're sure?" Doctor Daniel asks mildly.

"Sure of what?" Emily tries to delay by asking for a clarification, "Sure that there wasn't somebody else there?"

"The elderly sometimes revisit their memories."

"Pardon my French, Doc," Fargo says, "but in this particular case, that's just so much crap! My father-in-law is clearly delusional! We asked him right to his face if he was talking to somebody!"

"And what did he say?"

Emily frowned, "He made a joke out of it."

"What sort of a joke?"

Fargo makes an insistent gesture to his wife, impatiently expressing the thought with his hands: come on, out with it!

"It was about Fargo being named after a town." She has gotten over the anger she had felt at the moment her dad said it. Right now, in this meeting, she feels puzzled and empty of emotion. The recent weeks with Fargo have taken a lot out of her.

Dr. Daniel tries to make light of Jack's comment. "At least he didn't say a movie." He realizes he should have arranged for their on-call psychologist to be at the meeting, even though the cost cutting Goozer would have sniped and griped about that.

There is a pause. Nobody laughs. Fargo glares. "Doc, you don't seem to be getting the seriousness of Jack's problems."

"Well, I'm just trying to get to the bottom of this. You know, older people do talk to themselves sometimes."

"That's just another excuse!" Fargo is shouting. He catches himself, and puts a calmer expression on his face. "Look, Doc, I think he should be committed. The guy's a danger to himself. He's going to get in trouble or hurt somebody."

Dr. Daniel clears his throat and refers to his notes. When he looks up again, he ignores Fargo and speaks directly to Emily, "Haven't you told me he's always been somewhat of a distracted guy?"

"Well...yes."

Fargo stands and flings his hands high over his head. There is a look of astonished outrage on his face. He sees the flaming asteroid heading for New York City, but nobody is listening to him. "Distracted?! Old Jack's no longer in the ball park!"

Emily lays a hand on her husband's arm, hoping to calm him down a little, but he shakes her away.

Dr. Daniel studies his notes further, trying to ignore the uncomfortable scene, "It says here you already have conservatorship of his resources."

"That what we know of!" Fargo blurts out.

"You're saying you want to know everything he's got, and you suspect he's hiding his assets from you? I don't see how you can – "

"No, not like that." Emily's face reddens and she quickly interrupts him. "There's more than enough set aside for his expenses, even if he lives to be a hundred and ten."

"God forbid," Fargo mutters under his breath.

"Then you think he's being victimized?"

"Yes!" Fargo blurts out.

Emily frowns at her husband's behavior, shaking her head no, "Maybe my husband does, but honestly, I don't. Dad isn't spiteful or paranoid...and his family trust – I manage it, so I know – is bigger than we ever imagined."

Fargo gives them a sour look. "Well, yeah, but we can't really get at it until he dies. And what if he changes his mind? Irrevocable trusts are revocable, you know. And what if there actually is money that's not in that precious trust?"

Dr. Daniel clears his throat again. He likes to think he is a fair and reasonable person, and yet the direction of this conversation has him feeling professionally and personally embarrassed; this is no longer about Jack's mental capabilities, which, as a geriatric physician, he feels fully capable of evaluating. This meeting is deteriorating into a family quarrel about resources, and the discussion has become more about personal matters he feels are not his business. He talks to Emily, ignoring Fargo for the moment. Emily seems more willing to listen to a medical appraisal.

"Emily, I'm a doctor, not a lawyer. In my professional opinion, medically speaking, for now your dad seems okay. He's already under supervised care, and he can be moved to our more intensive care ward when it is time."

Fargo shakes his head. "No! When it's time?! What exactly does that mean?"

"When it's decided that such a move is what is needed for the patient."

"And who gets to decide that?"

Fargo stares at the two of them. He realizes that, clearly, it is not him. He frowns and shakes his head, frustrated but powerless to do anything more.

Twenty four

Mid-July in Sherman Oaks is hot and dry. There is a lid holding the smog in the valley and the air is so acidic you can taste it. Sales of eye drops are going way up, the restless black widowers are on the prowl and the big Chermundo swimming pool is overcrowded during the daylight hours. It is lit at night, but the water is so tepid I personally am not tempted even a little. Most evenings after dusk I take a short run on the nearby streets and come back to a cool-down shower. This evening, I am on my way out when I spot Jack wheeling into the hobby room on the far side of the lounge.

He sees me coming and gives me a weak smile and a limp, one-handed wave. "No lounge chairs in here." He points to a sofa, but it is too low for my taste, so I pull up a ladder-back wooden chair with a plump cushion tied on to the seat. The hobbyists and crafters have knocked off for the night. We are alone in the room, surrounded by sewing and scrapping projects, and the far side of the crafts area has woodworking and model building, birdhouses, balsa wood airplanes and an old piece of driftwood that someone is whittling away to resemble a ghastly spirit or a frightened gopher, it is impossible to tell which.

"Where is DoubleSpin?" I ask.

He shrugs as if he does not know and does not care. I know nothing could be further from the truth.

"I guess you have been avoiding me." I keep talking just to fill the silence.

"Not really, Lucy. I just don't know what to say. I know you can see him, too. I'm grateful for that because it means I'm not totally delusional."

"Or we both are," I joke.

Jack takes that seriously. "The odds against us both seeing him have to be incalculably huge." He is quiet again, and I can see he is sorting out his thoughts. "And I'm grateful to you for not telling anybody."

"Nobody would believe me any more than they believe you."

"Right. I wonder what he's really doing here." Jack scratches his face. It looks like he hasn't shaved for a couple of days.

"You better get to your electric razor, my friend," I tell him. "Don't give the Goozer a chance to stick the Z to you."

"Right. Or my son-in-law."

"We've got a world to save," I kid him, but Jack is not in a joking mood.

"What in the world would he want with an old man who can't even get out of his wheelchair?"

"You can stand up a little?" I do not know if this is true or not. Nobody outside of Herbert knows just how Jack gets around without a full-time nurse's aide.

"I have bars all over my place," he tells me. "I use my arms for most of it; I just drag my legs around and use them to prop me up."

"That cannot be pleasant."

Jack shrugs. "My own fault. I fell and broke my back." Then something occurs to him. He digs in one pocket of his sweatshirt and comes up with three of the little tangerines some marketeer named Cuties. "Look what DoubleSpin taught me," he says, and in a minute he is juggling the tangerines like some circus marvel. "Toss me that spool of thread!" Somehow he catches the spool on the fly and he is juggling all four.

He finally comes to a triumphant stop and starts peeling one of the Cuties. "Impressive," I say. "The earth is doomed, but I hear Ringling Brothers is looking for a few good jugglers."

"Funny."

"Well, do I get one?" He tosses me the one he has peeled. The silence lengthens between us as we eat our tangerines.

"I want to show you something else DoubleSpin taught me," he says, but at that moment the spool he used in his act rolls from the spot where he had set it and falls off the table.

I bend down and pick it up. I set it back on the table and give Jack an inquiring look, "Okay, now show me."

"I just did," he says. And the spool, which I had set on end on the table a few seconds before quivers of its own accord, topples over, and rolls off the table again.

"Hey…" I protest.

"Hey, indeed. I can move objects with my mind."

"That is amazing, Jack!"

"It's harder than juggling, but still, it's just a trick. DoubleSpin says a few humans can do it, if they know how."

We look at each other and I feel a little shiver that is somewhere between fear and amazement. Jack nods once, and gives me a quick smile, probably the first genuine smile to cross his face since I have known him.

"And now," he says, "I want to see if I can teach you."

"Trade you," I tell him. "Our friend taught me something I think you will like, as well."

Twenty five

Meanwhile, far and away in another part of the galaxy known to humans as the Milky Way, a fuzzy holographic image of DoubleSpin stands at attention before a group of ancient beings who are shrouded in grey silk-like materials. These elders are six in number, and they communicate through mental wavelengths. The youngest, the recorder, flicks a tablet from time to time, an instrument that is to the Apple iPod as a pulp novel is to a stone tablet.

We said you were not ready for your first big show, the eldest of the ancients rumbles.

You are a goof-up. You will never be ready.

All this time. All this energy spent. You enlist a handful of decaying people to save a planet?

A rustle of doubt and displeasure moves through the elders, a chill wind in an old stand of pine trees.

DoubleSpin gulps, *Well, I haven't actually got them all on board yet, but things are moving in the right direction. And look, six of the contestant planets are already out of it!*

Another of the elders frowns *I knew it wasn't time to move you up. Too green, too raw, too untried.*

Another elder disagrees, *We had no one else, and we had to fill the show.*

Yes, but now we've meddled, and the stain is on us.

Wait! DoubleSpin raises his hand before they can come to a decision.

The full intensity of their god-like intelligence swings to DoubleSpin. *What is it, little Spinner?* The elder asks.

We cannot give up on them! I don't care how small their chances are.

The elder looks dubious. *If you fail after consuming so much energy, you will never get another assignment. Not in a galactic cycle! Cut your losses now. We'll retrain you to collect cosmic dust or something.*

No! DoubleSpin is shimmering with a golden intensity. His image looks frayed and unstable, like he will explode. *Please! Give me a chance! This race is worthwhile. They show glimmers of courage and honor. They can self-deprecate and have an advanced sense of humor.*

Murmurs of angry dissent ripple through the gathering of elders; but the leader raises one arm for silence.

A little more time, then. So be your wish come real. Go. Prove our decision wise. He turns to a bulky electron holographic inciter. *Listen up, sentient universe! Let it not be said that we were inflexible. Let it not be said that we were unfeeling.*

Jack and I are still in the Villas hobby room. It is after midnight. Curfew has come and gone and I am still not getting this mind-over-matter thing. On the other hand, Jack is a total dud at mental-speak. I believe he is going to have to risk looking like he is talking to thin air unless he gets hit by lightning or run over by a truck and that somehow clears a path in his brain.

Jack has become bored with the mind-speak trick of mine that he clearly cannot do, and he has gone back to lifting objects. He has a pocket full of tangerines; and he manages to get the one a few inches off the ground, but it is a tremendous struggle. In that moment, DoubleSpin materializes out of nowhere and nothing right before our eyes.

"DoubleSpin!" Jack and I both say, shouting his name like a greeting. It is a moment before we see how upset and frazzled our alien friend looks. His impeccable grey suit is actually tattered and a bit frayed, and his hair looks rumpled and out of sorts.

Travel, he says by way of answering my concern. "Travel," he repeats out loud for either Jack's sake or the invisible cameras, it is hard to be sure. *I know*, he says to me. *Jack and you are not capable that way or I would have taken you with me.*

He sees Jack is idly trying to lift a scissors from the scrapping table. "No, Jack. Think this way: the apple hit Newton on the head, so he discovered gravity. But mental moving doesn't have anything to do with the weight of the object."

"But…" Jack starts to protest.

"How much distance is there between particles?" DoubleSpin asks him.

I can see Jack's mind going. I remember that here is the guy who is at ease in a room full of JPL scientists talking about things like remote transmissions and rocket vectors.

Suddenly the heavy scissors takes off straight up like an arrow and buries itself handle deep in the ceiling.

"That's better," DoubleSpin says. He smiles a little, but I can see worry lines on his grey forehead. Something is really bothering him.

Twenty six

Mid-July in Lagos finds the rainy season in full swing, but, through some quirk in the weather patterns, the recent heavy squalls have died down. There is a momentary break in the heavy cloud cover, and a few rays of sunlight are turning the moisture laden atmosphere into an unbearably hot and muggy presence. Because of pressures that are more political than financial, Big Mo has moved his operations from the office building in downtown Lagos to a water-soaked cabana in a suburb that many decades ago was elegant but is now run down and in squalid decay. The cabana was once decorated in Hawaiian-casual, and it still sports plenty of varnished bamboo, dry palm frond decorations dyed poison green, and cocoanuts spray painted bright Nigerian orange. But tropical decay is moving in fast and hard. There are buckets on the floor half-filled with rainwater that drips endlessly from the ceiling, and more buckets sit on three large moisture-bowed tables stretched across the center of the room.

Outside, through the wide open side of the cabana, rain casually pocks the surface of a deserted swimming pool that is filled to overflow with dirty water and floating debris. A month or two ago, when Mo first rented the place, the pool was nearly empty with a small puddle of brackish, foul-smelling water at the deep end; then it was little more than a convenient hollow the last tenants had used as a garbage dump.

Mo leans on one corner of his desk, the same cheap wood veneer desk he brought with him from the last site of his highly mobile operation. Today everything is running smoothly, maybe a little too smoothly; Mo has a sixth sense that he uses to keep track of how his luck is running, and this lack of ripples in his operation has him worried. Mo's team – the operators, the letter openers and the talent stars – sit around the damp fiberboard tables, positioned just about the same as they were in the high rise building. Some of the crew amuse themselves by tossing a half-size Nerf football. They do not have a clue anything might be out of the ordinary, and that is the way Mo likes it. A worried team cannot operate at top performance levels. His job is to do the worrying.

Albert launches a high one that is nearly clipped by the nearest of two sputtering overhead fans, "OJ throws for a big score!" Mo eyes the wobbly flight of the ball, idly wondering why the fan's ancient electric motor has not shorted out long ago.

Super-star Charles neatly one-hands the Nerf, "OJ Simpson is dead, idiot! And he was a running backer A running backer catches the ball, he does not throw it."

"OJ not dead, he in jail in Las Vegas," someone volunteers.

"OJ never in jail!" someone else protests, and this starts another round of jabbering about the crazy Americans and their decayed Elvis lifestyle.

Maba grins. Her breasts spill alluringly from her halter top; she dresses for success. "You peoples know nothing at all. Mister OJ does not catch the ball, the quarterboy give it to him!"

Quarter-*back*, Maba," Charles corrects her. "You best stay in the kitchen, mamma. You no good on the field!"

Maba's grin broadens and she waggles her fingers tauntingly in his direction. "I plenty good on de field, Charlie-boy, and you knows it!"

This gets a titter of laughter and approving nods from around the table. BuBa and BeBe steadily open envelopes and send out prayer shawls. They are the daily bread-and-butter of Mo's operation and they know it. In another corner, the little flock of dial-up callers is busy with their outgoing calls. Morning in Africa is the middle of the night in the United States, prime time for waking sleepy old rich men from their slumber.

BuBa is a dark-skinned black man. His wife BeBe is much smaller, almost like a doll in her colorful turban and multi-flower patterned robe.

Buba laughs out loud and waves a letter. "Listen up, good peoples! We be miracle workers yet one more time right here! 'Your wonderful blessed prayer shawl has cured my aching bones for good.' See, BeBe, we doing so much good in the world!"

Bebe is a no-nonsense gal; she frowns and indicates the pile of unopened letters on the table in front of them. "Quit funning round, mister. We got the actuality of real money waiting right here in front of your face."

"Naw, this is good stuff, baby. Listen up now: 'Honored, sir, since I have used my prayer towel to dry my back end, I am totally germ free. To prove it, I have urinated…uhh, ur-in-ated…uhh… on this paper, and I have AIDs real bad.'"

BuBa drops the letter. The room erupts in laughter as he rushes out of the room to wash his hands in the dank and foul-smelling water of the swimming pool.

One of the dialers waves for attention. "Hot line, number 16. Charles, for you. Herbert Miller. Old Viking Shipping."

Charles thinks a moment and then snaps his fingers, "Got it!" He digs through his box of file folders and pulls out the appropriate one, scanning it to refresh his memory as he prepares to answer the phone. "Oh, yeah, I'm a prince. I'm a prince. I actually am a prince...I'm a bloody royal prince!"

Mo is standing next to dialer number one. "Quit goofing around, Charley. It's your 'Old Viking' pal. I want to hear this one.

The operator gives them the quick look over to make sure they are both ready and after Mo gives her a nod she clicks a switch. Both Charley and Herbert's voice can now be heard on the loud speaker system. Star-power Charley does not like this. He is annoyed by the slight delay in his own voice as it goes through the system, but he has no choice other than to put a hand over one ear and plunge into it. He starts his end of the conversation with a phony heartiness and a noble, if only somewhat-British accent, "Herbert! Prince Bukamba, here in the Nigerian capital. Good fellow, it is so pleasant to hear from you!"

In return, Herbert's irate voice comes bellowing out of the loud speaker from half a world away, "Gol-dang it, Prince, I thought you was going to help me get my 35 million, 500 thousand dollars pronto-tonto!"

The actor's eye's widen. He holds the phone from his ear and blinks once or twice as he tries for a dignified frame of mind before continuing, "You may call me, 'Your Excellency,' Mr. Miller. Refresh my mind about your situation, please."

There is a low mutter and the far distant and yet distinct sound of shuffling papers. "Refresh your gol-dang mind! All right, I will! Holy Cripsers, now where is that...? Oh, here…" The American's scratchy voice bellows full into the phone, "Contract NNPC-slash-PEJ-slash-WRKL-slash-36! In the amount of 35 million and 500 thousand dollars, U.S. American money! Is that there refresh enough?!"

"Ahh, yes, how could it have slipped my mind? I was at the cabinet meetings just yesterday pleading your case, dear friend Herbert. Everything is ready; in fact, your check in the full amount is cut for you and already signed by the administrator. We are exceedingly, extremely very sorry for the holdup."

"Damn it, it's been months, Prince!"

Charles frowns at Mo and makes a confident gesture with one hand, assuring the boss that he has things under control. "Call me 'Your Excellence.' And we do not use profanity in the presence of the royal court, Herbert!"

Various members of the talent nod at each other in amused appreciation of Charles' quick rejoinder.

"Oh no, we don't never do that," Maba chuckles, risking a dark look from Mo.

There is a pause in the long distance conversation, and when Herbert speaks, the edge is somewhat off his anger. After all, the prince has said his money is in the works. "Right...*your Excellency*...but it has been many months, and my company needs that money for our operations."

"You say we received the...err..." Charles hastily refers to his notes, "...the refrigerators?"

"Yes, and the microwaves, the electric ranges, the compacters and the dishwashers. A whole ding-dang ringa-rang boatload. I have the invoices right here. The shipping instructions, the bill of lading, the dates shipped, I got everything."

Charles allows a hint of concern to slip into his voice, "Clearly, such paperwork can be manufactured?"

This sends Herbert into a sputtering rage, "Manufactured! Why, I – what are you trying to say? I don't get it! Look, what are you trying to pull?"

In point of fact, Herbert also needs to put on a bold front because both men, each on their own side of the world, realize there are no dishwashers or refrigerators. No nothing, in fact. This scam, like many of the 409 bait-scams, depends on the implicit understanding that they are both defrauding the Nigerian government through the Bank of Nigeria. Of course, it is a double scam, and the only cat to be skinned is Herbert. But thirty five million five hundred thousand dollars is an extraordinarily tempting sum of money for someone no longer as sharp as he once was, and the Old Viking is well on the hook.

"Herbert, calm down. I said your check is ready and waiting. All you have to do is come to Lagos and pick it up!"

That is the last straw, and the old man's voice fairly screams out of the loud speakers, "God damn it, Prince! I can't come to Lagos and you damn well know it!"

"Well, why not, my good fellow, if you are the big time businessman shipper importer-exporter, the head of the giant Old Viking Shipping Company, as you claim to be? How can you bill us $35 million for just a few kitchen items, in the first place? Just curious, you know."

Charles knows there is very little chance the old man will get on a plane and come to Africa. His passport is probably out of date, if he ever had one. And they would love it if he ever did. In such a case, hopefully the gullible American could be persuaded to show up with a suitcase full of money. Herbert would be escorted to a special room by special inspectors. He would be stripped clean of all valuables. If there was any way to gain long distance access to his funds, he might be kept alive a few weeks so they could drain his accounts. After that, he would be lucky if he was still alive, lying beaten, broken limbed and naked in some urban outskirt of Lagos proper with very little chance of finding his way to the U.S. embassy.

On the other hand, while Herbert does not realize these specifics, he is not a complete fool. He has heard Nigeria is a very dangerous place. Foreigners go there and do not come back out of the jungles. They get eaten by snakes and tigers and such.

"That there ding dang money is owed me! I have a valid contract! It's right here – Contract NNPC-slash-PEJ"

This yelling is beginning to annoy Charles, who again holds his free hand over his ear, "Herbert, gather your calmness about you! I, Prince Bukamba of the royal family have given you my personal word – your check is waiting for you! If you cannot come here, you can hire a representative to pick it up for you. We will make all arrangements for you!"

Charles signals Albert to get ready to pick up on his line. "If you find travel to our lovely city inconvenient at this time, if you would prefer, I can connect you with an able attorney who will conduct your affairs for you for a very modest fee; this will be a nominal and insignificant payment for services rendered, considering the sum of money you will soon receive."

When Herbert speaks again, he sounds distracted. His voice becomes furtive and whispery. "Shush, the walls got ears around here, Prince."

This puzzles Charles, but Mo spins a circle around his own ear. This new twist to the conversation confirms his

belief that Herbert is loopy. But Charles is not yet willing
to cut bait and give up on his fish. He patiently speaks into
the phone, reminding Herbert to address him by his title.
"*Your Excellency*, please, Herbert. What walls have ears?
Is your telephone bugged by the CIA? What are you
talking about, Mister Herbert Miller?"

"Yeah, right. *Your Excellence.*" But the mood has
changed and the American is still speaking hurriedly. He
does not answer Charles' questions about the line being
bugged, and by the tone of his voice, whatever his problem,
it has not gone away. "Look, Prince, send me an email
with your lawyer guy's number. Maybe we could work it
that way."

But now there are complications on the Nigerian end
of the line. BuBa, returning from washing his hands, bursts
in the door.

"They coming! They coming! They coming!" he
shouts. But before anyone has time to react, three
uniformed soldiers burst in the door.

One soldier yells, "Stop! I shoot!"

A second soldier shouts, "Nobody leaves!"

The third lets loose a short burst from his stubby
automatic rifle. Dusty debris and bits of bamboo float and
flutter down from the ceiling. One of the two ancient fans
comes loose and hangs by the electrical wiring from the
rafters, sputtering but with its fat wooden paddles still
slowly rotating as if that is their job and they will go on
until the end of time.

There is bustle and general tension, but no wild panic.
The team has been through raids like this, they are part of
the scammers' hectic way of life. Mo signals his people to
be calm; after all, it is his operation and he will be taking
the financial hit, and even this unwelcome visit is just
another part of his overhead costs.

In the initial confusion, several of the letter opener
people quickly slip various amounts of money off the table
into their pockets. BeBe would like to do the same with
her prayer shawl proceeds, but the money is on BuBa's side

of the table, and she is sitting too far from the stacks of cash to make a hasty grab without getting caught.

A haughty military man struts into the room looking as best he can like a West African imitation of General George Patton. He is blue-black skinned, short of stature and middle aged. He wears the insignia of a colonel and exudes an overall impression of short tempered self-importance. His pants and shirt are so neatly starched that they have only begun to soften and lose their sharp creases in the heavily humid air. He may be a small man, but he has a large army issue automatic pistol in a white leather holster at his waist. He also carries a riding crop that he whacks against backs, tables, chairs, arms, walls, desks, human heads – whatever is nearest – to show he means what he says.

The Colonel smiles when he sees Mo, and gives him a half-bow that is little more than a nod of recognition. It is not a pleasant look, and, in the middle of his bow, his glance flickers around the room as if to reprimand any onlooker that his gesture does not imply weakness.

As an eleven-year-old boy, the Colonel's family farmed a patch of swampy and unresponsive land for a remote missionary outpost of the Southern Baptist church. Approached by a hungry band of desperate rebel soldiers, they gave every bit of food they had to the soldiers, who then raped his mother and forced him to kill her and his father with a pistol that had only two bullets in it. Surrounded by dozens of jeering ragtag soldiers, his life's path was laid out before him.

The Colonel's bitter little grin fades, "Mohammed Kahn... Mohammed...Big Mo, for short."

Mo nods in resigned acknowledgement, lowering his head more and more, and saying the title Colonel in response each time his name is shortened.

"Colonel...Colonel...Colonel," he repeats. "What may we do to your honor?"

The Colonel is not happy, and Mo's appeasing attitude does nothing to lighten his mood. He knocks paperwork off the nearest table with his riding crop. "Mo. Mo. Mo. I close you down, you open up. I close you down, you move, you open up again. Friend Mohammed, you are a regular Mo-in-the-box."

"I pay..." Mo tries to protest. "I pay you good. I pay what you ask."

"Yes...you pay...but you must know you crawl around in the grey area between our slight affection and our extreme displeasure. And now I find out that you are an embarrassment to our President, who is receiving pressure from our dainty, white-gloved congressmen for your many sins against the good name of Nigeria."

"Surely, it is not just me! Why, there are thousands of similar operations to mine!"

"Yes, Mo, many hands are in the pot, so many, many hands that we are getting pressure from our friends across the sea with their fat pockets. The Americans threaten to cut off their investments in a bright Nigerian future. What a disaster that would be! Do you not see I am caught in the middle?"

"But...tell me, what can I do?"

"I do not know, Mister Mo. You are truly in a very bad position. As you say, there are so many just like you. Convince me, what do we need you for?"

As they talk, the Colonel walks over to the prayer shawl operation. He ignores a pile of personal checks and picks up the large stack of money next to it.

BeBe's grim expression and twitching hands show her upset feelings, but she is smart enough not to say anything. The Colonel expertly shuffles through the money, rejecting the dollar bills and keeping the 5s, 10s, 20s, 50s and even a 100 dollar bill.

He looks up at Mo, "You do everything we ask, and still you flourish like a poison jungle mushroom underfoot. Your unwelcome presence is everywhere I step. I tell you, it sorely tries my patience. Allah knows I do my best to be a good and gentle man, but these are difficult times, and so we come to the place where you sadly owe me something more.

"But – yes, anything! You just have to ask!"

"Yes. And it has come to this asking part. I fear I need an important favor of you, Mo."

The Colonel taps the money he has taken, folds it and puts it in his pocket. Clearly, money is nice, but it has nothing to do with the favor he will be requesting. He moves to Mo's side and puts his arm around the bigger man's shoulder. He has to stretch to reach up that high because Mo stands at least a foot taller than he does. This would be funny, but the Colonel is a notoriously unstable customer, and no one in the cabana dares even the slightest chuckle.

"Come with me, Mo. We walk a little ways only. Not a big favor, just a small thing, you do it for me."

Mo casts a worried look around the room. When people go for a walk with the Colonel, it is known that sometimes they do not return. But the Colonel has his soldiers and the soldiers have their guns, and Mo sees he has no choice. The two men walk out the door together. After a moment, the three soldiers follow, leaving Mo's team behind to stare uncertainly at each other, both relieved and worried for what their own futures may hold.

Looking out of the cabana through the dirty, moisture stained floor to ceiling windows they can see a little of what is taking place between the two men, and it is not reassuring. The Colonel is jabbing his finger in Mo's chest and making demands. Mo at first seems not to understand. Then, once he understands, he shakes his head 'no.' Whatever the Colonel is asking, Mo does not want to be involved. A third man, this one wearing an Arab headband and a dark, expensive suit, has been quietly watching from the shadows. Now he steps forward and shakes his fist, not at Mo, but at the Colonel. He seems to be urging the military man to increase his efforts to bend Mo to his wishes.

From inside the cabana, Charles shakes his head. "No good, no good at all. That Arab guy, he be Maloof Urdveen."

BuBa starts to say something, but BeBe hushes him, biting her own lip until it bleeds. They can see the Colonel is brimming with red-faced anger. Easily shamed to fury by his superiors, he becomes more insistent. Mo, backed up against the dirty pool by the smaller man, still vigorously shakes his head. His body language is clear; whatever the Colonel and Maloof Urdveen want, Mo cannot and will not agree to do it.

Then the critical moment, if there actually was one, when Mo could have changed his mind has passed, and the Colonel is done persuading. With a swift and entirely unexpected motion, he takes the pistol from his belt and in one smooth gesture brings it up and shoots their boss squarely in the forehead. Mo's arms fly out and he falls backward with a splash in the dirty pool without making a single cry. The Arab gives the body a faint, coldly appraising look and then nods his approval. He speaks briefly to the Colonel, pointing to the people left in the cabana, and then walks away. Mo's body floats face up on the surface of the water with his open eyes staring unseeingly at the clouds overhead, which are now darkly threatening. The first spatter of a coming downpour hits the skin of his face as it glazes the surface of the swimming pool.

Not thirty seconds later, the Colonel re-enters the cabana. He frowns, intent and aware that he has to quickly gain authority over Mo's people. He is followed by the three soldiers, guns at the ready.

BeBe makes the sign of the cross over herself. The talent huddles in their seats, ready for the hail of bullets they are sure will come.

Rene babbles in a whispering voice, "Oh, Jesus, God, no Jesus God, no, no, no."

There is a loud crack, but it is not from any of the rifles. The Colonel has slapped his crop against the nearest table. He walks around, studying each of the people in the room. He stares for a moment at Albert, then flicks Albert's tie over his shoulder with his riding crop, a gesture of dismissal.

Albert starts to blubber, "But I didn't do anything!"

"Qui-et!" The Colonel beats his crop in time to his words, one beat per syllable. "Qui-et! Qui-et! Qui-et!" He is finished looking around the room. He has made up his mind. He points to Star-Power Charles, who is still holding the phone, still connected to The Old Viking, his fish half way around the world.

"You."

Charles eyes widen, but he manages to speak in the phone. "Herbert. I call you back later."

Star-Power Charles carefully sets the big plastic receiver down on its cradle and slowly comes to his feet, not sure what to expect.

Twenty seven

Evening falls on the western edge of the Brave New World side of the globe. It is twilight in the dining and lounge area of the Chermundo Villas. Mid-August finds the dry smog of Southern California settling like poison gas over the San Fernando Valley. The L.A. Times has exhaled the unpleasant air in the form of editorials that try their best to whip up the sentiment against automobiles, which are as much a way of life out here as eating tacos, burritos and Bob's Big Boy hamburgers. As a long time valley dweller, this amuses and angers me. I have read my history and I have taken the tours. Smog has been a problem since the Spanish missionary priests came over the hill from Santa Monica and noticed the Indian campfires rising to hit the inversion layer and form the thin but nasty brownish-yellow cloud layer. I suppose you can blame it all on Henry Ford and Mercedes Benz; just do not ask me to believe you.

I put down the newspaper and go back to my frustrated attempts to read "Straight," a novel by Dick Francis that George has loaned me, something about an English jockey. George swears it is the greatest detective novel ever written. I am not sure that is true, but it is interesting, about a jockey who inherits his brother's gem business, and what with the murders and greed involved in both horse racing and diamonds, plus a fling with the deceased brother's mistress and her ties to British royalty…well, it is something to take my mind off the unbelievable super-normal happenings that are swirling around Jack and me.

As I try to concentrate, I am distracted by the clink and clatter of a nickels and dimes game of blackjack that is going on in the background. Jack sits in his wheelchair, looking out the wide French windows at the dark garden where nothing is happening. The strange creature who has informed us his name is DoubleSpin and we are the sole hope of our planet is lying on a nearby sofa, dipping a celery stick in a jar of peanut butter; but, of course, only Jack and I can see and hear him.

"What if you had superpowers?" DoubleSpin asks.

Jack doesn't answer right away. "Would I have to die to get them?"

"I guess that's a good question, when you consider the source. You humans are enormously preoccupied with your own exit from your current dimension."

"I didn't used to be," Jack tells him. "When I was twenty, I didn't think about it at all. Now I think there might be things I still could pass on to my granddaughter. So, you see, I don't really want to go just yet."

"So, aside from that, you wouldn't mind?"

"Of course I'd mind – how would you feel about falling into a black hole?"

"I wouldn't like it," DoubleSpin agrees.

"Why humans, anyway?" Jack asks. "Why don't you contact elephants…or the whales?"

"It was a close call, but when I appeared the elephants tended to freak out and fall over with heart attacks. And what are we going to do with whales, wait a million years so they can grow hands? We don't have years; we have months, at best."

"Chimps, then."

"No time left. This is good stuff, Jack. Our little interchange shows your kind can be empathetic."

At that moment, I get up and wander over, hoping to interrupt the conversation before the staff's attention is drawn once again to Jack's behavior. I ask Jack if he would be interested in a game of chess. Jack is a good chess player, and every once in a while he lets me win one.

"Not tonight, Lucy," he tells me. "I think Delrina was looking for someone to hang out with."

I am afraid my disappointment shows. I tell Jack, "Del plays chess like checkers gone wild."

"How's that?" I can see he is interested, in spite of himself. I like to verbally mess with Jack to keep him on his toes.

"She mashes the pieces; she squishes them around, gets the knights to move like the bishops do." Jack goes quiet for a moment, and then he says, "You get older, and your final end-game starts to preoccupy your thoughts. You start to wonder if elephants and dolphins go to heaven."

I think Jack is talking to me, but then I see DoubleSpin shrug. "We don't know any more about that than you do."

"Say, you don't put creatures like us in zoos, do you?"

Jack has taken DoubleSpin by surprise, and I catch a rift of mental images, a wild assortment of creatures behind one way glass while on the other side another set of creatures looking more or less like DoubleSpin shuffle past.

"Well, no, we…" DoubleSpin sees me watching closely and knows I have tuned in on his thoughts.

It might help if you were a little more guarded, I tell him.

"It will never happen to any of you, Jack," he promises.

More promises you cannot keep?

Jack eyes me. DoubleSpin waves a celery stick at him in warning, "Be nice, Jack. She likes you."

Jack now has his attention on me. "Here's the problem, Lu. DoubleSpin here seems like a nice enough fellow, but can we trust him?"

I take a seat nearby. "You mean, what is his motivation, right?"

"Exactly," Jack says. "Assuming he's real and we're not totally psycho, what's this all about?"

132

"If we take his word for it, he says it is a game show," I tell him. "Wacky as that seems, some sort of Save-A-Planet contest. He's worried about his career in galactic show biz."

Charity, DoubleSpin interjects.

"A charity event, he claims."

DoubleSpin looks guilty as charged. "We don't have the resources to save everybody. We just can't! And we can't run around spending all our time being cosmic do-gooders! We do what we can."

Jack frowns. "You don't know anything at all about us, our fears, or how we think. You live a thousand years."

I can't help it. DoubleSpin looks directly at me. *Individual sacrifices have to be made. Look, you humans have a spark, something wonderful. You are going places. But I've never met such a stubborn, backward, superstitious, and obdurate race – and you're right on the edge of elimination.*

Jack learns fast, I tell him. *So do I.* At the time, I swear, I do not realize what I am pledging, but even the way everything turns out, there are times in my life when the realization of how close we came haunts me.

Jack eyes me. He is not aware of our mental conversation. He does not say anything.

Then I hear it again, a booming voice in my head, a voice from somewhere in the galaxy saying, *You vouch for Jack?*

I do.

You vouch for George and Millie and Delrina?

I do.

And the Old Viking?

Even the crabby Old Viking. He is a good person at heart.

I do not know what gets into me. I think I must be tired with my life, with the lies of my marriage, with the dull half-life of existing at the Chermundo, just waiting around to die. Time for a change. Time to stand up and be counted. Time to stop being afraid. I think Jack would agree with me, if he hadn't been so flattened by his accident. *Yes,* I say. *And for me. All of us are all in.*

We're going to get on with it, then.

DoubleSpin nods once to us both and shrinks to a tiny point of grey, and then winks into nothing.

"He must get lonely," I say to Jack. "You think he really lives a thousand years?"

"At the very least."

I am finding the silence deafening as it lengthens between Jack and me. "I know what it is like to be lonely," I say. "Since Ted passed away. He was a phony and a fraud and he probably wanted to kill me, but sometimes we would play two handed pinochle, and he had a hat full of traveling salesman jokes."

"I didn't know he was a murderous person. That would make it hard to trust anybody." Jack is giving me a curious look.

"Oh, yes. After Ted, I didn't even try."

"Why do you think that is?"

"Afraid. I am sure of that one. I made such a mess of it the first time around. What about you?"

"We were happy enough."

"That doesn't sound like a true eternal love story."

"It was an arranged marriage." He grins when he sees my skeptical look. "No, honestly, it was. But not the usual white-handled shotgun. My brother was dating Doreen, who later on became my wife. He had to go to the army. This was the Vietnam era, and they had the draft and he got a low number. He was killed in action; he stepped on a primitive land mine, something they called a 'bouncing betty'…and a few days after that Doreen figured out she was pregnant."

"You married your wife to save your brother's honor?"

"No, not exactly. Doreen's father was a banker and kind of a mean guy, and he pretty much ran our small town. He held the paper on my dad's hunting and fishing store." Jack gave me a sad look. "The banker explained to me the way the world went. I married Doreen and saved the family store, and the bank threw in my college education to sweeten the deal."

"Does your daughter know?"

"Sure. Doreen told Emily, and she probably told Fargo, and he probably told Amanda.

"Is that why Fargo…disrespects you?"

"It's that obvious, huh? Fargo thinks I inherited my money from Em's rich old dad. Actually, that's not true. The guy died broke. The irony is he invested in plastics. He had to be the only unfortunate in the 1950s who lost money on plastics. He went down hard and took his bank with him. That's when we moved from Kern County to the west end of the valley. Doreen was very conscious of our social status. I was only a high school math teacher, but it was better than being the daughter of a disgraced financial criminal."

"Criminal?"

Jack grins. "Did I fail to say he used bank funds for his plunge into plastics?"

A white coated nurse appears in the doorway. "Ten o'clock," she says. "Meds. Meds reminder, everybody."

One or two people wave and acknowledge her presence. Life goes on.

I look around the room. Everything is normal, just another night on board the good ship Chermundo. Across the lounge, the game of blackjack winds down to boos and guffaws. Then the players decide they can get away with a last hand. Somebody chuckles and there are furtive looks to see if the nurse is coming back. I sit in my favorite padded leather lounge chair with the cheater-lifter. Jack is in his wheelchair, unaware that some seriously bad raindrops are about to fall on his head, actually on all our heads. A feeling of uncertainty washes over me. I have guaranteed an alien player in a cosmic game that I do not understand that we are going to be the saviors of the world. I believe from what I have read in history books that fate is unkind to those who prop halos on their own heads and attempt to bring salvation to others.

"See you later, Lucy," Jack says. "I have to go lift some weights."

Twenty eight

To his own way of thinking, Maloof Urdveen has spent far too much of his evaporating time schedule whipping Mo's crew into shape. His plan, as he sees it, will re-awaken the sputtering so-called Mother of All Wars. It would be such an unexpected joy if he, isolated in the backwash jungles, turned out to be the catalyst for that war and not his fabulously wealthy cousins with their nettlesome air of superiority. But this enormous, earth shaking project has been stalled by insignificant flea-speck matters and stymied by irrelevant details that rise up seemingly out of nowhere.

Maloof has been concentrating particularly on Super-star Charles, whom he has ordered the Colonel to savagely beat senseless on a regular basis. Charles has been given a personal guard so he does not simply escape and run away to his homeland tribe out in the god-awful back country where it will be impossible to find him. The Arab has seen the potential in quietly exerting some influence on scam enterprises like the one Mo had going, but none of the other scam outfits the Colonel had under his thumb has panned out, and Maloof is left feeling helpless and frustrated.

Charles is their one dimly shining hope, the last available key to success, and this foolish and ungrateful young man must be made to perform flawlessly. Maloof's theory is that the right amount of physical and mental torment can bring Charles to this state of excellence. Oddly enough, Charles' imagination and his ambitions are stunted by his very success as a thieving petty scammer. The enterprising young felon sees only the small picture. He cannot be trusted, and so he cannot be brought on board the grand scheme. Having no real world standards to judge by, Charles thinks it is still okay to extract relatively small sums of money from the Americans – even his affection for scamming is dangerous, even though Maloof has explained repeatedly that petty theft is no longer the order of the day.

Time is important. The schedule is critical. Charles must help them set their plan into action. But Charles responds by explaining how the Americans are not just stupid gulls; they have to be motivated through their greed. Maloof is, to a certain degree, forced to admit the young scam artist is right. To this end, he has entrusted Charles with certain sums of cash that he may use to get a shipment into the States. He does not care exactly which port of entry becomes their window of opportunity, though Washington D.C. or Manhattan would be nice. After some weeks of education, Charles seems on the right track. He thinks he has made progress in Los Angeles. This will involve passage through the Panama Canal, but Charles says he has a contact in Southern California who assures him this will not be a problem.

Once Maloof is convinced that Charles' part of the plan is at last on a schedule, the Nigerian Arab books a flight from Lagos to Egypt and makes his way to the office of a distant cousin, a specialist who is doing business in the financial district of Cairo. The cousin is not Egyptian, though he can pass as well as the next man. Egypt is made up of so many ethnicities and languages that few bother or have reason to sort them out. The English language is the mild glue that in this age keeps everything more or less in one gigantic mess that somehow manages to stumble along from day to day and year to year, just another stuck together socio-politico-religioso monster that feeds on itself as it shambles along.

"I have big money for you," he tells his cousin. "Bigger than any you have ever seen." The cousin's eyebrows rise in twin skeptical half circles, but Maloof can see he has his attention.

Meanwhile on the other side of the world, Jack is wheeling through Herbert's office in their shared living room, and the Old Viking seems even more off-kilter than usual as he madly pounds away at his laptop.

"Treat me like dirt!" he growls. *"Your Excellency!* I'm going to shove this dirty crapper a taste of excellency right up his royal kazoo!"

Herbert prints off a page as Jack is rolling past him.

"What's up, Herb?" Jack asks. The Old Viking's high level of verbal venom is a bit over the top, even for Jack's unpredictable roommate.

Herbert grabs the closest arm of the wheelchair, "Well, get this – I arrange for a shipment of expensive Nigerian ivory, all carved stuff, and I do all the spade work from this end, and we're supposed to be partners, me and the prince – and now I get the invoices?!"

Jack gives him a skeptical look. "Hey, you dying your hair?"

"Course not."

"Bet you are. Got the hotsy-totsies for Delrina of your dreams."

"Stay on point, my friend. My shipment from Nigeria."

Jack frowns. "Isn't it illegal to import ivory? I read about it somewhere."

"Not ancient carved artifacts, it ain't! Shows you what little you don't know, Jackster-boy-wonder!"

"You're right about that one, Herb." Jack tries to wheel past, but his friend has not let go of his wheelchair. "Wait – Jack, wait! Here, take a look at this." The Old Viking shoves the newly printed page in Jack's hands. "I need an opinion. Do you think this is strong enough?"

Jack reads out loud:

"i AM OF A THINK YOU ARE NO BETTER THAN THE REST OF THEM BUSTARDS!!!! MAYBE YOU

ARE NOT EVEN NO REAL PRINCE AT ALL AFTER ALL!!!!"

Jack hands the page back to his friend, "I don't think 'bustards' is a real word, Herb."

Herb dismisses his correction with a wave of one hand. "Hell, the Prince'll get the main drift of it!"

"That he will." Jack starts to wheel past, but he pauses, thinking he will try one more time. "These guys are all crooks, Herb. I'm glad you're finally seeing the light.

"Crooks who owe me money! And I aim to get it, my friend!"

At this point DoubleSpin places a hand on the wheelchair, preventing Jack from continuing on to his room. Jack is surprised; the figment has acted in his physical world.

"Ask him what happened lately to rile him up."

Jack stares open-mouthed at the Stranger, who insists, "Ask him!" Jack stares at DoubleSpin's hand on his wheelchair. The Stranger lets go of the chair with an amused fake expression of guilt that says, okay, you got me!

"Herbert. Just exactly what happened?" Jack asks.

Herbert gives him a grateful look. He has been hoping to vent about this with someone.

"Well, it all started when I was talking with Prince Bukamba on the phone, this was some time ago, weeks or months, it's not important, but then…"

"'Prince Bukamba.' This that same prince who turns out to be one of your scamster friends?"

Herbert's look sours. "I thought you wanted to know what happened, Jack-ster."

Jack glances at the Stranger, who gives him a stern look as if to say he might try a little harder. Jack sighs, he will try again.

"Okay, sorry, Herb. I do want to know. Go ahead."

"The Prince is a member of the royal family of Nigeria. It's like England, except they have tribes like American Indians but they are all black people running around there mostly in robes and shorts and the women half naked and-"

"Right, Herb. I know about that part. Let's focus on the shipment of ivory."

"Anyway, the Prince has very high connections in the government. I got his stationery right here." Herbert fumbles through his fat file and hands Jack a letter with an ornate crest at the top.

Jack nods, impressed with the trouble these people have gone to extort money from his friend. Jack glances at DoubleSpin to convey his feelings, but he does not communicate his reservations out loud. He's going to do his best not to upset Herbert again.

"Right. Okay. I see that here," Jack says in a matter-of-fact way. "What about it?"

"Well, I'm talking with the Prince and something happens, like maybe an interruption. I got the feeling some soldiers showed up."

"Soldiers?" Jack interest sharpens, in spite of how he feels about Herbert's dealings with the African scammers. "How could you know that, Herb?"

"What, you think I'm dumb? I'm just old; I'm not stupid. I was in the army, Jack. From my end of the phone I heard shouting, like orders in the military, and gunshots!"

"Well, it's a very unstable country. They're always doing a civil war or a military coup or some other form of population reduction over there. You saw the internet stuff I pulled up for you."

"Yeah, I saw it. Thanks for nothing, pal. Next time I need a little encouragement – "

Jack cuts in on his sentence " – you'll buy a parrot that agrees with anything you say. 'Yes, Herbert. No Herbert. You're so clever, Herbert!'"

"Are you going to hear me out or not?"

"Yes, Herbert," Jack says in the parrot voice.

Herbert gives him a snarly look, but continues anyway, "So here's the real deal, Jack: me and the Prince were talking and then I heard these soldiers come in and there was yelling and gunfire and then I got hung up on."

"Sounds like your pal the Prince got his butt busted."

Herbert's mood switches to nasty. "If I ever meet his royal royal-ness in person, I'm going to be the one doing some busting!"

Twenty nine

We are slogging through the last dregs of late summer and at the Chermundo we are all wishing for the Santa Ana winds to start whistling down out of the high desert to blow the acidic atmosphere out to sea, but a change in the weather does not seem to be in our immediate future. For now the San Fernando Valley is ringed with a series of fires blazing in the hills to the west toward Simi Valley and in the mountains to the north and east. The smoke stings the eyes and lungs worse than just the ordinary smog. We are blessed with an occasional dusting of grey ashes on the curved sidewalks and the umbrellas and tile-topped tables in the center garden outside the lounge area; San Fernando Valley Snow, the cynics call it.

Meanwhile, Jack and I are struggling to come to terms with our adventures with an alien. I cannot keep it a secret that I have pledged his life – all the Old Bunch's lives – in a highly improbable enterprise to save the planet, though I had done it before I realized what I was saying.

Jack takes it seriously, but in his light hearted way. "Really, Lucy, I would have done the same for you."

"I have the feeling DoubleSpin is not as experienced at this rescue of civilizations business as he would like us to believe."

"What do you mean?"

I do my best to put my reservations about DoubleSpin into words, "Well, he has these powers and tricks, and so we are in awe, like he might be an angel or a demigod or something. But sometimes he seems uncertain of himself and he keeps telling us we are the long shot underdogs."

"Maybe he's an angel-in-training, like that apprentice with wings in 'It's A Wonderful Life.'" Jack is looking at me in that half-joking, half-grave way of his and I think he has had similar feelings to those I am trying to express, but then he makes a joke of it. "You worry too much, Lu. I think maybe your first novel might not be a romance after all. Could be it turns out something science-fiction-y, something that stars the guests here at the Chermundo."

"Right," I say. "At least the interesting ones who may be a little over-the-hill, but not quite ready to be under the dirt."

"Yeah. That's us," Jack agrees.

But more mundane happenings are going on in Jack's life, and we talk about that, too. His son-in-law, the one named after a town in North Dakota, has been like a fool with a bee up his butt and in a moment of truce or weakness, Emily has confided to Jack that the wretched fellow intends to hire a private investigator, though his thinking is anything but clear on what can be gained by doing that. Emily told Jack because she does not want him to think she has anything to do with it.

A day or two later, the gang is occupying our usual table in the dining area for lunch. Jack is sitting there, gazing off into space and I am picking at a made-it-myself Cobb Salad. Millie is working on a piece of cold chicken left over from Sunday's Bountiful Brunch, and George has a plate piled to overflowing with cottage cheese strawberries and pineapple slices. Delrina comes over, shaking her dark maroon curls and looking perplexed.

"Delrina," George prods her. "Get yourself some food. Line closes down in ten minutes."

Delrina looks at us like we are not making any sense, and it comes to me in a flash without her saying a word that she has been talking to DoubleSpin. Delrina is a healthy, well-rounded Texan of Hispanic origin. Where a man like George lets his retreating circle of hair grow over his ears

and to where it approaches his shoulders in what he calls
The American Patriot Look, Delrina crops her curly head of
hair short and dyes it with henna, which, with her dark
complexion and ear-to-ear grin, gives her somewhat the
look of a demonic pixie out for a good time. You would
never know that her husband owned a string of Wendy's
Hamburger drive-ins and after he died she ran them herself
probably lots better than he did.

"I just met the new guy," she says.

"What new guy?" George asks.

"Foreigner. From India, maybe. Strange complexion
and slicked back hair."

"What did he say?" Jack asks.

"Not your ordinary getting to know you stuff."
Delrina looks puzzled. "We get to talking about life and
stuff, and pretty soon he wanted to know if I was willing to
die for my planet."

"What did you tell him?"

"I said sure, of course. I mean, who wouldn't?"

"Not me," Millie says with that mischievous grin of
hers.

"Come on, Mil. If the planet blows, you wouldn't be
here anyway."

"Oh," Millie says, thinking it over. "Well, in that case,
okay."

It is a moment of light hearted comradeship, at least for
some of us. Jack grins at me; he's found a way to take the
pressure off my guilty mind. He reaches his hand to the
center of the table. "Who's in it for saving dear old Mother
Earth?"

"Yea! Save the planet!" George yells in that too loud,
exuberant style of his. "I get the screenplay rights!" He
places his hand on top of mine, like we are picking sides
for a baseball game.

George yells to the Old Viking, who is in the adjacent
lounge banging at the computer keyboards, "Herbie, want
to get in on this?"

"There any money in it?" Herbert asks in that high-
pitched, querulous way of his.

"Tons and tons," Jack yells.

"Count me in on that one!" Herbie does not even know what he is agreeing to, but if there are profits legal or illegal to be made, he wants his share.

I hesitate before putting my own hand in. "Wait a minute, George. You cannot have all the rights. I get to write the novel: 'The Chermundo Bunch Saves the World.'"

"Fair enough, but then I get to option your novel."

"Shame on you people," Millie says. "We rescue the world from disaster and five minutes later you're carving up the profits."

Delrina grins at us as she slaps her hand on top of the pile. "Actually, it's even before we save it."

"What world?" The Old Viking says as his wrinkled old hand slaps in on top of the pile.

"How many are there?" George asks good-naturedly. "Try the pork chops, Delrina. They're pretty good today."

Thirty

Dick Burkle, Private Investigator, newly hatched, wonders just what variety of nut-ball has landed on his little chunk of the planet as he looks up from the crossword puzzle in the Los Angeles Times to see Fargo rush into his office. Dick is practicing sizing up people. He guesses his prospective new client is mid-to-late thirties, about his own age, but lighter in weight and with a tick in his right eye and an overall nervous attitude. Twitchy guy, is the first impression that comes to Dick's mind. He's hiding something.

The restless newcomer, who, Dick prays fervently, is a client, will not take a chair. He walks around in a fitful little pattern, four steps one way and four back the other. Dick decides he is probably on drugs.

Dick himself is wide across the shoulders. He has light brown hair standing up in a style that is half spike and half crew cut, the haircut of an ex-military guy newly trying to go civilian.

"Don't you want to sit down, guy?" Dick asks for the third time. "You are going to wear out my carpet."

"It's a tile floor," Fargo tells him.

"It's an expression of speech."

"It's a mixed metaphor," Jack's argumentative son-in-law snaps back at him.

"Right, a metafloor," Dick quips, getting in the last word, but the pun is lost on Fargo and that is a good thing because Fargo is the client here, and detectives only get away with smart-mouthing in Robert B. Parker novels.

Once Fargo lays out the broad strokes of The Deteriorating, Delirious & Demented Jack Hamlin Situation, the new detective's mind is filled with questions and reservations.

"I've got to get the goods on my father-in-law and get him committed to an insane asylum!" Fargo declares. "That's our goal."

This direction makes Dick nervous, and he says the first thing that comes to mind, "Shouldn't your wife be here? After all, it's her father you're accusing."

"My wife will do whatever I decide for us," Fargo says.

"I don't want to be discouraging, but you can't just commit somebody in this state…" Dick's voice trails off. He is conflicted and it shows.

On the one hand, he certainly does not want to talk Fargo out of employing him. Dick needs this assignment; he is trying to establish himself in the somewhat shady trade of private investigating, a profession that, without decent connections with the police force, is arguably harder to break into than show business, and he could use the money. Dick is an ex-military M.P. who did two tours in the Mid-East, and he needs to find a way to put all that spit, polish, dust and blood behind him. He figures detecting is a baby step, like a half-way house back to real ordinary life.

"This is California," Fargo says.

"I know where we are," Dick replies. "I'm talking about your father-in-law's state of mind." Dick is not used to taking guff from anybody. He is well over six feet and massive across his chest. He runs and he pumps iron, both out of habit, a man no longer sure why he does the things of his daily life, but convinced it is the right thing to do. His rough features would be attractive and he might even be considered handsome were it not for the perpetual cynical scowl on his lips and the furrowed forehead.

Dick Burkle's worry lines might be mistaken for those of a man of lesser intelligence, but Dick is smarter than he looks, in fact, too smart for his own good. He outguessed his commanders in Afghanistan on several occasions, disobeying orders to save some lives, including his own. In the army, you must promote or dismiss a man like that, and the officers in charge chose the latter. Now he is back in the real world trying his best to find the romance in his new career, which so far does not seem nearly as romantic as Raymond Chandler and Robert B. Parker made it out to be in their novels.

Fargo gives the big fellow the cold eye. For his part, he would like to make a statement by leaving, but he copied this address from the Yellow Pages at a health club he used to belong to. It is not only the closest detective service to where he was, it is the only agency he wrote down, and he hopes he will not have to run around the block to all the nearby bars and restaurants in order to find another Yellow Pages that probably no longer has the pages he needs, like five out of the last six he opened.

Fargo decides he is talking to a near idiot, but maybe they are all that way. He sighs impatiently. "My point is, in California, what's my wife's is half mine – and that includes her father."

"You mean her father's resources."

"Whatever," Fargo dismisses the possibility of extenuating circumstances with a wave of his hand. "You want the job or not?"

Dick Burkle has a hangover and three day's growth of shadow. He wears a disheveled look that matches Fargo's. Fargo thinks, sure, he's big, but so was the Hulk. He can't remember if the Hulk was a good or a bad guy. This hulkeroo looks borderline respectable and cop-tough, but they are all supposed to look like that, and if this is the way he is coming across with the questions, maybe he will not be able to stalk a mayfly.

"So all you want is a financial?" Dick is definitely looking disappointed.

"Jesus Christ, I'm the client here," Fargo says in a too loud voice. His nose is running and he is definitely feeling an approach of the major jitters. He would like to pop a mellow yellow, but sucking them down dry can be a bitch. He backs himself off a little and takes a deep breath, trying for utmost deadly serious.

To Dick, his prospective client is coming across like a puffy toad or a blowfish, pretending to be everybody but who he really is.

Fargo is oblivious. In his fried condition, he has no idea how he comes across to anyone.

"Yes, exactly what I want is a resources report. Not just the obvious stuff. Old Jack has got a lot more money stuffed away somewhere, lots more than he's saying! I just know there's a hidden stash of cash out there, maybe tons of it!"

"What about me tailing him for a while, I mean, the old fashioned Sam Spade way?"

Fargo may be cunning, but he is not very deep, except in the suspicion area. This suggestion of Dick's convinces him that the detective is trying to take a big chunk out of his wallet. Dick can see it on his face.

"Christ-sake," Fargo complains, waving his hands to describe the helpless mess that is his father-in-law. "The old fart's in a wheelchair in an old fart's home! Come on, man, where would you tail him to?!"

Dick shrugs. "Okay, gotcha. No tail." He looks crestfallen, but then he has another idea. "What about visitors?"

"Oh, yeah," Fargo says. "He sees visitors on a regular basis. From outer space."

Dick lets that one fly by. "So you don't want me to check out that angle? Your Jack Hamlin character has to have a pile of dough to live in Chermundo Villas, and if he's a drifty old balloon head, any slick talker can come along and squeeze a bundle out of him. You know as well as I do that there are con-men who ride the old folks circuit, send out fliers, pepper the internet with oldster emails, pretend to give seminars and stuff, just looking for soft touches like your father-in-law. That ton-o-money you think he's got could disappear before you know it."

This gives Fargo pause. "Well...okay, maybe hang out there for a couple of days. But no more than that."

Having given his approval to hire his very own detective, Fargo is feeling a desperate urge to move on down the road. The irritating tick starts up again, this time in his left eye. He has to get to his meds. He spins around and faces the door. He is ready to leave, but Dick appears standing in front of him. The big guy is faster than he seems.

"Oh, right." Fargo takes a worn check from his wallet and unfolds it. "Got a pen?"

Thirty one

A few minutes later, Fargo is seen exiting the dark and hidden doorway to the rundown and shabby office of Richard S. Burkle, Private Investigator in a bustling downtown section of L.A. crowded with Orientals and Hispanics. The signs are in Spanish, Korean, Chinese, Japanese and occasionally something perhaps Arabic with gracefully looping letters few people not from the Mideast can recognize, much less read. It is noon on a scorcher of a day, and the dry winds in off the high desert have finally blown much of the smog from the city air. Overhead, the harsh sunlight makes the busy and bustling street a place of light and shadows, all images too bright or too dark to be easily interpreted by normal human eyesight.

The somewhat strange person who calls himself DoubleSpin watches the passing flow of humanity with an avid curiosity. He is conducting a running commentary for his galactic audience when he is interrupted by the approach of a desperate looking woman who is wearing little more than a soiled sleeveless UCLA basketball t-shirt and thin, faded and stained yellow cotton shorts that leave nothing much to galactic sentient imagination, much less interest.

She says, "Want a good time, Johnny Boy?" Her look is one of glazed blankness under her dark shell of plastered down hair.

"No, thank you," DoubleSpin tells her. He points three doors down the sidewalk to where Fargo stands, blinking to adjust his vision to the harsh sunlight. "However, see that man down there? He looks as if he may be looking for some medication."

The woman's beady-eyed stare follows his gesture. She squints for a moment in Fargo's direction, and then she nods and quickly disappears into the crowded street scene. A few moments later, two street people move in on their new customer, trailed by the hooker in the UCLA t-shirt, who wants to make sure she gets her small cut of the business deal.

The two street salesmen call out, "Mister, over here, we got what you need!"

But Fargo barely notices them. He wants to get out of this overcrowded and seedy area of town, and he has spotted a taxi moving slowly on the other side of the busy street; a rare stroke of luck in Los Angeles. Fargo moves quickly between two illegally parked cars as he lets out a shrill whistle and yells, "Hey, taxi!"

As the cabbie brakes to wait for him, Fargo remembers the precious pill he is still holding in his clenched fist, and he quickly slaps his hand to his mouth and sucks it in. The squad of three – Jeff-the-Def, Harley D., Jeff's squat and burly muscle-boy, and the hooker in the thin college threads – see him down the pill and think to themselves, oh yeah, he's a live fish, all right! However, they recognize at nearly the same moment that their hot prospect is in danger of getting away before they can even make their pitch. They will have to move fast to close the distance.

"Hey, Dude," Jeff says in a loud voice. "Look what I got!" In a single arm motion that manages to be both furtive and dramatic, the street dealer opens one side of his rip-stop jacket to reveal a colorful pharmaceutical display, rows of plastic bottles held in place with carefully sewn elastic bands. "Ups, downs, red, blue, green, yellow. Powder, pills, you name your poison. Your voyage of choice, man!"

Fargo, who has been caught in the act of downing his own yellow, has a momentary panic attack, and the pill sticks in his throat and he chokes. He reaches out his arm in an automatic gesture for help. But Harley D., the enforcer, sees the move as a threatening gesture. This guy must be a pig or something! Harley D. steps between the customer and his boss and gives Fargo a shove.

Fargo is caught off balance and trips over a cement block that shouldn't be there, falling backwards in the direction of the busy street.

There is a screech of brakes. Tires squeal. Fargo throws up his hands in stunned surprise as a big pickup truck bears down on him. There is an unmistakable sound; the mind-sickening thump of metal hitting a body. Fargo is thrown half way across the road into oncoming traffic. He looks up in dazed horror as an even larger truck bears down on him.

The odd looking man with the slicked back hair accepts a paper wrapped burrito from a sidewalk vendor. He looks over his shoulder at the commotion blocking the busy street half-a-block away.

"Do you have them with peanut butter?" he asks politely.

"No, señor, only hot sauce and the chili pepper."

DoubleSpin hands across several dollar bills and selects a light green pepper from a small tray.

"Be careful, señor." The vendor warns.

DoubleSpin pops the entire pepper in his mouth. His eyes widen, but then a big smile lights his wan features. With his shiny jet black, slicked back hair and grey complexion he looks like the Count from Sesame Street, but without the fangs.

"Cosmic wowsers!" he says.

Thirty two

Fargo's funeral is a mixture of sad gestures and the unique type of wistful joy found in farewell parties. It is not uncommon for last rites to be this way in Southern California where death is passed off as something like an extended holiday on board a Carnival cruise ship to the Mexican Riviera or a radio listener prize vacation to Maui; four days, five nights and the rest of eternity in the tropical sun.

Two weed-thin young singers of indeterminate sexual orientation attempt a drawn-out, off-key duet accompanied by an organist who stumblingly plays a variety of nearly in-tune notes on an electric organ. Their pseudo-nymph-like voices are reedy, uncertain and sour, and the part-time singers hope nobody notices the missed notes or the lyrics they cannot recall, and that they actually will get paid. They need not be concerned; it is an event where nobody rails, rants, comments or even gives much attention to the presentation.

Fargo's mangled, broken remains lie inside a closed casket, with a picture of him smiling and looking young and healthy on an easel set up in front of it. The seats are about half full, with a sprinkling of family, friends and business associates coming and going.

Emily sits in the front row with her daughter Amanda next to her. Emily sobs and tries to keep up appearances by daubing her eyes and concentrating on sitting up straight. Amanda knows she should be grieving, but all she feels is a lightening sense of relief. Kids have an inner centering for what is real and true, and she knows that the happy-go-lucky father of her infant years left them long ago. She is feeling guilty at the dawning awareness that her father will no longer be able to hurt their family, particularly no longer able to wound her mother's spirit or to slap either of them around as he has begun to do.

The Old Bunch, our group of six, has vanned over from the Villas. As the service seems to be dragging fifteen minutes past forever, Millie and I take Jack's granddaughter Amanda off Emily's hands for a while. "Come on, Emily, we'll take her outside for a bit," I say, and Jack's daughter nods in numb agreement.

Amanda seems alright to us, but Emily looks like she is coming through a train wreck, which is understandable considering the sudden circumstance of her husband's death. After all, the sudden and unexpected disappearance of a husband happened to me. Believe me, no matter the circumstances, there is nothing calming or ordinary about the experience, even if the husbands were rotten eggs like Fargo and Ted.

Jack sits next to Emily with Herbert on his other side the Stranger standing on an end seat. This may seem odd, but nobody can see DoubleSpin except Jack and me. I am thinking he is probably up there to get a better angle for his cameras and his galaxy-wide audience.

Totally right on that one, he projects his thoughts in my direction. *Lucy Weiler on target yet again with that way of hers of zeroing in on what is going on in her little corner of the cosmos!*

No respect for the dead, DoubleSpin?

Not true, Lu; we respect them as discontinued from their former reality.

I am left to wonder just how that could possibly be different while he goes into some chatter about uniquely Earthian customs.

Meanwhile, Herbert is relentlessly conducting his international affairs with his Nigerian contacts, busily composing a letter on a yellow notepad. "Jack, Jack – how do you spell 'rascal'?"

"R-A-S-C-A-L." Jack whispers in a hoarse voice. "Is that as in 'Prince, you dirty rascal?'" Herbert nods, grins and waves him off; he is too busy to get into it with Jack.

Fargo's ex-boss approaches Emily and says the necessary things about insurance and how much the firm is going to miss him, quickly adding that they were planning on hiring him back as soon as things turned around. He wanders away with a last look at the photo blow-up of Fargo. In the picture, Fargo is displaying his famous top-of-the-world sales-guy's winning smile. The ex-boss shakes his head and moves on. He looks a little shaken.

Jack sees the expression on the man's face as he walks away, and that starts him thinking, *Maybe Fargo had one friend in the world that will actually miss him. Maybe they were drinking buddies or went to the same school. That's the thing about life, you just never know.*

Somehow DoubleSpin is able to broadcast Jack's private thoughts to just about every sentient being in the Milky Way without Jack realizing he is doing it.

Emily's attention settles again on Jack and Herbert, who, to her majorly distressed mind, have been acting too much like little schoolboys. She shakes Jack's arm, trying to be stern and yet proper.

She nods toward Herbert and hisses in a loud whisper, "What-is-he-doing?!"

Jack speaks calmly in his normal voice, "It's alright, Em. He's just writing a letter to his friend, The Royal Prince of Nigeria."

"Dad, no! This is my husband's funeral!"

"Well, I don't think Fargo will mind."

Jack pauses for a beat and looks past her over her shoulder. Fargo's ex-boss's boss approaches them, intent on extending his sincere condolences. He is a big fellow and he wears an expensive vested suit that would fit well on a smaller man.

"Dear Emily," he begins. He holds her hand a little too long. He makes her uncomfortable; he has tried to hit on her at company parties, not once but two or three times when Fargo was too drunk to know the difference. "I'm so sorry," he says in a smooth tenor voice that has all the necessary tones of regret but none of the sincerity.

"Thank you Mister Warburton." She tries to take her hand back, but he will not let go. His hand feels moist. "It must have been a terrible shock for all of you down at the office," she says, still trying to get out of his grasp.

The Stranger looks at Fargo's boss's boss. "Who's that, Jack?" he asks.

"I don't know him, but if I did, I wouldn't like him." Jack speaks in a normal voice, loud enough so everybody can hear him.

Warburton gives Jack a nasty glance, but says nothing directly to him, and he still holds Emily's hand. "We are going to miss good old Fargo. He was one hell of a worker. Reliable. And dependable, too!"

"It means the same thing," Jack says. "And you did fire him without proper notice. My daughter could sue you, you know."

Herbert looks up from his yellow notepad, not really aware what is going on around them, but willing to say anything in support of his pal Jack. "There's no fairness left in the world at all. Nobody cares. Nobody gives a damn. Ding dang government don't care. It's all going to hell in a handcart."

The overweight fellow clings to Emily's hand and drones on and on. DoubleSpin stands and puts his hand on the fellow's neck, above his shirt collar. The man lets go of Emily's hand as if he has been bitten by a bug. He puts his hand to his neck, where a big red welt is growing. "Ouch! Bee sting!" he cries, and quickly excuses himself, swatting imaginary flying insects as he walks away.

"Thanks," Jack tells the Stranger.

"Never a problem," DoubleSpin responds with a polite little nod of his head. In the next second he is explaining to his audience how that minor bit of action on his part cannot actually be considered a positive action that might constitute interference.

The prayer readings drone on and Jack's attention drifts back to Herbert's letter.

"I'm not sure 'rascal' is strong enough," Herbert snorts. He vigorously applies the eraser end of his pencil to his notepad. "Maybe 'scoundrel'?"

"S-C-O-U-N-D-R-E-L." Jack whispers.

Emily shakes Jack's arm. She nods her head in Herbert's direction. "Why did you have to bring him?"

"Herbert liked Fargo better than I did."

This seems to confuse Emily. "They had nothing at all in common."

"They both were spies in the service. Herb was a Korean linguist, and Fargo – "

"Shh! I don't want to hear!"

But Herbert has overheard the conversation and will finish the sentence in his loud whispery old voice, "Fargo was a ding dang ditty-bopper in the Ir-aq-ee-an conflict!"

"A what? Oh, I don't want to know. This isn't the place." She catches herself, but it is too late.

Herbert answers in a very loud voice, as if she is deaf or an idiot, "Morse code. Dit-ty Bop-per!"

Emily stiffens up and looks straight ahead, hoping to disassociate herself from Herbert.

"Tempus Fugit," the Stranger says.

"Yes, it does," Jack says. "I was just thinking that, myself."

"Nice ceremony. I certainly admire the roses. So fresh and fragile! And all these colors! Smell one for me, Jack."

"You mean your audience, don't you?" Jack asks. He wheels over to the flowers and smells one, and the Stranger shudders in pleasure.

"No flowers where you come from?"

"Crystals, actually. But they are quite pretty."

"I'll bet they are."

Emily is beside herself. Here it is, her husband's funeral and she is talking about nonsense ditty betty boops and Jack is talking to the air and rolling around in his wheelchair, happily sniffing the peonies and the roses. She is at the end of her rope. She speaks in a hoarse whisper,

"Dad. Please! Be quiet!"

"What's that, Em?"

"Dad! Please stop talking to thin air!"

But Emily's timing is unfortunate. The awful organ music that had seemed to be going on forever suddenly falls silent, and her latest sotto voce command is loud enough to be overheard by everyone. She looks around and breaks into tears. Jack puts his arms around her and comforts her. In a rare moment since she grew up and went away from home to college, she allows him to hold her in his arms.

Somebody starts singing Amazing Grace at a soulful, slow pace. The voice is old and it quavers, and yet it is beautifully in tone. Herbert, the Old Viking, has gotten his hands on the mike. In another moment, Millie and I are beside him, and I know our harmony is spot-on and true.

Music is a gift, and maybe it is all we have to give this broken family, this tortured woman and her confused young daughter. George and Delrina join in, and I can feel Jack, even as he holds Emily, softly singing:

> Amazing grace, how sweet the sound
> That saved a wretch like me
> I once was lost, but now am found
> Was blind but now I see.

I see the poor strange alien man who calls himself DoubleSpin standing still as the statue of some glorious demigod with his stone-grey face displaying pure wonder, caught in an unexpected web of golden human emotion. He is too moved to give direction to his invisible cameras, but I am somehow sure they are steadily whirring away in their other dimension.

> T'was grace that taught my heart to fear
> And grace, my fears relieved.
> How precious did that grace appear
> The hour I first believed.

> Through many dangers, toils and snares

I have already come;
'Tis grace that brought me safe thus far
And grace will lead me home.

Thirty three

Maloof's cousin is a middleman, a ten-percenter who seeks advantage from the needs and desires of people from all walks of life. Nominally a devout Muslim, he has no real beliefs except that everyone alive can be bought and every single thing in this world can be sold if the price is right. His most worthwhile connections are not the incredibly wealthy of his world or the angry fanatic believers, but the dangerous and unstable providers of killing devices who swim in the murky world between. His contacts on the dark side are a cold hearted loose association of enablers; it would be wrong to call them a pack, for they are too individually paranoid and greedy to form more than brief-lived alliances that soon fester and decay.

These specialized merchants of death accept Maloof's cousin as a necessary weakness in their way of doing business. He, in turn, understands his own low and troublesome status is such that, once a bit of exchange is consummated, they would prefer him dead rather than alive. So the precautions he takes with this savage group have thus far been sufficient to keep him from meeting a premature ending. Unfortunately for his own personal outcome, he is less concerned about his own blood relative.

As for the opportunity that Maloof has brought to his attention, the risks will be above the usual, but the rewards will also be beyond his wildest dreams. The cousin knows people and has knowledge that can make what Maloof asks of him come true. He has no suspicion of Maloof. His Nigerian cousin is crazy, but he will do nothing to jeopardize their relationship, which has proven mutually beneficial. They have done smaller deals three times before, and each time all parties involved were rewarded handsomely. This time, however, the project will be of historical proportions.

The way it works out, once events are set in motion, Maloof Urdveen's cousin errs on the side of confidence, and accepts with an ungloved hand an expensive leather valise that Maloof passes across to him as they sit together in the back of a taxi cab. Maloof's hands are ungloved as well. But there is no way the cousin can notice the thin coating of matte finish plastic sprayed on the Nigerian Arab's wrists and hands. Maloof simply passes over the suitcase he carries and asks to be left off from the taxi at a nearby busy intersection.

Shortly thereafter, in spite of his legendary caution, Maloof's cousin dies of massive heart failure while still on the way to his bank. There quickly follows a seemingly unrelated string of deaths as the taxi driver, a low level policeman, two higher-level police detectives and even an Egyptian army officer of high rank all consecutively expire of similar heart problems.

Finally a military security man who has had dealings with the modern version of the old Russian KGB, and hence has heard of such things, pulls on a pair of heavy rubber gloves before carrying the cursed valise to a stairway deserted at that hour that leads down to a pier for mooring small boats along the banks of the Nile. There he begins to submerge and wash away the evil. However, his is a plan that, for success, requires greater caution than that of which he is capable, and, as some skin on his wrists above the gloves is exposed to the current, in a matter of seconds he feels dizzier until he topples face first into the muddy water. His pants leg snags on a tie-up bolt at the edge of the pier and there his body will remain until someone finds him early the next morning. The valise, now heavily waterlogged, drifts about a hundred feet before it sinks down to the garbage littered silt and comes to rest on the river bottom. For a week or two, a surplus of dead fish will be found downstream, and scores of the poor who have no alternative but to bathe in the tepid river waters will fall sick for no apparent reason. Some of these will die, as the unfortunate of the world often do, and still others will become terminally ill from eating tainted fish, and yet another scattered bunch from eating the flesh of water fowl found floating in the reeds and presumed stricken by a divine act. But a few hundred deaths is not even one hesitating tick on the population counter in that part of the world, and the evil compound from the valise eventually thins and destabilizes of its own accord and life stumbles on, as it always has in the past in that part of the world.

Thirty four

Evenings nearly always find the carefully clipped
garden and wide walkways of the Chermundo Villas central
courtyard nearly deserted. I think it has something to do
with the habitual lack of moisture in the air of Southern
California. The dry desert atmosphere does not hold heat
very well after the sun goes down, and with the approach of
night and a frequent chill breeze venturing in from the
Pacific it becomes uncomfortable for thin-blooded people
like us to be outdoors. The sudden coolness catches us
unaware in our halter tops, cotton Hawaiian shirts and
shorts, and we duck indoors without thinking about it.

But this has been one of those days when the first hot
Santa Ana winds have been pumping in off the desert, just
a tentative push, but one that is strong enough to last into
the evening hours. The Old Bunch – we are more and more
calling ourselves that these days, a reference to those
maverick cowboys, The Wild Bunch – have been feeling on
the restless side, and maybe even what Millie calls peppy.
I think it is the fact of summer winding down, and any
change from the urban smog and stifling heat is welcome.

Morton Procter, the black widower who calls himself
'Foxy' Procter, power-walks toward us with each of his
fists pumping a half-pound chartreuse-colored dumbbell.
He ignores the rest of us, but he stops to talk to Millie.

"Hi Mil-babes," he says, flexing his arm so Millie can
admire the mild bulge of his scrawny biceps. He is

probably older than any of us, even Herbert, but he does not appear to know it. I have to admit he does stay in shape. He is wearing one of those spandex biker outfits with a swirling black and orange design and the word IBEX like a poster for the nearly-blind on the front. Foxy is lean as an old crow, with bushy black eyebrows under a bald head that features a rim of white hair running around behind his ears. Either the eyebrows are too dark or the hair is too white. I am thinking chemical enhancements when Foxy gives us a startled look. *I do not!* He thinks indignantly.

"I didn't know they made barbells that puny," Herbert drawls in that scratchy old voice of his.

I am thinking a bawdy thought, the sort I have not had in twenty years. *If he's going to dress like that, he should stuff a sock in his crotch.*

"Mil-babes, now you and I have to – " Foxy cuts off whatever he was going to say to Millie in mid-sentence and glares at me. We are staring up at him from our seats around an outdoor table. Not that we had that much going on in the way of conversation, but he did interrupt, so what does he expect, that we are just going to leave so he can have a private conversation and try for the two-thousandth time to hit on his Mil-babes? Then I see that is not what is bothering the pretentious old fart. Somehow, he has gotten the idea that his penis is small and shriveled up and he looks ridiculous in that outfit he is wearing. It occurs to me that I was the one thinking that. I try to look innocent as Foxy's gaze darts from person to person at our table.

"What's going on, Fox-babes?" George asks. "You having a heart attack?"

"Take it somewhere else," the Old Viking says. "This is our table."

Foxy gets an ugly expression on his face and I see he is about to let loose some blistering observations on life in general and us in particular. This does not seem fair to me; after all, we were minding our own business before he came along. I like to think I am one of the milder mannered people you will meet, but I have a sense of right and wrong, too. I feel a sudden little flare, this guy annoys me. I look right at him and think, *Get out of here before we squash you like a bug!*

Foxy's eyebrows arch up and his mouth drops open. He clamps it shut with a "Humph!" and power-walks away from us.

"Odd fellow," Delrina says, grinning at us, and when nobody answers, she bursts into song. She has a pleasant tenor, and she sings, "I can only sing the middle part…"

George's deep voice joins her, "I can only sing the low part…it's the only part I know."

Jack sings from his wheelchair, "I can only sing the middle part; it's the only part I know."

I add in an unsteady tenor, and Millie does alto…with Herbert's scratchy old falsetto somehow topping things off, "We can only sing the high parts, it's the only parts we know!"

And just like one of the Mills Brothers or the Four Freshmen we grin at each other and then burst into harmony like the band of old singing fools that we are, "But we all can sing the music, 'cause music is what makes us glow!"

We clap and give a few whoops of self-congratulations for the sheer fun of it. Being honest, it did not sound anything much like professionals might sing it, but it was not all that bad either for a gang of over-the-hillers just trying to pass the time.

We may not be pro singers, but we are loud enough to attract Mason's attention, on his way to his car after his shift is over. "Wow! You people are great!"

"Don't butter us up, Mason," George growls. "We know great when we hear it, and it ain't us!"

"What else can you sing?"

"We can't sing anything else," Millie says, even though we all know that is not true.

"Well, you should come up with something for the Thanksgiving party, or maybe Christmas."

I concentrate on Mason, my mind burrowing until I get in, and Mason is indeed a good person, and his surprise at our talent is genuine. But there is something else. His surprise is tinged with his pleased notion that we are peppier than he has ever seen us. Mason is writing a paper for a college course he is taking, and he makes the mental note to see if healthy group interaction might be a key to old people living happier lives. I do not know how to tell him, but that is not exactly a new or revolutionary idea. We wave goodnight and we sit together in contented silence at our table in the gathering darkness.

Later that same evening, Jack's room is illuminated by the dim light from an ivory colored plastic night light, an intaglio impression of a famous scene: an angel guiding a young girl who in turn guides her baby brother across a dangerous bridge. Jack is completely under the covers with a pillow over his head. The Stranger is in one of his favorite places, sitting cross-legged on Jack's desk, using a finger to lick the last of the peanut butter from a jar.

"It's called The Momentum Effect, do you know what that is?" he asks.

Jack's voice comes out muffled from under the pillow. "Like the snowball effect, I suppose, only with other stuff that's not snow."

"Right. They do something awful to you, you do something awful back. Pretty soon you wreck the planet."

"Does it happen a lot?"

"All the time."

"This is something you made up, right DoubleSpin?"

The Stranger pauses and turns his attention from the jar. "No, there's a formula."

"Where'd you get it?"

The Stranger wags a finger at Jack and shakes his head. "Nice try, Jack. I can tell you this much: if you input the formula correctly, you can measure the chances of survival of any civilization with a fair degree of accuracy."

Jack sighs and shoves the pillow away. No matter how he tries to trick him, the Stranger is not going to give away any information he does not want to. Jack decides to be agreeable. "Well, sure. Getting the data right is everything. Garbage in, garbage out, they always say."

The Stranger smiles. "I like talking with you, Jack."

"What's our survival quota? Here on earth?"

DoubleSpin gives him a grim look and shakes his head. "Right now it doesn't look like you're going to make it."

"Huh. Too bad."

"You don't seem very upset. No, I get it. You don't believe me."

"It's not that I don't believe you; I just don't know what to do about it."

"Can't help you there."

"Yeah, I know. Rules of the game." Jack eyes him skeptically, saying nothing for a long time. "By the way, how's your gravity tonight?"

"Getting full of it."

That amuses Jack. "You sure are."

Herbert's voice floats in from the other room. "Hey, Jack – can it, would you? I gotta catch a little shut-eye here."

Jack shrugs and reaches over to switch off the night light.

"'Night, Herbert. 'Night, DoubleSpin."

"Good night, Jack."

"Good night, Jack."

Herbert sits up, thinking he heard somebody else say good night to Jack. No, he decides, that just could not be. He clamps a set of headphones over his ears and turns on the Bloomberg Channel, hoping to see what the stock market is up to.

Thirty five

When it is night in Southern California, it is morning in Africa and inside the Colonel's interrogation room, dawn reveals a Star-Power Charles who is haggard, worn and much the worse for wear. He has bruises on his cheeks and a split lip. His clothes are ripped and stained.

The Colonel smiles in his bleak way. "I told you weeks ago, my dear Prince Charlie-boy, that we are in urgent need of a monstrously stupid American businessman. You have been here three times, once at the end of each week. No one. Ever. Lives. Through. A fourth." He slaps his crop on the table.

Charles, whose mind has begun to drift, startles and looks around with a wild stare. "Yes, yes! Our mission must go on!"

"Stop babbling, idiot! You promised you would find me one of these stupid Americans who would work for us. No problem, you said."

"Yes."

"Someone who understands import and export."

Charles is an automatic agreeing machine: Yes, yes, I understand. Please stop hitting me. Please let me live.

The Colonel slaps his crop on the table, inches from Charles's hand. "Someone foolishly greedy in the American way."

"I - I do have the acquaintance of many people like that," Charles gives a rubber neck nod like a plucked chicken.

"You have said so before, and your declarations were followed by no positive results. If you do actually have greedy American fools who are willing to do what you ask, get going! Now! Or! You! Are! Finished!"

By this time, after weeks of the Colonel's mind bending tricks, Charles will say and agree to anything. The unfortunate thing is the Colonel knows it.

"Yes. Yes, I do. Of course I can. Yes, I certainly will."

"Good. Go do it."

Charles stares at him in uncertain disbelief.

"I can go?"

"Yes, Charles. But you should know I am a results-oriented individual. You have 24 hours. Last chance. Do or die."

Charles scrambles to his feet and stumbles for the door. He looks back in disbelief, trying to convince himself he is not going to take a bullet through the back of his head.

But there is no bullet. He makes his way out into the light of day. It is coming closer to the end of the tropical rainy season now, and the muggy heat is enough to beat a man to his knees. Yet there, in that moment, under the intense glare of the African sun with the blossoming white clouds piled high in the sky, Charles feels the momentary rush of his unexpected release, the giddy sense of freedom and of being intensely alive. Then his spirits collapse as he realizes he is not free at all. Nothing has panned out for him. Every rich sucker he knows has flown the coop, turned him down, jeered at the idea of yet another business deal with him.

His very last hope is an unstable old coot named Herbert Miller who might do the job if he had even an ounce of brains left in his head. Maybe he is a rich, crazy man full of wild talk and no actions. But a slim chance is better than none at all. It is going to have to be Herbert Miller. Star-Power Charles stumbles down the street like a zombie, aware that in the future his life will be in the uncaring hands of a Nigerian machete man and an

American fruitcake. Yet he has no problem making that choice; it is better than no future at all.

Charles makes the necessary telephone calls, emails and faxes and it only takes a few days after that, and Herbert is filling his pal Jack in on his latest fool-safe venture that absolutely cannot fail.

Jack looks less than convinced. "So that's it?" he asks, ready to wheel away.

"No, that's not it! Not at all, Jack! You see, a day or two later the Prince calls me back, and pretty soon we got a deal."

Herbert has delayed his friend, hand arresting the motion of his wheelchair. Jack only wants to get some porky links and scrambled eggs for breakfast, but he is going to have to get past Herbert to do it and the Stranger is not helping.

"We want to hear this," DoubleSpin says.

"Is this about the millions he owes you?" Jack asks in an irritated way.

"No, not that," Herbert shakes his head. "That one's still in the works, and believe me, I am going to get that money for sure, Jack! This is something different, a show of good will from the royal family! They know they owe me, you see. This is their way of good faith, because the Bank of Nigeria been stringing us out so much, the Prince put in the word for me!"

"The word," Jack says. His vision of a fine breakfast is evaporating before him. The pork sausages always are the first to go, and that is why it is important to get to the serving line early, and there seems no end in sight to the glowing description of Herbert's new business venture.

"The Prince's Royal Will, a special decree to give me a juicy piece of business!" Herbert says.

"He's giving you the business, all right."

"Jack, listen!" The Old Viking shakes Jack's wheelchair. This has the effect of shooting pain down Jack's injured spine, but he grits his teeth and does not say anything. The sooner he lets Herbert get his story out, the sooner he will be free to go on his way.

"The Prince gets his family to hire me personally to be the importer of record on this whole royal treasury of gold crust spears and jeweled elephant tusks and stuff!"

"Is this that old ivory deal again?"

The Old Viking gives Jack a crafty look and nods his head 'yes.' "And gold bracelets and a pair of marble-size blood diamonds, to boot!"

"But okay, Herb, there is all this great stuff, but then he made you pay the freight, right?"

A shadow crosses Herbert's face, but just for the moment. "Yeah, he tried that, but I held firm and they had to pay on their end. He don't dare double-cross me this time! I got the power because that shipment is coming to me! That right there is an Old Viking consignment, and I can hold things up pretty good on this end if I see some shifty business. I'm in the driver's seat on this one, Jackie-boy!"

"Well, I hope it works out for you."

Jack looks to the Stranger for further instructions, but he is gone. This gives Jack his blessing to roll on through. DoubleSpin may find the Old Viking's latest venture interesting, but Jack is not impressed with Herbert's endless dickering with scam artists, and this latest conversation has only confirmed his belief his friend is being taken for another bad ride.

"Why can't you just play the stock market like every other rich old idiot?"

"Boring, Jack. Bor-ing!"

Herb gives him a lopsided grin and Jack wheels on past, heading for his breakfast.

Thirty six

However, that brief conversation is only the beginning of Jack's reluctant involvement in the mad adventures of the Old Viking. Urged on by DoubleSpin, Jack has Herbert keep him in the loop on this latest project, his shipment of ivory and precious crown jewelry, which is now up to two cargo containers. According to Herbert's updates, over the next few days, there is little progress with the transport of these supposedly priceless and fabulous Nigerian treasures.

"The bling-blang international export-import process is complicated and sticky," the Old Viking complains.

"It's just another scam," Jack says.

Herbert gives him a sour look. "Okay, Jack, I'll admit it and take my medicine like a man. I did have to come up with a few extra thou on this end – but my percentage of the deal is up to 45 percent!"

"O-kaaaay…well then, what's holding things up?"

Herbert grins. "I tied the treasure deal to me getting at least a couple mil. of the 35.5 they owe me."

"I don't think any of this is real."

"You don't know how business is done outside the United States Jackie-boy," Herb shoots back at him, a heated tone in his voice. "Greedy people got their hand out all over the world—China, Bermuda, Pakistan—everybody wants their cut."

Jack blinks and scratches his head. "Bermuda?" he asks. He's been trying to get past Herbert to his own room, but that is not going so well.

"An island in the Atlantic Ocean," Herbert lectures him. "You've heard of the triangle, right?"

"Ahh, yes, I believe I have. A sunken continent, inhabited by underwater aliens."

"Don't you go believing in that alien crap, Jack. Ain't no such thing."

"You figure?" Jack asks.

"Take it to the bank, my friend. That there lost civilization was the victimization of volcanic explosions. It's a historical artifact."

"You're probably right, Herb." Jack shoots his strange invisible pal with one of his fingers. DoubleSpin flies backward as if he has taken one in the heart. But for him, falling has nothing to do with gravity, and he ends up flying sideways and sticking soundlessly to a wall. Jack finds himself thinking, *It has to be one of the great moments in galactic broadcasting.*

One of Herbert's pictures, the one of him with some Japanese businessmen cutting a big ribbon outside a tractor factory in Nebraska, falls to the floor with a clatter. Herbert hurries to dust it off and re-hang it in its rightful position, and Jack takes the opportunity to glide on past him to his own room.

It may still be raining in Nigeria, but it is a great day at the Chermundo Villas half-way around the world from deepest Africa. Acorns and autumn leaf decorations and paper streamers in yellow, scarlet, gold and brown give a festive air to the community lounge area, and there are stuffed straw scarecrows in odd corners of the spacious room. In another two weeks, pumpkins will sprout here and there, in advance of the jack-o-lantern carving contest, and black plastic bats, plastic black widow spiders and spray can cobwebs will appear as if by magic.

The gang of six is on the move. Actually we are seven, if you count the Stranger, and eight with candy-striper Melody, who has put on her thick glasses as she is driving. We are in one of the Villas vans, on a trip to the supermarket. This particular van has been modified with a motorized ramp. Jack sits in his wheelchair between shelf seats with Delrina on one side and Herbert on the other. George is in back with Millie, while I sit up front next to Melody. She does not seem to notice DoubleSpin, who is crowded in between us, feet up and holding his knees so his long legs are out of the way of the automatic shift stick.

Herbert insists we do a run past the post office, where he intends to send off several thick envelopes. We wait impatiently as he trots in. "Got to be certified," he calls back over his shoulder, as if that explains everything. Jack sighs. Certified means waiting in line. But Melody hardly has time to break out her road version of the brain tease game before the Old Viking scurries back out of the post office. "Didn't like the look of things," he explains, casting another cautious glance back over his shoulder. He still has the fat envelopes with him.

"Yeah," George kids him. "UPS is better. They haven't been infiltrated by the FBI yet."

Herbert gives him a puzzled, half-believing stare, and George cannot hold his face straight any more. "Just kidding, you old geekster!"

Herbert huffs and crawls back in the van. "You can't be too careful, Georgie-Porgie, pudding pie," he says.

"That is true in every parsec of the platter," DoubleSpin agrees. I notice he has a tendency to reference the Milky Way as if it is a pizza. The van is full of us ordinary people, so he has shifted to find a place for himself, sitting cross-legged on the ceiling.

His upside down face is inches from Jack's. "You're in my space," Jack tells him.

"Actually, I'm nowhere near you," DoubleSpin says.
"How so?"
"Let's say you are in a fishbowl."
"Right. Okay. Easy to imagine. I'm in a bowl, quashed in with a bunch of other fish. But the fish that is you is finning in my space."

"No, Jack, I may look like I'm in there with you, but actually, I'm not."

He's sitting on the rim, looking in. I try to keep my thought calm as I float it into Jack's consciousness. Jack is stunned into silence. I am trying to make him feel normal but maybe he now thinks I have become a part of his madness; there is no way I can be sure.

Very good, Lucy, DoubleSpin says. *Go to the head of the class.* But, of course, I do not actually hear him, the human way. It is just that a thought like that sentence seemed to present itself in my thinking, not like I was actually hearing it, but more like a sixth sense, something that might relate to hearing like an e-book reader to an ordinary book. I did not actually hear it; I in some way am able to sense it. I do not know why that does not totally freak me out, but by this time it does not. Maybe I am just a tough old broad. Maybe it is because Jack likes his strange invisible pal, and any friend of Jack's is a friend of mine, you know?

So I reach out to DoubleSpin with a thought, *Why doesn't Jack just send you thoughts?*

I think perhaps he can, but he doesn't know it.

That is kind of...slow.

Jack's abilities are abstract and theoretical. It hasn't occurred to him.

I tried mental-speak on Jack before and he couldn't.

Well, if you do find a way without insulting him, it would be lovely.

I wouldn't do that, DoubleSpin!

You can be sharp-tongued, Lucy Weiler.

So I am accepting the amazing notion that I have an extra-special human ability, and also that our designated team leader Jack is in some ways about as normal as the rest of us (or maybe we are all a flock of koo-koo birds) and while this is going on in our heads the regular bubble of ordinary conversation rolls around us in the van.

Jack has not noticed the stunned expression on my face, and neither has anybody else. George has come up with a new story for Herbert about CIA involvement in the green pea business, which is where the numbing elements are put so nobody can notice how all the wooden items are being replaced with plastics. Herbert is not happy with being the butt of any more jokes, and a strong debate is about to break out, but Delrina and Millie start singing "One Hundred Bottles of Beer On The Wall," and by the time we get to six bottles, the trouble is averted and everybody is harmonizing, even Herbert, but not before he grumbles he will take a good whiskey over Budweiser any day of his life.

Thirty seven

Friday is the first day of the weekend special promotional price savings at Albersons, and the supermarket shoppers are more than half oldsters like us, all gunning for the deals. The other half is mostly coupon addicts, so there is a general excited sense of the hunt, of the flag is up attitude that pervades race tracks and casinos like Circus Circus in Vegas. I am pushing the group cart while Jack wheels himself along in his wheelchair. I can see DoubleSpin is in seventh heaven, cart wheeling along as he eyes the wealth of available energy sources.

Herbert keeps up with us. He asks for the hundredth time, "Why don't you get one of them motorized wheelchairs, Jack?"

"I don't know, Herbie, somehow that feels like cheating to me."

There is a lot going on all at once. George takes the opportunity to slip a can of Green Giant green peas in Herbert's cart, and DoubleSpin keeps trying to sneak a medium sized bag of dark chocolate M&Ms into mine. It is there and I set it back and the next time I turn around it has returned again.

Stop it, DoubleSpin! I tell him.

A voice in my head asks, *Please?*

So I put the purple colored bag of M&M's back in my cart. *I didn't know you were going to turn out to be a freeloader,* I tell him.

"Thought you hated M&Ms," Millie clucks.

"Girl can change her mind," I say.

"Jack doesn't really need a wheelchair at all, Herbert," DoubleSpin says in response to the Old Viking's question about getting a motorized chair. Herbert can't hear him, but Jack can.

He frowns at DoubleSpin, "Why don't you just shut up? Nobody can hear you anyway."

"I can hear him," I say. Jack blinks and bites his lip.

DoubleSpin shrugs. *Humans are nine tenths ice under the water.*

What do you want from Jack?"

The Stranger gives me some sort of alien on-camera look of disbelief. *You do want to win this thing, don't you? Jack Hamlin is a major key to saving your world. One of the keys.*

I just do not get what is going on, and that makes me lose patience. *You can do all this mind-stuff and defy gravity and whatever else I do not know—why not just save us yourself?*

DoubleSpin gives me an empathetic shrug. *Well, for one thing, it's against the rules. We would like to help everybody everywhere, but our resources are very limited. I'm like somebody talking to you on the end of a very long, very thin piece of string.*

You would think this would be a moment for thunderclaps and drum rolls, but it is nothing like that. On one level, I am communicating with an alien; but, in the here and now, everyday life goes on as before. I am pushing my cart along. Delrina says not to let her forget some Diet Snapple. Jack is rolling quietly at my side. The strange fellow ambles along next to Jack, hands in the pockets of his soft grey slacks. He looks at everything, seems interested in everything, as if it is his first time in a supermarket, which, I suppose, it is. He stops to read the labels in the spice rack.

"Celery Seed. Cardamom. Cinnamon. Jack, what does cinnamon taste like?"

"Like itself," Jack says. "You have to taste it."

A chubby young stocking clerk wearing a stained white apron and a furrowed brow has noticed Jack is muttering to himself. The stock boy frowns; something is going on that he does not understand. I am thinking this fellow is more proficient at stocking shelves than relating to customers, so that probably happens to him a lot. The guy could be trouble for us; the first thing he is going to do is make a nasty fuss. By now I am alerted and looking around to make sure nobody else is watching us. I bump Jack's arm and nod in the direction of the stock clerk to warn him we have to be careful. But the game has been set in motion.

"You know I can't taste things the way you do, Jack," the Stranger says. "Not the genuine sensation."

"I'm at a loss here, DoubleSpin."

"You taste it for me."

"But I…okay, if you insist."

Before I can do anything to prevent it, Jack snatches the nearest bottle of Saigon cinnamon from the shelf. He screws open the lid of the jar, licks his finger, sticks it in and takes a taste. I try to move my cart to block the clerk's view, but I am too late.

"Hey! You can't do that!" The stock boy moves toward Jack, holding out his hand for the jar of cinnamon.

I manage to push the cart in between them.

"Just as we thought, you are selling out of date spices!" I say, grabbing the little metal can out of Jack's hand. I snatch up another can and point to the use before date. I cannot really read the date, but at a moment like that, I decide he probably cannot, either. "Way out of date!" I yell at him.

Jack takes the open jar back and tastes the cinnamon again. DoubleSpin shivers in delight."

"That's wonderful! More! More!"

Jack pours out some more and takes a big lick."

Our odd alien pal shudders and falls to the floor like he is having an orgasm.

The stock boy is livid. "I'm going to call the manager!"

Meanwhile, I am thinking the best defense is a good offense, just like in football, "Get away from us!" I yell indignantly at him. "We are buying this spice! You don't want old people in your store, is that it!? Elder abuse! I'll sue you blind, you little twerp!"

That is about all it takes, and my ploy is a big success. The stock clerk retreats, looking back over his shoulder at me like I am a dangerous breed of witchy monster.

DoubleSpin stands, brushing himself off and slicking back his hair. "I owe you for that one. Thanks, Jack. You too, Lucy."

"No *problemo*, weird guy," I say.

Jack looks uncertainly from DoubleSpin to me.

"How is it you and I see DoubleSpin and nobody else does?"

"Because he wants it that way," I tell Jack.

Before Jack or I can say anything more, DoubleSpin points down the aisle. He indicates a big, tough looking guy who is awkwardly pushing his own cart. He has loaded it with a mop and four gallons of milk, and as if that is not enough, he looks as out of place as a vegetarian in a butcher shop. It certainly feels to me like he does not want to be seen by us. He makes a show of snapping his fingers, does a 180 degree turn and heads back the way he came.

"Oh, I forgot onions!" he says.

The big guy narrowly avoids Delrina, who is walking along with a basket full of a mix of her favorite things – ice cream, Sunkist prunes and Oreos cookies. "Hey, look out, Moygan from Sheboygan!" Delrina warns him.

The Stranger, who has recovered from his cinnamon lust, exchanges a look with Jack.

"I think that guy's been following us since we left Chermundo," Jack says.

"Very good, Jack. What do you think he wants?"

"Probably looking for the nutmeg." Jack gives the Stranger a look of dismissal. "And you're going to save the planet?"

"We are."

But my mind is now in overdrive. The stranger called DoubleSpin is more than a figment of our overworked imaginations. He does not do anything for nothing, and his gaze is on me.

"We are going to save it," DoubleSpin repeats out loud, looking directly at me.

Thirty eight

It is an hour or two later in the day, and our Oldsters Outing has taken a turn into a nearby McDonald's restaurant. Herbert is sitting next to Delrina, scarfing down a big double cheeseburger while his cell phone sits nearby on top of his yellow notepad, quiet for the moment but ever on the ready.

Jack is not eating. He is watching DoubleSpin, who has climbed a corkscrew stairway to the top of the indoor play yard and is staring at a cute four-year-old girl who gapes back at him in wide-eyed innocence with her mouth open and the palms of her hands spread wide as if to say, *Do you want to play patty-cake?*

Jack looks at me. "Old people and little girls can see him, when he wants them to."

"Just some old people," I say. "And probably just some kids. Just the ones he decides he can trust."

"Or put on his show."

The big, tough looking guy we saw in Albertsons is sitting two tables away from our group. I guess he figures the bustle and confusion at the old people's table will somehow make him invisible.

"You should eat something, Jack," I tell him.

"Jack's too cheap," Herbert grumps.

"I'll buy you something, Jack," I say.

"He's cheap, not poor," the Old Viking confides. "Jack has more money than Midas. The king," he clarifies, "not the muffler people."

The Stranger returns and sits next to us. Jack looks up at the top of the indoor play yard.

The little girl is looking around in wonder. "Hey, where'd he go?" She spots the Stranger. "Hey, how'd you get down there?"

"You move fast, DoubleSpin," Jack says.

"Faster than a speeding bullet," the Stranger agrees.

"About as fast as light," I say.

"Okay, fast as light…well, just under." The Stranger nods towards the tough looking man. "Ask him over, Jack."

Jack looks at the man and then at me.

I shrug. "What harm can it do?"

Jack eyes the Stranger for a moment, thinking about it. He nods, making up his mind, and yells across the noisy room, "Hey! Yes, I mean you over there!"

Herbert looks a little wide-eyed, wondering what he has missed. I shrug as if to reassure him there is nothing much up. But from forty feet away, the tough guy gives Jack a surprised "Who, me?" gesture.

Jack nods. "You! Get over here! You've been following us all afternoon!"

The Old Viking chides him, "Jack, don't be rude."

"Now that's the pot calling the kettle black," Delrina says, patting Herbert's hand. I start to think something really is going on between those two. Del is in his personal space, and the Old Viking doesn't seem to mind at all.

Jack calls again to the fellow across the way, "Come on over here, right now! Sit down right here."

The man takes his Coke and hamburger and hesitantly moves across the room to stand next to our table.

At the same moment, the little girl comes near. "Hey, we weren't done playing."

DoubleSpin indicates with a finger to his lips that she is to be quiet. He pats a nearby vacant seat, and she sits next to him. She pulls a Happy Meal toy from her pocket and starts to take it out of its wrapper. It is one of those little plastic flying super characters with a black eye mask and a green cape. The Stranger makes it fly through the air for her. Nobody in the room seems to notice.

Jack stares at the big man, sizing him up. "Who are you?"

Dick unhappily realizes his cover has been blown. He says his name is Dick Burkle and introduces himself as a private detective. "I don't mean you any harm," he says.

I think he seems like a genuinely nice man. I find myself thinking he should find another profession, something involving less cunning and trickery.

I wish I could, Lady. The thought comes unbidden to my mind. The man shakes his head in confusion. He clearly does not know what just happened.

Jack frowns. "Who hired you? Was it Emily?"

Dick shakes his head grimly, realizing the game is up. "Fargo," he replies.

"Fargo?! What the hell did he want?"

"A financial checkup on you."

"Fargo's dead, you know."

"What?"

"Jack's son-in-law died in a car accident," I tell him.

I can tell from the confusion in his mind that he really knew nothing about it. "Look, I'm sorry," he says to Jack. "Fargo hired me to tail you."

Jack shakes his head. "Unbelievable. Christ, I left them more money than God."

"It wasn't your daughter. Just Fargo. The man came to my office; he seemed all concerned and agitated. You sure he's dead?"

"Dead as a stone," Jack says.

DoubleSpin perks up. "Actually, stones have a form of life. Everything that exists has some form of – "

Jack waves the Stranger quiet. "I hope he paid you."

"Yeah. He paid me." Dick sighs and gets to his feet, "Shoot, I guess I'll be going."

Jack and the Stranger exchange glances. The Stranger shakes his head. "He can't go yet, Jack. He has to stick around for a little while."

"Uh uh. No. Sit back down," Jack tells the detective.

"Why?"

I can see Jack's mind is racing to come up with something that makes some sense. "Cheating a dead man," he says. "What sort of person are you, anyway?"

Dick thinks about it. He doesn't know how to respond to that one. "Well…this is my first job."

"Listen sharp now," DoubleSpin says. "Something is about to happen."

In the next second, Herbert's phone rings and he looks uncertainly at me. I think I get it; Jack and Delrina are okay, but I am not one of his insiders. I look across the room, pretending to ignore him, but Herb is also eyeing our new friend Dick Burkle, who he is sure definitely cannot be trusted. Still, the phone rings insistently, and Herbert finally snatches it up. He turns away from us, shielding the phone so we supposedly do not know he is talking on it and cannot hear a word he is saying. But with his hearing problems, he talks so loud it is like a crazy little bit of madcap nonsense out of a Marx Brothers skit.

While Herbert talks, the four-year-old girl starts playing patty-cake with thin air.

Doublespin, stop that, I tell him.

"Yes, mother," he says.

"She's your mother?" the little girl asks him.

DoubleSpin eyes me as he puts one of the too long fingers on his slender hands to his lips. "In a way," he says.

Meanwhile, Herbert sounds elated, "You're coming to California?! With my money?! That's great, man!...err, Prince-man." He looks around and realizes where he is, then gets twice as furtive in his silly way, putting his hand over his mouth as he talks into the phone in his whisper that anybody can hear half-way across the room. "Yeah, great, Prince...just put it in my account...what? You're bringing my cash?! I got to see that one! When? Where? Okay, send me an email! No, no, no, I can do anything on this end. *Any*-thing!"

Herbert pulls his crumpled McDonald's receipt from his pocket and straightens it a bit. He lifts the pen from

Jack's shirt pocket and starts writing. "Pier 53...right...right...can do, no problem...sure; you do me a favor, I do you a favor."

Herbert clicks his phone shut and stuffs Jack's pen back in his pocket.

"They don't call me Mister Shipping for nothing!" he shouts triumphantly. "The Old Viking rides again!"

He gazes around the McDonald's, looking a little dazed and for the moment not really sure where he is.

Jack and Delrina and I exchange worried looks. Delrina reaches over and places a hand on his shoulder. "Herbie, are you okay?"

"I – what? I – I...yes, yes Del, very fine, indeed!" He catches Jack's eye. Jack is always Jack, his stabilizing influence. Herbert puffs air in and out, getting control of his thoughts. When he next speaks, he is again his gruff and crotchety old self. "Of course I'm okay, Missy Delrina. Just another day, just another dollar." He looks at Jack, a big silly grin on his face and silently but wildly over-exaggeratedly mouths the words, "Thirty-five million clams!"

George grins. "You're about as inconspicuous as a wart-butted rhino in a ladies powder room, Herbie. Gonna let us in on your good fortune?"

Herbert leans forward and rubs his hands over his face. He lets out a loud breath of air. Then he sits up and speaks in his regular, every-day voice as if nothing has happened, "Come on, gang, let's blow this joint!"

I am thinking what an extraordinary afternoon this has been, but I do not say anything, and neither does anybody else.

Herbert gets up and starts out the door, carefully placing the phone in his pocket.

Dick Burkle stands. "We done here?"

"Get his card, Jack," DoubleSpin says.

Jack visibly starts. "Well, how do we get in touch with you?" he asks. "And you probably should report your findings to Emily."

"You want me to…? Well, yeah, of course you do." The detective seems doubtful, but he gives Jack his card and slowly walks away. He looks back over his shoulder, not sure what just happened.

Jack watches the detective leave. Herbert has forgotten the receipt with his notes on the table. Jack smiles at me and quietly picks up the notes and places them in his pocket.

DoubleSpin nods, showing his approval. "There's hope for you yet, earthling."

"You too, cosmic show-boater."

DoubleSpin grins, the game on. "Puny fourth-dimensionalist!" The Stranger pauses, hand to mouth, a little miffed at himself.

Jack is very pleased, "So…there are at least five...Broke one of the rules, didn't you, DS."

"Sometimes you get to me, Jack."

"Yeah, me and cinnamon, the loves of your life."

"Don't forget peanut butter," he says, brushing back his straight black hair.

I am too flabbergasted by the extra new dimensions in my own life to say anything at all. I stumble along with Jack and DoubleSpin and the others to the waiting van. The rest of our normal day awaits us back at the Chermundo. But for me, I know nothing will ever be the same again.

Thirty nine

Sometimes I try to see it like Jack, the way it must
appear to him. Maybe there are just too many things
happening all at the same time that he cannot explain.
Maybe after that long interlude when the current was just
drifting along toward Nowhere Town, our lives are picking
up again. Maybe he has had a premonition of things that
are to come, or maybe he is even acting on the advice from
his special invisible friend and actually does have a plan to
save the world. Whatever his reasons, one day the
following week, he has Emily drive him to Tom
Fennerman's office so they can update his will.

Tom Fennerman, who has always been the very model
of a family lawyer, is courteous, understanding and
efficient as ever. He pushes copies of the plump new will
across the desk, and Jack and Emily sign them.

Amanda is seated nearby on a sofa, busily filling in a
coloring book. Occasionally she looks at the strange man
with the slicked back black hair, sharp nose and the
somewhat pointy ears sitting on the sofa beside her. The
man looks a little like that Vulcan on the old Star Trek
shows Mommy watches, and he always was her favorite.
He smiles and says nothing, and so she figures he is waiting
for her mom and grandpa to finish so he can do his own
lawyer business with Mister Lawyer Fennerman.

Tom Fennerman smiles at Emily. He likes this family,
and, to his way of thinking, this is the way generations are
supposed to handle their affairs.

"You see, we are just basically taking your departed husband's name off the trust. It's standard procedure. The rest stays exactly the same."

Emily looks to Jack. "You don't have to do this, dad."

"I don't want to worry about it. No loose ends, Em. Frankly, from time to time, Fargo's family has seemed a little flint-eyed to me."

From his seat on the sofa, the Stranger raises one eyebrow. "Flint-eyed?"

"Grasping and greedy," Jack says.

Emily thinks he is explaining to Amanda. "Grandpa just wants to make sure you get a good education, honey."

The lawyer nods to Jack. "You're doing the right thing. You earned it. Your family should keep it."

"Damn straight."

"It is a great deal of money," the lawyer says.

"How did you make so much money, anyway, Dad? Someday Amanda will want to know how clever you were." She smiles; easy to see things are on the mend between father and daughter.

Jack returns her smile, thinking back on the successes of his life. "Microchips back in the Neanderthal Age of electronics. You know I was a math-head, and I thought it made good business sense to let the computers do the heavy lifting." Jack glances at the seat where the Stranger is sitting with Amanda. "The fortunes that could be made, if we only knew the future."

DoubleSpin has a 'maybe so-maybe not' expression on his face. He knows the odds on the future and it does not look too bright around this part of the galaxy.

They are about to leave the lawyer's office when Dick Burkle is shown in by the receptionist. "Sorry I'm late. I got lost in the building."

"Some detective," Jack kids him. "Dick, my daughter Emily...Fargo's widow."

"I didn't know my husband had any detective friends."

"Fargo hired him," Jack tells her.

"Fargo hired a detective? Whatever for?

The Stranger gives Jack a warning sign.

191

Jack nods. He has this one covered. "Oh, just trying to protect me, I suppose. Keep me away from the bad guys."

"But that's horrible! He never told me!"

"I know you didn't have anything to do with it, Em. And it's not so bad on Fargo's part. Understandable."

Amanda waves at the Stranger. The Stranger waves back. There is a picture of a clown on the wall behind him. Emily thinks Amanda is waving at the clown.

That is a cute clown, honey," she smiles at her daughter. "Hi there, Mister Clown." she says.

Amanda nods and waves at the clown, too.

The Stranger grins at Jack and waves back at Emily. He is enjoying himself. Jack and Amanda see him, but Emily does not.

Jack has an idea. "Well, come on, let's go to the park. I don't get enough chances to see Amanda."

"Your husband was trying to do the right thing, Mrs. Rafferty," Dick says. He still feels Fargo trying to hire him was not quite right, and he is trying to work it out in his own mind. "Him passing like that, I guess I owe you people."

Emily looks across the table at her father. "Hamlin, not Rafferty. Emily Hamlin. I'm taking my old name back."

Jack is mildly surprised, "I didn't know that."

"Me, either," the lawyer says. "Now we'll have to re-do the will."

"Do it," Jack says. "We want it right."

"I just decided…but why is he here?" She indicates Dick Burkle with an unfriendly nod of her head.

"I need him to work on something else. Dick, do you know old Herbert? That's the guy you met at McDonald's."

"Sure. Kind of a pop-off old fellow. Talks too loud."

Jack nods. "That's the one. Herbert Miller. He may need a little help from us…"

"Sure. What you have in mind?"

Jack sits up straighter in his wheelchair and stretches his arms high over his head before grabbing his wheels. "Come on, we'll talk about it in the park."

Half-way around the world, it is night along the south facing coastline of Nigeria. While heavily populated, this area is, in between the low sandy dry spots, little more than a swampy land mass, a place where the spongy interior jungles reluctantly release their dank moisture into the sluggish river estuary that leads to the Atlantic. A thick layer of dense fog cuts visibility to little more than the end of the nearest dock, and the tramp steamer Cyclops slowly moves away and disappears into the night, pulled by a lone tugboat. The dock steward, the last man to sign off on the two rusty red containers that he personally crane-lifted into the hold, approaches with one hand outstretched to Maloof Urdveen.

"Two containers," he says. "As per instruction, loaded at far ends of the ship."

"I have it right here," the slim Arab says. But even as reaches in his jacket, supposedly for a fat envelope with a payment for services rendered, the Colonel is standing nearby. There are two spitting sounds as a pair of bullets leave a silenced automatic pistol and turn an unsuspecting man's heart into a briefly spouting fountain of red blood.

"Payment enough," the Colonel says politely to the steward, even as the unfortunate man stiffens and then slowly curls into a ball and drops to the rough wooden planking on the dock.

"Next time not so close to me," Maloof reprimands the Colonel, frowning as he inspects his suit for flecks of blood.

In the bright noonday sunlight of Southern California, Jack easily rolls his wheelchair along the curving sidewalk that runs around the pond in the center of MacArthur Park. His young granddaughter Amanda runs alongside him. As they go along, she points out trees and birds and wonders if the pond holds dragons or monsters.

"Maybe alligators," Jack tells her.

She gives him a skeptical look.

"People buy the little ones as pets when they go to Disney World in Florida," he explains. "But once they get too big to keep in their bathtubs, sometimes they dump them off here."

Amanda nods. That makes sense to her.

Dick Burkle and Emily walk behind them. The Stranger is bringing up the rear, walking about ten paces behind their small group.

It is noontime in the park. Office workers and couples enjoy their lunches, and kids on skate boards and two or three on power motor scooters buzz around and in between the people walking along on the wide and gently curving concrete pathways. Emily takes a closer look at Dick, appraising him. "Could I hire you to look after him?"

"Two for the price of one?"

Emily's face reddens. "No. I don't mean like that. Just see what's going on."

Dick sees his wise-guy detective attitude is getting him in trouble again. "I didn't mean it the way it sounded, either. I'm not good with words."

"I...I think my father may be losing touch with reality. Just sometimes."

Dick runs a hand over his blond crew cut the way ex-army men do to make sure it is standing up the way it should. "Your dad's in the right place. Chermundo really looks out for the guests."

"I used to think so, but they've got a new director and he worries me a little."

A dozen steps ahead, Jack watches as Amanda runs in a circle, holding her dolly up like an airplane.

Emily smiles and turns her attention back to Dick and the problem at hand. "Sometimes Dad seems so sharp, like he is right there with us...when I see him like he is right now, I think he shouldn't be in that place at all. He should be out in the world. He is not that old, you know. And then his mind seems to drift off into outer space and I think maybe I'm just kidding myself.

"He can leave any time he wants, can't he?" Dick thinks about it. "How did he end up in Chermundo, anyway?"

"After Mom died, he took a bad turn for a while."

"That when he started hearing voices?"

"No, that is just a recent thing. But he wasn't eating, and he would just sit there, staring at nothing.

"He was already in the wheelchair?"

The kids on the motorized skate boards and scooters are an annoying presence as they buzz and weave in and out, playing a game of tag.

Emily looks at her shoes, remembering. "That happened at Mom's funeral. Jack wasn't watching where he was going. He fell in the open grave and broke his back."

"I already promised Jack I would finish out the month."

Emily frowns, bristling a little. "And so it would be a conflict of interest to look after him?"

"I didn't say that. Geez, don't be so spiky."

I'm not being spiky! I just want him to be alright and I thought – "

"Emily, there are no bad guys here. Jack's interest is your interest, so I don't see a problem. We're on the same team. I will do my best to look out for him...but honestly, I think it's a slam-dunk. He's not in any trouble. I don't see him on the internet. He doesn't even have a cell phone. What kind of problems are you looking for?"

"Fargo thought he was into business dealings with scam artists. He overheard him talking with his friend Herbert."

"This Herbert has his own set of problems, but I don't see him pulling Jack in with him. Didn't Jack just tell us as much?"

"Still."

Dick grins at her, throwing up his hands in mock defeat, "Okay. Okay, I'm on the case for you."

"Promise?"

"I promise!"

Three of the teens on their motorized scooters and boards buzz through the groups of slower moving people on the sidewalk, and suddenly are bearing down on Amanda.

Jack is the first to see the danger. "Amanda! Look out!" He lurches forward, and then falls back in his wheelchair.

In that moment, the Stranger moves forward faster than any earthly creature could and snatches Amanda out of harm's way.

"They almost ran me over!" Amanda pants.

"Almost doesn't count, Little Lady," DoubleSpin says.

He ushers her over to Jack, who now has no alternative but to believe in him.

"Thank you," Jack says. In the next second they are surrounded by Emily and Dick. Emily hugs her little girl so tightly that Amanda loses sight of the strange man with the slicked back hair that she is sure is grandpa's friend.

"Dad, what happened?" Emily asks.

"Where did he go?" Amanda is looking around for the man who saved her.

"Who?" her mother asks.

Forty

Millie and I are enjoying our afternoon at a hair and nails place called The Lovely Lady. We walked the short distance, a couple of blocks west on Ventura Boulevard from the Chermundo. We are having our nails done when my favorite nail gal Luisa steps back from my chair and gives me an appraising look. "You have your hair color new. Look pretty good to me!"

"Nothing out of the ordinary," I say, feeling good that somebody has said I have still got it, at least for an old lady.

Millie grins at us from her own pink padded plastic chair. The Lovely Lady is all about pink-and-cream, carnations and lace, cotton candy and butterflies. "Lucy is coloring her hair," Millie says. "But gradual, so nobody notices."

Now this is my best girlfriend in the world sitting in the cushy chair next to me, and so I do not take offense, but that is absolutely not a true thing she has said. "Mil! Do not tell tales out of school!"

"I think the modern expression is 'What happens in Vegas.'"

"To tell you true, young Miss Milliford, I have been thinking the same thing about you!" It was true. I had a similar thought about her the week before. Millie has a swarm of tight blond curls wrapped around her sweet heart-shaped face. "Come on, confession is good for the soul. You have been highlighting your gorgeous hair with the right touch of Garnier Nutrisse. I am thinking light natural blond or maybe medium gold?"

We smile affectionately at each other; neither believing for a minute the inconsequential lies that vanity is bringing to our lips. It is only later that evening, looking in the mirror in the privacy of my own bathroom, that I see what the ladies were talking about, and I am willing to play along with my delusion that the impossible can actually become a reality. How can it be that I am looking at an impossible darkening, my hair seriously darker than the iron grey mane it was one short week ago?

That evening at the Chermundo Villas at just about the time I am staring quizzically at myself in my mirror, Jack is sitting alone in the game area of the lounge. Jack has turned his wheelchair to face out the window. The fading garden pansies and snapdragons in the central courtyard area have been replaced with yellow and gold chrysanthemums, and garden looks fresh and new in its autumn harvest presentation.

The Stranger is lying on a nearby sofa eating peanut butter on original flavor Triscuits. "Time for a little tough love here, Jack."

"What is that supposed to mean?"

"It means now is the time when you have to get off your butt. The boat's in the water, Jack."

"Right. The fish are in the sea, the birds flock in the air, all is right in the world."

"Not exactly right in your world, Jack. By the way, when did you start taking the easy way out?"

Jack's eyes narrow and he frowns. This is something new. "I resent that. You save my granddaughter's life so now you think you can take me apart?"

"You don't really need the wheelchair, do you Jack." The way DoubleSpin says it, it is not a question.

"What do you mean?"

"You just gave up after your Doreen died. You married for honor and you got too little out of it, you settled for a lesser profession and then the wife dies on you."

Jack glares at him and starts to wheel away.

"Jack, wait..."

"No. You go too far, otherling."

Jack rolls away, stormily heading out of the lounge area. He passes right by me without even saying hi or acknowledging my presence. I am bored with squinting at myself in the mirror, and I am just looking for a game of chess or an alien encounter or something.

"Jack, where is DoubleSpin?"

Jack doesn't answer me. His face is set in an angry mask.

I look around the room and then I try to talk to the Stranger. I cannot see him, but I am guessing he is only visible when he wants.

"What did you do to him? Come on, I know you are here."

He appears, sitting cross-legged on the table where the gang usually plays blackjack and Melody's brainless word games.

I need him to meet me half way, he says. He is looking a little guilty, like maybe he does not know exactly what he is doing and maybe he has screwed up big time.

What do you mean?

Our Jack has to get up and walk. He has to. Everything depends on it.

That would be a miracle, my oddball friend. His back is broken in three places.

What? Why didn't he tell me?

Because you always act like you know everything.

Yes, DoubleSpin says with a sad look on his face. *I'm sorry about that, but in the real galaxy I don't.*

The strange creature begins to disappear before my eyes from the bottom up, like a television screen wiping itself invisible. *This will take some fixing,* he thinks at me just before he entirely winks out. I am so upset that I do not even realize what a neat disappearing act that is.

There I am, standing in the lounge, staring at the space where DoubleSpin was a moment before, and at the same time, Jack is rolling his way to his small suite. He has to pass the exercise room to get there. He stops to look in at the workout machines. The room is deserted. Jack sits in his wheelchair, thinking about his life.

"I don't quit," he mutters. He looks into the wall mirror and sees an old man muttering to himself. Not as old as some, true enough…but old enough. "I don't quit. I don't quit."

His face becomes a fierce mask of resolve. He clinches the arms of his wheelchair with both hands and tries to stand. This is absurd and dangerous.

"I can lift a Diet Sprite can with my brain," he mutters. "Why can't I lift myself?"

A lot of effort on his part, but as he tries to stand up, Jack has forgotten to set the two little chrome plated levers he uses to brake the wheels on his wheelchair. The chair rolls backward away from him and he falls to the floor with a heavy thump.

A night nurse rushes in.

"Jack! What in God's Name is happening here?"

Jack looks at her with a dazed expression on his face. "Exercise," he says, trying his best to smile through the agonizing swarm of pain he is feeling in his spine and lower back.

"Who told you that you could exercise, mister?" There is real concern in her voice.

Jack thinks about it. He sees invisible people. He can lift light-weight objects with his mind. What harm is there in one or two little white lies? "My doctor," he says. "My doctor told me I should."

But he is not going to get off so easily; everybody who works at Chermundo has seen his file. The nurse knows his spinal injuries are massive and permanent, and she also is aware that there are no doctor's orders like he claims. Her lips thin. "The doctor? What doctor?"

"Oh, right. I forgot. My spiritual advisor. That's who told me."

"Your spiritual mentor gave you physical exercises?"

Jack is out of gas. He simply cannot come up with a good fib on the spur of the moment. He remains quiet as the nurse lifts him and half-carries and half-drags him back to the wheelchair.

"Listen to me, Jack. You twist your spine the wrong way and you'll be in big trouble."

He gives her a bitter smile. "You mean I might be paralyzed?"

They are interrupted by a loud bong, a melodious sound. The nurse sighs, "Oh, damn it! When it rains, it pours. Look, Jack, I have to go. You get yourself back to your room right now." She exits in a hurry.

"Thanks. Appreciate the help."

Defeated, Jack starts to wheel himself out of the room. But he finds he cannot move the wheelchair. There is a hand holding it back. It is DoubleSpin.

"One try and you're done?"

"Yeah. One and done."

"We need to talk," the Stranger says.

"We already talked."

The Stranger gives him an appraising look, "Look, I'm sorry. I should have known about your back. But I honestly, absolutely don't know everything. Low research budget on the show, you know. Still, my bad. I'm sorry."

Jack shrugs; he does not hold a grudge.

DoubleSpin blows out a puff of breath.

"You just did that for show, didn't you?" Jack asks. "You don't really breathe air."

"Well, no, I mean, yes…look, Jack, you love your granddaughter, don't you?"

"Of course. Goes without saying."

"And you tried to stand just now because you've seen that I'm real and you know I'm asking you a favor and you maybe even can believe it's important."

Jack nods yes, and spins his wheelchair in an impatient circle.

"I guess that's right."

"Well, your granddaughter is in danger. You are all in danger."

That gets Jack's attention." You keep saying that."

"Jack. Listen, please. I know this sounds crazy, but the sum total future of everything that you know, love and believe in depends on you getting up out of that wheelchair."

Jack hesitates. This is the biggest, goofiest delusion of them all, and yet DoubleSpin will not let up on him. "Somebody saved your granddaughter in the park, Jack. Now that somebody is asking you to do something in return. And I can help you. I will help you."

"Get out of here. Let me think. Let me think by myself. "

DoubleSpin nods, but he does not walk out of the room. He does a spin dissolve, staring at Jack with his eyes as the rest of him turns into a whirlpool of a blurred something that disappears into nothing.

Jack sighs. He does not need to think; he has already made up his mind. He doggedly takes both hands and tries to lever himself up and out of the wheelchair.

"This is really the dumbest thing I've ever done."

He pushes and heaves himself upright, and for a moment, he actually stands. Then, a series of distinct click noises come from his back. There seems like nothing magical about it and the pain overwhelms him. Jack cries out and crumples to the floor.

When he regains consciousness, he is lying face down on the carpet. DoubleSpin is hanging upside down from a hanging exercise machine, calmly watching him. Jack sits up and shakes his head.

"Holy Jesus, that hurt!" He does a double take when he sees the Stranger. "I thought I told you to get out of here."

"You didn't say 'stay out'…How are you doing?

"I feel like I was hit by lightning."

"Realignment is always painful."

Jack reaches behind to feel his back with one tentative hand. He stares at DoubleSpin, who is still upside down, though no longer hanging from the bar. The Stranger slowly drifts across the room.

Jack shakes his head. "You know, you are one odd fellow." He is trying to concentrate on anything but the foolish thing he has done to what was left of his spinal cord. "How did you get your name, anyway?"

"I was named after a particle. Sub-atomic. How's your back, Jack?"

"Don't remind me. I'm trying hard not to think about it. DoubleSpin is a particle?"

"Right. Has to go around twice to go around once. Kind of neat, right?"

"That's impossible."

The Stranger, still upside down, floats into a wall and gently bounces off it like the ball on a primitive electronic table tennis game.

"I guess it is." DoubleSpin slowly rotates in the air until he is standing on the ceiling. He starts to walk away. He has to step over the door jam to continue out of the room. Jack realizes his wheelchair is half-way across the room, where it rolled when he fell. He starts to get up, and then, remembering the pain, sits down again.

The Stranger pauses and looks back at him. He is still upside down. He turns and smiles.

"Come on, Jack. Time to get up."

Jack looks at him and shakes his head. "Not me. I'm a cripple."

"No, you're an idiot! Come on, weakling-of-earth!"

Jack's face darkens. He is remembering DoubleSpin accused him of being a quitter. He pushes himself up – and lurches to his feet.

"Good," DoubleSpin says with a fierce nod of approval. He turns to his ever-present invisible camera. "Now we can get on with saving the earth."

Jack stands alone in the exercise room. He is weaving unsteadily back and forth and he looks as if he will fall over at any moment. He takes a first hesitant step toward his wheelchair. He eyes himself dubiously in the full wall mirrors. He is taking actual small steps by himself for the first time in years, and at the moment, the salvation of the planet seems more ridiculous than any miraculous healing that Jesus or Edgar Casey ever performed. Yet, Jack's wobbly legs are able to support him. He places one hand against the nearest wall and begins to make his slow progress out of the room.

Our two day time nurses are seated at the duty station down the hall from the exercise room. They are working late, going through their records, clicking alphabetically down the screen full of names as they review the patients.

"Bella. What do you think of Herbert?" Jane asks. Jane is in her mid-forties; thin as a rail and has short-cropped bleached blond hair and the lined features around her eyes and mouth of someone who knows the next bad thing is right around the corner.

Bella frowns. "Herbert Miller? Now there's one crafty old son of a bitch." Bella pops a See's white chocolate caramel in her mouth.

"I think he's getting worse," Jane says. She takes a bite out of a tuna sandwich. "Eww, gag me with a spoon! It's actually spoiled!" She spits the bite from her mouth into a wastebasket and throws the wedge of bread in after it. "Damn machine vending. This place is going to hell in a hand basket."

"The rants?" Bella asks.

"What? Oh, Herbert. Yeah."

"Should we recommend him for the Z ward? I'm feeling pressure from the Goozer. He sure wants him over there."

"Gooze-baby wants everybody over there." Jane shrugs, "I don't know. One school of thought says it's better now than after the Old Viking goes berserker on us."

Bella types in her opinion. "Okay. We need the shrink's opinion for that one. But I can hear the howl from the director's office clear as a vampire wail."

Jane grins at her friend. "Vampires wail, huh? Well, I'll leave a note for Dr. Daniel; that will take the heat off us."

Jack rounds the corner of the door and walks along the hall, taking hesitant steps toward the nursing station.

"Look. I can walk!"

The nurses stare at him.

Bella leaps to her feet. "That's not possible."

The night nurse comes running in. "Where's Jack? Jack! I thought I told you not to – "

She is about to lunge for him, but he motions her back with one hand.

"I got this one, Mabes."

Bella shakes her head. "You seen his X-rays? His spinal cord is disconnected in three places!"

"Was," Jack corrects her. "Look."

He takes another step and does a timid pirouette. They are small and hesitant steps and his attempt at a fancy little turn just about does him in, but it is an incredible performance, the first time anybody at Chermundo has seen Jack out of his wheelchair.

Bella crosses herself and gives him a bug-eyed stare, and then enfolds him in a big hug. "Mother of Mary," she says.

Word spreads faster than the speed of light about the miracle, and in ten minutes half the Villas guests are down in the lounge to see Jack for themselves. The general feeling is, if poor old Jack Hamlin can get up and walk around, there is hope for the rest of just about everybody. A festive, party-like atmosphere rustles through them all; Showboat George and Delrina break out some apple cider and Ritz crackers and we all toast him and people who hardly even know Jack including one or two black widows looking for their next meal ticket that come around and poke him once or twice if only to be able to say they witnessed the amazing event.

Forty one

After the sun goes down and the night crawlers come
out, Hollywood Boulevard is one of the sleazier areas to be
found anywhere in the City of Angels. Innocents, fools and
folks on the downslide attract a variety of creatures offering
cheap good times, and police cars patrol, trying to serve
and protect as best they can. Albert, who has arrived with
Charles on the plane from Lagos, is standing uneasily
outside a clothing store with a window full of silk hats and
snake leather boots highlighted by flashing strobes. Young
Albert looks out of place as a bible college student in a
Nevada whorehouse.

Charles' bruises have healed and his spirits are on the
rise. "Not dead yet!" he keeps telling himself. He says it a
lot, just to be sure. But the Colonel is nowhere around, so
Charles does a joyful 'ta-DAH!' as he comes out the door,
attired in his new purple velvet cowboy hat. "I love
Hollywood!" he yells to nobody in particular. He still
wears his sporty and colorful leisure suit attire. He does a
self-satisfied little bow, showing off his hat, and eyes his
reflection in the store window. "Land of the flea and home
of the freed slave!"

Making any commotion in that contested part of town
is easily misunderstood, and Charles' fleet moment of glory
has caught the attention of Wolfango Dango, a black pimp
with gold capped teeth and a glittery nest of gold chains
hanging heavy around his wide neck. "Hey! Hey, you!
Yeah, you, mudderflecher wit' the purple doffer!"

Charles turns to stare at this new development. He flinches a little, expecting to see one of the Colonel's men step out of the shadows with an instrument of torture. He has not caught up to speed yet; this misunderstanding has the potential to be almost as bad as anything he's ever known. Wolfango moves aggressively and postures in front of the new African immigrant with his chest out, hands on his hips. Albert tries to shrink into the shadows; he is an urban survivor, and he knows the smell of trouble.

"Ahh, now be the time to retreat to the rear, Prince Charley," he says in a low voice. But it is too late to run or hide. Charles is caught in the headlights of Wolfango's ire. "What? Me?" the kid from Lagos stutters.

"What you doing' here, nigger black boy?" Wolfango growls. He is black, if not blacker, than Charles, and this makes no sense to the Nigerian. Wolfango pushes a finger in his chest. "Casing out the turf, right?"

"No, see, I'm new to this area and I'm just looking around at the prospects, and such..."

Wolfango's expression grows mean. "That's what I just said, pussy-punker!"

Honey, a heavily made-up hooker, hustles up to Wolfango. "Dango, baby I got's to take five for a pee break."

"Not now, Honey-bunny."

Honey sees Albert and a smile lights her face. "Say now, sweet-face, you looking for a time?"

"N-no...I—I..." Albert stammers.

Wolfango barks orders. He points to Albert. "You, dandy-hopper. You go with Honey. I'm going to have a few words with our purple hatted outlaw interloper here."

Wolfango pushes Charles into a dark corridor between two buildings. Charles protests, "Wait, there's some mistake!"

His sentence is cut off by a blow to his stomach.

"Yeah, there is. I told you this be my turf, man."

I wake up in the middle of the night gasping for air. I am having another of the drowning dreams that I have had ever since I found out my husband was probably going to murder me. I gasp for air and try to slow the racing beat of my pounding heart. *Lucy, Lucy, Lucy!* I scold myself. I do calm down a little, but I know I am not going to be able to go back to sleep. I see by the glowing hands on the little clock by my bed that it is after midnight so it is officially lights out and we are not supposed to be wandering around, but the night gang is pretty lax about that rule, so I wrap my favorite purple wooly robe around my flannel nightshirt and slip into a pair of fuzzy slippers and wander out of my rooms and down the hall to the self serve nook between the kitchen and the lounge area. I have started heating up water for some chamomile tea when Millie wanders in looking all sleepy eyed. I get out a second cup to fix her one of her own when Delrina shows up patting her rumpled up curls and looking for Diet Coke in the big fridge.

"Who called the meeting?" she asks.

"That strange new guy," Showboat George says as he staggers in, looking like he is hung over. Georgie-Porgie is a sight to behold, wearing an old Terminator t-shirt and sagging extra-large desert camo pajama bottoms held up with suspenders.

We move into the lounge and Jack is already there with Herbert. At least, Herbert is physically in the room, though he is over on the far side, banging away at a computer keyboard.

Jack is on the floor, trying a few sit-ups. "Five," he says and falls back on the floor, looking exhausted. He gets on his hands and knees and pulls himself up using the edge of one of the tables. "Five is enough," he says, and slumps into a seat next to me.

DoubleSpin comes walking in, just like he is a regular earth-bound human.

I give him a questioning look, and he responds with the thought, *Believe me it uses up a lot of extra energy to walk around like I'm a normal earthling, but I didn't want to freak the team out.*

Everybody is looking at him, so I get the picture right away. He is finally letting all of the Old Bunch see him.

"Okay," he says out loud. "I know you were joking around last week when you vowed to save the earth."

"No, we were not," I protest.

"Yeah. We were tootin' fruitin' serious." This from the Old Viking, getting in on the conversation even while he is still pounding at his computer.

"Who are you, anyway?" George asks.

"I'm Jack's friend," DoubleSpin answers. "I'm a little...strange."

"Strange how?" Herbert pipes up from his position crouched over the keyboard.

"I can do stuff like go invisible."

"Yeah, yeah, yeah," Herb says. "Just like my money."

"He sends it to Nigeria," Jack says. "And presto-*invisibilo!*"

"Do it, do it, do it!" Delrina says, clapping her hands. She is thinking we have an amateur magician rooming at the Chermundo.

DoubleSpin fades out, and then pops back into view. A ripple of astonishment goes through our gang, and a "Holy Cow!" erupts from Showboat George.

The Old Viking asks from his corner of the room, "Jack, how do we spell 'avaricious'?" When Jack doesn't answer, he yells, "Hey, who's the new guy?"

"A-V-A-R-I-C-I-O-U-S," I call over to him, and Herbie goes back to his typing as he mutters, "Thanks, Lucy," and adds a few grumbles about ungrateful old fart Jack.

"Okay. Settle down and listen up," DoubleSpin says.

I figure we are about as settled as we are going to get after seeing his go invisible act and our alien friend probably agrees, because he starts right in with his pitch.

"Something bad is going to happen," he says. "And you are the only ones who can prevent it."

"How bad?" Jack asks.

"Nuclear bad."

"But, Oh Invisible Man...shouldn't you be talking to the CIA and Homeland Security and the FBI and folks like

209

that?" Del waves her hands in the air and waggles her fingers.

"That won't work. We've...we have run the numbers."

"I still can't get over that disappearing act," Millie says, looking at me. "Just like that Predator movie."

George nods. "Look, I personally believe you, 'cause ordinary folks don't go dissolving in and out...and you do look a little weird, like you came from Ju-pit-er or something...but we are not comic book heroes here. We're just a pack of old crappers—uhh, pardon me, ladies, I mean us guys are."

"Our calculating analysis has determined you are the best way," DoubleSpin tells us. "The only way, really."

"O-kay, Dough-kay," Delrina says. "What do we have to do?"

DoubleSpin leans forward and places his hand in the center of the table. "Just do this for real. Promise each other you will do your best...to save the earth."

"What are the odds, if we do this for real?" Jack asks.

"Umm, 50-50, maybe."

"And if we don't?"

"You have nothing, that way."

Jack sighs and reaches his hand in toward the center of the table.

It is a little like we are kids again, taking the secret society oath. One by one, we each place our right hand palm down on DoubleSpin's. Last of all, Herbert's hand comes slapping in on top of the pile. "He does not know what any of this is about and really, none of us do, but he wants in. Hey, you guys were going to go without me again, weren't you?"

"Of course not, Herbert," DoubleSpin says. "We need you."

"Yes, you do," the Old Viking chuckles happily, still without a clue but content to be a member of the team.

I would like to tell you this is the moment when electricity sparkles everywhere and we are all invested with superpowers like bullet-bouncing and elasticity and high speed flying, but that actually doesn't come until later. Well, some of it. Or maybe it is that we only realize later some of the things that have happened to us. Looking back, I like to remember that I felt a faint disrupting tingle of energy or something, and maybe I did and maybe I did not. I do remember we all laughed a little self-consciously and took our hands back out of the circle and that DoubleSpin was pleased. Very, very pleased.

But that did not last but a few seconds and then he tells us he has to go somewhere to report in and do something complicated and then he will be back in time for whatever will happen next. We get the part about him going and reporting and coming back, but the rest is blurry, as if he said it but it got scrambled by a bad transmission. By this time I am aware of his tricky ways. That was a something-something-something he did not want us to know. Or maybe couldn't tell us. *Rules of the game,* he would say.

"See you later, alligator," Georgie-Porgie says.

"Don't forget your passport," Herbert says, looking up from his station at the computer keyboard. DoubleSpin promises that he will remember, and then does a fast fade to invisible.

We look at each other, but there is nothing much more to say. We are all aware that it is the middle of the night, and so we wander off to our rooms, wondering what particular brand of madness we have gotten ourselves into.

I personally am convinced that I will never ever get to sleep, but after all it is close to two in the morning, and the moment my head hits that pillow I am out like a light. I fall into a deep sleep; a better slumber than it seems I have had in years.

Forty two

There is one sneaky thing about the normal, everyday process of getting old; you are so slowly robbed of your youth that you forget how joyful it is to have younger muscles and the rush of blood through your veins. The next morning, not quite awake, I shuffle into my bathroom and am greeted by my face in the mirror. I am not sure what I am hoping for, but there is no miraculous set back of the old DNA clock staring back at me, just the same old wrinkles, and the same thin face with the high cheekbones my mother always assured me were elegant.

Maybe my hair is a shade darker, although maybe that is just hopeful imagining. I stare hard at myself and finally decide my iron grey locks do look like they are thinking they might want to revert to the glossy black of my youth. Wishful thinking. If a thing like that could actually become real, I would be happy to tell Millie I took her advice and started coloring my hair. Now how do I conjure up a cure for the wrinkles around my eyes and the loose and sagging skin on my turkey neck? I cover my hopeful head of hair with a woolen cap and pull on a light jacket. I look like what I am, a foolish old lady who is ready to go for a shivery stroll in the brisk morning air.

I dawdle and fuss around, finding excuses not to leave my room. By the time I think I may be somewhat presentable it is closer to noon than breakfast. I take off my cap and wander into the lounge only to find that most of our gang has already eaten. The sandwich and salads line is still open. I feel more hungry than usual so I fill up a heaping plate of cottage cheese and load it with blueberries and pineapple chunks, and then I claim my favorite lounge chair next to our regular table. It is almost as if nothing extraordinary has happened, and Jack, Herbert, George, Millie and Desmond are going through the motions of playing quarter limit blackjack.

An interesting thing about Jack this morning; I can see he is doing chair exercises from his sitting position. He sees the expression on my face and says, "You forget what you've lost until you try to get it back."

"I was thinking something like that earlier this morning."

"Me, too," Millie says. "I was remembering how I used to bounce up and charge into the day."

"Visualization is everything," DoubleSpin says. He has returned from wherever he went to report and is sitting in a chair like a regular human being. "You have to see it to believe it to be it," he adds, with a wise tilt of his head.

"True enough," Jack nods in agreement and smiles, looking in DoubleSpin's direction and then at me. He shrugs his shoulders. There is no easy explanation why the Stranger behaves the way he does. We are both hoping that he actually has a plan, that it works out for us and that we are not all the victims of mass delusion.

From the number of empty plates stacked around our table, it is clear the Old Bunch has finished breakfast without me. The business of Chermundo goes on as usual. Mason, the orderly on duty, is conducting one of his surveys to get our opinion on upcoming events.

"Okay, who votes for the L.A. Zoo?" he asks.

I must look a little startled, being brought back to the mundane world by the question.

Delrina puts up a hesitant hand, but there is a chorus of "Boooo" and "Nooo" from around the room, and somebody says "The zoo sucks!" just loud enough so everybody can hear.

Somebody else sounds off, "I don't ever want to smell elephant poop again in this lifetime!"

"Okay, how about Universal Studios?"

There is another round of groans, hisses and catcalls.

"We already been there three times this year!" the same whiner complains.

"Aardvarks and mechanical sharks, oh my!" somebody else pipes up.

"Well, how about the Chumash Village?" Mason asks.

This time there is no response. This is a new destination, and nobody is certain what such a day trip might involve.

Showboat George eyes Mason suspiciously over his cards, and then grins at me. "What's a Chew-Mash, Lucy? Can you eat it?"

I pretty much know the history of the San Fernando Valley so at least I have some idea about where Mason wants to take us. After World War II, the Rocketdyne people fenced off a big isolated section in the hills west of Valley Circle Boulevard. They might not have realized it at the time, but Chumash Indians had been living there for centuries, and there were caves with paintings and old pottery and other artifacts, and because it was fenced off with a ten foot high cyclone fence and plenty of keep out signs, the Indian imprint on the area was accidentally not destroyed or built over as the Los Angeles population rushed to expand out in that direction.

I explain to our gang, "The Calabasas Historical Society found remains of an Indian village in the hills at the west end of the valley. They have been keeping it a secret so people do not sneak in there, but Mason told me he has been taking a course on it over at Pierce College."

Delrina twirls one of her reddish curls around a forefinger. "Gol-dang it, Lucy, I could have known that if I had known it."

"Del, that makes no sense at all." Herbert shakes his head.

Unpredictable George has lurched to his feet and is war whooping it up around the table. "Whoop-whoop-whoop-whoop! Goooooo—Chew-mash!"

Mason eyes us uncertainly, but I can see he is particularly interested in taking us on this outing. "They are doing an archeological dig," he says. "So we have to stay out of certain areas they have roped off. I can get us in, but you have to promise to behave."

Herbert lights up; he has an idea and I suspect I know what it is. A deserted Indian village out in the deserted hills is a perfect place where he can make his calls to his Nigerian pals, the Prince of Benin and other assorted rascals and scam artists. Herbert stands, giving us a glimpse of his former self, the boss of Old Viking Shipping. "Sit Down, Georgie-Porgie!" he barks. "Don't be silly! It sounds like an amazing adventure, Mason. I'll make sure my friends here behave."

"I actually would like to go," I add, just in case Mason thinks we are kidding.

Mason looks around the room. He cannot decide whether to be delighted at this show of support from the Old Bunch or astonished at Herbert's sudden display of responsibility. Some of the guests at the other tables nod, and most everybody in the room looks like they are in general agreement; at least it is something new and different, it will be free and sounds like it might even be fun.

Mason happily makes the decision. "Okay, people, the Chumash Village it is. The sign-up list will be on the bulletin board."

"You are going, right, Jack?" I ask.

"I don't know, Lu." I guess he has taken to calling me Lu now that we are in some secret invisible-alien society.

The Stranger speaks from the ceiling, "I'd really like to see that village, Jack." He is also still sitting in the chair near us, so I am guessing the upside down image is invisible to everybody but Jack and me.

"It's just a bunch of cave paintings...and rocks..." I cannot be sure Jack is talking to me or to the alien.

"I'm not asking for much, here," the Stranger says.

"Oh, alright," Jack says. "Sign us up all around."

Herbert chuckles, "Our invisible friend can't come, Jack.

"How would you know if he did, Herbie?"

"I guess I could smell him or something," the Old Viking says. "Aliens all stink like goop, don't they?"

Jack and I look at DoubleSpin, who does a backward swan dive that ends with him frozen upside down in the air a few inches over the Old Viking's head. Herbert brushes his hand over his head as if he feels there is a pesky insect buzzing around up there.

"Careful," Jack says. "You'll hurt his ultra-dimensional feelings."

Mason has overheard the joking. He quietly moves over to the blackjack table and sits in the chair that is quickly vacated by DoubleSpin. The orderly is seemingly looking at the papers in his hand that have some information about the Indian village, and he watches as a hand is dealt and the card game continues.

"Say there, Jack," Mason says. "What's this about an invisible person?"

Jack eyes him over his cards. "What are you talking about, Mason?"

"There's gossip around, you know? I keep my ears open; I hear stuff."

None of the guests at the table says anything; everybody is quietly studying their cards. It is Jack's call. The Stranger puts two fingers to his ears, wiggling them like he is a rabbit.

"It's not a person, Mason." Jack says, getting the Charades clue from DoubleSpin. "It's a giant bunny."

Mason is a little set back by the reference to Harvey, that movie from 1950 that stars James Stewart and a six-foot invisible rabbit, but he is not going to give up. "Don't make fun of me, Jack. I'm serious."

Jack sits back and eyes Mason; he has a thought of his own. "Mason, do you ever hear voices?"

Mason smiles; now they are getting somewhere. "Me? No. We're talking about you, Jack."

"No, Mason, you were talking about me. And now I'm talking about you."

Mason eyes Jack with a new respect; this is going to be trickier than he thought. Still, he has sat through lectures on

the cunning of the delusional person. He decides to play
Jack's game. "Okay, Jack. What about me?"

Jack nods agreeably. "Right. Just last week you were
talking about how you used to feed your Mamma's
pancakes to your dog Woofie under the table. You said, 'I
can still hear my Mamma yelling: 'Mason, you get that
mutt out of here right now!'''"

Mason knows he has been played. A slow frown
gathers at the corners of his normally cheerful expression.
"Well, that was different."

"Everything's different, Mason." Jack eyes the orderly
sitting next to him. "Different from what we would think."
He breaks eye contact and turns his attention back to the
game. "Give me another card, George."

Mason eyes Jack, who sighs as he goes busted at 23.
Jack is either the world's sanest person or the craziest.
Mason thinks of himself as a good person; he takes his job
seriously and he wants to do the right thing. He looks at
me, but I give him a shrug that says if I know anything, I
am not talking to you about it. From the look in his eyes, it
is clear he cannot make up his mind one way or the other.

"How soon 'til lunch, Mason?" Delrina asks. "I could
eat a horse…put it in a bun, of course."

The Old Bunch breaks out in song:

Kill a tree and eat a horse
Put it in a bun, of course
And I – I – I – I – I just want to cry.

 The orderly has given up, but he gives Delrina a last
parting shot, "I saw you just had two breakfasts." "I'm in
training, my good man, Mason," she tells him. "I need my
protein and my carbs."

"Yeah," Herbert nods in agreement. "She weight lifts
the fork up to her mouth."

"Crabs, not carbs, Millie," George adds. "It's what
makes you so crabby."

"Quite the gang of jokesters," Mason smiles, his spirits
lifting.

"We are the Old Bunch," I smile up at him. "Like the Wild Bunch, only old and not so wild.

"Yeah," Jack adds. "And we're here to save your world."

"Naw," George says. "To rock your world!"

And we treat our orderly to another verse:

Here's paradise / now treat it nice
Keep it green / it's good advice
Yet here we are/ spittin' in God's eye
Why, why, why, why...I just want to cry

Forty three

The Jack-In-The-Box restaurant on the northwest corner of Hollywood and Vine is decorated with iconic black and white blow-up photos of touched up and highly romanticized moments from the lives of Marilyn Monroe, James Cagney, Humphrey Bogart, Mae West, and Elvis.

The early morning patrons are a mixed bag of tourists, dawn hustlers and tired zombies leftover from the night shift. Charles and Albert sit at a table littered with the remains of their morning meal of Cokes, burgers and fries. Charles' face is newly battered and his recently refreshed spirits have been dampened by the events of their previous night on Hollywood Boulevard. His hat is ripped and crumpled.

"You could have come to my assistance, Albert!"

Albert is not, to Charles' mind, appropriately sympathetic, "My humblest apologies, 'your Royal Excellency,' but I had my hands full."

"Oh, right." Charles groans and, with his elbows on the table, puts his head between his hands.

"She had a very big knife, Charles. These Americans are unexpectedly resourceful and dangerous." Albert spreads his arms wide in a show of astonishment. "I had to actually pay her for sex!"

"I'm getting my brains kicked out and you are getting your rocks off!"

Albert shrugs. "Well, it was just oral sex. That is not real true carnal knowledge in the law of this land. I have it on good authority. A former President of the United States has said so."

Before Charles can think of a worthy comeback, two newcomers enter. It is the Colonel, dressed in khaki casual, and Maloof Urdveen, wearing the usual dark suit and his Arab headband.

Charles sees them and whispers to Albert, "Does not our Arab leader look silly with that handkerchief on his head?"

"Well, Princely One, I would agree with you, but look around you." Albert waves one hand, indicating the people at the surrounding tables. This is Hollywood and there are east Indian turbans, slinky hooker dresses, black afros, dark sunglasses, cowboy hats. "Here everybody pretends to be someone that they are not," Albert says, pointing to the Hollywood pamphlet he has been reading. "It is their hope to be uncovered for the movies."

"Dis-covered, Albert. Dis-covered." Charles waves the Colonel and Maloof over. "Have you eaten yet?"

"Food is nothing," Maloof Urdveen says. "We have our great enterprise to pursue."

At this same moment in earth time, DoubleSpin is watching Jack do knee bends in the lounge area of the Chermundo. Jack has been warned by the staff to use the exercise room, but he has never been one to follow instructions, and so he is getting in a few extra whenever he can.

"You know that's only physical," DoubleSpin informs him from a nearby wall that he is drifting in and out of.

"You keep saying that. Should I be doing mental push-ups?"

"Well, yes." The expression on DoubleSpin's face changes. "Jack? Why does Bella dye her hair white?"

Jack looks up to see the black nurse with her platinum curls is at the very top of a ladder, reaching high over her head in an attempt to attach a huge plastic black widow spider near the ceiling in a corner of the room. The spider has a suction cup on the bottom of its belly, and Bella wants to get it as high as she can possibly reach.

"Because she thinks it makes her pretty," Jack says. He notices Bella's position on the ladder. "Jesus, that's dangerous!"

"Don't warn her, Jack. She'll fall for sure."

"But – "

"She's going to fall, anyway. She will die horribly of a broken neck. Unless she lands on that sofa over there. Whoops – there she goes!"

Jack looks from Bella to the cushioned sofa. It is as if he is watching a tragedy in slow motion. At the last second he grits his teeth and strains his will. The heavy piece of furniture trembles for a split-second and then shoots across the room to break Bella's fall.

Lucky for Bella…but unlucky for Jack and DoubleSpin is the fact that Mason has entered the room and seen everything from Bella on the ladder to the sofa shooting across the room to rescue her. Then again, double-lucky for everybody, I also have been making my way to the lounge to see what Jack is up to. As Mason opens his mouth to say something, my thought rushes across to him, *Mason that could NOT have happened! It did not happen! Did not! Understand me, that did not happen!*

Mason looks around the room. He feels confused and then he sees Bella, who has rolled off the sofa and is getting up from the floor. "Hey, Bella," he says. "You okay?"

I hurry over and help her adjust her wig, which has come askew in her fall.

"I just had a bit of a fall," she tells him. "I'm alright, I think…"

The big plastic spider was not stuck with enough suction, and in the next second it lands with a plop on the floor next to her.

"Next time, get somebody like me to do that for you," Mason scolds her. He picks up the spider and scrambles up the ladder. He is taller and in a few seconds he has it attached in the corner up near the ceiling. "I'm going to take this ladder so you're not tempted to get into more trouble."

"Oh, I'm done for the day," she assures him.

As they leave, DoubleSpin nods to Jack. "See, it doesn't have anything to do with how heavy a thing is."

The Stranger turns to me, *Well done, Lucy.*

That leaves me wondering how much of what just happened was luck and how much was a carefully controlled exercise to help us discover more about our new selves. DoubleSpin is turning out to be the alien I love to hate. He is smiling at me. I have not been able to figure out his exact way of doing things, but from his ear-to-ear grin, I am on the right track with my own training program.

Forty four

The executive office at Chermundo Villas is bustling with more activity than usual. The morning meeting is spearheaded by director Dr. Humphrey Goozeman, and in addition to the regular senior staff members, there are various investors of The Chermundo Villas Company, Inc. and three quietly observant bank representatives. Humphrey begins the meeting by declaring the company is afflicted with serious financial problems, and he is eager to let everyone in the room know it is a community problem, to be shared by everyone attending the meeting. Dr. Daniel, the sales staff of four young people, several senior nurses and Mason sit around a large oval table. The investors and bank people flank them from behind, sitting in a row of chairs against one wall. The staff members are not surprised by the director's announcement, and they do not seem to be in any way sympathetic to his concerns. Since Goozeman was appointed, these meeting occur on a regular basis, and the subjects of profits and cost cutting regularly come into play.

Goozeman, this small potato shaped man who presents himself as an academician, is decked out in a brownish tweed suit, and decorated with a prep tie and matching handkerchief for trimming. Today, he carries a tan plastic tobacco pipe, the type molded to look as if it is ornately carved. He is trying for the air of a successful clinical psychologist, although he has never practiced medicine, and the few who know his background are not impressed with his uneventful career selling medical equipment.

Now, seeing the lack of staff enthusiasm, the Goozer frowns and chews on the end of his pipe. No one has ever seen him light up a bowl, and that is probably a good thing as the general impression is that he would burn his tongue or start a small fire in his own wastebasket.

"Look, people—nobody here seems to understand," he says. His voice is a melodious whine, interesting at first, but a sound that wears on the ears with any repetition. "Nobody here understands our dilemma," he repeats. "I have a problem that affects us all. I need space for new guests. This is a team and we are all in this together, to better serve the needs of our clientele. Alzheimer's is a one way street. We all know this. A big percentage of our guests sadly dead end over there anyway, sooner or later."

Dr. Daniel sighs, "We've been over this before, Doctor Goozeman. Alzheimer's is not a cut-and-dried, black-or-white diagnosis. I will not go along with pushing marginal or subjective diagnostics so you can dump guests in the Z ward!"

Goozeman frowns at the inflection on his title. His business cards say he is a doctor, but no one has ever seen real validation of a medical education in his background. "I'm certainly not saying dump them," he protests. "Look around the Z. Nice food, new rooms, new facility. We clean their rooms, we clean their clothes, and we even wipe their butts when they need it. Ain't life grand and sumptuous! What you are not understanding is, we all report to shareholders, and the good ship Chermundo is running on a very thin margin around here."

"But you can't…" Daniel is outraged. He stands and throws one hand in the air.

Goozeman backs away, momentarily afraid Daniel is going to lash out and strike him. He recovers, takes a deep breath and clears his throat, "I would like to introduce you to a new member of the staff." He claps his hands twice and on cue, a tall, lean and dour man in a white physician's coat enters from Goozeman's office through an adjoining door. The newcomer is lean as a rake and has an unhealthy pallor.

"I am Doctor Ray Culbert," he says, using the same inflections on the word doctor that Goozeman uses when proclaiming his own questionable status. "I have been hired to head the Alzheimer's Ward."

This is a demotion for Dr. Daniel, who stands to voice his protest, "Nobody talked to me about this!"

"You are a good geriatric doctor," Goozeman says in his purring cat voice. "But the remedies for Alzheimer's control have advanced beyond your experience."

"Control is the operative word," the new doctor adds. "Through an entirely new set of experimental drugs, we can provide a tranquil state of mind."

"You want to drug them senseless!" Bella stands alongside Dr. Daniel.

Dr. Daniel points at the director as if he is charging him with murder. "Rumor at the San Diego convention was that you are trying to sell this place!"

Bella glowers at the diminutive Goozeman, "I see it now. You're just filling the Alzheimer's unit to make room for new people! And if they are quiet in the Z ward, you can jam more people in!"

"New guests. That's my job, Bella. Mason. Dr. Daniel. My job. And how I do it is my responsibility. Let me remind you, this little cruise ship has to operate using the most modern methods or we all sink. And as to whether I'm looking for new ownership is none of your business."

Mason grumbles, "I think it is, and I think your methods stink!" He throws down his folder and punctuates his point by walking out of the room.

Goozeman yells after him, "Orderly, this meeting is not over!"

But Mason has already gone. Humphrey glares around the table at those remaining. "I don't think that boy knows what's good for him! Anybody can be replaced. Anybody! Are there any more questions?"

The nurses stare down at their paperwork in front of them, saying nothing.

Dr. Daniel unhappily shakes his head. "I'm going to make some calls."

"You do that," Goozeman snaps. "You can call your way right into a new job somewhere else."

Forty five

Herbert has been pacing and fidgeting about for hours. He has never liked the part of his business when he was waiting for a deal to be signed, a shipment to be delivered or a payment to be made. It is after lunch, and the dining room is almost empty when he gets a call on his cell phone. He goes through his furtive routine, trying to keep his secrets while talking too loud at the same time.

"Yeah. Herb Miller here...yeah...yeah...of course I can...of course I did."

Jack is doing sit-ups while talking with the Stranger, who is sitting eight feet up on a shelf-wall divider between the dining room and the lounge. From the count, Jack is over ten. There is one other change., today the Stranger's face, usually a grayish hue, is a light blue, as if he has been dipped in pastel dye. That is a new development, but nothing is predictable about DoubleSpin.

"You talk about principles, earthling, but you just find reasons to do what you want."

Jack shrugs. "Okay, so we're all pricks. So what?"

"No, not pricks, Jack. Not at all. At least, not all of you. You are simply self-delusional."

"Well is it some kind of optical trick or are you turning the color of an Easter egg?"

"That's not funny, Jack."

Herbert yells from a few feet away as if Jack is across the room. "Jack! Jack! We got to be there at four this afternoon!"

"Where, Herb?"

"Jack-In-The-Box at Hollywood and Vine!"

"Oh yeah, like that's going to happen. They're not going to van you to get a hamburger in Hollywood when you can walk to a Wendy's a half a block from here!"

Mason sees Herbert and moves to talk to him. Herbert catches sight of the orderly coming in their direction. He has time to send a loud whisper Jack's way, "Suitcases of money!"

Mason is not sure exactly what he has overheard. He examines his clipboard, "Ahh, Herbert, we're moving you to a new room this afternoon."

"Hell, I don't care," Herbert says. "Don't bother me with the small stuff."

Jack eyes Mason. "I'm getting a new cellmate?"

"No. You're going with him." Mason doesn't look happy about it.

Jack can read Mason pretty well; he is quick to fill in the blank spaces.

"Un-be-*liev*-able! We're going other side," he says.

Mason nods, "Yes. Don't worry, Jack. It's …nearly the same as this side."

Herbert is slower than Jack, but after a quick look at Jack, he also realizes what this means. He stands, suddenly alarmed at the unexpected turn of events.

"What? I ain't going other side! Sidney! That rotten, sneaky nephew of mine is behind this! That dirty little rat! Nobody said zip to me about moving to the Z ward! The Doc never said nothing!"

Mason gives him a tired look. "They've been holding meetings the last couple of days and this morning the order came down from Goozeman's office."

"No, no, no! I don't care, they can't do this! I – I got to have evaluation!"

Mason looks to the doorway, but the other nurses and orderlies are nowhere around. He tries to calm down the old man. "Now, Herbert."

But Herbert's reaction is one of increasingly alarm. He's so close to the deal of his life and now this! He looks around wildly, "No, no, no! You can't! I won't! No! I want my wife! My Rhonda would never allow it!"

"Rhonda has been dead for ten years, Herbert."

Herbert has reached his flashpoint. He yells, "No! That's garbage! Don't say those crazy things! I – Rhonda! No!"

Herbert overturns the table and dashes from the room. Mason reluctantly goes after him.

Jack looks around the room. It is empty, except for Bella, who comes in and looks around. "Jack! What's all the noise?! What's happening?"

Jack shrugs. "Nobody ever tells me."

The nurse rushes back out. Jack looks up at the Stranger. "What are you doing up there, anyway? I thought you were getting gravitized…err, gravitated, gravelated…whatever."

"Wallowing in my weight, Jack." The Stranger is struck with a sudden thought. He reaches his hand up to his own face. "You said I looked unusual?"

"There isn't anything normal about you, my friend."

"No...I mean different."

"Well, you painted your face blue as a robin's egg."

The Stranger gives Jack a sudden look of nervous fear. "No...say it ain't so, Jack."

"Oh, yeah. No kidding, robin's egg blue…hey, what's wrong?"

The Stranger looks stricken. He stares at nothing, gapes as if he is seeing the most horrible thing in his life.

Jack reaches out a hand. "At the risk of repeating myself, what's wrong with you, DoubleSpin?"

The Stranger is silent.

"Okay, don't tell me." Jack gets to his feet and with some effort starts to walk out of the room.

"They're calling me back," DoubleSpin says. He is still cross-legged, but is now floating in the air, a foot or two to one side of the wall divider on which he had been resting.

Jack turns to face him, "Why?"

"They don't think you're worth the resources to keep you in the show...the numbers haven't been that great."

"Well, clearly I'm not."

"Not you, Jack. The whole planet," the Stranger says. "You haven't made the cut." He turns to his invisible camera. "I apologize to the entire sentient galaxy, and particularly to the loyal and devoted members of the Spin-Spin Fan Club."

This proves to be too much for Jack, and he angrily turns on the Stranger. "We take the vow for you, and then Herb and I get sent to the Z ward and now the earth is under attack and you decide to pull up stakes! I have to find Lucy, get our team together!"

"They'll be here in a minute." DoubleSpin nods unhappily. "I put out a call."

DoubleSpin is telling it right; in less than thirty seconds I walk in with Delrina, Millie and George.

"You called, sire?" I ask, trying for light humor. Word travels fast at the Villas and everybody already knows what is happening to Jack and Herbert.

"How do I look?" DoubleSpin asks me.

"Like somebody sprayed you with Seafoam Blue interior latex paint," I tell him.

"We need another meeting," he shouts. "Right now!"

This is something new. I have not seen what anybody might consider strong emotion from our off-planet friend, but right now he looks like he is totally losing his cool as my students would have described it.

The lounge is too crowded for the kind of privacy we need, but as it is an uncomfortably brisk autumn and nobody is in the center garden, we go out there and stand around, rubbing our hands in the cool breeze, making jokes about our thin California blood and trying our best to look like we are just a bunch of nature loving fools.

"One for all and all for one," DoubleSpin says, putting his hand out and urging us to add our own. Jack reaches his in without any hesitation, and so do I. Delrina, Millie and George look at each other and do the same. This time, the very instant we have all joined hands we experience a glitter of blinding illumination, at least I do. It is nothing like a physical flash of light but some hard-to-explain type of energy that leaves us all tingling and weird inside.

"Good," DoubleSpin says. "At least they can't take that away from me."

"Take what?" George says. "Your vibrator?"

"You earthlings," the strange blue-faced fellow says. "I love you all."

"What did you do to us?" I look at my own hands, which are feeling somehow different, as if they are inhabited by some unaccountable new force that is crawling everywhere and in every direction through my body.

"Turned back your DNA a little more." He must have seen the alarm on my face. "No, don't worry, just another tweak."

"Otherwise we'd be crawling around like babies," Delrina jokes.

"That's right," DoubleSpin says. "Or worse."

Jack gives him his reflective little smile. "This means we get to go around twice to go around once."

DoubleSpin returns his smile. "Something like that."

"Now we're all double-spins."

"Sort of," DoubleSpin nods in agreement, but the thought does not seem to make him any happier.

I do not have time to say or do anything; because our strange alien friend is doing one of his dramatic movie-time fades to nothing, this one from both the top and bottom with both of his ends snapping like window shades to his waistline.

"You're not leaving us?" I ask.

"No. I have to call my…office…" His voice comes at us out of thin air.

None of us has any real idea what we should do next. We all feel strangely unsettled and a little jittery.

"I guess he's going to get back to us," Jack says. "Meanwhile, I have to go pack my things."

"Jack, you are not going to let them move you!" I glare at him.

"Don't worry, Lu, I'm not quitting. Fennerman is on vacation. I think the Goozer knew that. But Tom will straighten everything out when he gets back."

"I think you have to call him."

"No service. I tried already. His office says he's hiking in the High Sierras."

"But – "

"Lu. I've got this one covered."

He smiles and I find myself believing him.

Forty six

The rest of us decide to hang out in the lounge, to keep each other company while Jack makes his way back to his old room. The Jackster does not have much in the way of worldly goods, so packing should not take him very long.

Wherever DoubleSpin took himself off to, he must have gone at top speed, because he has already returned and is waiting for Jack when he gets there.

Jack and Herbert's rooms are already stripped bare, with their personal possessions packed in boxes and in the process of being carted away. Only the generic Villas furniture that comes with the lease remains. A man with a dolly cart is puffing and grunting to show how hard he works as he wheels cardboard boxes out of their joint living room and down the hall.

One of the nurses sees Jack. Many on the staff became friendlier since he miraculously regained use of his legs and became somewhat of a celebrity in their lives. The nurse tries to find the right words to comfort him, "Jack, Jack…it will be okay."

"Of course it will, Jane," Jack says. He turns to DoubleSpin, "So you're just going to dump us."

Nurse Jane thinks he is talking to her. "No, nothing like that, hon. Don't even think that! There will still be plenty of field trips, and someone to take you to the supermarket."

But Jack has already moved from her to the doorway to Herbert's old rooms. The Stranger is in there, leaning against the wall, eyeing him.

"You're dumping me," Jack says, lowering his voice.

"I have no choice."

"I went the extra mile for you."

"But…"

"No buts, DoubleSpin. I did the impossible for you."

DoubleSpin has no answer for that. He shakes his head as if to clear it. Moisture gathers in his eyes.

"I thought your kind couldn't cry," Jack tells him.

"I'm not crying. Look, you are something special, Jack. I can't do much, but I'm still here for a little bit and I'll do what I can. Here—get the revolver."

"What?"

"Jack, why do I have to repeat everything? What is Herbert's favorite movie?"

"The Godfather.'"

The Stranger points to Herbert's bathroom "Get the gat, man."

Things are moving too fast for Jack. He looks around uncertainly. "Maybe we should tell someone."

The Stranger snaps. "JACK!" His voice roars in Jack's head like thunder. "Get the revolver, now! You have fifteen seconds!"

The Stranger is not kidding around. With his face a deepening blue, he looks like the very strange other-worldly creature that he is. Jack hops to it, hustling into Herbert's bathroom. The revolver is in a plastic bag taped inside the water reservoir of the toilet. Jack pulls out his shirt and slips the revolver in his belt behind his back.

"Cold, wet and slimy," he says, making sure his shirt tail covers the weapon. "I don't think that was in the movie."

He is just in time as Nurse Jane calls out from the next room, "Did we get everything, hon?"

Jack whirls around. "I guess," he says. He collects his wits, "Old Herbie isn't very big on deodorants."

Jane laughs, "I noticed that myself."

That evening finds Maloof, the Colonel and Charles sitting at an outdoor table at Pink's Hot Dog Stand on Santa Monica Street in Old Hollywood. The Colonel carries two medium sized metal suitcases. A happy, chattering and self-absorbed bunch of kids in their late teens walks by. The girls are showing a lot of flesh, as well as a variety of piercings and tattoos. The stand is now deserted except for Maloof's group and three homeboys sitting nearby on one of the tables. The young delinquents are noisily passing the time with handheld computer games that give off the sounds of explosions, growls and shrieks of pain and horror, the usual sound tracks of make-believe violence and electronic bloodshed.

"Where is Albert?" Charles asks.

"He is otherwise occupied," the Colonel says. Charles does not see this as a good indication of his own chances for survival. He has been taking hope, now that he is in America, that he may actually be safer, but the news that his assistant will not be here probably means that he is dead.

The Colonel may not be a mind reader, but he can read Star-Power Charles pretty well. He slaps him on the side of the head. "Charles, your assistant is fine. Do not worry about him."

"He was my friend."

"You are an ignorant fool. You know nothing. Mo corrupted you with money and fancy clothes."

Maloof takes a bite from his hotdog. "Very tasty," he says.

Charles nods, affecting his princely attitude, and before he can stop himself, words come out of his mouth, "Pork, you know."

Maloof spits it out and looks at Charles as if it is his fault. The Colonel cuffs Charles on the head, harder this time, as if he is a dog that has to be constantly reprimanded for bad behavior.

'"You should have alerted him before he ate."

This constant slapping around of Charles amuses the three homeboys, who have been watching this little bit of action as much as paying attention to their electronic games of bloody battle and mayhem. The three of them are most likely black, white and Hispanic, but they are so heavily tattooed that, in the dim outdoor light at Pinks, there is little enough to know for sure.

"Cruel blow, man!" the black boy gasses off to nobody in particular.

"Big hands for a little asshole," the white boy giggles.

The Hispanic says nothing. He sits back, jiving to the music in his ear, his eyes glittery as he watches the two suitcases the Colonel has passed off to Charles.

Maloof glares at the Colonel, "So, this wonderful and reliable Old Viking of yours is late."

The Colonel in turn gives Charles a cold stare. Charles shrugs, "I tried to tell you, but you insisted on coming here. He could not meet us at that Jack Box place and he will not meet us here, not now. I told you. He insists we get together at an old archeological dig."

"What? Where?" The Colonel raises his fist.

Charles cowers. "In the west end of the San Fernando Valley."

"That is entirely stupid and dangerous! He wants his money, he should come to us! He must!"

Charles sees a chance to at least temporarily dodge the deadly end-game punishment that is moving ever closer. "No! It's perfect! A deserted place. Nothing but rocks and trees. Nobody goes there. The Americans care nothing for their ancient heritage."

"When do we do this?" Maloof asks.

Charles stands and straightens himself. He's not going to be shot through the head, after all. "Tomorrow. The only problem I see..."

The Colonel draws his fist back in a warning gesture. "We don't keep you alive for problems, Charles."

Maloof smoothly grabs the Colonel's hand. This frustrates the Colonel, but he dares not say anything.

"Colonel. Let him say his concern. What is the problem you see, Charles?"

"Well...if we give him the money, why will he do what we ask?"

"That's why there are two suitcases of money, Prince Charley."

Maloof places one of the metal suitcases on the round metal table in front of them and cracks it open enough to reveal it is full of tight packets of American currency.

The homeboys go quiet. They have seen enough. They eye each other expectantly.

Maloof closes it and places it on top of the second suitcase. The Hispanic moves forward a notch, placing a hand on the metal case as Maloof snaps it shut. "Gracias, gentlemen. You can leave these on the table, right where they is."

The white boy says softly, "Oh, yeah, gentlemen. We gonna take it from here, lighten your load, so to speak."

The Hispanic flicks open a huge switchblade knife, something Rambo's bad cousin might carry. The black boy grins, smacking his brass knuckles into his other hand. The white boy also grins, pulling out a length of heavy chain.

The Colonel and Maloof give the Hispanic a cold stare, saying nothing.

Charles' jaw drops open and he shakes his head sympathetically. He looks apologetic. "Oh, no...you guys don't want to do this!"

The Colonel is quicker than lightning or the wind; before any of the three homeboys can move, he whips out his pistol with the long silencer already attached, and the night vibrates with a spitting hiss.

The Hispanic is closest to the Colonel, and he is the target. He folds over with less sound escaping from his dying lips than anyone not accustomed to these matters would believe possible.

Maloof snarls, "My suit!"

The Colonel looks at his Arab leader. "Sorry, sir. Sorry, sorry, sorry. He wipes a few flecks of blood from Maloof's suit with one of Pink's paper napkins. "He was close, and he had the knife…"

"If you had any idea how much this suit cost – never mind." Maloof turns his attention to the remaining two punks. The tattoo across the white boy's bare chest reads "Money for nothing And Chicks for free." The boy shrinks back as Maloof reaches his hand to tease one of his nipples over the tattoo.

"Nothing is free," Maloof says with a shrug. "This is why decadent people are destroyed by their vices. In this case, the sin of greed." He clicks open the top case and takes a packet of money from it. He holds it out to the two remaining punks. His gaze narrows. "Do the two of you want to work for me?"

Take the money or die, Maloof leaves it up to them.

Forty seven

Geoff Mumfrey, nicknamed Mumzey, runs the Z ward with a policy he likes to think of as fists in velvet gloves. He is a dapper little senior orderly with quick wits and a mind that likes to fit all the parts of his life into neat little compartments. He thought he would quit when he heard he was getting a new boss, but after he met the tall, gaunt and dour Doctor Culbert he realized the new head honcho of the Z believed in progressive medical ideas exactly in line with his own: a quiet ward is a good ward and meds are the orderly's best friend.

Culbert introduces him to an entirely new range of pacifier drugs that are experimental but showing great promise. Mumfrey loves it when the patients show such immediate effects as he sees. His decade of experience with Alzheimer's patients has been frustrating, and he now finds he wants to personally stick as many of them as possible.

"We do things a little differently," Mumzey tells Jack and Herbert, and two other pairs of oldsters who had been handed over to him the day before courtesy of the Goozer. Mumzey figures the two oldster pairs are nodders, not much in the real world any more, and he is sure they will not give him or his crew any trouble. They better not, with Doctor Culbert standing right there like a hungry old stork. Everybody knows Goozeman has had it in for Jack since he turned the tables on him and Herbert's nephew in their earlier attempt to get the Old Viking into the Z, and the Goozer has warned Mumzey to be extra careful, but the fellow seems like just another aimless nodder, staring at the wall the way he is. Herbert Miller, on the other hand promises to be a handful. All it takes is a quick glance to see it. Here it is first morning and these two bozos are standing in front of the locked door expecting to just walk to the other side without help so they can eat their scrambled eggs or whatever with the regulars. Scrambled brains is more like it! he thinks.

"We escorted the breakfast bunch over there ten minutes ago," Geoff says. "You missed it. Get an energy bar from the machine in our Quik Café."

Jack smiles, realizing things are about to go south for both the CEO and the President of the Z ward.

"I don't care how you do your things," Herb says with a rough edge to his voice. He is not interested in energy bars or food of any type. "Where's my stuff?"

"You don't have any stuff anymore, my dear Old Viking friend."

"I ain't your friend. Did you sell it on Ebay? Christ, that bronze with the horned helmet alone was worth a ding-dang fortune!"

Mumfrey tenses up as he gives Herbert a closer look. The wrinkled old fart is supposed to be in his mid-eighties, but he doesn't look a day over sixty. Fifty-five is more like it. That is the thing in elder care, you have to be ready for anything and you can never tell about the wire thin old crappers; they are quick as snakes and they can hurt you. Mumzey flips open his cell phone and is about to call for the quik-stik needle when Mason buzzes himself in through the main door from the other side.

"Oh, there you are," Mason says to Jack and Herbert. "Field trip." He looks at Geoff, dismissing him with a cheery wave of his hand.

"You can't just…" Mumzey wants to say Z ward people do not just go on regular field trips. Everybody at Chermundo knows the Z rule is that from time to time the ones on good behavior are escorted for small trips to a local city park where they can watch the flowers, and the spotted dogs and the stupid kids bumbling around with their doting cow moms – but that is the extent of their liberty privileges.

However, Mason is a really big guy and Mumzey gets the feeling today is no day to mess with him. In spite of the deepening frown on Dr. Culbert's face, Geoff knows if he crosses Mason here and now, it will create an unpleasant scene and might even cause him some personal physical pain. So he does nothing, and just like that, his two new troublemakers are heading out the door. Mumzey is sure it is a conspiracy from the other side, an attempt to lessen his ability to handle the Old Crappers Ward, as he calls his domain, and this suspicion is reinforced when he overhears Jack asking Mason, "What took you so long?"

And Herbert's comment, "Yeah, ten more seconds and I was going to take that little weasel out."

Mumzey swears under his breath, vowing that this little incident is going to come up for discussion at next week's directors meeting. Happy-Go-Lucky Mason is going to find himself in a heap of trouble!

Our trip to the Chumash Village is so popular Mason has had to rent a larger van from a local bus service. Not counting the enthusiastic Old Bunch, over twenty people have signed up and are waiting out in front of the Villas when our ride shows up. Mason has enlisted candy-striper Melody to help him count heads and keep track of the strays. Since he convinced her to wear her glasses, she is squinting a lot less, and he is finding her pleasant to be around. It does not take a matchmaker or a mystic to see something is going on there.

Our rented Fleet Van smells brand new and is painted a shiny two-tone white and light green. Melody checks off the guests as they climb on board. They have a rear loading platform, but nobody from the Old Bunch bothers with it. This surprises Mason, because he knows all our ailments.

"No thank you, Mason, you dear boy," Millie declines his supporting arm. "I'm going commando on this one. That's an expression I hear the young people say."

George snickers, "I think that means you're running around without pants."

She tickles his ribs. "Oh Georgie-Porgie!"

Mason shakes his head as the pair get on the van, giggling like two teens. He catches my eye. "What do you think, Lucy?"

"Something's in the air, Mason," I tell him. "Like with you and Melody."

He gets a shy look on his face and tries to change the subject. "You're doing something different with your hair."

"Oh, you noticed," I say. "That's sweet of you." Actually, I am wearing a broad sun hat, anything to cover the fact that my hair is well on its way to jet black. I have to get to Albertsons fast and buy some Lady Clairol. Old ladies can be excused for coloring their hair; it is just part of the drill. Maybe skin cream can explain the way my skin is tightening up. On the other hand, I am certain there is no way to explain the return of an old familiar curse. I had my period last night, and I do not believe there is any other seventy-five-year-old woman on the planet who can claim that.

Jack and Herbert sit together. From the seat behind them, Delrina and I can overhear them chuckling like schoolboys. "You weren't really going to karate chop him?"

"Naaw, Jack – Korean *ju jitsu* I learned in Seoul back in the day. I was going to let him come for me with his pack of needles and then I was going to bust his arm!"

Mason gets behind the wheel and steers us out of the Chermundo parking lot and we soon find ourselves speeding on the North 101, which actually heads west, and that makes about as much sense as anything else in Southern California, which is actually Central California if you count Baja, the Mexican California south of the border.

We are approaching the Valley Circle Exit when Delrina pokes me in the ribs. "You know, Melody is prettier than she looks."

"The girl needs a little help."

"Shame about those glasses," Delrina grins at me.

Talk about Jack and Herbert getting giddy. Del and I both have the idea at the same time. "You think we can?"

"Let's give it a shot," she says. "It's just simple myopia. Let's do the left one first."

We concentrate on the imagery, visualizing the structure of Melody's left eye.

"Wow," Delrina says. "No wonder she squints."

"We make a great surgical team," I tell her. I find it is not really all that difficult. Delrina freezes her in place and I do the reshaping.

After thirty seconds, we work on the right eye, which is not as bad, and a few seconds after that, Melody is squinting so badly through her glasses that she takes them off.

"Better talk to her," Del says. "I feel a panic attack coming on."

I send Melody the idea. *You do not need those silly glasses. You never have.*

Melody quietly puts her eyeglasses in her hiking knapsack, on the floor between her legs. Mason takes the Valley Circle off-ramp, but we catch the red light. He turns to Melody and smiles. "Hey, you got new contacts. Nice!"

She smiles, saying nothing.

Delrina has thought of something else. She smiles brightly at me, "What do you think, a little strawberry blond touch to the hair?"

"Good idea," I agree.

Forty eight

At first glance, Burro Flats looks like nothing more than a deserted Southern California picnic area, but without the redwood picnic tables or fire pits. Imagine a clearing set among old oak trees in the middle of a rocky glade. Upon closer inspection, it will seem a little unkempt, with the ankle deep grass and boulders lying around that people might trip over. A closer look and you will make out the faint chalk outline of a stick man on an old rock wall, and the curious may wonder at the rows of concave holes scooped from the rocks, these where generations of Chumash Indians used to grind up acorns they had gathered to make a mash they then cooked into unleavened bread.

Today it is over a hundred years since the Southern California Indian tribe that once camped here was chased away from this hilly rim in one corner of the valley, vanquished by disease or the encroachment of the farmers and ranchers, nobody knows for sure, not even the Calabasas Historical Society, though my guess is, their disappearance was due to all of the above. The land itself looks much the same as it did in the hundreds of years that marked the Indian times before the coming of the Mexicans and the Europeans, though everything else is different. White contrails of jets from Burbank International track high overhead, and the faint distant flapping sound of an unseen police helicopter can be heard carrying up from the valley that slopes away and below us to the east.

The two dozen or so of us guests from Chermundo Villas who have signed up for the outing are decked out in straw hats, flowered skirts, gaily flowered Hawaiian shirts and walking shorts. For the most part we carry bright yellow daypacks provided by the home.

We members of the Old Bunch are a glorious sight to behold. George has three extra canteens of water slung around him. I am front and center, of course, in my wide straw hat and with my zoom lens Nikon on a strap around my neck, with a somewhat younger and more nimble Jack and our blue-faced pal DoubleSpin. Others along on the outing include Fumbler Fred, Awful Arthur the Letch, and Tangle Toes Tillie.

The Old Viking seems to have entirely forgotten the monumental fuss he made over his move to the Z ward. I am fairly certain that he looks younger, but it is hard to tell just what is under the floppy ranger hat and outsized olive colored camo outfit he has on. He has told everybody who would listen that the Z ward is nothing. Jack will take care of it, and meanwhile he has bigger fish to fry. I have not had a chance to ask Jack in private what he thinks about it. I can only imagine after the conversations we all have had about going other side that he cannot be pleased. The Z ward is a prison sentence, a life sentence…or, more appropriately, since the Z-sters are in there for good, a death sentence. Beyond our old fears, the rumored methods of the new Alzheimer's doctor are chilling to even think about. But the truth is, we Old Bunchsters are not the same people we were a few days ago. We are somehow advanced; we are not exactly sure what has changed, but we know it is something new and big and amazing and true. We are not just imagining things here.

But we are in the tour mode here at Burro Flats. As we are being moved right along, Mason energetically points out hard-to-imagine details under a grove of gnarled old oak trees. "This was the Chumash Kitchen."

My pal Millie gives the area a skeptical look. "Doesn't look like a kitchen to me. Looks like an outdoor forest. What do you say, George?"

"Forest," George nods and agrees. "Big enchanted forest. Surprised Walt Disney didn't turn it into a theme park for fairies and such."

Delrina nods. "Put in Neanderthal Land right over there." She points to the dark cliff face with the chalk stick man on it. She has her hand idly linked in Herbert's arm. He is not paying attention to anybody. His eyes flick around, looking for something or someone in the distance. I swear, he does seem to be standing straighter, with less curve in that old spine of his.

Mason waves one arm in a half circle, indicating the gnarled old stand of trees around us. "These oaks look ancient, but most are probably the children and grandchildren of the trees that fed the Indians."

"Trees don't feed people," George says.

"Acorns," Mason says. "The Indians ground up the acorns to make a type of unleavened flat bread."

"Man cannot live on bread alone," Millie says.

"Let them eat cake!" Delrina sings out merrily.

"No," Mason says, refusing to let his lecture disintegrate into joke time. "Millie is right. In the summer, the whole tribe migrated away from here through Topanga Canyon and they would spend the summer fishing. But in the winter, the weather at the coast was bad and they would trek back in here to harvest the acorns. And they hunted deer and rabbits."

Jack tries to get Mason's attention. "Look at this string of notches." He points to a flat stone that has a line of half-inch holes in it.

Mason puzzles over it for a moment. "Probably the rock wore away like that."

"No, I don't think so. Look at this."

Before the orderly can stop him, Jack breaks a small twig off a tree. "Don't worry, Mason, it's just a dead branch." Jack breaks the twig and sticks pieces in the holes.

"But what?"

Jack smiles patiently. I can see what a good teacher he must have been. He points to a distant ridge to the east of us. "The sun comes up over there, Mason. Right through that crack in the rock. Each day the shadows move a little bit this way. He points to one of the holes that has a line scratched in the rock surface to indicate it is somehow special. "I bet that is planting day."

Mason's face lights up. "Jack, that's wonderful!"

"Yes, it is, Mason. Yes it is."

Mason rushes around to gather Melody and some of the other guests to share the discovery.

We move a little away from the hubbub and I am walking along with Jack, Herbert and DoubleSpin. The strange fellow from some other edge of the galaxy asks me in the mind-speak way we have, *How do I look, Lucy Weiler?*

I am not sure exactly how to tell him the bad news about his complexion problems, but, like my daddy always told me, honesty is the best policy, and so I say, "Like a blueberry talking head." He looks so troubled that I forget I do not have to say the words out loud.

DoubleSpin's lips tremble and I am starting to think that maybe honesty is not the best policy after all. I tell him, *I meant no personal offense.* But I can see it is not simply a question of his vanity.

He says, *I don't know how much longer they will let me stay.*

Delrina scoffs at me. "No, Lucy, acorns! I didn't hear Mason say anything about blueberries."

In that moment I get a good sense of how Jack's been feeling over the past months, carrying on two conversations at the same time. The whole thing is odd because apparently Delrina can only hear my thoughts when I direct them at her.

DoubleSpin nods at me, *Of course it has to work that way. Your intent is your tuner. Otherwise your brain would be crushed by a thousand thoughts all at once.*

Mason looks over at us and I am worried; even with my new tuner capabilities, two or three conversations at the same time could get out of hand.

Jack sees my predicament and tries to cover up the fact that now I am talking to invisible people, too. He claps Delrina on the back. "Maybe it is cactus pears, Del. Mason said there was a lot of cactus."

Arthur the Letch, trying to walk along with Jack and me, trips over a rock and goes sprawling in a heap. He is not hurt, but the rock turns out to be one of the round grinding stones and this is another pretty rare discovery, and so it takes Mason's attention away from us.

The Stranger tugs Jack's arm. "Jack, Jack – we have to talk."

Herbert pauses next to a half-dead old oak tree. I can see he is looking to get a little distance between himself and the main group. It is a good moment for him because Mason's attention is still on the grinding stone. Mason is pretty sure he has found the exact kitchen groove that stone once fit into.

Melody looks back at us, but Jack waves her on. "Lu and I will stay with Herb. He's tired. We'll catch up to you guys in a minute."

Meanwhile, Herbert is taking the opportunity to talk a mile a minute on his cell phone, "Well, damn it, how can you get lost? There's nothing here to get lost from! Jack, tell these guys."

Things are suddenly very busy in Jack's life. The Stranger is pulling at his arm, I am trying to keep an eye on what is going on, and Herbert has handed him the cell phone. Jack motions for DoubleSpin to hold on a moment and nods to me for pretty much the same reason as he takes the phone from Herbert.

"Yeah, Herbert's pal Jack here. Oh, the Nigerian Prince!" Jack can't resist a half snort of amusement. "Hey, Prince, how goes things in the kingdom?"

Even as he speaks, Jack takes a look around. He spots three men sitting in a patch of shade under a tree across a small ravine. "Look, Prince, you're going to be okay. I can see you guys from here. You're less than a quarter mile away. Look towards the sun. We're under the big oak that's split in two, looks like half a giant green bush. Right. That's me waving...right."

Jack hands Herbert his phone. "They'll be along. We can wait here, if you want."

Mason yells at them. He has caught up to the main group. With some effort, he is carrying the round grinding rock they found, and he does not want to have to come back for Jack, Herbert and me. He yells at us, "What's holding you guys up?"

Jack smiles. "Mason hasn't been doing his daily workouts." He cups his hands and yells back in Mason's direction, "We're tired, Mason. We're going to take a snack break here. We'll be there in five or ten."

Even at this distance I can see our friendly orderly and guide's face clouding up. "Well, okay, but we have a whole bunch more to discover. We haven't even seen the cave paintings yet."

That perks my attention. I cup my own hands and yell, "How far is that?"

"Less than a mile. Scouts honor!" Mason crosses his heart.

Delrina gives out a sigh, "Can't I see this on National Geo?" She winks at me. *Anything to help the cause.*

I yell at our intrepid orderly, "If we do not rest now, Delrina might need a stretcher or something."

Like I figure he will, Mason caves. "Okay, we'll take a break. We'll wait for you here."

Herbert frantically pulls at Jack's arm. "Jack. Jack! What did they say about the money?"

"One guy's bringing it. It's in an aluminum case. Look, I'll be a minute."

Jack looks around for DoubleSpin, who is sitting nearby on the low branch of an oak tree, puffing like he is about to explode. His face is stained a deep blue like the faces of the men in the Blue Man Group with their famous act at the Luxor in Las Vegas.

"Okay, DoubleSpin, what's going on here?"

"They're pulling me back. No grav left. I'm running on empty. We've only got a few minutes."

Herbert has tagged after and wants Jack's attention. "Jack, Jack!"

Jack looks to me for help. "Lu?"

He does not have to say more than my name; I take Herbert by the arm and firmly lead him away, talking like a stern schoolteacher. As we walk away, I hear DoubleSpin say, "I've never tried to fight it before." I sneak a look over my shoulder and DoubleSpin is shaking so violently that it looks like he might disintegrate.

Jack shakes his head. Too much is happening at the same time. "Jesus...!" he exclaims.

Herbert and I are standing ten feet away. Herbert is looking back at his buddy Jack. He whispers to me, "You think he really sees Jesus Christ Lord Almighty?"

"Herbert! Shush!"

"Dag nab it!" he says in frustration.

Herbert is on a very short fuse today. The Old Viking is finding it impossible to stay still for thirty seconds. He looks around, and he is not seeing the people he was supposed to meet. He rips open his lunch bag and pulls out an apple. Disgusted, he throws it to the ground.

"Jack!"

I have to take Herbert's arm and pull him away. "Let's walk to meet your friends," I tell him. "That's what you want, isn't it?"

Back by the tree, Jack reaches out and places a hand on DoubleSpin's shoulder. "Maybe you have to accept it," he tells him.

"No!"

"You came here for a reason."

The strange being seems terrified, and Jack tries to find words to comfort him, "You're being called to do something greater."

"But this will ruin me! I haven't succeeded, and we're out of time. You all are out of time!"

"I'll finish up for you."

"You don't know what you're saying!"

"Have faith in me, little blue face from outer space."

The Stranger does not stop shaking, but a grim smile lights his features. "Jack, when you talk like that, I almost think you could. You've come a long way, my friend."

"Let's give it a shot, DoubleSpin. I'm the best you've got here."

"I would have to jump you a few levels…I don't even know if I could."

"Don't give me that dimensional crap. You look terrible. Just elevate my crap or whatever and get on out of here. I've got your back…wherever it is."

"Let me give you what I can." DoubleSpin closes his eyes. His body goes totally still as if he is meditating. He floats in the air for a moment, and then he begins to fade.

Jack says, "I don't feel any different."

"Remember, it has nothing to do with gravity. It's all about intent and willpower. Harmonics might help."

"Right. Harmonics. Got it, chief!" Jack gives him a smart little salute.

"Jack Hamlin saves the world," the strange being says. He smiles as he fades into thin air. "Stranger things have probably happened in the galaxy, though I don't know where or when."

Jack reaches out, but DoubleSpin is gone. With a last look back at the spot his strange alien friend vacated, he turns away and catches up to us. Herbert has been digging further in his lunch sack, but he stops and stares accusingly at Jack. "Jack, where are they?"

Jack eyes the bag in Herbert's hands. "You going to eat your peanut butter sandwich?

Herbert looks at him. "Jack, you hate peanut butter."

"So do you." He takes the peanut butter sandwich out of Herbert's bag.

I am puzzled by Jack's behavior, but he does not look sick, just maybe a little dazed and out of it, which is normal for the old Jack but maybe not this one.

"Is everything okay?"

"He's gone, Lucy."

"Gone for good?"

"I'd be surprised if he came back." Jack takes a big bite out of the peanut butter sandwich. He seems annoyed by the taste. "Disgusting! Maybe it didn't take…oh well, make the best of it. I never liked castor oil, either." He grimaces and takes another big bite.

The two of us are alone. We look at each other, thinking the same thing.

"Where's Herbie?" we say at the same moment.

Forty nine

I spot the Old Viking about fifty yards from us just as
he is hot-footing his way around a big grey boulder. He
has found his contact, the Prince of *Africanus Rex* or
wherever, and Jack and I hurry to join their group of five
suspicious looking characters. There is a puffy, self-
important black man in a trim khaki outfit, a narrow-eyed
Mid-eastern looking guy in a dark suit and a younger black
fellow in a purple hat and tiger-stripe lounge pants. My
first impression is that, if this is an up and coming young
prince, royalty has come down a notch or two. Finally
there are two young guys who look like thugs or street gang
people. The purple-hatted prince is carrying an aluminum
case and huffing more than the others. He looks like he has
taken some punches to the face. As we join them, Herbert
gives us a triumphant ear-to-ear grin. The Old Viking
looks like he is in his crowning moment, a man who is
ready to join the royal circle of the super-rich by signing
off on the deal of a lifetime.

"Herbert?" The black fellow in the battered velvet hat
extends one hand for a polite handshake.

"Prince Bukamba!" Herbert yells, and engulfs him in a
big hug. "Good to see you, your Excellency!"

The Prince seems uncomfortable, as if he is not used to
displays of affection from commoners. "I know I do not
look at my best right now. I am not used to such physical
exertion in these mountains of California."

Herbert waves this off. "Oh, I don't care about that. Did you bring my money?"

"Half of it," the black man in the khakis says. He has a golden eagle colonel's insignia pinned on his shoulders. I am thinking that makes him about as much a real colonel as Goozeman is an actual doctor, but nobody asks me.

"Well...where's the other half?" Herbert growls; he is clearly still on the prowl for his millions.

Charles pulls out of his grasp, steps back and puts on a haughty look that might resemble the way Nigerian royalty treats commoners like us. "Trust, Herbert. Trust. We have a deal. Remember, 'The Old Viking rides again.' You come through on your end, we come through on ours."

The two thugs are more rough-and-tumble than royal aides; I have the impression they are looking for any excuse to tear us apart. In fact, it is my impression that everybody in the Prince's group is eyeing us like hungry jackals examining a few tasty rabbits.

But if Herbert is intimidated, he is not showing it. The Old Viking returns the Prince a look of haughty disdain of his own, frowns and then lowers his bushy eyebrows. When he speaks it is with a crafty sense of measured reserve, "Yeah gentlemen, but I already have done my part. The Cyclops is already unloaded. Our shipment is waiting on the dock and you already double-crossed me with two containers for the price of one."

This moment of negotiation is interrupted by a distant shout. "Hey, you guys! Let's get going!" Mason yells.

The Colonel's hand automatically slides inside his open jacket. Even a novice murder mystery reader like me can see he has a gun.

Charles places a hand on his arm, "No need, sir. Everything is in order. This is right, is it not, Herbert?"

"Let's see the money," the Old Viking grumbles unhappily. "I'll be the judge of that."

I am not sure this will be enough, so I send the thought *Everything is going to be alright. Don't be a stupid blithering fool from Benin.* Our man in Khaki looks a little bewildered, but his hand drifts away from his jacket.

Charles cracks open the metal case. It is filled with what appears to be neatly stacked bundles of 100 dollar bills.

We hear Mason calling us from the distance, "Fellows, let's go! The cave paintings are waiting!"

Herbert ignores the call. He cannot take his eyes off the money. He smiles and says softly, "Okay. A deal's a deal."

Maloof frowns. "Exactly where is our shipment, Herbert?"

Herbert fishes in all his pockets. "Jack…I wrote some notes on a piece of paper when we were at that McDonald's."

"Right," Jack says. "Something about Pier 53."

"That's it! Pier 53. We're okay."

"Hey, you guys!" It is Mason, our trusty orderly, retracing his steps to see what sort of trouble his delinquents have gotten into. If he only knew!

I hurry over to slow him down a bit with a question about the cave paintings. "Is it true the Chumash used chalk they found in an outcropping near here?"

Mason pulls out the color pages he printed off the internet to show me that yes, there is a place even today known as Chalk Hills.

I can see over Mason's shoulder that the Arab looks nervous. The Prince in the shabby purple hat is hastily closing up the suitcase, but the Colonel has his automatic pistol half drawn.

Herbert grins at the Arab and confidently claps him on the back. He does not even see the Colonel's pistol. "Pier 53," he says in a loud whisper. "Seven thirty or eight. We'll be there with a truck."

This makes the Colonel unhappy. I am thinking he is a control freak. "Shouldn't we bring the truck?" he suggests.

Herbert shakes his head. "Yeah, sure. They are going to let the likes of you in there with a truck! No, fellows, you just figure out how to get yourselves in."

Maloof nods. "Okay. You bring truck, Mister Old Viking. It is all settled."

Mason finishes up informing me about the chalk and we join Herbert and his small group.

"What's going on here, guys? Who are these fellows?

"Just another bunch of amateur tourists like us," Jack tells him. "They got lost. We're showing them the way to hike back out."

Mason is about to accept Jack's explanation when he sees the suitcase.

"What's that?"

"Tenderfeet," Jack says. "They didn't have a knapsack."

"They carried a suitcase out here?"

"Yeah, stupid, huh?" Herbert says. The Colonel looks angry enough to kill.

I send him the thought, *You don't need to kill anybody here. You don't want the police.*

"Don't worry," Jack assures Mason. "We'll help them carry it. Herbert takes the opportunity to wrestle the metal suitcase from the Prince. Mason eyes them for a moment, and then accepts his role as the tour guide. "Sure…okay. You guys are welcome to join us. You're going to like this! You are about to lay your eyes on wonderful cave paintings that date back to before Europeans came to California!"

Mason grabs the Colonel's arm as they walk toward the main Chermundo group. "You'll be among the lucky few who get to see rare examples of Chumash Indian cave paintings of Coyote throwing stars across the heavens. It's the medicine man's grotto. The holy man of the tribe, you know? The keeper of the legends. The only reason it still survives is this area was fenced off by the government back around World War II."

The Colonel walks along without causing a scene; he still wants to shoot Mason but he realizes there are too many witnesses. Charles smiles; he is relieved and so very happy to still be among the living.

Jack sees Charles's expression. "He can't kill everybody, can he?"

Charles shakes his head. "No, my friend. But he would if he could."

Unfortunately for the easy resolution of our world-saving problems, at about this same time back in the Z ward at the Chermundo, the cleaning lady is discovering Herbert's revolver in Jack's toilet tank. She holds the dripping bag up with two fingers and gives it a distasteful grimace. "Aiii Caramba and Holy Moley!" she says.

Bella comes in just in time to see her holding the dripping bag with the gun inside, "Maria, what? *Oh-my-God!*"

In the next half hour, Harvey Goozeman, who has been hoping against hope that Herbert and Jack's lawyer will fall off a cliff in the mountains, is trying hard to hide his joy. His two new Z-sters caught with a concealed weapon! He gets on the phone to alert the local police. In under a half hour an LAPD squad car pulls up to the Chermundo with its lights blazing. One of the police officers traces the registration number on the weapon from the computer in their car and they find that it is legally registered to one Herbert Miller.

"But we expressly forbid firearms here at the Chermundo Villas," Goozeman pretends to protest in outrage.

"That's not our problem," the officer assures him. "Mr. Miller has the right to own it and it was not loaded. No bullets."

"But—we simply cannot have our guests running around with guns!" Harvey sputters.

The officer shrugs. "If you have something like that in his lease, I suppose you can boot him."

That does not make Goozeman any happier. His mission is to fill the Z ward, not empty it. He is even less thrilled when three federal agents show up in an unmarked car. They are looking for the president of Old Viking Shipping, and they tell the director they believe Herbert Miller is involved in an illegal business deal with national security implications.

Fifty

Meanwhile back at Burro Flats I get pesky Arthur the
Letch to use my camera to take pictures of the Old Bunch
with our hands raised in the V for Victory gesture. We are
standing next to each other with the cave paintings in the
background. We are hot, sweaty and happy as we troop
back to the bus. When Arthur hands me back my camera, I
direct him over towards Tangle Toes Tillie. *She's really
kind-of sweet on you, Artie.* Having powers is certainly
helping with my brush off techniques. Way to go, Lu-
babes! I compliment myself, figuring nobody else will, but
Millie and Delrina are both grinning at me. *You go girl!*

Jack now has the aluminum suitcase under one arm.
He boards the bus and I climb the three metal steps right
behind him. It looks like we are the last ones in. Mason
checks us off his list, at which point he discovers Herbert is
missing. Everybody else is on the bus.

Mason figures maybe he just forgot to check him off,
but it is his job to make sure. "Herbert? Herbert!" He
climbs off the bus and yells into the brushy area
surrounding the cave with its paintings of fireballs in the
sky and crafty old coyote scattering stars across the Milky
Way. I find myself wondering if DoubleSpin's folks had a
hand in sowing that legend in prehistoric minds. But Mason
is getting no positive results in his effort to locate the Old
Viking. Our trusty orderly climbs back on the bus and
hurries down the narrow aisle for a last check. "Herbert?
Herbert?!"

Mason gives Jack and me an accusing frown. "He was with you two. Lucy, where is Herbert?"

I feel sorry for Mason, but we have an earth to save. I shrug. "His new friends said they would give him a lift."

Mason looks near to panic. "That's against—you can't—he can't."

Jack looks up at Mason with his patented mild-mannered smile. "Nobody tells Herbert anything, Mason. You know that. He's like a mule."

I tell Mason, *Everything will be alright,* and that seems to calm him down.

Events have moved swiftly back in the Z ward at the Chermundo since the maid found the 38 revolver hidden in Jack's bathroom. Goozeman is thinking maybe it was Herbert's pistol and maybe it wasn't, but it will be a good chance to sew a little confusion in the ranks of the enemy. Before he's through, he hopes to have the two of them locked down as permanent residents in the Alzheimer's side of the home. He phones Jack's daughter Emily and tells her she would do well to come right over because Herbert and her dad have created a situation.

Emily in turn has had the presence of mind to call Dick Burkle. In under an hour they are seated in Humphrey Goozeman's office with Doctor Daniel, nurse Bella and the maid who discovered the firearm with two angry federal agents who are taking this situation more seriously than Emily believes is warranted.

"But my father doesn't own a gun," she protests. "He is clearly not implicated in whatever is going on here. He signed a petition promoting the Brady Bill."

"Not that you know of." The agent sitting closest to her gives her a doubting look.

Emily is not used to men she does not know acting superior and contradicting her. She barks angrily, "Look, I don't know what you're getting at!"

Dick Burkle places a hand on her shoulder. "Calmness here, Emily. They are just doing their job."

Emily shakes his hand away. "You calm down yourself, Dick Detective! This is my father we're talking about!"

The second federal agent gives Dick a cold stare. "Who are you?"

"Family friend," Dick says, and now he is frowning. He is not that far removed from his Military Police days, where he was in command and not likely to be answering questions."

Emily blurts out, "He's a private investigator. He's looking out for my father." She doesn't understand how these people think, and she has said too much in the wrong direction. The federal agents look at each other.

"Which is it?" one asks Dick.

"Why does he need a P.I.?" the other asks.

"It's both," Dick says. "And my client's needs are confidential." His tone implies it is none of their business.

"I'll bet they are," one of the feds sneers.

Dick tries to talk common sense with Goozeman, "You found an unloaded firearm in the toilet tank. That is in no way a federal offense."

"It is illegal to – " Dr. Goozeman starts to speak, but both federal agents hold up hands at the same time to silence him.

The agent closest to Emily gives her a hard look. "We have reason to believe your father is operating as part of a vicious international terrorist ring."

"What??"

"He and his partner, Herbert Miller are in association with known criminals, mass murderers and terrorists.

"That's impossible..." Emily is stunned into silence.

Even Goozeman is flabbergasted. If that charge proves to be true, Jack and Herbert will be guests in a federal penitentiary for the rest of their lives. But that is not his real problem. Goozeman's mind is churning; he sees the bad publicity could ruin any chances he might have to sell Chermundo Villas for a top price. "I have to agree with the lady, that is more than a little outside reality! Between the two of them, Herbert Miller and Jack Hamlin couldn't terrorize a cocker spaniel."

Goozeman's protest is interrupted as Mason enters, escorting Jack. Both of them still wear their yellow daypacks and Jack is carrying the aluminum suitcase full of money.

Mason sits down in the nearest chair and wearily wipes his forehead with a paper tissue. "You wanted to see us?"

Dr. Daniel looks out the open doorway behind Jack. "Where is Herbert?"

Jack smiles. "Not here." He closes the door behind him. "Emily! Pleasant surprise!"

"Where is Herbert Miller?" one of the agents repeats the question.

Jack eyes them for a moment before saying anything, "Herbert is among the missing."

Dr. Daniel picks up the damp bag containing the revolver. He holds it away from him with two fingers as if it might have an infectious disease. "Jack – is this your gun?"

"No. I don't own a gun. Ask Emily, here."

The agent's ignore Emily. One of them yells at Jack, "Do you know whose gun it is?!"

"Who the hell are you?"

"Federal agents."

"Huh. Where did you find the revolver?" Jack gives it a closer look. "What is it, a Luger?"

"Nice try, fella," the agent scoffs. "Not even close."

"One of the maids found it in your room," Dr. Daniel says.

"We'll do the talking here," agent says.

"My old room or my new room?" Jack asks.

"Your new room," Dr. Daniel says before the agent can stop him.

The government man slaps the palm of his hand on the table to show his irritation. "So you're telling us that firearm belonged to the person who was in that room before you?"

"I'm not telling you anything. I don't know who owns it."

"So what's in the suitcase?"

"Money. Supposed to be a million dollars."

Emily barks at him, "Dad, this is serious!"

"Well, I haven't counted it, Em."

Emily bites her lip and looks around the room.

"Open the suitcase, Jack," one of the agents orders.

"I'm afraid I can't do that."

"Why not?"

"Not me. What if it's wired to explode?"

The agents both reach for their cell phones. They look at each other and then one punches in a number. After a few seconds, a third agent enters the room and gingerly takes the aluminum suitcase.

Jack holds up one hand. "That's Herbert's money."

One of the agents makes a deprecating sound with his lips. "Right. We'll see that he gets it back. Even if we have to shred it first."

Jack shrugs, pointing to a camera mounted in a corner of the office. "Take a bow. You are stealing a private citizen's money on closed circuit television."

The federal agent stands on a chair and rips the camera off the wall. "Jesus! We're all on the same side, here!"

This angers Goozeman. "You're going to have to pay to for that!"

Dr. Daniel leans over to Mason. "Where is Herbert?"

"He got a ride with some friends of his."

"What friends?" one of the agents asks.

Mason looks at Jack, who eyes his daughter as if to say he is not responsible for any of this. "Well, there was a beat-up guy in a velvet purple hat who says he is Nigerian royalty, a Prince of some sort…and a dorky but mean looking little fellow in khaki threads that they called the Colonel, and an even more scary guy in a dark suit And two punks with a lot of tattoos."

This upsets the federal agents. They stand and lean over Jack as if they are willing to beat answers out of him.

"Where did they go?"

"Where are they now?"

Emily clenches her fists. "Stop bullying my dad! Can't you see he doesn't know anything?

Jack smiles at his daughter. "Thanks, Em, but I'm alright. They said they were headed for L.A. Harbor."

Everybody in the room stares at Jack.

"Herbert used to run a company called Old Viking Shipping. He kept his license up, even after he retired."

"And?"

"And those guys are paying him a lot of money to bring in some cargo.

"What kind of cargo? Come on, fellow, do we have to pull it out of you?"

"I don't know what it is. Herbert thinks it's gold and red diamonds and ivory tusks."

The agents are not happy. One of them activates his cell phone. The other groans and looks around the table as if anybody there can help, or at least try to be a little sympathetic, "That's twenty miles of wharfs and warehouses."

Jack pulls two slips of paper from his pocket. It is the Jack-In-The-Box receipt and a crumpled notepaper on which Herbert has scribbled his reminders, "Here's the pier number. Maybe we've got time. My guess is Herbert will drag his feet."

The closest agent snatches the paper from his hand, "We've got time. You don't. You're not going anywhere. He looks at Goozeman. "You said this guy is in your Alzheimer's ward?"

The diminutive administrator nods. "Yes, he is."

Emily indignantly stands. "My dad is not an Alzheimer's patient!"

"And leave it up to you fellows not to screw things up?" Jack asks.

"Nobody asked you, pal," the agent says. "We'll come back for him."

"He'll be here," Humphrey Goozeman says.

Jack shakes his head as the two federal agents leave, "I don't think so."

He turns away from the group remaining at the table and stares at the wall.

Goozeman orders Dr. Daniel, "Get Mr. Jack Hamlin out of here. What if word of this hits the local news?" He looks at Emily. "We'll sue your family."

"My dad does not have Alzheimer's," she angrily repeats.

Dr. Daniel takes Jack gently by the arm, "Seeing invisible people again, Jack?

Jack gets to his feet, offering no resistance to the doctor, "No, Doctor Daniel," he says. "I see possibilities, courses of action, things to do and things not to do. Later, Em. Later, Dick. Thanks for coming. Hope you enjoyed the show." He waves to his daughter as Dr. Daniel conducts him from the room.

Jack has been staring at the bulletin board on the wall. It is covered with photos of guests and their families, with thank you letters, with directives and with the rotating list of code numbers that unlock the doors to the Alzheimer's unit. Nobody with normal human eyes could read that fine print from that distance, and nobody with a normal human brain could be expected to memorize the entire page at a single glance.

Fifty one

The piers, warehouses and truck yards of Los Angeles harbor can look as cold and forbidding as any military installation. Herbert, up to his old tricks, scratches his head and looks around in puzzled dismay. He points to the nearest semi-truck cab. "Maybe this one?"

The Colonel has his hand on the automatic pistol inside his khaki jacket. "I say kill him now."

Maloof gives Herbert a less-than-friendly shove. "My colleague is losing patience with you, Herbert."

This clarifies matters for the Old Viking, who realizes he can probably stall no longer. "No, no, no, now I remember. I am sure it is this one over here."

He leads them to a red truck cab, and gestures they are to climb in.

"You first," the Colonel growls, opening the door and half pushing and half lifting him up into the cab. After a moment of fussing around, Herbert finds the keys under the seat pad.

"Ahaa!" He triumphantly holds up the keys and then fires the engine.

Charles gives him a skeptical look. "You are not going to drive this by yourself?"

"Don't be such a ding dang dandy-hopper, Prince. Hike up your pantaloons and climb on board – The Old Viking rides again!"

Jack is sitting alone in his new room in the Z ward when two unwelcome visitors arrive. It is Mumzey, accompanied by the dour Doctor Culbert, whom the staff and guests at the Villas have wasted no time in nicknaming Evil Doctor Stork.

"Oh, hi Stork. Hi Mumbles." Jack gives them a little wave. He seems listless and as drifty as ever.

Mumbles looks at the tray of needles in his hand. This is going to be the easiest stick of the century.

"Why is everyone calling me 'Stork'?" Doctor Culbert asks.

"Because that is your name?" the head orderly answers.

"That-is-not-my-name! And I wasn't asking you. Why is everyone calling me by a derogatory nickname, Jack?"

Jack's smile lightens a little. "Because I told them to," he answers. The Stork quickly realizes that the sane world of his former reality is crumbling around him.

"You're certainly looking for an overdose, Mister Hamlin." He nods to Mumfrey, who is neatly injecting himself with one of the needles. Another needle, already empty, hangs from his arm.

Culbert cannot believe what he is seeing. "Mumfrey, you idiot! What are you doing?"

"My j-j-job," the head orderly manages to stammer before he collapses.

"You!" Doctor Culbert's eyes go wide in amazement. His brows furrow as he struggles to fight off an idea in his head. *You are no longer Doctor Culbert. You are Doctor Strangelove, and your left hand wishes to present you with a gift.*

"No!" Culbert shouts as his right arm snakes out to grab his left wrist. *Oh yes, Doctor Strangelove. Oh yes!* The Stork is powerless against the allure of the senseless crazy idea taking over his will, and the needle that stabs him in the chest is quickly followed by a second and then a third. He glares at Jack as he crumples and falls on the floor next to Geoff Mumfrey.

As night gathers on the street out in front of the Chermundo Villas retirement home, Emily is sitting in her car, a late model Toyota. She does not want to leave, but visiting hours are over for the Z ward, and she cannot come up with a plan to help her dad. Dick Burkle stands by the open driver's side window, reluctant to leave her.

Emily pounds the steering wheel with both hands. "I don't know what to do!"

"Jack is not mixed up in this. It's that Herbert."

"You don't know that!"

"Common sense tells me he isn't. And you know it, too."

"Well…yes…okay. Okay." She tries to collect her thoughts. "I'm sorry I yelled at you, Dick…but I can't think what we can do about any of this now. Maybe Tom Fennerman knows a good criminal lawyer. They'll catch Herbert and you know he'll implicate Dad. Dad is just living in his other world. He's gotten to where things are just... too... complicated."

Emily's sentence slows to a halt. She can do nothing more than stare. Her father appears at the front door of the main entrance to the Chermundo Villas and starts walking in their direction.

Jack gives Dick a friendly pat on the shoulder. "Hi there, Burkle." He gets in the back seat of Emily's car.

A taxi pulls up behind them.

Jack taps his daughter's shoulder, "Emily, move over. Let Dick drive."

"Dad…how did you get out?"

"A four number code unlocks the doors, and they use the same code on the whole corridor. They change it every day...even though, if you're in the Z unit, they presume you can't count past three. Come on, Dick – let's go."

"Go?" Emily asks, "Go where?"

"L.A. Harbor."

Emily locks the car doors from the driver's seat. She is not moving over and Dick cannot get in.

"Dad, I'm not taking you anywhere."

"I think I agree with you, Em. Probably too dangerous, anyway."

The lock on his door clicks open. Jack gets out of the car, and firmly closes the door.

Emily pounds the arm rest on her door. "But I locked…"

"Take care of her, Dick. Love you, Em."

Jack gets in the taxi that is still parked behind her car and the taxi pulls away.

It takes a beat before Emily realizes what is happening. "Dick! Stop him!"

But the doors are all still locked and Dick cannot get in. Once she unlocks them, she fumbles for the keys, and they fall to the floor. Dick finally opens the door and gets in, but she is still feeling around on the floor for her keychain. She almost finds them but they scoot further under the seat. When she finally grabs them and hands them to Dick he drops them and they have to start all over. Meanwhile, Jack's taxi is moving further and further down Ventura Boulevard away from them.

Jack grins at his cabby. "Hey, I'll give you a hundred bucko's if you make sure nobody follows us."

"You got it, boss!"

Fifty two

Like some impossible, terrible implosion, the footage of disaster running backwards, the unlikely terrorist plot that DoubleSpin warned us about is beginning to come together at Pier 53 in Los Angeles Harbor. Herbert is showing the three fellows from Nigeria that he actually can drive a semi-truck cab, after a fashion. He pulls the cab to a jerking halt in front of a battered red container. "Okay, three wise men, there's the first container. The other one is over there, parked exactly a hundred yards away, just like you ordered. Now where's the rest of my money?"

"One moment, please," Maloof tells him.

Herbert jumps down from his side of the truck. The Colonel, Maloof and Charles exit from their side and warily approach the first cargo container. The Colonel skeptically eyes the trailer truck cab.

"And how do you expect us to get our containers on this truck?" Maloof asks.

"I suppose you need a big fork lift. That's not my problem."

The Colonel takes out his automatic pistol and begins screwing a long silencer on the end. "No, Herbert Miller, this most certainly is your problem."

Even this modern version of the Old Viking has his limits, and Herbert goes bug-eyed at the sight of the gun. "W-wait a minute...you can't expect...I mean...that's not in our agreement."

The Colonel tightens the silencer to his satisfaction. He raises it, aims it point blank at Herbert's right eye.

Herbert babbles on as if his life is at stake, which it is. "B-but it's the middle of the night. Nobody just has fork lifts out here. Tomorrow morning it will be easy.

Maloof shakes his head, no. "We cannot wait until tomorrow. And we cannot take these two containers together, so it is two trips from here to downtown Los Angeles."

The Colonel frowns, considering the problem, "What if we use the truck to push the two containers together?"

"What, *here?*"

"Yes, here. We attain critical mass; we take out the biggest harbor in West United States." Maloof considers the idea, studying the distance between the two containers.

Herbert shakes his head, "This truck will never be able to – "

"*Shut up!* Shoot him! I can't think!"

But before the Colonel can raise his gun to shoot Herbert, Jack walks out of the shadows.

"Hi, Herb."

"J-J-Jack! Jack, boy am I ever glad to see you!"

Jack talks as if the three Nigerians aren't there, "I told you these were bad guys, Herbie. Nigerian scam artists, I said. Look at them. This guy's no Prince. And this guy's just a military murderer. Jack sizes up Maloof. "This guy…"

"Kill him!" Maloof urges the Colonel. The pistol with the big silencer moves in Jack's direction.

"That would be really foolish."

"And why is that so?"

Jack points to a nearby bulk, "There's a fork lift under that tarp. And I know how to drive it."

Herbert frowns at his friend, "Jack, you can't drive a fork lift."

"I've jumped a few levels, Herbie. I can drive anything."

Maloof signals the ever-eager Colonel to put down his weapon. "Show us," he says.

Jack goes over to the forklift and pulls off the tarp. He climbs in and starts the engine. He puts the lifter in gear and asks, "What now?"

"Change of plans," Maloof says. "We do it here and now. Lift this container and move it over next to that one." Maloof indicates the second container.

Jack is not the master driver of forklifts that he has said, but he does manage to get the prongs under the closest container. He hoists it a foot off the ground and spins the fork-lift in a small half circle. He is about to head for the second container when a half dozen federal agents step out from behind nearby containers.

"Hold it right there!"

"Federal Marshalls!"

Back at Chermundo, the minute we get word that Jack and Herbert have escaped from the Z ward, I get a mental fix on Jack. He is heading south on the 405 freeway. Who knew the Old Bunch had GPS in our heads that we could use to track each other? Amazing! It seems we all have talents: Showboat George somehow jumpstarts the Villas Van without the keys. Delrina, Millie and I scramble on board and we take off out of there with me driving.

We show up at Pier 53 to see a stalled fork lift with a rusty red container on it about half a football field from this other red cargo container. It is an odd, nightmarish scene; bright blue zaps of charged energy are arcing between the two containers.

What a confusing situation! Our Herbie is down behind the lift like he has bricks in his butt (his words), and the Colonel and Maloof Urdveen have guns and about a dozen federal agents are shooting at them and bullets are impacting everywhere or singing off into the night sky – and like some princess of bad timing, Emily rushes into the scene, followed by Dick, who knows enough about warfare to not want to be there. The detective tries to tackle her to get her out of the line of fire, but Dick misses and Emily is just walking around, looking this way and that for her dad, and in the next second Jack is there, right in front of her getting hit by what must seem like ten or twenty bullets, only he is still standing with the crumpled bits of lead falling off him like dandruff or dead fleas.

The government men must have a thousand bullets; their guns are blasting away, and there are two young thugs who disappear as if by magic, running into the dark night as if their lives depend on it. There is a fffittt! – fffittt! - fffittt!-sound from the Colonel and Maloof's silencers. The damp dockside air is thick with gun smoke mingled with fog and the smell of powder.

I'm feeling bewildered because Jack pushes Emily toward Dick and safety, and then he disappears, only in the next moment somebody very much like him knocks the pistol from the Colonel's hand. It looks like mild-mannered Jack is the hero who saves the earth, but not yet, because Maloof has climbed into the fork lift. The Old Viking tries to stop him, but Maloof clubs him with his pistol. He grinds some gears and has it moving slowly but steadily toward the other container. It is a frightening scene; both containers are now supercharged with zaps of bluish green lightning or radiation or something that I have never seen or even had any idea existed.

But the feds know, and they rain bullets in the direction of the slowly moving fork lift.

"Stop him!"

"If those two containers get any closer!"

"It's an atomic weapon," Jack whispers to Herbert, pushing his old pal out of the way.

Emily thinks she remembers seeing the Colonel shooting again at her dad from point blank range, but in the next second Jack has used the cutting edge of his palm to dislodge the pistol and Emily remembers thinking she never knew her dad knew karate and then Dick grabbed her and pulled her behind the same crates where Herbert was trying to hide.

The two federal agents who had been at the Chermundo must have called up heavy reinforcements because it sounds like a squad of men is blasting away at the terrorists.

The Colonel is caught in the hail of bullets and his body jerks around like he is a stunt double hired to play the death scene from that "Scarface" movie starring Al Pachino.

And yet he must have wedged his foot on the pedal; the fork lift, now only inching forward at a slow crawl, still continues its relentless march toward mass destruction.

Crazy as it sounds; Jack assumes the lotus position, one of DoubleSpin's favorite positions, and he calls for the rest of the Old Bunch. Not that it matters, but later Herbert will swear that he is absolutely certain his friend is floating a foot or so off the ground, and maybe he is shining a bit with a pale yellow glow.

Although it is totally out of place in a scene that will end in the destruction of our world, Jack begins to sing, and at that same time he makes eye contact with me.

He sings, "I can only sing the middle part/ it's the only part I know."

I understand that Jack is trying to go into that place of his strength, his special power to move things with his mind. But he cannot do it alone.

The Old Bunch sings with him, as if it is the most natural thing in the world.

Showboat George sings, "I can only sing the low part/ it's the only part I know."

Millie and Delrina and I join in. "We can only sing the high parts/ they're the only parts we know..."

Then the Old Viking's quavering voice comes in on top, "But together we make music/ And music is what makes us glow!"

There is a pause, and in the next second the fork lift, along with the container on it and with Maloof Urdveen's body still in the driver's seat takes off like a rocket. It shoots straight up in the air. There is a tremendous clap of sound as what has to be the oddest projectile ever launched breaks the sound barrier, and then all we see is a bright streak in the sky that glows reddish yellow as it heads out of sight through the upper atmosphere and off into the night sky. We look at each other, feeling wonderful and yet totally exhausted at the same time. I need a hug, and I look around for my pal Jack. But I do not see him.

In all of this madness, Star-Power Charles staggers around with his hands in the air, even after being hit once in the shoulder and again in his arm. One of the federal agents slams him to the ground and stands on him, with the Nigerian protesting the entire time that he is a Prince and has diplomatic immunity. It appears his wounds are shallow and what you might call near hits, the opposite of near misses. They cuff him and haul him to his feet.

"When the royal family hears of this..." he protests.

"Yeah, right," one of the agents says. "You're the Prince of Nuka-buka-duka and we're gonna get a royal summons from deepest Africa!"

Herbert, Emily and Dick slowly get to their feet. Emily looks dazed.

Dick gives her a worried look. "Em, you alright? You're not hit?"

"No...Jack pushed me out of the way...I think."

She looks around, but cannot find her father. "Dad? Dad!!" There is no answer from Jack. There is, in fact, no Jack to be found in the area.

What happens after

Emily remembers the oddest things, disjointed parts here and there about the incident that even today are still hard for her and Dick to patch together, to figure out exactly what happened.

The two of them never understood it, not even after they got married a year or two later. For them, the memory of the events at Pier 53 will always be a patchwork of confusing moments, a chaotic bit of business, everything happening at once.

At the government debriefings, various people remember Jack on the fork lift, then the government people showing up and a lot of gunfire and the terrorist leader Maloof on the fork lift with a rusty red cargo container. And one or two of the agents remember some odd chanting or singing, or maybe it was the buzz of all that radiation pouring from the containers. Some remember the container on the fork lift taking off like a rocket. Emily was sure her father had stood between her and a hail of bullets, and she "sort of remembered" that oddly out of place singing, but that could not have been, because when everything was over, her dad was not even there. In fact, the last time she had talked to him was by her car in front of the Villas. The last thing he had said was "I love you, Emily."

Even that was a little strange. One moment he was there, having somehow gotten out of the locked Z ward, and then he found a way to get out of her locked car and the next he was speeding away in a taxi.

So Emily and Dick thought they were seeing Jack at the dock, but it could not possibly have been. Perhaps it was the tarp lying crumpled on the pier. It was dark, nobody could be sure. Whatever it was, after the shooting stopped, they rushed around looking for Jack but there was nothing but some worn bungee cords and a crumpled pile of dusty canvas. Jack, who Herbert swore had started up the fork lift; Jack, who had pushed Emily out of harm's way and taken a swarm of bullets; that Jack was nowhere to be found.

There are other loose ends. The government brain trust decided that one container must have held a rocket that took off, but then, how did it fit with the other half of the bomb that had been left behind? Where was the missing other half of the bomb needed to reach critical mass? Where had the rocket landed? Questions without answers, missing pieces of a puzzle that never would be solved.

Southern California has dodged a nuclear bullet, and, if DoubleSpin is right, the entire world has dodged it, as well.

Since the federal agents had seen Jack at the wharf, they decide and agree that he must have fallen off the pier and his body floated away. There was no blood, but since, when it is all over, he is cleared of any part of the scheme to blow up Southern California, they did not look all that hard. They even send Emily an important looking signed parchment paper with a golden seal on it for heroic citizenship and the case on Jack Hamlin is closed. I have to mess with their minds quite a bit for that one, but in the end all they remember is the one container with half a bomb, still there at Pier 53. No barbershop quartet singing, no other half rocketing off into the sky. Okay, I confess: I did have a small hand in blurring memories of that particular bit of barbershop harmony.

As for the Old Bunch, we all give our own vague interpretations of what happened, and as our stories are about like those of the federal agents, we are patted on the back and given free rides back to the Chermundo Villas.

It is some weeks later and the days are once again moving along in their mindless flow around here. What is left of the Old Bunch realizes that we are going to have to move on. If we want to, we can probably last for another week or two before the questions really start. So far, we have gotten by with the excuse that we are using new vitamins, hair color, wigs and makeup, but we are just too damn bouncy and full of energy to pass for oldsters any more.

Halloween has drifted by and the pilgrim paper decorations and pumpkins indicate our world is floating on toward Thanksgiving. One really great thing—the Villas were bought out by some trust fund, and nasty Goozeman and his henchmen are gone. Dr. Daniel is once again in charge of all medical aspects of the Villas, including the Z ward. I am certain Tom Fennerman had something to do with it, as well as getting Herbert back on the right side of Chermundo. For now, the Old Viking is back in the room he had before and his green neon sign is back up on the wall, "Old Viking Shipping."

He has contacted some of his old business associates and it looks like they still need telephone poles in Abu Dabi. Delrina has moved in the adjoining room that was Jack's, and she and Herbie are talking about getting married. The only thing holding them up is the paperwork – not the marriage license, the pre-nup, which our gal Del is insisting on. When they heard that news, George and Millie had a quiet sparkle in their eyes, and I am thinking they will be the next to tie the knot. Wedding bells are in the air; here and there and almost everywhere…even shy Mason has popped the question to Melody.

Today the gang is sitting around in the lounge area, most of us still in our best we-have-been-to-a-wake clothes. There was a memorial service for Jack, everybody had a chance to say how much they missed him and what a good guy he was. Now we are having a reception with those big platters of cheese and cold cuts from Costco, and pretzels dipped in chocolate and soft drinks all around.

Herbert raises a Diet Coke can in salute. "That Jack! You couldn't find a truer friend. And he could think up a storm, too – he had prizes on the wall proclaiming he was a champion genius math whiz."

George grins. "They gonna give you back all that money?" Georgie-Porgie has thrown out all his lounge lizard outfits and is wearing up-to-date Hollywood player gear. Millie tells me he is pitching a re-hash of one of his old screenplays around town, passing himself off as his own illegitimate son. It looks like he is having the time of his (new) life. Some of the producers and directors still in the game swear he looks like a chip off the old block. His question about the suitcases of money gets everybody's attention, and Herbie laughs in a booming way.

"They ding dang damn well better!" He lowers his voice and whispers with his best Old Viking grin, "They don't know I got the other suitcase."

That gets George's interest, "How did you do that?"

"I don't know. When I got back to my room, it was there."

"Maybe Jack…" The two men look at each other in silence; they are certain Jack was responsible but just not quite sure how.

There is a new air of freedom and optimism around here, even though I know Dr. Daniel and Mason are worried about me because they know I miss my pal Jack; they now worry about me somewhat the way we all used to fret over poor old Jack. But they do not know what to do, and I am sure it will take a week or two for them to sort at least some of it out. The truth is, they do not know what to make of any of us. The Old Bunch is just too full of juice and vigor. The after-funeral party begins to dissolve a bit; the guests drift off to their rooms and a game of blackjack starts itself up, coins all over a big, eight-person table.

Herbert is on his cell phone, and you can guess how that is going, his side of the conversation is one big hoarse whisper that a deaf man could overhear. I think I got it wrong about Herbie. Maybe he was drifting into dementia at the Villas, but he was probably always a reckless, devil-may-care entrepreneur with a cunning and devious streak. Well, he is going to be Delrina's problem, and if anybody can handle him, I would put my money on the lady with the henna hair.

I am sitting in my favorite chair, my feet up a little, and my fingers playing over the keyboard on my laptop whenever I catch the next threads of my story. It is a little hard to concentrate. Writing is not that easy, and Herb is now yelling into his cell phone.

"Don't give me that bull; you ain't no Presidential Widow! I know a little more than that...Nigeria is ruled by a prince!" he shouts.

Time goes by until I am the last guest left in the lounge. I pretend not to see Dr. Daniel standing in the doorway with his prescription pad. He is talking to Mason, and they both look over in my direction.

I suddenly see Jack is sitting on the sofa near me, just about where DoubleSpin used to sit! He is eating a peanut butter sandwich, go figure. Jack used to hate peanut butter. Here is the thing: I can see him but nobody else in the room can!

"Hey Lu," he says. "Mason's talking about you, you know."

"I know, Jack."

"How's the story coming?"

"Nobody is ever going to believe this."

"Science Fiction," he gives me a knowing look. "You'll sell a million."

Across the room, Mason and the doctor are still talking about me. They do not think I can hear them, but the new improved model of me can focus in on every little detail in the room.

Mason is saying, "I don't know; she seems distant, you know, since Jack passed." Mason has that frowning look on his face. He is a very caring person, and I know that Dr. Daniel is worried about me, as well.

"Easy to understand," the good doc says. "They were good friends."

"I guess."

"That it then?"

"Yeah, I guess…" Dr. Daniel exits. Mason starts to take his exit, then looks back and catches me talking to Jack.

Minutes pass and the lounge is deserted, except for me and Jack. Clever Mason has come back and is watching me again, and now that there is nobody else in the room, he can make out enough so that he is sure that I am talking to the invisible Jack Hamlin and I do not care.

"What did it feel like?" I ask Jack. "I mean, if you do not mind my asking?"

I take a look over at Jack, who is sort-of sitting on the Stranger's favorite sofa cross-legged and floating several inches above the sofa.

Jack scratches his head. He has probably thought a lot about this and I do not think he is holding out on me, but it looks like he does not really have a good answer. "Well, you know how, as a writer you are looking at your characters, and even if one of them is you, it's different than when in real life you are just yourself, if that makes any sense."

"In a way, I guess…"

"I'm not really here, you know."

"Oh, I know," I say, as I feel the old familiar feeling of being alone again sweep over me.

"But I'm not dead, either, Lu."

"What?!"

"I'm up here in Washington State. I bought an apple farm. A couple hundred acres.

"We had a ceremony for you, you know!" I say angrily.

"I know. I'm sorry, Lu. I couldn't help it. I had to stay with that container to be sure it hit the sun. And then I had to find my way back. I got lost and found myself in some other place. I didn't know where I was. Not earth, for sure."

"Oh." I take a deep breath, the air rushing back into my lungs.

Jack gets down on one knee…well, that is not exactly the way it was. He is actually still in the air, but I get the gesture. He says, "And I'm hoping – I mean, I don't know how to say this, so I'll just come out with it. I love you. I want to marry you. Would you like – could you find a place for me in your heart? Could you consider me?"

I am so furious with the man I could hit him with a brick. I am not one to hide my emotions, and he sees it right away. "What's wrong, Lu?"

I do not know where to start. "Jack, we are no longer the crazy young fools we once were! I am not ready to leap off cliffs of passion and dive into the surf of love or however you think of it."

"I bought a farm for you."

"For me. You bought a farm for me."

"Sure. It even has a little grove of crabby apples."

"And just why did you do that, you hopeless man?"

"That's what friends who love each other do."

"Is that what we are?"

"I hope so, Lu. Remember when you shared your story with me…I thought you got robbed of your life, the first time around. It wasn't fair, the way I see it. I thought maybe this would make you happy."

The silence extends between us for such a length of time that I think he might turn blue and explode like DoubleSpin. Or maybe I will.

"Well, I do not know about this…" I start, trying to puzzle it through in my own head. I am not going to be rushed or pushed or pressured by this self-centered idiot of a man, or any other, for that matter.

"I want to share my life with you, Lucy," he says. "I need you, but only if you want to come."

I am thinking how exasperatingly persistent men can be, and then I find words coming out of my mouth, "Maybe…maybe I could come up there just for a day or two."

"That would be a good thing," he says.

"No promises, Jack. But I could look you right in the eye and give you a chance to redeem yourself and if it feels right, you could try your miserable best to woo a girl the proper, old-fashioned way."

When I see the look of pure joy light up his face, I know I am doing the right thing. Washington is a big state, but I visualize my old pal Wheelchair Jack and a small clump of crab apple trees – and there it is, a warm and glowing home point, as steady as the North Star. I am not going to have any trouble getting there. I will not even need a road map.

While Jack and I have been talking, Mason has quietly moved across the room to stand next to us.

"Lucy...? Who are you talking to?" That startles the dickens out of me for a moment, until I realize it is just kind Mason. Looking down at me; the dear concerned man can see that I am alone.

I decide to fess up. I smile up at him. "I was just saying a few words to Jack..."

"You actually think you see Jack, or you're just talking to his memory...?"

Jack raises one hand; he has an idea – but I think we both have the same notion. I nod to Jack and turn to Mason. "Oh, his memory, I guess...Like you talk to your own Mamma sometimes, even though you know she has been dead over ten years now."

Mason nods, accepting my explanation. "Okay...good night, Lucy."

Mason turns to leave, and then turns back to face us. He cannot see Jack, but he glances past me to the blank space on the sofa, looking in the direction that I was talking. "Good night, Jack," he says, and then there is a note of whimsy in his voice as he adds a twist on an old Jimmy Durante farewell, "Good night, Mister Calabash, wherever you are!"

Jack's warm and friendly reply comes softly at him out of nowhere, "Good night, Mason."

On hearing Jack's unexpected farewell, Mason looks like he will die of fright. He turns to me for confirmation.

I just say, "Good night, Mason.

Our good orderly gives me a wide-eyed stare, and then blesses himself and backs out of the room.

Jack smiles. "DoubleSpin tells me he didn't get demoted. Earth couldn't win first place because we'd already been eliminated as a hopeless cause and they had a rule against it. But we got Honorable Mention, along with some sort of pink crystal flower trophy. Our pal DS is now a show regular."

"He deserves it. He tried hard for us."

"He's working on his show-biz look. He's got a gal-pal assistant, Verona Bandana or something like that. She's a real looker, though who knows what she looks like in real life. DoubleSpin actually has tentacles and an elephant trunk nose."

"Not really?"

"Yes, he does. But he assures me his eyes are the same." Jack's smile fades a little, "Please come and see me soon, Lu," I see Jack has been practicing his own dissolves. "I miss you," he says as he slowly fades to invisible.

And here I am, Lucy Weiler, left alone in a big room in a place where old people come to be taken care of until they die, but it is not sad for me because I am growing younger every day, and I am going to go up there and see what young Jack is all about, and with a little luck we are going to share our second spin on life together.

I will get up soon and start to make a list of things to do: packing; a talk with Tom Fennerman and another with the rest of the Old Bunch so we stay in touch; figure out some way to break the glorious news to Emily and Amanda so they will come visit us (and not be too freaked out that Grandpa Jack looks as young as his daughter); ship the furniture I got from Aunt Clara, and the rest of the things from mom and dad's farm that I have in storage; figure out how to send my novel manuscript to a publisher with some other pen-name on it, and I am going to have to change all the names and places. But for the moment I settle back in my comfortable old lounge chair. I know how to do all that work-a-day practical stuff, I tell myself. I find I am thinking – no, feeling amazed at – what a wonderful universe we live in and how little we know about it. Tomorrow will come for me and for almost everyone on the planet as well. I am in the heart of something new and big and wonderful. I will take a train up north and drive a tractor and shake apples down out of apple trees. I have an intuitive notion that Jack and I will have children, and they will be special in ways I cannot begin to describe. I am feeling certain something like that is about to happen, but for now, it is just so very great to be alive.

And now…

A special excerpt from

John Klawitter's

ORANGE GLORY
The Zoomins Must Die

Coming from
Double Dragon Publishing
In Summer 2015

ORANGE GLORY: *The Zoomins Must Die*

ONE – The late 1950's and some years later

Jesus is talking again. "Pull the trigger, Kate," he says in that softly persuasive way of his. "Pull the trigger."

Kate is out of options. She is over two months pregnant, courtesy of Grandma Lulubird Twillinger's crusty old lover, and now she has been raped again, this time by a biker gang. The work shed spins around her. She has lost too much blood. She staggers back against the big red-painted gas tank Granma Lu's crew uses to fill the tractors and the picker-crane. She doesn't have the strength to crawl into town for help. And yes, Jesus, the man-the myth-the legend, is still standing right there, watching over her with his warmly encouraging smile and flowing robes, for all the good that does anybody. He cannot possibly mean actually pull the trigger, can he? *What, shoot herself? What trigger?* There is no gun. Then what does he mean? She puzzles it out. *Do something, anything.* She grimaces, forcing herself to act, pushing back against her pain. She picks up an empty beer bottle from the floor, and then another. She carefully fills them halfway with gasoline from the tractor tank, wads dirty rags in the top, then gives each one a little shake so she can feel the cold liquid sting her fingers. She knows the pickers leave plenty of matches in the bathroom. *Fuck Jesu Christi, she's going to have to do this one by herself, just like always.*

Charley Birch touched the cute little blond girl's nose with the tip of his Rambo knife, not torturing her or anything like that, but just to get a reaction. There was none, of course, but he dutifully scribbled No Reaction on his note pad. No answer was an answer, just not the one he wanted. His mind was swarming with questions, he felt like a dull dunce in fifth grade. The girl had extraordinary pale skin and blue eyes. She was a porcelain doll, not really a human, at least not to him. Nothing made sense. The experiments were failures, all of them, and this was just one more example.

In a sudden fit of exasperation he jammed the Rambo blade through her left eye and deep in her skull. It easily slid in and exited from the back of her skull, shiny steel appearing abruptly between her golden hair. But there was no reaction, no death-jerk, no blood, and upon withdrawing the deadly knife her skin moved back to its unwounded wholeness like water in a pond. The girl was there, and wasn't there, half way in their dimension and half way somewhere else.

"I am in deep shit here," Charley muttered to himself. "I don't know how deep, but it is most certainly shit all the way."

A man in military fatigues shifted uneasily at his side. Charley knew it had nothing to do with the girl, who was simply test subject #7641f, the 'f' standing for female. The fellow was recruited from Argentina, an ex-German technician who could be trusted, in fact was trusted with a Z clearance, the one that meant if you even look funny at us, we kill you. It was lunch time, and the fellow was hungry.

"Send her to the island," Charley said with a brief nod at the motionless blond doll. "Then you can head for the mess hall."

Charley made his own way past mess to the restricted executives dining room where the food was marginally better. Ike's man showed up for lunch as planned, hungry to see where all their money was going. He wore a baggy blue suit and a pair of the thick tortoise shell plastic rim glasses that were all in vogue. Charley wrapped an arm around his thin shoulders and led him into the project projection room, where the unit cook had laid out a feast of ham-and-cheese sandwiches with crunchy pickles, bicycled over from the local deli.

They sat on uncomfortable metal chairs pulled up to a folding metal table. Charley snapped his fingers and a young fellow wearing a short crew cut, summer fatigues and the rank of a corporal clicked the lights off and started a short silent film. It was a crude black-and-white film shot in 35 millimeter. The projector clacked and on the screen appeared the image of a heavily bearded man wearing nothing but a pair of white army white briefs, He had a dirty white turban wound over his wild mass of dark hair and was standing motionless as a statue. They had other footage of women, young boys and girls, but Charley had thought this out carefully. Better to stay on point.

"That a real person?" Ike's man asked with a note of disbelief. "He's not moving. That's a manikin, right?"

"No it isn't. That's test subject #3228. They're all like that when they get in their vegetable state."

"What state is that?"

"Like that," Charley said, pointing at the screen. He didn't want to have to say he didn't know.

The footage pulled back to reveal two soldiers with M-1 rifles pointing at the fellow in the turban. Their intention was so clear that Ike's man raised one hand, but before he could protest, the soldiers fired point blank at the man. To his relief, nothing happened.

"Huh, missed," Ike's man said, feeling the knot in his stomach unwind. "Some marksmen."

"Watch now," Charley said. "We had a Mitchell hi-speed running at the same time.

The next footage was a close-up of the man's abdomen, cut off so it just showed the top of the white briefs he was wearing. Two bullets moved in slow motion toward fragile skin. They penetrated the man's body. The flesh made way and closed up behind them like pale peach jello.

"What the hell just happened there?"

"Bullets can't kill them. Or grenades. Or bayonettes."

"In-CRED-ible! Our dream of the unstoppable warrior…The President will have to see this to believe it!"

It might have annoyed Charley that Ike's man had appropriated the project as his own personal dream, but he had other problems.

"We don't know exactly how this works," he said, smoothly trying to get past the fact that nobody on the project could explain what was happening – plus the test subjects had other characteristics that made them less than ideal soldiers.

Someone other than this bureaucratic pencil-pusher from D.C. might have asked if there were problems, and, if so, how long might it be before they had a willing army of these super-warriors. But Ike's man was an appointee, not a man of science.

"We've made our big breakthrough!" he bubbled.

Charley nodded, going along with the flow. *Feed the fool his treats, take the funding and run with it.* Maybe they could fix things, claw their way out of the shit pit. He ran the footage again.

"I call them 'zoomins' because I don't think we can really look at them as ordinary human people any more. They look like humans, but they really are something else."

"They certainly are! And you can't kill them?"

Charley nodded, looking at the ice cubes floating in his tea glass rather than directly at Ike's man. "They are nearly impossible to kill. We hope to get one or two in at Ground Zero out in Nevada, but I'm pretty sure even that won't affect them."

But Ike's man proved to be a little smarter than he looked, "*Nearly* impossible?"

"Well…one or two of them have died. We'researching that." Actually, the research was brutal and thousands had died and they still didn't have answers.

"You're not sure why?"

"That's right," Charley repeated. "We're not sure why."

Of the eight thousand and some few hundred unsuspecting people quietly kidnapped and folded into the project, only a few hundred had survived. Of these, several dozen were physically and mentally shaped into something vaguely prehistoric. Ninety percent of the rest were like the blond doll of a girl and the man in the white shorts, unkillable but also unreachable, as if floating in a dreamlike state not of their world, not of their dimension, really. The few remaining were of prime interest. They seemed just like ordinary humans, but would unexpectedly display a range of talents that could only be described as unprecedented and amazing.

The name zoomins stuck, and in the years that followed, the project hadn't learned that much more about what made them tick. But among the many unknowns they were experiencing was the real reason Charley called them Zoomins. He named them that, because while some of them could heal at will, others could zoom in and out of sight, and then reappear somewhere else in the blink of an eye. Nobody could figure out how they did it, and it was something the zoomins didn't themselves understand and didn't seem to be able to control. *If they ever did gain mastery over that particular talent, look out!*

Some years after the high-point meeting at which Charley convinced Ike's man to advise the President of the United States to continue funding his project, enthusiasm for their prospects had dwindled to the level that one of their most promising subjects, young Kate Twillinger, was being triangulated for elimination, even though Charley was convinced they wouldn't be able to *take her out*, as the cruel Nam expression went . This was in late August, pushing toward September. Their mission was to take place in rural Central Florida while dawn was coming uneventfully to the sleepy village of Orange Glory. Yes, Orange Glory, where their project had originally gotten its name. It was dozens of miles from the ocean one way and from the gulf the other, and isolated from urban Orlando by miles of suburban development that thinned away to farms, orchards and undeveloped low swamplands.

That morning moved on to become a sultry afternoon. An uneasy silence settled in like a bad memory. Birds and the usual scatter of small wildlife creatures slipped into their quiet and unconscious hiding mode. Though the sky overhead was a hypnotizing deep blue, a bank of towering white clouds hung over the southern horizon, creeping in so slowly it seemed as stationary as a far-away mountain crested in snow and shining in dazzling sunlight.

At the local Orange Glory general store, a primitive and rusty dial on the paint-flaked red Coca-Cola barometer plummeted unnoticed into the red zone. Buck Owens wailed *The sun's gonna shine in my life once more.* An Orlando disk jockey interrupted with a static-impeded report warning of heavy rain moving up from the Keys. Oh yes, hurricane weather, but this was Florida and it was, after all, *the season of the wet,* so nobody was much paying attention.

At this time the old Twillinger home still endured the harshness of the tropical climate, located as it was in the middle of Twill Grove, the generations-old family owned orange grove. The original settler, Great-Great-Grandaddy Eban Twillinger had chased off the devil thieving itinerant Seminoles who were camping on his property and had personally planted the first little citrus saplings he'd stolen from a local Catholic priest's property after the holy padre died of old age or something else. Eban's first wife used to bring baskets of food to the wandering redskins, but after the devils stole the wife and his first-born daughter and sold them as white whores in the Caribbean slave trade his practice became *get out Ol' Betsy and shoot on sight,* although his attitude righted itself considerably when his new wife turned out softer and more cuddly than the old one.

A tattered ghost of forgotten dreams, the house itself had been built in the 1880's by Eban's son, Great-Granddaddy Hubber Twillinger. Those were the flush days as Hubber sold off about two square miles of property, including the entire present day town of Orange Glory. Eban had got there first, not counting the devil Indian

savages, so of course it all was his by right. The home
Hubber built was splendid for its time and place, but the
years and the humid, buggy climate wore it into a shabby
two story, paint-peeling, broken-lace Victorian structure, as
out of place in that rural area of shacks and trailers as a
prim chapel in honkytonk pork town city.

Worse, the old homestead house suffered the indignity
of a brace of what the locals referred to as *them damn
gov'ment 'lectrical intrusions* draped uncomfortably close
over the front porch.

The encroachment of the electrical wires was an old
story, though it had not spread beyond local legend, and
that for reasons as vague and undecipherable as *that damn
gov'ment bid'ness.*

Back in the day, the Twillingers fought hard that
nothing of that sort should cross their property, but nobody
in memory had ever won against *gov'ment bid'ness*, so
there they were, those heavy strings of wires on their
strutting steel legs, all the way from the coal burning
Itchimoli power plant, thick buzzing metal ropes that
swung down too low without so much as an *excuse me*
before snapping on east in the general direction of Orlando.

Any hour of the night or day, the wires overhead might
think to give off a brief high-pitched hum, and this time
when it happened, Granny Lulubird Twillinger snapped
without warning. Granny Lu had been inside the summer
kitchen hunched over the old Formica topped table sipping
her cold coffee and digesting the obits from a two week old
Sunday Sentinel. She suddenly threw her heavy coffee
mug across the room at her granddaughter Kate. The mug-
fling was an apparent afterthought, a wild and
unpremeditated pitch, or it might have struck the intended
target, the soft side of Kate's skull above her ear. To the
original Orange Glory Project way of thinking, this would
have been an absurd waste of resources, but they now had
new objectives. The suppressed documents showed
Granny Lulubird always had been as unpredictable as they
come, not that any of that mattered once the entire
adventure was tagged, bagged and burned so no trace

remained of what it was, how it got out of control, or what it did to the world.

August, in the summer of 1964, probably about when the first cracks began to appear in the known universe. Back then few of the agency's *cogni scenti* suspected anything so astoundingly absurd. In those days, nobody was trying to connect the dots; nobody had any idea of the changes to come. The world was complicated enough, what with the devious communist menace, the godless love bead children, the black people's discontent and Elvis running around like some lewd Godless clown in full hip gyration.

It was no secret that Granny Lu liked slapping her granddaughter around; let's just call it her own private exploration into the unknown. Granny had tried to explain her seemingly cruel behavior to her friends; her fond hope, she said, was that maybe a couple of hard knocks on the kid would bear interesting fruit of the whacko-bird tree, that is, bring out some of the witchy unpredictability so much a part of her daughter, Crazy Tillie's, unpredictable persona. Tillie was Matilda Twillinger, Granny Lu's own daughter and Kate's mother, and she had been quite mad even before she went missing with the passwords to the Twillinger money locked up tight as a drum. Where had the Twillinger genes run so amuck? Grandma Lu swore it couldn't be her fault. *Couldn't be!*

Other than the rock solid conviction it had to be Crazy Tillie's failure, withered and dried up old Grandma Lulubird wasn't exactly sure why she herself was so hell-bent on smacking her granddaughter upside the head. Them damn *gov'ment wires* would get to buzzing overhead and Granny Lu would get to the end of her patience and the only thing to do was smack the annoying little whelp.

Maybe the truth of it was the way the old woman from time to time confessed at church prayer meetings, demonic pure evil Satan – or more properly, outer space aliens! – had imprinted bad notions in her brain. *But no, that had to be just crazy talk, there warn't no such thing as aliens from outer space, was there?* Bottom line, the old lady fervently

293

and privately hoped Kate would begin expressing things normal folks did not, like maybe talking to the poison swamp flowers and the pythons, possibly holding conversations with snapshots in the old family album, and even lie down in the warm dust between the orange trees and ask a favor or two of the saints and beasts of burden, as had her mother Tillie, that is, if the savored and oft repeated gossip was true. *Should any of those odd wonderments happen, they could all praise the Lord for small favors!* Because Granny could then petition the state of Florida to dress Kate in a plain brown straight jacket and hopefully unlock her great granddaddy's family trust, because of Tillie's devious cunning as out of reach until then as the last juicers high on the tree.

Everybody in Orange Glory Junction could see it bothered Granny Lu no end that Kate was still alive, though the kid looked barely a teenager and from the drift of things was not destined for a long or fruitful life. Lord knows, Lu had done her best to get rid of the problem; she once pawned the kid off to a Jamaican crop duster who claimed to have connections to descendants of the same sex slave trade that had whisked away her ancestors, but that damn skinny little teen bitch Kate with her kinky reddish blond hair had slipped off into one of her secret swampy places and wisely elected not to come out of hiding until the islander's rotten wing old biplane took off for Georgia.

Nobody normal around those parts knew it, but Granny once tried a little arsenic powder, left over from spraying the trees, to solve her problem. But that day Kate said she wasn't hungry, even though Granny Lu angrily warned her that was all she was getting to eat until come tomorrow. After the old lady realized her ploy had failed, the damn wires started buzzing and she got onto a fit of temper and threw the oat meal out the back door and it killed two of her dogs who fought nearly to the death over it before it killed them.

Kate's naturally curly hair was bowl-clipped almost short as a boy's, the strawberry blond by-product of an angry semi-annual ritual, the scissors snipping like shark bites, Granny Lulubird's claw-like hands, arthritic with the plucking of countless Florida oranges, hip-hopping about the young girl's face without regard for eyes or nose, her high-pitched, rackety old voice warning, "You don't want to get mite-fleas, girly-girl!"

Kate survived through the long seasons and dangerous times by practicing invisibility. She grew alert, and clever at slipping out of range. But this time in the afternoon of the day in late August of 1964 she was too slow, and when Granny's favored cracked ceramic mug only glanced off the side of her head before it shattered against the wall, somebody had to pay.

Even so, Kate nearly made it to the back screen door, but not before Grams lurched from her chair and caught her a good one on the side of her head with the heavy end of her knob-gnarled cane. Not her head! Not again!

At that moment the kitchen timer dinged, alerting Granny Lu it was nearly time to take the citrus pies out of the oven. Granny was distracted from her mission of beating Kate's brains out long enough to reach for the shelf over the sink and screw another ten minutes on the timer. Kate, lying helpless on the floor, focused on the stubby white finger on the timer. She heard the steady beat of the seconds, loud as a hammer in her ear. And then there was a pause when she seemed to blank out and she heard and saw nothing. And then – impossibly – the ticking increased and Granny's movements seemed to slow down until she was barely moving at all. This was a gift from the angels, as Granny had been moving in to deliver a killing blow on her granddaughter. Regardless where it came from, Kate snapped to her feet and bounded out the door before her astounded grandmother could move a muscle.

"Oh no," Granny Lu moaned, settling back down at the table with her head between her hands. "That little bitch done learned to twitch like her momma."

Just as an aside, you should know that, up to that time the very heart of the Orange Glory project had demanded cranial impact to their subject's heads on as regular a basis as might be instigated, with a schedule matched as closely as possible to the electro-magnetic impulsing from the power lines and the spray of particles from the big grey box the power and light representatives had assured everybody were step-down transformers. *Mental transforming*, more obfuscation, you see, the truth wrapped in a convenient code word. The military, as you probably know, loves riddles. But that is the other side of the story, unimportant for the moment, and, as Granny's furious outbursts had never been controllable, all future military historians would have to go by might be a series of unverifiable local events and their unintended consequences.

Regardless, Kate was moving too fast. The door frame loomed up and smacked her on her left ear and she tasted blood in the back of her mouth. She darted out the rusty old screen door and skittered from the back of the house like a dizzy colt, wearing only her underwear. She thought nobody would see her. That, of course, was a mistake, but understandable in her panic, and even supra-humans are not perfect. Due to ill-luck, fate, the predetermined course of the universe or the next spin of the cosmic prayer-wheel, the army was watching.

An army specialist with the rank of Private First Class was the first to spot her blurred image. He was the driver, little more than a low class vehicle-handler trained to get behind the steering wheel of medium-to-heavy weight trucks. He had been cleared to drive the MGT387, a ten wheeled vehicle disguised to look like a big garbage truck because it was a part of the Orange Glory project. He was short and had a round, generally blank face, bristly blond crew cut hair and the embarrassing habit of idly reaching his right hand down to readjust his balls in public.

His name was Fritz Harper, and he was promoted to driver because he had failed at every other task they gave him. They stamped a clearance code at the top of his file because if he became an embarrassment, which was likely because of his surly disposition and presumed low I.Q., it would be easier to dispose of him. As it turned out, he did screw up a lot and they did keep track of all that, but sometimes a demotion or reassignment is just easier than burn-body, and, beyond that, the actual truth they were all trying to ignore was they had tried to kill him a dozen times and nothing had worked, and that, of course, meant either that their specialists were not all that accomplished or, unthinkably, Fritz was actually one of the supra-humans. This last notion was the least likely, they believed, because Fritzy-boy was so damn stupid he was one step removed from Neanderthal, while the zoomins were quietly, frighteningly superior in dozens of unexpected ways.

This couldn't have been more than a few seconds after Granny Lu had flung her coffee mug at Kate, on that muggy afternoon with the crystal blue sky and sno-cone clouds moving up from the south. Fritz, short at five foot seven with his chunky worker-bee body and stiff blond buzz cut fortified with a max load of Brill Cream, was driving the militarized garbage truck through the actual swampy little backwash town in Central Florida that had given the project its name, Operation Orange Glory.

Charley Birch was there, too. Charley, who had personally fronted the project in its glory days, now was saddled with the dishonor of dismantling it. He tried his best to ignore Fritz as he looked out through the grey one-way glass, both of them morosely eyeing the endless groomed rows of citrus trees as they stood at attention like parade soldiers. Charley Birch, nearsighted, middle aged, balding and pot-bellied, gone to seed as he'd slipped out of the service and turned civilian in a quietly desperate attempt to escape at least some few of the consequences of his failure.

Charley picked at his McDonald's scrambled eggs and pan cakes from Orlando, now rewarmed a second time in the MGT's portable toaster oven. A third passenger was jammed in the close interior of the vehicle. General Filbert Redelak had invited himself along. He was a prissy, thin-lipped twin star from the agency. The General was clearly not impressed with any of their preparations for the subject elimination, and, after the latest bits of messy mischief involving the missing squadron of fighter planes and the unfortunate mess on board the Philadelphia Experiment, Charley was sure the general had shown up to shut him down again, only for good this time. *Jesus H. Christ, the Philadelphia Experiment! Though there were some similarities in the disastrous results, Charley had nothing to do with that, and he could prove it!*

The fourth man onboard was a sniper, a specialist named Ollie Krell. Ollie was a thin Nordic with cancerous, pockmarked yellowish skin stretched over a skull head of a face. Charley Birch had asked he come along simply to prove a point, that even a top kill specialist couldn't take down a zoomin.

"How did this craziness start in the first place?" the General asked in his whispery-thin voice. He had finished his own sausage-and-eggs meal and was slurping the last of a giant Diet Lime Coke.

Charley tried to toss it off to post-war innocence, pretty much the way he always did. "Well, you know, we had the girly troopers doing the DC bars and they ran into some very interesting dudes from the USSR who didn't know how to keep their mouths shut while their trousers were down around their ankles."

But Redelak knew Charley too well to hum along with that old tune.

"Birch, quit blathering; get to the heart of it. Anybody who has read the files knows it started in Chicagoland."

The general's quiet but holier than thou act annoyed Charley no end. In referring to the specially designed particle accelerators in their grey metal boxes, General Redeldak thought he was cutting to the chase, but to Charley he was acting more like an accountant than an agency man. Hadn't he even read the confidential grade briefings?

"Sure, looking back it is easy to dismiss Sexual Intercept as some sort of spy game of little consequence, but what you dismiss as a rude exchange of fluids for info was once at the heart of our intelligence gathering. That was the late 1950's, not all that long ago…"

"Right, except 'heart' is the wrong organ."

"You can snigger and sneer all you want, but the information we got proved conclusively the Russians were making big progress developing superhuman intelligence."

"Right. Conclusively," the General's tone showed his disbelief. "Only somewhere they lost it along the way."

Charley's face reddened and his tight lips betrayed his anger, "You blame me, but I had the go ahead for Orange Glory from the highest levels. Nobody can pin this on me."

"I'm not forgetting and nobody's blaming you, Mister Birch."

"They better not try."

Charley knew how hollow his words sounded, but he had no choice other than to hopelessly argue his case. "The Ruskies had been, so the story went, creating wonders through an exotic blend of chemicals, electro-magnetic brain cell warping on levels assumed to be sub-atomic, and the fairly rough physical damaging and re-healing of those cells. Charley had thought to do them one better with his heavy grey-box accelerators.

"Comic book stuff," Redelak sniffed.

"Yes, but theoretically possible."

"You never did have more than a vague notion what you were doing."

Charley shrugged,"That's what research is."

"And you still don't to this day."

Charley went silent, turning his gaze to watch the orchards, ponds and undeveloped swamplands drift by. Truth was, the General didn't know the half of it. The bright boys had built their first particle accelerators outside the old German town of Batavia in Northern Illinois, Codeword Chicagoland, and Charley had managed to get any number of his experimental subjects into the particle showers, not in a direct line with the protons themselves – they found out soon enough that killed about 99% of them right away – but in what they calculated as an extremely narrow effective range during the mille-seconds after particle impact when the fundamental recreation of the universe was taking place, in that tiny moment of opportunity, som very strange things happened.

Wonderful, terrible, exciting things. Nobody knew much about any of that, and they still didn't. Dark matter, hell – it was a dark subject. Over a decade the Orange Glory project had blossomed like some unknown and unknowable poisonous night flower, and anybody in the agency with even a half-assed clearance was aware it existed. And yet here was a tight assed know-nothing two star General sticking it to him, Charley Birch, like it was entirely his singular personal fault.

"Your curiosity got a little out of hand, didn't it, Mr. Birch."

That was more a judgment and a condemnation than a question, and Charley had to fight to keep a lid on his temper. *How like the army to go looking for people to stick with the blame!*

Charley felt he had to admit to a little something to keep the bigger disaster out of the discussion,

"Well, a little at some point in time, but we have been able to put things back on track."

In truth, things had gone terribly out of control, and when they had, Charley had started the first lie, that the abnormalities cropping up in his test subjects were minor aberrations and nothing they could not handle. That had probably been a mistake. They should have simply clean-slated all the Zoomins before it was too late. The good old burn-body solution.

"We told you to clean up your mess, and you didn't. You defied direct orders."

"No!"

"Oh, yes, Charley Birch."

"Well, I-I did hesitate, but that was because I couldn't figure out how to get rid of them. They become not strictly human, you know."

"What do you mean?"

Charley couldn't believe it. Hadn't this fool read anything? "You can't simply kill them. You can't. We can't. I can't. Maybe nobody can."

"So you bottle them up and fly them off-shore where it is costing us half the national debt to contain them."

Charley shrugged, pointing to the distance where the top floor of an old Victorian house was poking its eaves over a green quilted blanket of orange trees, "There. Right there. That's the Twillinger place."

"And there she is!" Fritz yelled with a bob of his round melon head as he took one hand off the wheel to point. In the next second he slammed on the brakes and the truck skidded to a stop. "Gift from God!"

"Shut up, Fritz," grim faced Ollie Krell muttered as he fiddled with the scope on his rifle. Krell hadn't said anything all morning. In fact, he hadn't spoken a word for three days, some sort of offshoot Buddhism he was working on for self-improvement.

"Kate Twillinger. Confirmed."

Charley caught a fleeting glimpse of a slim girl darting through the orange grove. He couldn't shake off his sense of foreboding. No way this could turn out well.

Ollie Krell squinted into his riflescope and shook his head. The target wavered in his vision, watery and indistinct as she moved through the foliage in the grove.

"Where? Where is she?" the General was shouting like an excited schoolboy, clearly thinking they could solve their problem with one quick shot.

"Right there! Running from the house!"

"But she's just a skinny teenager!"

By now Charley was beside himself, "Jesus Christ, shoot her!"

But the General was now on a new tangent. "I don't see what is so dangerous about her, Mister Birch. Are we now exterminating little girls?"

The Two Star held up one hand, indicating the grim faced shooter was to wait. That was a relief to Ollie Krell, who had unaccountably lost his target in the scope sight, something that had never happened in all his experience shooting men, women, cows and dogs in World War II and Korea.

Fritz started the truck lurching forward in low gear, barely managing to keep Kate in sight as she hurried away from the house.

Charley spoke through clenched teeth, "She-is-no-longer-human."

The General shrugged, "What's wrong with that? Monkeys and cows and dogs aren't human, either."

"She-is-better," Charley said.

"How better?"

"Beyond you and me."

"And there's something wrong with that?"

"Ask your children's children."

"What? Why?"

"They'll be her pets."

"Bullshit! She's just a little teener bitch."

Ollie Krell was disgusted, "I could have offed her a dozen times already. That's what you wanted to find out, wasn't it?"

"But you didn't," Charley said with a grim tone that implied he couldn't.

The General sighed and nodded his go ahead. "Well, Charley-boy, let's just see what the hell you're talking about. Okay, now we're into snuffing out little girls. I've changed my mind. Go ahead, take the subject down, Specialist."

There was a slight delay, as the firing angle had changed. This forced Ollie Krell to move further back in the vehicle and crank down another small window. So it was a few more precious moments before he again had Kate swimming in his sight, but that was when Fritz unexpectedly slammed his foot on the brakes. The scope gave Krell a nasty rap near the big scar on his forehead and the GT387 skidded to an abrupt halt.

"God damn it, Fritz!" Ollie shouted, rubbing his bruised eye socket.

But the stubby little driver had already hopped out of the truck and was jogging up to a man wearing undershorts and a faded fireman's shirt who had parked an aging fire truck in the middle of the road.

"Damn, get out of the way, you stupid backwoods hick! We got a bad batch of contaminated garbage here!"

The local man didn't seem impressed. "All garbage is contaminated, and who you calling a hick, you pumpkin headed lame-brain?" Clearly the local wasn't impressed with Fritz, outfitted as he was in his fake garbage man uniform.

Fritz's diseased garbage ploy was totally bogus, but that was what the operations manual said to do and these were dumb locals anyway, what did they know? Still, by the time Fritz got the local lame-brain scooted out of the way, Kate had disappeared.

"Shades of Nam," General Redelak muttered. "I tell you we have to kill them all."

"Except," Charley insisted, "zoomins are un-killable."

"There is no such word in my dictionary," the General said.

"Or mine," Krell added, but with less conviction.

"Supra-humans, then," Charley sniped back at them. He suspected the general had conducted his war from a boardroom and had never been anywhere near Southeast Asia, "You can't even kill one dinky little girl. How do you propose we kill them all?"

"A few of the big busters, laid on the island in the middle of the night. We claim it's a big meteorite. Boo-hoo, too bad, a few dozen unknown victims turned to cinder and ashes. Problem solved."

Fritz, who had returned from his encounter with the local fireman, took it all in from his driver's seat, but he said nothing. Yes, he'd heard rumors of bleak and barren Santa Barbella, where the agency kept their subjects. *Kill them all*, the General had said. That sounded like a direct order to Fritz, and this was an order from the top. To his way of thinking, there was no deadline on such orders. They were in effect until they were countermanded.

Charley angrily shook his head, not bothering to point out that something had yet again interfered the moment their shooter had raised his rifle to take out Kate Twillinger. Was it simply bad timing? Charley was certain it was something else, though exactly what that something else was, he couldn't even begin to imagine. Something bad, though, he was sure.

"We're late," the General said, eyeing his watch.

"For what? Pork sandwiches and grits?"

That caught Fritz's attention, and he grinned, showing a mouth full of pointy yellow teeth. "I could go for some of that."

"No,", Redelak said, idly dusting the gold stars on his left shoulder with the soft cloth towel he'd been using to clean his Ray Ban aviator sunglasses. "I've got meetings. You've had your little show, Charley, and we learned nothing. We give it up for now."

Fritz threw a careless salute to anybody who cared and started up the truck's big twin-diesel engines. In a half hour they had bumped their way back along the unimproved oil coated gravel roads, finally hitting an asphalt two lane and then the expressway.

The cloud bank was now towering in the near distance, the white anvil tops of thunderheads showing a violent promise; but these were grown military men and veterans of the Floridian climate, trained to ignore the unpredictable vagrancies of the weather. What was more, they had plans and important procedures to perform. They paid the clouds no mind and proceeded without undue haste until they pulled off the expressway to stop in a quite suburb north of Orlando city proper.

"You get out here," General Redelak told Charley. He waved to an inconspicuous brick building that was set back by rolling green lawns about an eighth of a mile from iron gates. "Your new home. Don't worry; we already moved your personal belongings."

"You, too, Fritz," the kill specialist added.

"But I'm driving," Fritz protested.

"No more," the General's lips grew even thinner. "You're assigned to guard dog Mister Glory-boy here."

Grim Ollie Krell screwed a silencer on his short barreled pistol as he scooted Fritz and moved over to take his place in the driver's seat. Charley waved off the show of force, "Violence is not the answer."

"It pays the bills," Ollie shrugged.

"Come on, Fritzie," Charley said, as if he was calling a pet dog, and the stubby little corporal doubled over and jumped out of a small side door.

"Yeah, Fritzie-boy, get out," Krell added.

Fritz put an unhappy face on his round melon head, looking like he wanted to say something else, but the silencer trumped any ideas he might have been forming in that slow brain of his. He showed his disapproval by pursing his plump lips and silently made his way out the door after Charley.

Standing on the roadside, Charley Birch breathed a sigh of relief. He had been sure they were going to kill him, had been certain a bullet was coming his way ever since they figured out he was lying about that disintegrating universe business. As if they could have come up with anything better! And, as is always the case with really believable fraud, there was an element of truth to the entire business; because of Orange Glory, everything of reality, as current-day humanity knew it, was a bit frayed about the edges. Unless space and time settled back down, life was never going to be the same for anybody.

Fiction

Crazyhead
Devils
Hollywood Havoc: *The Trouble With Fat Boy*
Hollywood Havoc: *The Llama Goes Up*
Foul
The Heart of Desire
The Rogue Pirates Bible Heretical
The Freight Train of Love
Codes & Decodes

Non Fiction

TANS (*That Ain't No S****)
Headslap: *The Life & Times of Deacon Jones*
The Book of Deacon
Vidmaker 101

ABOUT THE AUTHOR

John Klawitter is a long time surviving 'Hollywood hyphenate', that is, a writer, screenwriter, song lyrics composer, producer of award winning documentaries and TV Specials, and a DGA director.

Before Tinseltown, he served as a cryptographer/linguist at the National Security Agency Puzzle Palace in Maryland, and in a field office in Saigon.

Before his military service, he studied English, Philosophy, Religion, Geology, Logic and Oriental Studies at St. Joseph's College in Indiana, UCLA, and The Monterey Institute of Foreign Studies. He once was fairly fluent in the Vietnamese language, though no longer claims to know if he is ordering chicken soup or a bowl of rice with fish sauce down at the local Pho #10.

He has authored over a dozen novels and non-fiction books, available at www.double-dragon-ebooks.com, www.amazon.com, www.bn.com, as well as, upon request, your local bookstore.

For more about his experiences at Disney, Warner Bros, Paramount, Fox, Hanna-Barbera, and his film projects and books, see www.johnklawitter,com.